BACHELOR DOCTOR

A RICH INDULGENCE BILLIONAIRE DOCTOR
ROMANCE

REGINA MORRIS

CONTENTS

Author   v
Foreword   ix

Chapter 1   1
Chapter 2   13
Chapter 3   25
Chapter 4   35
Chapter 5   47
Chapter 6   60
Chapter 7   75
Chapter 8   97
Chapter 9   115
Chapter 10   139
Chapter 11   157
Chapter 12   175
Chapter 13   188
Chapter 14   200
Chapter 15   223
Chapter 16   239
Chapter 17   249
Chapter 18   259
Chapter 19   271
Chapter 20   289
Chapter 21   298
Chapter 22   327
Chapter 23   338
Chapter 24   344
Chapter 25   360
Chapter 26   377
Chapter 27   390

Acknowledgments   403
About the Author   405
Also by Regina Morris   409

AUTHOR

Silkhaven Publishing, LLC
Join Regina Morris' mailing list for games, freebies, and fun at http://newsletter.reginamorris.com
Please visit author Regina Morris on her website http://www.reginamorris.com
Regina Morris enjoys connecting with fans on social media. Please find her at:
Facebook: http://www.facebook.com/ReginaAnnMorris (@ReginaMorris)
Twitter: http://www.twitter.com/ReginaMorris (@ReginaMorris)
Pinterest: http://www.pinterest.com/ReginaAnnMorris

Chaos ensues when billionaire Thomas Stallworth, Chicago's leading breast reconstruction surgeon, has to stop his brother's wedding in Las Vegas.

Thomas needs to reveal a shocking secret the bride

is hiding, which will create a rift between the brothers. Worse yet, Thomas drunkenly gets married after the bachelor party to the bride's cousin and must annul the union without anyone finding out.

The bride has an agenda of her own and curtails Thomas's efforts with the one bridesmaid who would hate him the most.

Ashley Uxer, a breast cancer survivor who chose not to reconstruct, attends her cousin's wedding. After the bachelor party, she finds herself drunkenly married to the handsome groomsman she has been led to believe is a plastic surgeon whose specialty is rhinoplasty.

In this romantic comedy, Thomas and Ashley lose the bride's wedding ring, their emotional baggage, and their hearts in Las Vegas.

Silkhaven Publishing, LLC

ISBN: 978-1-948997-88-1 (EPub Ebook)

ISBN: 978-1-948997-89-8 (MOBI Ebook)

ISBN: 978-1-948997-90-4 (Paperback)

Library of Congress Control Number: 9781948997904

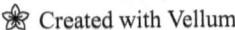 Created with Vellum

FOREWORD

Dear Readers,

As an author and avid reader of romance novels, I love it when two people can find true love and have a happily ever after.

I especially enjoy Rom-Com stories.

I've written nearly twenty romance stories and have never come across a novel where the heroine is a breast cancer survivor struggling to reclaim her femininity.

Cancer of any type touches nearly everyone at some point in their lives, whether you are afflicted or have a loved one who is.

Even with the seriousness of this disease, I wanted my novel to be a fun story that will have you smiling, laughing, and cheering for my two characters.

I am a skin cancer and breast cancer survivor. I understand firsthand how difficult these diseases can be.

I also have the BRCA2 gene mutation, giving me a higher chance of eight additional cancers.

I wanted to write a novel with the heroine facing such trauma in her life but being able to move past the disease and find true love.

Everyone deserves to find true love. Cancer patients who sit in infusion chairs and worry about the spread of the disease or the reoccurrence of it, deserve love especially so.

My novel, 'Bachelor Doctor,' digs deep into the main character's emotions (where I used personal experiences and my own feelings), but it is a romantic comedy.

They say 'laughter is the best medicine,' and writing this story was cathartic for me. I have the love of my life, and I want everyone to experience that as well.

Regina Morris

1

_____

E legance and class aside, Thomas had to admit that he hated everything about his brother's upcoming wedding. The location, the timing, and most importantly, the bride. Blond, beautiful, and an absolute fraud. His brother boasted his bride as the type of lady men dreamed of taking home to meet their mothers.

Thomas knew better.

The bride kept secrets. Unfortunately, Thomas personally knew how loose her morals were—and how flexible her body was.

His brother needed to know the truth.

Thomas turned off the highway and followed the GPS on his Lexus as he slowed to watch for his exit. The wedding resort sat nestled within the trees off a small private drive, and the wedding invite had mentioned the road would be challenging to find.

Nearly missing the turnoff, he saw the sign in time and cranked the wheel. *Bella Rosa Wedding Resort*. Painted red hearts sprinkled the white background of the marker and gave it a sugary-sweet, love-is-in-the-air flair—so he knew this hellhole had to be the place.

It made his skin crawl.

If he had not already needed to be in Nevada on business this week, he would have found an excuse not to come.

His tires skirted across the graveled road, kicking up small pebbles that clunked against the undercarriage of his car. He slowly pulled past the gate of the open white fence that encircled the place and came to another sign at the end of the dirt road. Parking was to the right, but his instructions told him to turn left to the manor house he saw in the distance, so he did.

A large, three-story, bricked chateau—complete with balconies that faced the canyon and enough flowers to cause any hay fever sufferer to run away—loomed in front of him. The invitation had said to drive past the manor, around the smaller carriage house, and to a parking lot that lay beyond.

Thomas glanced at the manicured gardens and the bright summer foliage as he slowly drove along the winding path. The place clearly earned some serious bank from lovestruck brides wanting the perfect dream wedding, all their money going toward one ideal day, even with nearly fifty percent of all marriages ending in divorce. With this place so close to the Vegas Strip, it would make more sense to have a quick wedding and save the money to create a life together.

But it wasn't his money. And Thomas didn't want to share his life with anyone. Not anymore.

He parked in a shady spot. Then, leaving his luggage behind until he checked in, he stepped out of the car, the summer heat toasting his skin and causing his eyes to squint. He put on his sunglasses and trekked to the main house.

The stone walkway wound around a large oak tree with flower beds and led to the house's side porch. Little niceties such as birdhouses, a birdbath, and small signs indicating the way to the lover's gazebo and the lover's grotto greeted him on his short journey to what would surely be a terrible week filled with gooey love stories and happy couples cooing at each other.

Just then, he heard the wedding march. An excited bride stood in the distance, ready to walk the aisle. This place probably had a dozen ceremonies a week.

If he didn't hate weddings so much, he'd consider investing.

A little bell sounded on the door when he walked into the main house. Air-conditioned air greeted him and cooled his face where tiny droplets of sweat had formed from the short walk. His Giacometti shoes creaked against the wooden floorboards as he crossed the foyer of what appeared to be an old, historic house and walked to the reception desk, where he removed his Ray Bans.

A man wearing a white button-down shirt and black slacks sat behind a circular wooden counter nestled under a magnificent staircase. An old-style cubby rested behind him with guestroom numbers, and a closed door with a simple *Private* sign stood to the left. "Welcome to the Bella Rosa Wedding Resort. My name is Hershel. How may I help you?"

I'm here for the Stallworth wedding. I have a reservation, and there's supposed to be a wedding package for me." Thomas placed his credit card on the wooden desk.

He did his best to match his voice to the upbeat smile Hershel beamed at him, but he must have missed the mark because Hershel took the payment and asked, "Did you have any problems finding the place?"

"No." Thomas glanced at the brochures on the desk showing sites visitors could see while in Las Vegas. "I parked behind the carriage house." Several cars were already in the lot, but he wanted to confirm that he had left his car in the correct place.

Hershel glanced at his computer screen for a moment and said, "That's perfect since the wedding party has chosen the Wedding Bliss package." He handed the card back to Thomas after swiping it. "The wedding party's arrangements give you a nice discount."

Hershel turned the visitor's book around. "Would you mind signing in?"

Thomas's eyebrow rose. "Why?"

"My wife likes the charm of having a guest book." A more severe expression replaced the smile on his face as his hand rested on the tome. "We don't spam you or anything. Brenda likes the hominess of it."

His mother's words, *"I'm sure you can get along with your brother for one week. Just smile and do all the wedding stuff because it's important to him,"* came to Thomas's mind, and he reluctantly signed the book with the red-feathered pen before placing the quill back down next to an old-style bell.

"Thank you." Hershel turned the book back around and read the newest entry. "Dr. Thomas Stallworth." He turned to the cubby, his hand moving as he went column by column and then row by row before pulling out a key. "This is the key to the carriage house. We ask that you lock the front door at night. The second key is for your private room. You have room #6."

Thomas took the keys—actual keys, not the electronic pass cards most other hotels had. A wooden fob dangled from the ring with a delicately whittled #6 inside a heart. He wondered if this wedding place had indoor plumbing.

"My mother will arrive on Tuesday. I reserved a room in the main house for her." He handed the credit card back to him. "Can you please use this for her?"

"Of course, sir. And the discounted rate will apply to

that room, as well." Hershel pointed down the hallway. "A breakfast buffet is served from seven to ten a.m. in the dining room. We have tables on the porch, and you're welcome to eat in the gardens, as well, provided you bring the plates back inside. There are also plenty of fantastic restaurants around."

Thomas glanced toward the dining room. Love seats with heart-shaped pillows, lacy curtains, and the romantic atmosphere dripping everywhere caught his attention—as did other patrons of the place, paired off as if this were Noah's Ark.

"And then there's this." Hershel reached behind the counter and picked up a teal-colored bag with silver lace ribbons. "The goodie bag is compliments of the bride and groom. The wedding itinerary is inside."

Thomas did a double-take on the ornate bag. His brother wasn't a "goodie bag" type of guy. This was from the bride, a woman he could barely remember other than the few hours of fun they had shared. All he really knew of her had been from the description his mother had given him. The bride was detailed oriented and leaned toward the controlling side, so a dedicated schedule was not out of character for her. Neither was color-coding the event or giving it a theme. "I only know that the wedding is Saturday, and tonight is the bachelor party." It seemed odd to have a week-long wedding celebration, especially at the prices the Bella Rosa charged, but he had promised to play along—

mostly since he was one a member of the wedding party.

Glancing inside the bag, Thomas found several coupons. Massage, horseback riding, Grand Canyon tour, hiking trails, etcetera. A slight smile pulled at the corners of his lips. With enough to do, he could avoid the wedding party altogether. If that proved successful, maybe he wouldn't have to tell his brother the bad news about his loose bride and ruin his life.

A small, typed booklet caught his eye—*Wedding Itinerary* with a heart above the *i*. Every day held an event. Pink for women, blue for men, and purple for joint activities. Nothing mentioned whether the events were optional, and every minute seemed accounted for.

He groaned inwardly, hiding his true feelings.

"Well, the meeting with the Stallworth wedding coordinator could have gone better," a woman said as she came out of the door behind the counter marked *Private*. "Oh, sorry." The woman's eyes widened as a smile quickly spread across her face. "Welcome to the Bella Rosa."

Hershel placed his arm around the woman's shoulders. Her outfit matched his. "This is my wife, Brenda."

Thomas nodded hello as he placed everything back into the goodie bag. "Are the massages done on-site?"

Brenda gestured to the closed door across from the staircase. "A licensed professional comes in. You can schedule thirty or sixty-minute sessions. We don't offer couples massages."

That wouldn't be a problem. The wedding party, the guests, and even the owners were all happy couples. Thomas took in a deep breath. It was only for a week.

"Brenda..." An energetic younger woman—her bright green eyes holding a sensual depth and her pert little nose giving her a dainty and heavenly appearance —came to the counter. She was a rare fresh-faced, auburn-haired beauty wearing a carefree T-shirt and yoga pants. "Sorry. When you have a second, I need to talk to you about a problem with the flowers."

"I'll be right there," Brenda said.

Thomas studied the young woman and her delicate features, his heartbeats quickening. Her auburn hair gleamed with shadows of deep gold and rich red, and the thick hair curled gracefully over her shoulders.

Brenda pointed at the guest book, her finger tracing his entry. "Is there a *Misses* Dr. Stallworth who needs a key?" she said, distracting him from the beautiful woman.

It took a second for him to process what she had said, but then he jiggled the keys in his hand, feeling the number six's smooth texture. "Not anymore. I'm sure I can find my way to the carriage house."

He turned to leave but gave the mystery woman at the desk a parting glance. Her hips tapered into long legs, and the light from the doorway silhouetted her beautiful curves. She looked like an angel, especially with the light dancing off her loose curls.

She didn't wear a uniform, so she probably didn't work at the Bella Rosa. And she seemed calm, so likely not a bride, either.

Places like this gave an illusion of love and suggested that everyone should be paired off. He would not fall for the false charm, even if she *were* the most beautiful woman he had ever seen.

Ashley's gaze lingered on the man's long, lean form as he walked to the door, the chime signaling his exit. "Who was that?" His powerful, well-muscled body had moved with ease and grace. His height nearly required him to duck to clear the door, and his broad frame filled the threshold as he left.

"That gorgeous man is Dr. Thomas Stallworth," Brenda said.

"Claimed to be a member of Linda's wedding party," Hershel added.

Ashley sniffed the air and inhaled the last of his cologne mixed with the heat of sunshine that had clung to him. Musky. Manly. A clean and masculine scent. "That was Thomas Stallworth?" When Hershel nodded, she added, "He's the groom's elusive brother. The two haven't seen each other in nearly ten years."

Mentally, she compared Thomas to his brother, Paul.

Thomas was taller and darker-haired, although probably still considered blond, and had a much broader chest. The brothers had the same eyes, almond-shaped baby blues, and possibly the same jawline. Thomas had a trimmed beard and mustache, though. She wouldn't have picked Thomas out of the crowd as a Stallworth, but few men were that handsome and had an innately captivating presence.

"You can tell he's a doctor," Brenda said, causing Ashley's eyebrow to rise under her auburn bangs.

Hershel leaned against the counter and crossed his arms. "And how is that, sweetheart?" he asked good-naturedly.

"Good posture," she said sheepishly as she stepped toward Ashley. With Hershel safely behind her, she mouthed, "*Muscular and built.*"

The two women walked back to the small office. Ashley thought about what Thomas had been wearing— a simple, blue, V-neck T-shirt that showcased his broad chest and Levi's jeans that were just a bit too tight.

Ashley mostly saw doctors in white lab coats, not out on the town, and Thomas didn't look like any doctors she knew. Her oncologist was a short, obese man with a ruddy complexion and a hooked nose.

"What type of a doctor is Thomas?" Brenda sat behind the desk in front of the computer in the tiny office. Her eyebrow arched, appearing as if an evil plot brewed, and the look she gave Ashley told her one thing: The woman wanted to play Cupid.

Since they had met in the ABC—After Breast Cancer Class—two years ago provided by the BCRC—Breast Cancer Resource Center—Brenda had tried to set her up with a few eligible bachelors. All were lovely men, all reasonably handsome, and none were her type.

"No clue what his specialty is," Ashley said. "Paul mentioned he made him an usher at the last minute, but their mother wants him to be a groomsman." She gazed past the now-closed door to where the man had stood. His profile had been sharp and confident, his hair thick and lush. Would he now be paired up with her to walk down the aisle?

Brenda cleared her throat.

"What?" Ashley asked as her neck swiveled so she faced her boss.

"Your jaw is on the floor." Brenda grinned as she studied Ashley, making the younger woman feel a blush flash on her face. "He's single and available. Obviously, good-looking."

Good-looking? He was sinfully handsome. "He's only here for the wedding," Ashley said, protesting and doing her best to belay her friend's Cupid-like intentions.

"A week. Your cousin paid for the Wedding Bliss package, which includes a week-long event. There's nothing wrong with some fun while you both stay here. Is there?"

"A man like that wouldn't be interested in someone

like me." Ashley pointed at her body as though something hideous lay hidden under her clothes.

"Someone like *you*? What? A strong, independent woman?"

"You know what I mean. Besides, I haven't dated anyone since…" She touched a strand of curly hair that rested against her neck. "I'm not ready." She wasn't sure if she'd ever be ready.

"Love lives at the Bella Rosa Resort. Don't sell yourself short."

2

Ashley stared into the mirror and checked her outfit one more time. The summer dress rested high on the neck and accentuated her messy-bun hairstyle that left tendrils of curls cascading down the sides of her cheeks.

Too bad she couldn't lose the last ten pounds she'd wanted to shed in time for the wedding.

She turned and lifted her arms high, mimicking dance moves. The fabric lay close against her skin, and the only way anyone could see the silver mark of her scar was from a side angle. She studied her reflection once more, letting out a deep sigh of relief knowing she was completely covered.

"We've got to go." Linda's voice came from outside the bathroom door. Whether Ashley needed another minute of primping or not, her cousin wouldn't allow her to have it. Besides, she wouldn't lose those ten pounds in the next few minutes. She applied bright red lipstick and noted that her thick, dark eyebrows set off her emerald-colored eyes before opening the bathroom door and facing the wedding party's ladies.

"You look beautiful," Imani said, adjusting her purse on her shoulder and admiring Ashley's hair. Her head tilted, and she glanced concernedly at the messy bun. "Your curls look a bit dry. Feel free to use some of my hair mask."

She spoke the words pleasantly, and Ashley took no offense. Imani had arrived with a margarita maker, bottles of wine, and some handmade souvenir buttons and sashes for the wedding party to wear tonight. Ashley considered women like her the givers of society and always enjoyed their company.

"We don't have time." Linda ushered the ladies out the cottage's door and asked that they walk the short distance to the barn, where the start of the joint bachelor/bachelorette party would be.

Ashley felt rushed. Linda was a perfect example of the takers of society. Ashley loved her cousin dearly, but Linda got her way when push came to shove. It wasn't an endearing quality, but there always had to be one within a group, and Linda had always held a special place in Ashley's heart.

"I want to talk to Ashley for a minute. We'll see you there." Linda gestured at the building.

The scent of Italian food wafted into the tiny house now that the door was open. The smell reminded Ashley just how hungry she was. Having been on a diet for the last three months had helped her fit into her bridesmaid dress, and she was grateful to be a size smaller, but she planned on celebrating with her cousin tonight.

"I didn't even know he had arrived," Linda said with a scowl as she halfway closed the cottage door and faced Ashley privately.

Drama already? Ashley had hoped for a fun night out on the town. But judging by the sour expression on Linda's face, that would not happen. "Who?"

"Paul's brother. Thomas. I hoped he'd arrive Saturday morning just in time for the wedding, but Paul texted me that he arrived earlier."

Ashley thought back to the ruggedly handsome man she had almost met at the reception desk: dark blond hair, piercing blue eyes, and massive shoulders. The image quickened her pulse. "I got a glimpse of him when he arrived."

She watched the other bridal party women walk along the stone pathway and past the lover's grotto to the barn where her friends Brenda and Hershel were setting up the dinner. A cool summer breeze had settled in, picking up the scent of jasmine from the gardens. It mixed with the smell of garlic bread.

Linda closed the cottage's door completely, making their conversation private and getting Ashley's attention. "The two brothers haven't gotten along since Thomas stole an old girlfriend from Paul years ago." A pinched expression crossed her face, the one she got whenever someone got in her way. "Tina was all wrong for Paul, but that is another story. Please do me a favor?"

Old girlfriend? That was a lot of info dumped very quickly. Ashley couldn't wrap her head around the news fast enough, but she knew better than to ask for a bunch of details when she saw Linda's jaw tense. "What's the favor?"

"Keep Thomas busy and away from Paul as much as you can."

As a bridesmaid, Ashley had expected bridal errands like steaming the veil the night before the wedding or getting emergency chocolate or wine for the bride. She hadn't expected something that sounded in the neighborhood of a cloak-and-dagger operation. "Keep Thomas away from Paul?"

"Just… I don't know…." Linda pulled cash from her purse. "Here. The men are all going to some show on the Strip tonight. If I know the best man, Brian, he'll take his duties to heart and have them drinking all night. I don't want Paul upset, so take Thomas somewhere else. Then, once the show starts, and he doesn't attend the performance with the rest of the men, he'll entertain himself. It is Vegas, after all." She let out a slight chuckle. "If he has a good time, we may not see him for days."

Being asked to entertain a gorgeous man wasn't without its charm, but Ashley shook her head. "How am I supposed to lure Thomas away from a night of drunken fun with the boys?"

Linda cocked her head and gave her cousin an are-you-kidding-me glare. She then counted off on her fingers. "This man probably doesn't want to be here anymore than Paul wants him here. He doesn't know anyone. And he is a total dog who won't turn away a pretty face." Her lips thinned regretfully. "I shouldn't ask you to do this, but..." Her eyes briefly shut, and the frame of her body slumped as though in defeat. "Be careful. The man went after his brother's girlfriend, breaking some sort of man-code. Only a manwhore would do something that sleazy." She placed the money in Ashley's hand. "You've lived in Vegas your whole life and know the town. Join us after you've lost him somewhere. The show starts at eleven p.m., so take him to a bar after we're done with dinner and then lose him. You have our itinerary and know where we'll be."

She sure did. The ladies were going to the Nuts & Bolts Club, a place known for their male strippers. Ashley didn't mind places like that, but she wasn't excited about it, either. She was usually the shy woman sitting at the table the men ignored while they singled out the loudest and most aggressive women.

Even though she wasn't excited about the Nuts & Bolts Club, keeping Thomas occupied sounded underhanded, though not in a wholly immoral or dirty way. Ashley didn't like being dishonest at all, but she had promised to help Linda with the wedding in any way she could. "The brothers don't get along?"

Linda shook her head and gave her a deflated look

as if the men's feud was reminiscent of the Hatfields and McCoys. "And I don't need anything else going wrong with this wedding."

True. The coordinator had called with a problem earlier. Ashley didn't have the heart to mention that the florist couldn't guarantee gardenias in the centerpieces.

Linda gave her the sad-puppy-dog eyes, the look she always affected as a kid when she wanted Ashley to do something. Ashley never could refuse that look.

"Fine." Ashley took the money, and Linda immediately engulfed her in a bear hug. "I can't guarantee I'll be able to distract him, but I'll do my best," she said against her cousin's shoulder.

The two left the cottage and trekked the short distance to the barn. They walked through the garden seating area, around the chairs encircling a decorative firepit, and neared the reflection pond. With each step, Ashley wondered how long ago this *Tina* fiasco had happened. Linda and Paul had been dating for the last three years, so it couldn't have been too recently.

The barn's double wooden doors lay open, allowing the delicious scents of the catered meal to waft on the breeze. A decorative sign stating *Stallworth Wedding* sat in front of the door, its picture already taken and documented by Mindy, the bridesmaid who loved scrapbooking and was the group's shutterbug.

Ashley entered the barn, this time as a guest and not as hired help or a friend who occasionally helped Brenda and Hershel. The rustic building's transformation always amazed her. White twinkle lights hung in rows of spiderweb-like designs from the ceiling, casting romantic shadows on the wooden floor beneath. Standing candelabras and long carpet runners paved the way, breaking the room's flow into separate seating areas, a dance floor, and an entryway. The space exemplified elegance mixed with rustic charm with its rough wooden walls and hay bales. It was a perfect wedding spot.

The wedding party stood within the entry. Hershel oversaw a waiter placing another stack of plates near where the caterer stood by the food, and Brenda busily walked around the tables with name cards in her hand. Linda's nearly week-long wedding celebration was about to begin, and excitement hung in the air.

What Ashley didn't see was Thomas.

She made her way in and knew better than to ask Brenda if she needed any help. Her friend had already told her not to offer since she was a guest this week. Instead, Ashley mingled with Matt and Connor—two college friends of Paul's he had stayed close to over the years. Linda called them groomsman one and two in all seating charts and wedding plans. It was nice to put faces and real names to the men.

During the small talk, Ashley spied Thomas, and an overall weighted feeling overcame her. He stood near the bar—alone and seemingly lost in his thoughts. Most would have said he looked bored, but his brooding only oozed a cool James Dean-ish flare to Ashley.

Ashley walked over to Linda and whispered, "That's Thomas." She had no need to announce it since Linda knew everyone at her joint bachelor/bachelorette party. However, Ashley still felt the need to mention who he was, especially since he now walked toward them.

"Paul." Thomas nodded at his brother and then smiled at Linda. "This must be your lovely bride."

The three exchanged pleasantries, and Ashley studied them. She caught a hint of distance from the brothers in how they stood apart and avoided eye contact. Thomas had a beer in his hand and sipped it as he looked away, and Paul seemed positively mesmerized by the white string lights hanging overhead. But there was something else. Linda wasn't her usual gushing self, possibly too afraid the ex-girlfriend would be mentioned, and a fight would ensue. Instead, she was polite—almost dismissive. The scene would be complete if they discussed the weather.

One thing was clear. Thomas wasn't welcome, and that was a shame.

How in the world did Linda not recognize him?

Thomas stood dumbly, looking into the eyes of the woman he was sure was the one he fondly called his *convention center hookup*. The tryst had been on the fourteenth floor of the Marriott in Denver about five years ago. After hours. A drunken night. Linda's last name barely fit on the name tag she wore. And Higgenbothem was hard to forget, especially since he had read it as *Hug-a-bottom* in his inebriated state.

Linda stared right past him without any hint of recognition, and a tinge of anger mixed with hurt stabbed at his gut.

She *didn't* remember him.

She played coy and cute, fiddling with her hair and giggling like a schoolgirl. Was it a game? Or had she slept with so many people that she honestly couldn't remember him?

He still remembered her smoldering gaze as she propositioned him, and the two left the bar together all those years ago. After the conquest, he'd left her hotel room with her red lace panties in his suit pocket.

The only thing he remembered about her, other than her last name and hot body, was that she had been newly divorced and wanted to be wild and free.

Wild. She was that night.

But she didn't remember him?

"Mindy, Sarah," Linda said, getting their attention. "Have you met Thomas? He's Paul's brother."

He greeted the two women he assumed were bridesmaids but then refocused on Linda, who was busy playing the charming host.

She let out a slight giggle, and he knew.

That laugh. That hair. Those eyes. He glanced down. Yep, those legs had been wrapped around him. It was her.

He'd always believed he was hard to forget. It wasn't as though he had a slew of past lovers...well, at least not back then. Until the convention center hookup, he had enjoyed three brief encounters in his life, plus two real romances. Not quite a scoreboard for being a hot-lover, bed-them-and-leave-them type of guy. The encounter with Linda had changed everything, though, and it was why he remembered her so well.

Linda's cavalier approach to intimacy had taught him that sex was just sex. No commitment, no strings, no feelings. Immediately after satisfying her needs, she'd shown him the door. He had never been with a woman only for sex without hoping for more before, and he liked it.

Now, she clung to Paul's arm like a lifeline. Thomas wasn't sure what she was saying since he wasn't paying attention, but she showed everyone her engagement ring and said something about getting a manicure. Exactly how superficial was she?

"We'll go jogging in the morning while the men get their tuxedos," she prattled on. "They had to wait for the last fitting because Thomas came in just today."

Thomas paid no attention to Linda as she rattled off even more wedding information, but her familiar voice echoed in his ears. His experience with her had convinced him to go on a wild spree of his own. Even though he didn't view her in any romantic way, he owed her a debt of gratitude. Sowing his wild oats and getting his wilder side out of his system was what he'd needed —at least at the time.

The years since Linda had been fun, and seeing her again could almost be enough for him to go on another tear with women. But things had been changing lately. Finding more gray hair, going through a slight weight increase, and feeling stiffness in his knee reminded him that he wasn't a young man anymore. Not that he was old, but he was *growing* old.

Growing old and still alone.

His breath hitched.

He wished he could find a woman he could spend the rest of his life with, but it seemed she wasn't out there. Women were always after his money, and he wasn't interested in being their rich doctor husband.

He heard his name in the conversation and said, "I'm thrilled to be included in the wedding." He wasn't sure if he'd answered whatever question had been asked, but it was good enough.

And then a notion occurred to him. If Linda didn't remember their one-night stand, perhaps he was off the hook. They had been consenting adults, and it had happened years ago. He wasn't interested in her now, would never try to break up the pair, and didn't want this to create an even deeper wedge between his brother and him.

But, deep down, he knew it would.

"We met three years ago," Paul said, "I recognized the right woman the moment I saw her."

And that confirmed the timeline. Paul didn't know Linda when Thomas had slept with her in Denver. He knew his mind was yo-yo-ing, but maybe no one needed to know about their little tryst.

Maybe.

He studied his brother. Other than the man not looking too excited to see him, Paul seemed happy. Close friends and people who cared about the couple filled the room. He had risen within his pharmaceutical company from sales to director of some division—or so his mother would have Thomas believe.

"I'm happy for the two of you." Thomas made brief eye contact with Linda, and she turned away, not entirely as if she had recognized him but more like she didn't care to look at him—which seemed odd. No desire existed between the two, but he wasn't sure if he trusted her. She may make his brother happy, but if Thomas knew of one lie she had told, how many other secrets did the woman have?

Her closet was probably crammed full of skeletons.

The list of pros and cons for tell versus don't tell was growing. If he told Paul the truth, he had to do it before his brother and Linda spoke their vows.

3

————

"We're ready," Brenda said, approaching them. She took Linda by the arm. "You and Paul are seated at the head of the large table." She swung her arm around. "The seats all have name cards...."

Ashley thought it was sweet how Brenda and Hershel were hands-on with the wedding arrangements. She had worked at the Bella Rosa for the last year and knew the couple, as owners, typically had their staff handle the little details. Brenda and Hershel being good friends gave the wedding an added special touch.

As Brenda explained who'd catered the meal, what wines and cocktails were available, and how rideshares would arrive to take them to their next destination, Ashley stood at the back of the barn and took in the beautiful room that sometimes served as a wedding venue, a restaurant, a reception hall, and even as a party room. Brenda and Hershel had done well when picking out this place.

"How are you doing, Ashley?" came a husky voice from behind her. She turned to find the best man staring at her.

"Brian, right?"

"Very good, sweetheart." He puffed out his chest and straightened his form. It was as if he were trying to look more muscular and taller—even though he was a good fifteen pounds overweight, and she overwhelmed his height in her high heels. His reputation preceded him, too. Three times divorced and a different bimbo on his arm every time Linda and Paul went to dinner with him. The man must have *some* saving grace or he wouldn't be the best man.

He held out his hand. "I don't believe I've had the pleasure."

And you certainly won't, she thought to herself. The tone of his voice set her off in a bad way. Still, she shook his hand. Linda had given her the rundown of the groomsmen. Brian was the player. Connor was the devoted husband. Matt was a dedicated husband and father. Ashley already knew Mohinder, her cousin. And now Thomas had been added to the mix.

"They're such a great couple," Brian said. "I've known Paul for years. I introduced him to Linda."

And there was the catch. It now made sense. "I had no idea."

It had been a long time since a man had hit on her,

but she remembered the signs. If they stared at your breasts instead of making eye contact, the chances were good they weren't interested in your mind. Judging by the leer in Brian's gaze, he didn't care if she had any gray matter in her head.

"That's a beautiful dress you're wearing."

"Thank you." She left her answer curt since she didn't want to add to Brian's fun-and-done tally. She tugged at the collar of her dress, wishing the man wouldn't stare at her.

When Brenda finished her speech, Ashley made her way to the open bar. A beer sounded good. Since Brian still had a drink in his hand, and because she wasn't responding to his advances, he didn't follow. Instead, he made a beeline for Sarah, one of the other bridesmaids.

Ashley's phone dinged as she waited for her drink. "Crap," she muttered as she read the text.

"Bad news?" Thomas placed his empty bottle on the bar and signaled for another.

Warmth flooded Ashley, and her breath quickened. She realized he was taller now that he stood next to her. His cologne's musk engulfed her, and she locked onto his beautiful blue eyes. They reflected the twinkling lights overhead and sparkled back at her. "What?"

His playful smile held a hint of concern. "Your phone. Bad news?"

He hadn't tried to stare at her boobs. Even with Linda's warning, Thomas seemed pleasant enough, and something about his reassuring voice pulled her in. "I was hoping to complete a geocaching game before the wedding, but it looks like an opponent just found the last container and won the prize." She placed the phone back into her purse and took her beer from the bar. "It's a game. A treasure hunt using a GPS or smartphone...."

"I'm aware," he said, unable to contain the smile on his face. "A cacher hides a container with a log sheet and some trinkets, then you download the coordinates and find it, sign the log, and move on to the next one."

A nerdy game for sure—one she rarely admitted to playing. She was surprised someone who probably reigned as his high school's prom king had even heard of it. "I lost because someone got to the last container first." She grinned awkwardly. "I don't play that often."

"I..." Hesitation sounded in his voice, but then he gave her a crooked smile and said, "I'm ranked."

"Ranked?" She wasn't sure if she was more surprised to be talking to one of the best players or that he'd willingly admitted to it.

"It's not that impressive. I'm number twenty-four of the top twenty-five in the Chicago area."

It was a weird flex, that was certain, but his voice's tone held pride.

"The treasures can be quite nice, and I'm competitive enough to enjoy a good game."

The small trinkets she played for were just that, trinkets. Maybe a ten-dollar Amazon gift card, but nothing of real value. Plastic trophies or beads were usually the norm. She figured a wealthy doctor like Thomas played for much nicer rewards.

"I'm Thomas," he said, holding out his hand. A smile filled his face and caught the twinkle in his eye that told her he was genuinely interested in meeting her. "What's your name, beautiful?"

His deep voice was resonant, and she smiled back at him. She wasn't used to such flattery—fake or honest—and his charm caught her off guard. The words didn't sound slimy coming from Thomas as they had with Brian, but she needed to remind herself that this man also played the field and supposedly couldn't turn down a pretty face. "My name is Ashley. It's nice to meet a champion sportsman like yourself."

He chuckled in an it's-nothing type of way, as if he had just realized that being a ranked geocacher may not be as sexy of a claim as he had been aiming for.

They took their seats, which were right next to each other. Ashley felt confident that Brenda was responsible for the seating because Ashley distinctly remembered being next to Imani when she and Linda had last reviewed the seating chart. She glared at Brenda, who had placed the name cards on the table. She was anything but subtle. Sitting next to a handsome doctor, especially one who needed to be distracted, was not a horrible way to spend an evening. She could certainly get through the meal.

She wasn't sure how she'd be able to keep his interest off the wedding and his brother. Him being a fellow geocacher was a good start, but he seemed so out of her league. He sat with perfect posture and sorted the sugar packets so all the yellow, pink, and white ones were grouped and faced the same way in the tiny container.

"The food certainly smells heavenly," she said, desperate for an opener. He smiled back and seemed out of his element. And why wouldn't he be? The only person he knew sat at the table across the room. Paul's chair was physically the farthest away from Thomas, and Ashley was sure Thomas felt the shun.

Even though Paul ignored him, Thomas gained the attention of other people. The first course was served with a side dish of envy. The other women in the room wished they were seated by the man. Imani, who Ashley knew to be a single mother, actually thrust her chest out every time Thomas glanced her way. Mindy and the other bridesmaid, Sarah, also made goo-goo eyes at the man.

Thomas may be a player, but the playing field lay wide open, and she imagined many women provided themselves to him. She couldn't blame him for taking advantage of the opportunities.

With all the pretty and single women at the rehearsal dinner, she must ensure that Thomas found her alluring enough that he could be distracted—at least long enough to be lured away from the party and dumped somewhere.

———————

Thomas gladly sat next to Ashley. She wore a modest summer dress that fastened at her neck in a seventies style that left her shoulders and arms bare. It reminded him of the old Farrah Fawcett look, and the auburn-haired beauty wearing it was an angel in every sense of the word. Unlike the other women at the party, her fresh face wasn't overly done in makeup, and the smile she wore summoned him like a beacon. Freckles lay sprinkled across her creamy white skin, and he wanted to connect the dots.

She held up her beer and offered a toast, so he tapped his bottle to hers.

"Bottoms up," she said, flashing her pearly whites and giving him a slightly devilish smile.

Bottoms up indeed, he thought, his mind already thinking of how creamy the skin under the dress was. He studied her delicate features, noting how her style in jewelry complemented her elfin frame. Simple and unassuming earrings hung from her lobes, and a tasteful golden band encircled her thin wrist.

He had only seen such beauty in paintings. And like in museums, she was off-limits. Which was such a shame because…well, she seemed so intriguing. He had found a woman who enjoyed the incredibly geeky hobby of geocaching. A sinfully gorgeous female didn't nerd-out like that. It'd be easier to find a herd of beauties at Comic Con than have one of them confess to a silly game of high-tech treasure hunting.

She also didn't go for a frou-frou drink. She liked the same beer he did.

Ashley was a unicorn.

She may be off-limits, but he needed to get to know her better.

"I thought you were the florist or the wedding coordinator." Her face pinched in an adorable what-are-you-talking-about way, so, he clarified. "You were at the front desk when I checked in."

"Oh, that." Her head swiveled as though making sure no one stood within earshot. "There was a mess-up with the flowers, but I took care of everything. Don't let Linda know another problem came up."

"Have there been many issues?" He leaned in and whispered to keep the confidential conversation a secret.

"Only one hiccup so far *today*. But stay tuned."

He watched her pert lips pucker when she sipped from the brown bottle, her mouth forming a perfect little *o* each time. She let out a delightful moan when the cold beverage quenched her thirst and then delicately licked her lips, her dainty pink tongue brushing across her full mouth.

"So, what do you do if you're not a wedding planner?"

She stared at him through long, luscious eyelashes. "I have a degree in kinesiology. I put myself through school working as a masseuse at hotels, but I hope to get on with a hospital. Maybe with knee rehabilitation."

Lovely. Caring. Smart.

Sexy.

Shit. It didn't get better than that.

Their salads arrived and were set in front of them. He was much hungrier than he had thought and had almost nearly devoured it when he heard Ashley laugh. She obviously knew the people at the table since she easily talked with them and even understood a private joke. He felt out of place but didn't care to have the joke explained. He remained too busy watching Ashley's face light up. He had the best seat in the house.

She answered a question from across the table. All he heard was that there were one too many groomsmen to match the bridesmaids now that Thomas had arrived, and there was a good chance his position would be elevated from usher to groomsman. They had directed the question to him, but he deflected it. His role hadn't been explained in Linda's schedule of events, but he assumed it would be thoroughly reviewed during their rehearsal dinner in a few days.

He was confident that his role was seat warmer, last-minute usher, or perhaps dog walker if someone brought in an emotional support animal. The role didn't matter. He suspected his mother had insisted he get an invite to the wedding and all the *fun* activities that came with the event. Paul had always been their mother's favorite, and even though he didn't want Thomas there, the man would do anything to appease their mom.

It still stung that Thomas wasn't more involved with the wedding party, but he hadn't been close to Paul in years. Only the most treasured family and friends should retain those few, cherished positions with someone at the altar if they were about to commit themselves to a life of misery.

He studied Ashley again. Young, beautiful, sexy. She must be close to Linda to be a party member. He wanted to engage her in conversation again and found a standard way to do so. "How do you know Linda?" he asked, assuming that a beautiful woman like her wasn't connected to Paul. He would have gone after Ashley himself if that were the case.

"I'm Linda's cousin."

Ashley, the beautiful woman and fellow geocacher he'd like to know better, was related to the bride.

Crap.

The bride.

The woman he'd slept with five years ago.

He was skating on thin ice.

This wedding party needed to be a dry dock for him. It *needed* to be no fun.

He shifted in his seat. Ashley was a woman he wanted to chat up and get to know better, at least for the evening. But she was off-limits.

4

_____

Every woman in the place needed to be hands-off. He had been introduced to everyone when he sat down, but he didn't remember anyone's name but Ashley's.

"So, what do you do, Thomas?" A female voice sounded from across the table. The woman wore what he considered a _Karen_ hairstyle, had a soccer-mom look about her, and was probably best friends with the bride since she kept busy snapping pictures left and right. Her gaudy jewelry, strawberry daiquiri, and the numerous times she played with her hair while talking to him told him one thing, but he wasn't interested in playing with her, not while the goddess Ashley sat to his left.

"You're a doctor, right?" another woman, this one an ebony beauty, asked as the catering staff served the lasagna.

"That's right," he said, gleaming a fake smile toward them and getting their names.

He didn't want to make small talk with the women, but the tomatoes from the lasagna would give him heartburn all night. There wasn't much choice. Talk or choke down Tums later.

He took a big bite.

The woman, whose name he now remembered as Imani, leaned across the table, flaunting her ample chest at him. Her breasts were pert, round, and natural. She was what he considered a chatty Cathy. If he showed any interest, the two would talk throughout the meal and then every free moment for the rest of the week. He didn't need clingy. "What's your specialty?" she asked.

"I'm a plastic surgeon," he said, his voice short and dismissive.

"Oh." Imani touched her nose like she already understood everything he did for a living. Everyone assumed noses when you mentioned plastic surgery, and he hated being stereotyped. He did reconstructive plastic surgery, not elective cosmetic surgery. But he would not debate the importance of his profession for more than vanity's sake, so he nodded and kept his mouth shut.

The attendees shared several stories between the tables. He learned how the happy couple had met, fallen in love, and how his brother had proposed. He had never given Paul credit for being a romantic at heart but meeting his soon-to-be wife at a pet adoption day and proposing during a dog training class sounded romantically cheesy, especially since both women sitting across the table—Mindy and…he wanted to say Sarah—cried during the story.

Toasts were made, but Thomas didn't offer one. He hadn't seen his brother in ten years, had ruined Paul's first chance at love, and felt out of his element since he didn't know anyone here.

Of course, he could get to know the goddess sitting to his left better.

He shifted his body toward Ashley as a waiter served the final course. Her eyes lit up when she saw him looking her way. He played a game he called *sexy eyes* throughout dessert, one where he stared at her as though looking into her soul.

However, this time, he felt like the game worked.

"I understand you're not from around here," she said softly. Her head was lowered, and her pouty smile drew him in.

God, she was incredible.

Her eyes narrowed, and a hint of a smile curved her lips as she peeked from behind her bangs in a shy, schoolgirl way. He'd always found that expression sexy.

"Chicago," he said, not taking his eyes off her.

She propped her elbow on the table and leaned in. "Are you enjoying Nevada?"

He was warming up to it, especially given how close Ashley now sat next to him. But did he enjoy Nevada? The question had consumed him lately. Ian Ostern Memorial Hospital had extended an invitation for him to be their next chief of plastic and reconstructive surgery, a coveted spot he wanted. Still, he would need to leave Chicago. Having his brother so close to him was not a draw, but the large sum of money Ian Ostern Memorial would pay him was.

He gave her his best smoldering look, even though he knew he played with fire and shouldn't. "I'm finding the state has some of the most attractive women in the country."

She let out a heartfelt laugh, followed by a feminine snort, which caused her to blush and quickly cover her mouth with her hand. "I'm sorry," she said, still giggling. "Does that line usually work for you?"

It did when tempting a loose woman at a bar. And it worked often, but not on those like Ashley. A quality woman could see through the cheesiness and keep him on his toes.

He felt up to the challenge.

He shrugged and tilted his head. In a low, husky voice, he said, "It got a reaction. Nice to know I can affect you, and I don't mind starting with your funny bone."

She blushed and looked away, so he knew he was getting under her skin.

"Thomas." Paul's voice sounded behind him. Paul leaned in like he needed to share something important. Thomas pulled back his chair and gave them some privacy. Paul whispered, "I need a favor."

A favor? Paul hadn't needed him for anything in a

decade. His brother wasn't frowning, he didn't look mad, and Thomas had no idea what he could need.

Paul straightened and motioned that he needed to talk in private, so Thomas rose, and the two men took a few steps away from the dinner party and stood in the back of the barn away from prying eyes and ears.

"Brian is nearly drunk, and he's already left this on the table twice." He handed Thomas a small jewelry box. "He picked up Linda's wedding ring from the engraver today. I need you to keep it safe."

Thomas glanced at Brian, who was hitting on Mindy and slinging back another drink. So much for picking out a good best man.

"Please put it back in the carriage house before we leave."

Thomas wasn't foolish enough to accept responsibility for something so valuable without confirming that he actually had the item, so he opened the box and looked inside. Three round, brilliant-cut diamonds curved in a row reflected the light and drew his eyes in.

"The ring set is called Cytser." Paul pointed to the row of tiny diamonds. "These curve around the engagement ring's larger diamond and match the six other diamonds in that setting."

He had seen Linda's engagement ring earlier and could imagine the combined setting. "Cytser?"

"The jeweler said the rings have names. I don't know. It means constellation in some language."

Thomas knew little about engagement rings or their names. He barely knew anything about diamonds at all except that they had carats and clarity. Even so, he didn't care to ask. "It's beautiful," he whispered.

"She picked it out a few weeks ago from Jay's Jewelers." His brother's smile held considerable pride as though pleased he could buy her the ring she wanted.

And Thomas realized he was happy for him.

This was the first brotherly moment the two had shared, and Thomas was surprised by how much he had missed Paul. "Linda already knows what the ring looks like, of course, so I had it inscribed. That way, there is *some* element of surprise for her."

"May I?" Thomas asked and placed his fingers around the ring to remove it from the box. When Paul nodded, Thomas picked it up and tilted it so the light caught the words inside. In script text, he read, *Love Everlasting*. "That's a beautiful sentiment."

Paul beamed from ear to ear. "It's also the title of the movie we watched on our first date. She's going to love it."

"I'm sure." He carefully placed the ring back inside the box.

"Please take it back to the carriage house. We don't need it to get lost tonight."

Thomas put the box into his pocket and assured his brother that he'd see to it before they left. Paul then moved away, and Thomas returned to the table where Ashley asked, "Is everything okay?"

Her eyes held concern. She loved the couple, and it showed. "Everything's fine."

"I hear you're Paul's older brother." A man's voice pulled Thomas's attention from Ashley. He turned to see a man standing behind him. He hated being interrupted, but it was probably for the best. Something about Ashley mesmerized him, and he didn't need to do something stupid at his brother's wedding.

"I'm Ashley and Linda's half-cousin, Mohinder." He extended his hand, and Thomas gladly accepted it. "Paul only mentioned having a brother a few weeks ago. I'm glad you made it to the wedding."

Of course, Paul had only mentioned having a brother a few weeks ago.

Thomas did his best to smile politely. "I'm glad I came, as well."

Mohinder's dark complexion and brown eyes contrasted starkly with Ashley's cool tones and reddish hair and Linda's Nordic appearance. "You're a half-cousin?" he asked.

The crowd stirred with people mingling, so Mohinder took a seat where Imani had been sitting. "Linda's and Ashley's mothers are sisters. My mother is a half-sister to them, making me a half-cousin."

"Our grandmother married twice," Ashley explained, leaning in and joining the conversation. "Grandma was in her early forties and went to India with her church on a retreat. That's where she met her second husband."

Even with the darker skin, the resemblance was unquestionable. "You and Ashley have similar facial features, but Linda looks different."

"Linda takes after her mother," Mohinder said.

"The two of them could be twins." Ashley gently touched her hair and twirled a curl around her index finger. "Linda's mother worked as a physician's assistant in the pharmaceutical industry like Paul and created her own moisturizing line. It's good stuff, but…"

"Expensive," Mohinder said.

Ashley's eyes widened as though agreeing. "She gifted her baseline set of products to the family every year at Christmas. It does wonders around the eyes." She glanced at her hands and showed off her glistening skin. "And everywhere else."

"So, she's successful?" Thomas wasn't interested in some miracle cream—although everyone on that side of the family had fantastic skin—but he did want to engage in more conversation with Ashley.

"She was fairly successful," Ashley said. Her expression turned sad. "She passed away a few years ago. Car accident."

Thomas saw the pain in both Mohinder's and Ashley's eyes. The family was close. "I'm sorry to hear that."

"Linda's mother came from money, but the inheritance has dwindled throughout the years. I think they suffered during the late seventies or early eighties, and Linda's paternal grandmother—no relation to us—squandered all the money."

Thomas let Mohinder's words settle in. He had assumed, or his mother had led him to believe, that Paul was marrying into a wealthy family. But, evidently, that wasn't the case.

"It's not like they're poor," Ashley said. "Linda has more money than Mohinder and me combined," she said, indicating her cousin and herself. "But the air of pretense is always there. That's why we're being treated to a week-long extravaganza instead of a typical wedding." She exaggerated the word *extravaganza* in a rich-sounding voice.

"Treated? Well, they had help paying for the wedding. Ashley and the owners are good friends, and she managed a good discount."

Ashley slapped Mohinder gently on the shoulder. "It was the least I could do."

Even with the discount, the place was expensive. Thomas counted the people attending the dinner. There was a good dozen here, with more coming to stay at the Bella Rosa. A catered meal at a private venue for that many people added cost to the weekend. There was the charge of the carriage house, the cottage, and the wedding itself, plus everything else in Linda's itinerary.

"You'll be able to meet our grandmother and my grandfather at the wedding, same with all the aunts and uncles and, of course, the Higgenbothems," Mohinder said. "We have an extensive family."

"Family is important," Thomas said, knowing how hard it was for him to honor his father's dying wish to mend his ways, reconcile with his brother Paul, and take care of his mother.

"What about your parents?" Ashley asked.

The beautiful unicorn had read his mind. He rarely shared personal stuff with people, but her compassionate green eyes melted his resolve. "My father died of a heart attack over a year ago, but my mother will be here in a couple of days."

"I'm sorry for your loss." Ashley touched his hand, and a jolt of excitement ran through him. Her warm, soft fingers did not stay long, and she pulled away once she noticed him staring at where their skin touched.

"I'm here to support my brother. Plus, I promised my father I'd get along with Paul. We haven't really spoken in many years."

The two nodded to tell Thomas they knew the Tina story and how he had supposedly stolen her away from Paul.

His one mistake.

And he had paid dearly for it.

"Okay, you two. We're out of here." Matt, a groomsman, stood behind Ashley, with Brian stumbling behind him. Thomas couldn't even garner the title of groomsman, at least, not yet. And Brian? Brian was Paul's best man—the position that should have gone to Thomas. If things hadn't gone the way they had, he would be standing next to his brother on his big day.

"Baby doll," Brian said, his eyes narrowing on Ashley, "the ladies are ready to leave." Brian gazed at Ashley, and Thomas saw the man's gaze directed at her chest and then move south to take in her legs. "We're heading out to give Paul one more night of freedom." He gestured toward the barn doors. "The cars are here."

Thomas noticed the guests were no longer seated and were now standing at the door. Hershel and his wife Brenda had disappeared once the dinner began, probably to have their meal at the house, but they had returned and were now putting *I'm the Bride*, and *I'm the Groom* sashes on Linda and Paul and telling everyone to be safe and responsible.

Even Brian had gone up to them. He was now getting a sash that read, *F*** me! I'm the Best Man*. The groomsmen had buttons on their shirts, but Thomas couldn't read them from where he sat.

"We're coming," Ashley said. Thomas quickly stood and pulled out her chair. He didn't want to go to strip clubs with his little brother all night. What if he got drunk and said something stupid like, "*If I remember correctly, that Linda of yours is super limber.*"

The men also planned to see a traditional burlesque show. But if he read Brian correctly, he took his best man duties seriously, and there'd be a stripper involved —maybe even a sex worker.

Thomas didn't want to see his little brother receiving a lap dance.

He walked to the door and heard Ashley thanking

Brenda and Hershel. The three stood close together and smiled warmly at one another in a way that told him they were close friends. He wasn't sure how much of a discount she'd received from the couple, but it made for a lovely wedding present.

All he had done was buy a place setting off their registry.

He stood aside and allowed her to walk out the door to find her rideshare, but she stopped and stared at him. In one of the sexiest invites he had ever heard, she asked, "Do you want to get out of here?"

5

—————

T homas heard his heart pounding.

He gripped his head with both hands and let out a soft moan. Something must have died in his mouth, but his body ached too much for him even to move to discover what it was.

Why was he so uncomfortable? He stretched his legs and hit the side of...a couch? He reached above him and felt the opposite arm of the couch behind his head. Why did he fall asleep on a love seat easily a foot too short of supporting his tall form? He pried his eyes open. The sunlight burned, so he closed them again.

Crap. Where am I?

He rubbed his temple and gingerly opened his eyes once more. Where was he?

He swallowed a few times, his tongue feeling as if it were covered in fur. A generic coffee table. A hideous floor lamp. Heart-shaped pillows?

He was alone. Whatever fun he'd had last night hadn't left him with an awkward sneak-out-the-door moment and a promise to call.

But, crap. If he hadn't gone home with a woman, where the heck was he?

Then it hit him.

The wedding.

The Bella Rosa Resort.

Ugh! He turned on the couch, his back aching. A long time had passed since he'd gone out and tied one on like this—an extremely long time.

His back and neck popped as he stretched, giving him some relief but not enough.

He needed eye drops, a shower, mouthwash for sure, and a lot of ibuprofen. He remained dressed in last night's outfit, and the distinct scent of peppermint schnapps hit him, making his stomach turn.

He didn't drink schnapps. And definitely not peppermint.

He squeezed his eyes shut as he tried to remember what had happened.

There was a bachelor party, Italian food—which explained his raging heartburn—and what else?

God, had he told his brother the truth about Linda?

Think, Thomas, he said to himself, knowing he'd need water, medication, and another good hour of sleep before his neurons truly sparked to life.

Snoring roared behind him, the kind that only a CPAP machine could help. It explained why he'd dreamed of being on a train. Thinking about the fleeting dream he'd had—traveling by train and getting motion sickness—made him want to retch.

It's only the booze, he reminded himself. *You'll live.*

It hurt to crane his neck to see who snored, but he did it anyway. A man lay naked and asleep on the floor, his legs spread wide, showing the world what little he'd been born with. The guy looked familiar, and Thomas knew him to be a wedding party member. He just couldn't remember his name.

Then it came to him. Brian. The loud, obnoxious, and overbearing best man.

Best man. Hardly. The man was crude and had hit on every woman within earshot last night, including…Ashley.

Ashley was her name.

He glanced around the room. What'd happened to her?

Thomas held his head as he stood, trying his best not to fall back onto the couch. A blanket lay on the back of the sofa—naturally, a woven one with hearts—and he placed it over Brian to cover the man. Brian seemed worse off than Thomas felt, and that was saying quite a bit. He rolled the guy so he lay on his side just in case he threw up.

"I'll get us both some water. Don't worry." Thomas then added, "And something for the headache I'm sure you'll have."

If Brian was here, then Thomas's brother and the other guys should have also made it back.

Thomas staggered to Paul's bedroom door, finding it open, and Paul clothed and passed out on the bedcovers. The strong smell of alcohol hung in the air. Paul seemed peaceful, and seeing him like this reminded Thomas of when they were kids. Being eight years older than Paul, Thomas had been a grown man when Paul entered his teenage years. The first time Paul got drunk was when Thomas—already twenty-four and old enough to know better—had bought him some beer to celebrate his sixteenth birthday. He'd had to hide the empty bottles and put Paul to bed early that night, keeping the secret from both their parents.

It was one of many secrets the two had shared growing up. They may have been years apart in age, but they had always remained close. Until Tina, Paul's girlfriend his freshman year in college. She'd broken up with him and had taken an interest in Thomas. He had been a fool to be seduced by her charms. The vixen had driven a wedge between the two men that had cut deeply into Thomas's heart, especially since their marriage was short-lived because she only wanted to be a doctor's wife.

Thomas stared at his brother, wishing he could undo all the hurt. He knew he would have to tell Paul the truth about Linda; he just didn't know when. The truth would have to be aired before Paul tied the knot; Thomas was confident of that.

Making his way to the second bedroom, he checked on…what was he? A half-cousin?

Mohinder stirred awake and moaned when he saw Thomas staring at him from his bedroom door threshold.

"Wherever we went," Thomas said, "it looks like we had a good time."

"Nothing is worth this." Mohinder groaned as he held his head and sat up. "I didn't even drink as much as you all did." He studied Thomas. "Well, I don't even know where you went. You missed the entire party."

A flash of fuzzy memories flooded Thomas's mind. Dinner, the rideshare, some sort of bar with lasers? Several images of Ashley—unclear and jumbled—crossed his mind. Had he not spent the evening with his brother and the other men?

His mind raced, which flat-out hurt. If he needed to operate heavy machinery or even fold some laundry, he'd need to ask for help.

His head pounded, and yet he sort of remembered having a good time last night. A good time with…Ashley.

But, evidently, not that much fun if he'd woken up fully clothed and alone on the couch.

Where did she go?

A slight panic engulfed him. Did she make it home all right?

The other two bedroom doors were closed, but he heard snoring.

"Matt and Connor made it back with us," Mohinder

said, waving a hand toward the doors. "I have to pee." He shakily moved from the bed and walked past Thomas to the bathroom, giving Thomas time to stagger to the carriage house's small kitchen to get six chilled bottles of water from the fridge. He placed a bottle beside each groomsman and Paul so they'd find it as soon as they woke up. He then put two bottles on the counter for him and Mohinder, wishing the man would hurry out of the bathroom.

He was halfway done drinking his water and dancing around the kitchen with an urgent need to relieve himself when Mohinder returned.

"We're not alone," Mohinder said, his voice sounding ominous as though he had discovered a dead body in the bathtub.

It was too early for shame or a *Scooby-Doo* mystery. Thomas handed the man a water bottle. "What?"

Mohinder's eyebrows narrowed, and he nearly scowled. "Why is my cousin in your bed?"

Thomas's gaze darted to his bedroom across from the living room, his head instantly throbbing with the motion. "Ashley is here?"

He stumbled to the bedroom with Mohinder and peeked in. She lay under the covers, still asleep but facing them, her hair splayed across his pillow. "I don't remember bringing her back here." That heartburn dinner, and a driver who spoke broken English. And again, something with lasers. Everything sounded bizarre. His mind had…nothing.

Mohinder pointed at Ashley. "Did you sleep with my cousin?" he asked, his voice louder than Thomas's ears could handle at the moment. Even though Mohinder could barely stand, he straightened and made himself seem formidable, although he was a good two inches shorter than Thomas. "She's been through a lot the last few years, and she isn't the type of woman to…"

"Relax." A one-night stand had never killed anyone. At least, not if protection was used. Besides, he was as surprised to find her here as Mohinder was. "I woke up on the couch." He tugged on his shirt. "Fully clothed." He then remembered Brian, naked as a jaybird and passed out on the floor, but Thomas dismissed him. Even covered up in the bed, he could tell Ashley still wore her dress. "Looks like I gave Ashley my bed to sleep in. Nothing happened."

God, chances were the two had been so drunk they couldn't even find her room—which was across the garden at the cottage.

How did they find their way back here?

And was he so drunk that he didn't sleep with her? That made no sense.

"Nothing had better have happened. She isn't that type of woman."

Thomas knew Mohinder wanted to sound menacing, but his words came out slightly slurred. Or did Thomas just hear them that way?

God, he felt as though he were moving in slow motion.

"I love my cousin, and if you hurt her, I will make sure you pay." Mohinder's voice, shaky as it sounded, was still filled with protectiveness, and his eyes shone with determination. He loved Ashley. Thomas saw that.

"We had a good time, that's all." He said it more to fill his memory gaps than to belay any of Mohinder's worry. He had no idea what he and Ashley had done.

Mohinder didn't look convinced but no longer puffed out his chest and tried to look threatening. "You disappeared last night. Paul figured you didn't want to hang out with us."

"Ashley and I went our own way after dinner last night." The words stung Thomas as he said them. Paul had been right, but it had nothing to do with spending the evening with the boys—not really. Thomas had wanted to keep his distance so the ugly truth wouldn't come out. Now, the opportunity was lost. Had he told his brother—and he was too drunk to process the information or even remember it afterward—Thomas would be off the hook.

Sort of.

A puzzled expression crossed Mohinder's face as though memories were flooding back. He pointed his finger at Thomas, slightly shaking it as though the motion helped him to remember. "You were passed out on the couch when we got home last night." His gaze focused on Ashley. "Ashley must have been back here, already asleep."

Thomas used his hand like a squeegee and rubbed his face. A tingling sensation, not necessarily unpleasant, ran through his cheeks as blood circulated and stirred him back to life. "She must have been." Soft snores came from Ashley. As bad as she must feel, she still had a beauty about her. Tousled hair and smudged makeup aside, she looked sexy.

Mohinder stepped back and stared into the living room. "Brian said his bedroom was too hot. Something about the air vents not working in there, so he stripped and slept on the floor since you were already on the couch."

"I'm glad he didn't try to share the sofa with me." Thomas took comfort in knowing the men had not realized that Ashley slept only a few feet away. Brian lived as a player, and Thomas suspected Ashley would not have appreciated his advances.

At least, a part of him—deep down and feeling possessive—hoped she wouldn't have appreciated them.

Thomas didn't remember coming home with Ashley or even putting her to bed last night. Although, he did remember drinking some lemon shots. She had never done shots, and all he recalled was a bar table holding many little glasses in columns and rows.

God, there had been enough not just to form a line but also to have columns and rows. He couldn't remember where they'd gone, only that Ashley was with him, and they had drunk a lot. Which reminded him of his bladder's urgent need.

Mohinder glanced over to where Brian's snores were coming from. "He partied hard and will be a mess today."

"I think all of us will be messed up today." Thomas made his way into the bathroom to relieve himself. Afterward, he brought out a bottle of ibuprofen. The cap gave him a moment of grief, but he finally got two pills out. "Here, take these," he said to Mohinder, who had finished his first bottle of water and was getting a second one.

Thomas took two ibuprofen himself before setting a couple of pills near the water bottles for each of the men.

His phone vibrated in his pocket. He always set it to do not disturb until eight a.m. while on vacation, and a slew of texts now flooded in. They were from Linda. He had not given her his number five years ago when they'd shared their one-night stand. He knew that for a fact because he never gave it out. Evidently, she'd gotten his contact information from Paul.

Many texts asked where Ashley was and if she was all right.

His phone read like a mini novel, with him written as the villain.

Several questions had come in for four hours last night. He read his replies, which were respectful at first, saying he and Ashley were having drinks, then having dessert somewhere, watching a show...basic stuff but definitely answers regarding what they'd done—things he also needed to understand. His last text to Linda wasn't so polite. He had called her a *batch* and asked her to leave him alone. At least, that's what he could make out, given the poor grammar of his last few sentences. Spellcheck had renamed her in the text because he was certain *batch* wasn't the word he had intended to use for her.

He checked the messages to his brother. He had told Paul that his bride was pushy and—well, of course, he'd spelled the word correctly when complained to his brother. His brother's replies were not kind. But, at the very least, Thomas found no evidence that he had told Paul the truth about Linda, even though he'd called her a liar in one text and said she should own up to what she had done. Paul sounded confused in his reply and told him to go to hell.

Thomas put the phone away. The same old fight remained between the two. Eventually, they'd stop talking about Linda and return to Tina, lack of boundaries, and the knife Thomas had supposedly used to stab Paul in the back all those years ago. "Last night seems to have been pretty lively," he finally said to Mohinder.

An eerie sensation crept over him and made him shudder. He may not have slept with Ashley—well, probably not—but his brother wouldn't believe that.

He'd accuse him of getting the woman drunk and seducing her.

Pain hit him square in the gut. He didn't need more strife between them. His bed may not remain empty for long, but he wasn't an opportunist. He wouldn't have gotten her drunk to take advantage of her. And he wouldn't have chosen the bride's cousin to sleep with a few nights before Paul's wedding.

Besides, Ashley had asked *him* out. The idea of breaking from the party had come from her after dinner last night.

His gut twisted more. Ashley was probably like so many of the women he met. They discovered he was a doctor, had money, a nice car, a full head of hair, and hadn't let himself go…and they wanted a piece of him.

Dammit.

Mohinder had said she wasn't like that, but in his experience, all women were well-versed in scheming to get what they wanted. What if he had slept with her? What if she claimed he did, regardless of the truth? She could already be pregnant by some other man and have seen Thomas as a meal ticket by way of a lawsuit.

Nah, there were tests to prove paternity. Plus, tests existed to confirm a pregnancy. Science would be on his side.

"What the hell is this?" Mohinder picked up a paper from the coffee table near the couch where Thomas had slept. His eyes widened as he read it, and then he glared at Thomas in a way that made him feel uneasy.

Thomas's head still pounded, and he needed no more grief today. "What?"

Mohinder turned the paper around, and Thomas's gaze zoomed in on it—especially the title of the document that read, *Clark County, Nevada - Marriage License.*

6

Thomas's chest tightened, and he could barely stand on his rubbery legs. He crossed the room and grabbed the paper from Mohinder's hands. "This has to be fake."

He tried to catch his breath but couldn't.

It wasn't a marriage certificate, only a license to get married. His gaze darted across the page and rested on their signatures. He swallowed the lump in his throat. He'd recognize his signature anywhere, but this was the sloppiest signature of his he had ever seen. The bold *T* and the swirly *S* were his, but the rest of the letters were munged together and unreadable. There was a word after his name that he couldn't make out, though. "What is this?" he said, pointing to the document. "Looks like *S, u*...something."

"Surgeon?" Mohinder guessed.

Name and occupation. His name had been written brazenly, firmly, and sloppily.

Which was utter nonsense.

"A license. So, are you married to my cousin or not?" Mohinder's reddened face and harsh words were not helping the situation. He puffed out his chest once again and took on a protective stance where his cousin was concerned. "I don't know you, but Ashley is vulnerable, and so far, you seem like a complete jerk."

Thomas held out his hand. "Hey, I don't want to be married. Your cousin is nice," he said, remembering bits and pieces of the night before, "but if we *did* get hitched, it was a complete mistake."

Thomas's gaze darted to the bride's name. Bold letters stared back at him, and he read her full name, which was more legible than his. "Ashley Uxer." Beside it in parentheses were the letters *H, o, t* and then something he couldn't make out.

"Ashley Uxer and hotel something?" He focused on last night's conversation. Kinesiology degree. Knee rehabilitation. What had she said? Then, he finally remembered. "She works at a hotel in town as a masseuse. Maybe that has something to do with the word by her name." At least he knew the vixen's full name now. "She must have tricked me into…"

"Shut it," Mohinder said, his voice booming and hurting Thomas's ears. "Don't be so full of yourself. Ashley is sweet and wonderful." He pointed his finger accusingly at Thomas. "Paul chose to keep you at a safe distance. There's probably a good reason for that."

Thomas's jaw tightened. The rift between him and Paul was not for public display but was evidently fodder for the bridal party. "That has nothing to do with—"

"Ashley recently got past some health issues and graduated college. She doesn't need to be married to some lowlife." Mohinder finally took a breath and glanced at the bedroom door where Ashley slept. "She's going to be devastated when she finds out she's married again."

Again?

"It's only a license. There's no proof we got married." Thomas slyly moved his fingers together on his left hand and felt a ring. His heart sank until it bounced off the floor. A frickin' ring rested on his finger.

A RING!

He glanced down, not allowing Mohinder to see him do so, and saw the cheesy jewelry. A surge of panic engulfed him, and he needed to sit. "I can fix whatever this is," he said in a shaky voice. "I'll make everything go away. No one needs to know what happened."

"You'd better make it right, or I swear…"

"It'll be fine," Thomas said, more to assure himself than to appease the other man.

Mohinder sat next to him, his eyes on Thomas's partially hidden hand. He saw the ring and grabbed Thomas's arm, gawking at the gaudy bling. "Honesty is the best policy. Explain what happened to Ashley and get an annulment. Lies can destroy a family, and Paul, *your* brother, is about to marry your new *wife's* cousin."

The word *wife* tore into Thomas, making him want to throw up.

"I'm a lawyer. Not in Nevada, but still." Mohinder handed the license to Thomas. "The marriage isn't legal until it's registered. So, if you two didn't go to a chapel last night…"

Thomas held up his left hand and waggled his fingers. The ring had been purchased somewhere. "I'm sure a chapel was involved."

Mohinder's face hardened, a reddish hue coloring his brown skin. "But if the chapel didn't file because the two of you were drunk, you may be able to settle this without any legal action."

"Legal action. Right." Thomas heard Mohinder's words but only focused on the ring that now weighed down his hand. He rose and walked toward the bedroom door where…where *his wife* slept. "We can get out of this."

"Yes, with an annulment." Mohinder followed Thomas's thoughts. "She annulled her first marriage, and since her family is Catholic, she still plans to be married in a church one day." He shook his head as though he knew this news would hurt her. "It's Sunday. If I were you, I'd get a blood test to prove you were drunk. It'd also be good for you to retrace your steps. Maybe find the chapel where you were married and see if they filed the paperwork." He shot Thomas a stern glare. "I'd also not consummate the marriage."

For the first time in his life, Thomas didn't think he could perform such an act. Now in his early forties, he had not been on a bender like this in years, and his body was punishing him for it. And Ashley? As tempting as she was, and he had to admit he remembered enjoying himself last night, there was no way he'd fall into a trap with her.

"I know of several doctors and clinics in the area," Thomas said. "I'm sure we can get some blood drawn. However, we may not get the results back for a few days."

He stared at his wife lying in bed, an earthy citrus scent mixed with the smell of whiskey tantalizing him and bringing forth a faint memory. The fragrance had engulfed him last night, teased and pulled him in. He hated flowery perfumes, but Ashley wore the strikingly bold fragrance with unmatched confidence.

He inhaled deeply, and his arousal surprised him, especially since the massive ring on his hand reminded him of the trap that lay before him.

His mind raced until his thunderous headache stalled his thoughts. He doubted he had slept with her last night. His hands stroked his shirt, finding each button still securely fastened. She was a perfect ten, everything he wanted, and he hadn't slept with her? That didn't make sense.

He'd wanted her from the moment he first laid eyes

on her. Plus, she had come on to him by suggesting they go to a bar after dinner. Where had they gone? Everything was fuzzy.

A soft moan sounded, and she stirred, turning from them and facing the window. If he believed Mohinder, Ashley was a sweet person. But for all Thomas knew, she could be a she-devil in disguise, wanting to trap him in a sham of a marriage to take his money.

God. Why was it so bright?

Pain stabbed into Ashley's brain. Curled in a fetal position on the bed, she held her head, the palms of her hands pressed firmly to her ears.

She wanted to die.

Date. She tried to think, pulling the blankets around herself tightly. *Day...what day?* She squinted her eyes and knew the time was late, but her head felt like it might explode. *Workday?*

It didn't feel like a Monday. Tuesday?

She rolled over and buried her face in the soft pillow. *Bright. Nine o'clock?*

Not caring if it was a workday or if she was late for work, she figured she'd claim a sick day.

Her eyes felt glued shut as if her pillow had been stuffed with pollen. Her throat hurt due to thirst. She was definitely sick.

She opened one eye a crack to see if she had placed

her water bottle on her nightstand. The light pierced like a dagger, but she weathered it long enough to see if water lay within arm's reach.

A bronze lamp stood on the tiny nightstand.

Where did that lamp come from?

She focused on something shiny that lay on the bedside table. Why was there a smartwatch? Her eyes popped open, but still didn't allow her to focus. She leaned toward the nightstand for a closer look, rubbing her eyes to see better. An Apple watch and a brown leather wallet...they weren't hers. Why would she have a man's watch and wallet on her nightstand? She studied the two items. They definitely belonged to a man.

Her chest tightened, and her body went rigid. This wasn't her room. And...she could hardly breathe...she wasn't alone.

No. No. No.

God, no.

Her heart pounded as her hands quickly inspected what she may or may not be wearing. She felt her dress and sighed in relief when she discovered that she still wore her underwear. She rubbed her feet together. No shoes. She was dressed where it truly mattered, at least.

Her mind raced, trying to remember what had happened last night. More importantly, did someone lie next to her in the bed?

She tried desperately to suck in some air, but the oxygen had seemingly fled the room—much like her dignity and self-respect. She knew a man slept next to her. She just had no clue who it could be.

An image of Thomas came to her foggy brain.

She had gone out with Thomas Stallworth! They'd taken a rideshare to the Vegas Strip. They went to a bar...yes, there had been a bar, she was sure about that. Some lemon shots.

She squeezed her eyes shut, and tears pooled. What did she do after the bar? Thomas may be the most handsome man she'd ever laid eyes on, but from what she had been told about him, he would likely be interested in only one thing.

And he was Paul's brother! Handsome and gorgeous for sure, but... No, no, no. This couldn't be happening. Linda would kill her.

Her first-ever one-nighter, and she had to do the boneheaded thing of sleeping with Paul's brother.

She let out a gasp. It might not be Thomas.

Crap. What if some stranger from the bar had picked her up? The plan was to ditch Thomas somewhere on the Strip.

What if he had ditched her?

No. Nope! She wouldn't even consider that. Thomas had not ditched her somewhere, and she had not hooked up with some stranger. She may have been blitzed last night, but she would have gone to the Nuts & Bolts Club to meet Linda if Thomas had disappeared on her.

She thought about that and reconsidered. No. She

would have gone home. Even drunk, she would have gone home.

Well, not home. Back to the Bella Rosa.

That lamp. She opened her eyes wider and stared at it. She had helped Brenda pick out the new light fixtures for the carriage house. Now eying the wallpaper behind the nightstand, she recognized the pattern. She had spent the night at the Bella Rosa, but not in her bed at the cottage. The color scheme of the cottage was pastels, and this room was decorated in blues and browns. This was definitely the carriage house, where the men stayed when the bridal party bought the deluxe package.

If her head would stop pounding and her eyesight stopped being so blurry, she might have the courage to turn over. She didn't hear any snoring but figured Thomas was probably so drunk he was passed out. Maybe he had been too drunk to want to have sex with her.

Yes. That might have happened. Also, Thomas was a doctor and therefore a respected member of the community. He probably wasn't the type of man to take advantage of a woman.

God, what was she thinking? A doctor or not, he was a man. But was he a *decent* man?

She focused on her body. Did it *feel* like she'd had sex last night? It had been ages since a man had been in her bed, but she was sure—no, she was positive—she had not slept with Thomas. A hysterectomy two years ago had changed her body down there. Her doctor had told her it would be painful at first to be intimate with a man, and she felt no different, other than the dryness she always woke to.

She felt positive she hadn't slept with Thomas. She was okay.

Good Lord, she needed to pee a river. Time was up. She had to get out of this bed.

She gathered her courage and carefully turned without moving too much.

The movement hurt her head, but she shifted her hips slightly and then her shoulders.

God, please let no one be naked beside me. She told herself to be brave and to find out. She had mentally undressed Thomas during dinner last night, but that was a different situation.

She took a deep breath and turned her neck toward the second pillow on the bed.

The bed was empty. The covers of the quilt remained tucked in on that side.

She stared at the open door and saw a number on it. At least she knew where she was. Room number six. Thomas's room. She had woken up in *his* room.

Drunk. In Thomas's room. Alone. He had the key to the carriage house and the one to his individual room. He must have let her in. Besides, his watch and wallet were on the bedside table, so he had definitely been in the room with her at some point during the night. She was drunk, in his bed...and... She'd woken up in the manwhore's bed alone?

A massive surge of relief filled her, but a small part felt chided. A handsome man like Thomas wouldn't be interested in taking advantage of her. Thanks to her cancer and all the operations she had needed, she had been cut up, cored out, and only resembled a woman when she had clothes on.

She had probably told him her medical history, and he hadn't wanted to touch her with a ten-foot pole. What man would?

Dammit. No. She was a survivor. She was a woman, no matter what had been taken away.

Tears welled and threatened to escape.

She may not be ready to date and be with a man, but dammit, she didn't need to be vulnerable and rejected, dumped in Thomas's bed untouched.

Hoping her spiral was remnants of her drunken night, she told herself to organize her thoughts and get off the stupid emotional roller coaster. She had never had a one-night stand before. Never in her wildest dreams had she *wanted* one. And Thomas had been decent enough not to touch her. She needed to be grateful that he was an honorable man. Getting out of this room was the top priority, not her little pity party about her cancer and surgeries.

A knock came from the door, and her gaze darted toward it.

Her blurry eyesight focused on where the sound had come from, and she found Thomas standing on the threshold, staring at her. Same with her cousin, Mohinder.

Her stomach sank. So much for sneaking out without anyone seeing her.

"Are you feeling all right?" Thomas asked, his voice husky and deep. If he felt half as yucky as she did this morning, he had no right to look as fantastic as he did—scruffy beard, tousled hair, award-winning smile.

The man was tall, handsome, and probably a good kisser—no! She needed to stop thinking like that. Had she been tempted, it would have been last night. This morning, she needed to slink away.

"I'm fine." Her voice cracked and sounded as horrible as she felt.

"I'll get you a warm washcloth and some water," Mohinder said, then left, headed toward the kitchen.

Water would be good. Rinsing off sounded terrific, too. She felt physically and emotionally dirty. Her makeup was probably gone. Her hair… Her hair! Some might say chemo had blessed her with curls, but she now understood the struggle to manage curly hair. Surely, she resembled the bride of Frankenstein with her hair sticking up in every direction since she wasn't sleeping on a satin pillowcase.

She needed a coiled scrunchy to pull it back. Checking her wrist, she found no hair tie. "What happened last night?" she asked, not making eye contact.

Thomas entered the room and sat next to her on the

bed. The mattress gave way to his weight and pulled her closer to him. His hand gently touched her shoulder. "I was hoping you'd tell me, beautiful."

Beautiful? His eyesight must be blurry, too.

He brushed a stray curl from her face and stared at her. His gaze was concentrated and concerned, making her think that, on some level, the two may have made some connection last night.

"Are you feeling sick?" he asked.

Sick? How bad did she look? Oh, wait. Thomas was a doctor. He wasn't gazing into her eyes in any romantic way. He was conducting a medical checkup.

God, she was a mess.

She nodded and cleared her throat. "I need to pee."

He rose and held out his hand to give her assistance. Her legs felt weighted, but with his help, she managed to get to the bathroom door, where she met Mohinder.

"Here," he said, handing her a water bottle and a warm washcloth.

She thanked them both and closed herself in the bathroom. Had she actually told that gorgeous man she needed to pee? Not even, "*I need to use the restroom*," or "*I need a moment to myself.*" Anything less crass.

The bathroom mirror reflected the frightening truth. How did mascara run this badly? The black smudges were the only makeup that remained, and it had smeared all over the place. She put the warm cloth on her face, and the heat refreshed her. She inhaled deeply into the fabric, and the sensation calmed her stomach.

A green stain marred her dress, but it was dry and caked.

Damn, she liked this dress.

Her back muscles twinged like they always did after vomiting. Yep. She'd thrown up at some point last night. That explained the horrible taste in her mouth. A toiletry bag sat on the sink, surrounded by shampoo, shave cream, and a bottle of Scope. She'd shared his bed, so a little sharing of mouthwash didn't seem like much harm.

She used the bathroom, rinsed her mouth, and then inspected her hair, which looked as though it had been styled with the help of an electrical socket. There was nothing she could do but wet it down and tame the rag mop.

The sound of a phone buzzing scared her, and she let out a slight squeal, her heart racing. *It's only a phone,* she told herself, searching for the cell. She found her clutch purse on the floor between the toilet and the shower.

Perfect. She'd just left it lying around? She must have been really out of it.

She fetched the purse, and a faint memory of ridding herself of the alcohol last night came back to her. The memory made her stomach twist, so she stood and took some deep breaths.

The phone buzzed again. Her iPhone's alarm was going off. Did she really believe she'd go for a morning run? Ha! She had actually thought she'd be awake at dawn to go for a run and burn off the calories from the party last night.

She shut off the sound. That would not be happening. She wanted to down some aspirin and then crawl back into bed. *Her* bed.

Doubting her cousin Linda would pick up if she called, she decided to text her. That was when she noticed a long text exchange between the two. Ashley scanned the conversation. *Having a great time*, *Don't worry*, *See you later*... The texts ended about three a.m.

She texted Linda. *I assume we won't be running this morning. See you later.*

Later was right. Ashley straightened her dress, and a thought occurred to her. Had she been stupid enough to get a tattoo? She didn't hurt anywhere but did a cursory check on her body anyway. Finding no ink, she straightened her clothing, making sure her mastectomy bra and prosthetic boobs were on straight and that her outfit covered the port scar on her clavicle.

"Are you all right?" The kind words from Thomas accompanied a soft knock on the door. "We need to talk."

God, she had never been so embarrassed. She didn't want to discuss anything that may have happened—or hadn't—last night.

"I have ibuprofen."

She wanted that.

7

Ashley led Thomas back to the bedroom, first signaling to Mohinder that she was fine and that he shouldn't worry or hover like a mother hen. From the pained expression and the heaviness of his brow, her cousin suffered from partying too hard last night. The man seemed grateful to return to bed. If he felt half as bad as she did, she couldn't blame him for wanting to go back to sleep.

"Here," Thomas said, handing Ashley an ibuprofen gelcap.

Hope sprang forth as she eyed the bright blue-green bit of heaven. "Two, please."

Taking another pill from the container, he said, "NSAIDs are hard on the liver, so don't take any more for at least six hours."

Liver, shmiver. She needed her headache to go away. Her liver must have been pickled in alcohol last night, so it was already suffering. She downed the medicine with one gulp of water before finishing the bottle and quenching her thirst. "I'm a bit dizzy."

He sat her on the bed and touched her fingers slightly. He then pinched her fingertips and the skin on her hand. The movement wasn't aggressive or passionate, yet the man held her hand. He caressed her skin and sat mere inches from her, his fingers gentle, patient, and…

"You're dehydrated."

She had forgotten for a moment that he was a doctor. An extra-sexy doctor.

He took her empty water bottle and returned a moment later with a fresh one. His head must pound as badly as hers because he picked up his bottle from the dresser and took a drink. "Thank you," she said, taking a gulp from her second bottle. She had never thought water could taste so good.

An awkward silence filled the room as they sat and sipped water. She hardly knew the man, yet she sat in his bed. She knew the situation should have been uncomfortable, but she didn't care. All she wanted was to feel better. Still, she covered her legs with more of the sheet—partly due to propriety even though she remained fully clothed, but mostly it felt nice to be covered since she wasn't feeling well.

"It's been a long time since I've tied one on like this." Thomas rubbed his temple and then tipped his neck from side to side. Tension was released from his face when his vertebrae popped. The man then twisted his body from side to side, and she suspected he was also adjusting his back.

"I never let myself go crazy like this." She set the water bottle down and stared at him. His hair was tousled in a way only men could pull off—a bedhead coif. When her hair was shorter, she had woken every day to a troll doll greeting her in the mirror.

His eyes stared deeply into hers as if he were beseeching answers from her—answers she didn't have. Usually, such a stare would make her feel uneasy. His lips curled up into a slightly sweet smile. A devilish one that wasn't snide but gave him the appearance of an innocent schoolboy.

She could get lost in his baby blues and genuine smile. Was that what had happened last night? Yes, he was devilishly handsome and charming, but had she really let her inhibitions down with this Adonis?

Or did she have help?

She'd have sworn he roofied her if he didn't look as sick as she felt. But only an idiot would rug himself *and* his victim. He appeared to be an intelligent man. Even if he had access to drugs as a doctor, she didn't think he had used them on her. Besides, she had woken up alone.

"What do you remember about last night?" Questions filled his voice, and his tone held a pleading lilt as though he genuinely had no clue.

What did she remember? Not much. "We had the dinner in the barn," she said, her voice still scraggly. Last night, she had initially been nervous to talk to him but had promised Linda to get him away from the men and ditch him somewhere. Studying his face now, he almost looked beaten down, and she realized she had done this to him. He'd come to celebrate his brother's wedding, not to go out on the town and get trashed with a stranger.

"We went to a bar," she finally admitted, omitting any guilt she felt and pushing the shame deep down inside her.

"A bar." His face pinched amusingly. "I'd say a few bars. Either that or we stayed at one place all night and closed the place down." He rubbed his head, which only made his mad hairstyle sexier. "I have an online directory of clinics and a network of techs in the area. We should probably get our blood-alcohol content tested."

Puzzlement rose within her. Yes, they were drunk and had clearly been three sheets to the wind last night. If he had drugged her, he certainly wouldn't be suggesting any blood tests now. Still…

"Why should we get a blood-alcohol test done?"

He pulled a piece of paper from his pocket. He carefully unfolded it as if it were delicate or super important.

Holding it upright so she could see it, he said, "We may have gotten married last night."

The pull on her gut was nearly strong enough to make her throw up, and she felt even dizzier. She grabbed the paperwork and quickly scanned the page, her eyes darting to the word *License* and then to the two names on the bottom. One signature, although more messy than usual, was hers.

"A license." She turned the page over, even though she knew a certificate wouldn't be printed on the back since it was a different legal document. "Did you find a certificate of marriage?"

Her heart raced as she glared at him. "Did you?" she asked, her voice nearly a shriek as she gave him only a second to answer.

He leaned in and took the paper from her hand. "Shh. It's okay. We'll figure this out."

"Nevada doesn't make you wait three days from getting the license before...before you can get married," she nearly shouted. She could hear her own heartbeat pounding in her ears. "As soon as we left"—she pointed repeatedly to the words on the paper—"the Clark County Clerk's Office, we could have gone to any chapel on the Strip." She closed her eyes. The Strip! Drunk and in one of those tacky chapels. Elvis had probably performed the ceremony.

She found it difficult to breathe. In one quick motion, she threw back the covers from her legs. She searched the bed, then her gaze darted from the nightstand to the dresser and then back to his baby blues. "A certificate would make us legally married." She figured he understood the difference between the two, but she said it anyway. Her hand dove into the empty side pockets of her dress.

"It's all right." His calm voice cut through her panic, and she took a deep breath. "If we did get married, the certificate will be filed with the state. A copy would be mailed to us or still available at the chapel."

This couldn't be happening. Not to her. She was a good girl. For goodness sake, she was a frequent blood donor and a churchgoer. She had a membership to the educational public television station for sponsorship, and she held an active public library card. Women like her didn't run off and get married on the Strip.

No. They certainly didn't. She was a mature and sophisticated woman now.

She wasn't stupid.

At least, not anymore.

She stared coldly at him. He was a doctor. And he was known for being a bad boy—at least, that was the rumor. Again, she remembered that he had access to drugs.

"It was you." Her finger rose accusingly, and she pointed it at him. "You drugged me!"

His body stiffened, and he pulled away from her. "I certainly did not!"

"I don't see how I could have landed in this bed"— her arms waved over the mattress— "without the help of some sort of date-rape drug."

His face reddened, and his lips pulled into a straight, thin line. "You think I'm an opportunistic rapist?"

"If the name fits…."

"If I am, then I'm a poor excuse for one. You woke up fully clothed in my bed while I slept so crooked on the couch that my back is killing me." His face twisted with disgust. "If anything, you are a bed-hopping whore who only wants to latch onto a doctor."

Something about the way he looked, or maybe the way he'd said it, had her breaking out in a fit of laughter. "Bed-hopping whore?"

The tightness in his face left, and a curl of a smile came to his mouth. "A rapist and a whore. Aren't we a great combination?" He leaned slightly toward her and flashed her a smile. "I'm sorry, I probably shouldn't call my wife that."

She laughed wholeheartedly, which surprised her… yet felt familiar. She remembered nothing about last night, but being comfortable with Thomas and joking with him seemed natural.

Before she even looked down, she touched the ring on her finger. She felt the loose fit of the band and knew it to be a wedding ring.

Crap.

Wedding certificate or not, she wore a wedding ring.

She glanced down to see a cheesy, cheap ring encircling her finger. Her heart pounded in a near-heartbreak sort of way. The silver band had a pair of dice on it, the spots on the dice made of fake diamond chips. She took it off and, even with a headache, squinted her eyes at the ring's interior.

"What are you doing?"

"Here," she said, pointing to the inscription. "Something is written on the inside of my ring. It's too small, though. I can't read it."

An inscription? If Thomas ever got married again— something he wouldn't do knowingly—the words on a wedding band wouldn't be flowery poetry with promises of eternal love. Not at all. The inscription would read *PUT ME BACK ON!* His ex-wife had taught him that hard lesson years ago.

His gaudy ring was bigger than Ashley's, so he removed it and held it close to his face with one eye squinted. The motion was painful, but he could make out the words. "Pair O' Dice Chapel Las Vegas, NV," he read, grimacing at the bad pun.

Ashley turned her ring and tried to read the tiny letters. "Looks the same." She palmed the ring as if holding a dead mouse in her hand. She then gazed at Thomas, eyeing him in a way that didn't quite place blame but came too damn close for his comfort. "Not an incredibly romantic sentiment."

"At least we know which chapel we got married in." The words came out strained. Her expression had hardened, and he wondered if Ashley's distaste for the wedding stemmed from the institution itself or the fact that he was the prospective bridegroom.

She tossed the ring onto the bed, discarding it like an unwelcome piece of fruit she refused to eat because she'd found a worm inside. "Let's see if there are any more clues about last night." She had placed her purse on the bed once she returned to the room, so she fetched it and took out her phone. She scrolled through what looked like several pictures.

Her head tilted as she studied an image, and her lips pursed in what he assumed was disapproval.

God. Had they taken naked selfies or something?

"What are you looking at?" he asked as he leaned closer to her phone.

"Is that a pirate?" She turned the device to better show him the image. "There are skeletons on what looks like a corner of—"

"That looks like a parrot." He leaned in and pointed to a green and red spot in the picture. "That corner is a cage." He had seen the inside of plenty of bars, although tasteful ones and not any Halloween-themed disasters. "Are there any pirate-themed places around?"

"Uh, sort of. We have the Treasure Island Hotel and Casino. But, trust me, this place isn't it. This isn't even Señor Frogs. It's…well, it's a dive. That's for sure."

She shrugged and flipped to the next picture. The two of them with drinks in both hands, posing with a pirate. "This is embarrassing."

"This bar is embarrassing." They must have found the only Long John Silver's-meets-Halloween Horror Nights bar in all of Nevada. Cheap plastic decorations mixed with pirate uniforms, complete with wenches falling out of their tops, glared back at him from the photos. But what made his skin crawl were the expressions on their faces. Was she doing duck face? And his image? It could only be described as his orgasm face. It was clear they were already drunk and three sheets to the wind by the time the pictures had been taken.

"This couldn't have been the first place we went to," he said, not wanting to believe he'd step into the freak show bar if he knew what he was doing.

She tapped the picture and pulled up the data. "It's the first picture *I* took after we left dinner last night. It's timestamped close to eleven, though."

"That's over three hours after we left." He took out his phone and opened the phone's album. He wasn't one to take pictures, and definitely not selfies, but he had taken a few. "We don't look drunk in this shot," he said, eying a nice image of the two of them at a classy bar, each holding up what looked like a lemon shot. "We may have gone here first." Scrolling through his camera roll was like watching them get drunk. "He had two nice pictures, followed by one of the Halloween fright nights, and then what appeared to be closeups of a tree."

"A tree?" She leaned over, and her citrus scent closed in on him. He inhaled deeply. He remembered being close to her last night, smelling her hair and thinking she smelled like orange blossoms.

But that was last night. Today, they had a mess to figure out.

He rubbed his brow with his fingertips. His headache subsided a bit, but then he noticed a mark on his wrist. *Yo Ho Ho's* had been stamped on his skin over another mark labeled *Corporate Room*. The blue ink of the latter lay below the word *Yo* and told him they had gone to the Corporate Room first. "Do you have these marks?"

When she'd done her body inspection in the bathroom earlier, she had found the Corporate Room mark on her left hand, but there was no pirate one. "I know I was there. She studied herself in the picture that clearly showed her at the place. Thomas had been slumped beside her, half falling off his barstool, and there were two plastic rats behind them on a shelf, doing the nasty. "I was there."

"Wait," he said as she scrolled to another photo. "What is that a picture of? Is it a map?"

The picture showed a cheesy treasure map hanging on the wall. There was no frame of reference, so she flipped to the next image. That's when she realized the two images had been taken in the ladies' restroom.

"If I knew who those women were, I would probably apologize to them. Those were not flattering images at all."

The doctor in him came out, hoping the young woman throwing up on the floor was all right this morning. He opened the backpack that sat on the floor next to the bed and pulled out a notebook and a pen. "So, we were here in the barn until eight p.m. or so. Then we went to the Corporate Room, and then this pirate place…."

"Yo Ho Ho's," she said, reading a sign from another picture on her phone.

"Let's see if we can estimate when we left the pirate place and where we went afterward." They went back through the images they had already seen and wrote down the place and the pictures' timestamps.

The next image showed a screenshot of what appeared to be a text on her phone. "Looks like a text image of random words from (773) 555-2020."

"That's my phone number." He studied the three words, his excitement building as he realized what they were. "Bamboo. Rod. Polar," he said, glancing at her with a wide smile. "What3words," he finally said.

"These three." A confused expression crossed her face as she held the phone closer to him.

"No, they're coordinates." He thought back to what he remembered of the night before. "You geocache, right?"

"I forgot I told you that." A slight smile tugged at the corners of her mouth as though a guilty pleasure had been revealed. She took a deep breath. "But I don't understand what the words mean."

"What3words.com. The entire world is broken into three-meter square grids." The giddiness rose in his voice, and his nerdy part came out, but he didn't care.

She was a fellow geocacher, and What3Words might interest her. "Each grid has a unique three-word address that will never change."

A beautiful auburn eyebrow rose and hid behind a wayward curl. "Really?" She sat straighter and gestured with her hands. "The whole world?"

He had learned about the measurements a year ago from a fellow treasure hunter who geocached with him. It elevated the game to a different level than just longitude and latitude coordinates. "Three meters by three meters. Every inch, including the oceans. Plus," he added, grinning, "every language has its own unique triple destination."

Her bloodshot eyes showed her slow response to capture the full effect, but eventually, she asked, "What about elevation? If the words are centered in a high-rise building, then…?"

"Exactly. It's the only flaw in the system. Each floor would be included." She nodded in understanding, her soft curls bouncing against her jawline slightly. He didn't want—no, he didn't *need*—to consider his *wife* in such a way, but she was genuinely beautiful. Her eyes showed that her headache probably matched his, but as miserable as she likely felt, she still beamed with beauty.

The fact that she sat on his bed probably added to the attraction.

No. He reminded himself that he needed to fix this marriage problem, attend his brother's wedding, and then get the hell out of town before anything else went wrong.

She glanced at her phone with half-shut eyes and then announced, "We were at the Clark County Marriage License Bureau at nearly midnight, so probably after our two bar stops." She paused for a moment. "That's a good distance from the Strip. We must have taken a rideshare."

That didn't seem right, yet they *did* have the license. She must have noticed the puzzled look on his face since she added, "This is Nevada. That office is open every day of the week until midnight."

Of course, it was.

She flipped to the following picture. "Pair O' Dice Chapel at one-thirty this morning." Her eyes glazed over, and her hand went to her mouth as a horrified gasp escaped.

He glanced at the image but focused more on her expression. A sinking feeling hit him—one that didn't sit well with him. She looked hurt and disappointed in a way that left him speechless. He had money, good looks, and was a catch. They were both hot and about the same age. There was nothing to gasp about.

"We were married within hours of knowing each other." Her voice sounded disappointed and withdrawn.

"Yeah, but we got married the day *after* we met." He shrugged and gave her a wry smile. "If that makes you feel any better." He noted the times and places in his notebook as he collected his thoughts. "Regardless, we didn't know each other, and we can certainly use that." He glanced at the picture she still had up where they could barely stand, and their eyes were glazed over, showing their drunkenness. "And the fact that we were zonked out of our minds. Both reasons to get divorced."

"Annulled."

"That's what I meant." She didn't even want it known that a wedding had taken place. She wanted it completely erased. He wanted that, too, but he didn't expect that kind of reaction.

"I don't work until later this afternoon, so we can drive…" She touched her head. "Or rather schedule a car to somewhere right away. I don't want this *marriage*," she said, making air quotes, "to get in the way of Linda's wedding."

"Thanks. And I can't have more issues between my brother and me right now."

"Linda has been two steps away from becoming a Bridezilla. I had to sidestep a floral arrangement crisis yesterday." Her shoulders slumped defeatedly. "Plus, my parents are attending the wedding. The fewer people who know what we did, the better."

Again with the shame, although he agreed they should expedite the issue.

It occurred to him to check his Venmo account. He used it all the time for online purchases. What if he had drunkenly bought a car or something last night? A payment of one thousand dollars caught his attention. "Who the hell is dot6vegasmom?"

"What?"

He pointed to the payment on his phone's app. "At two a.m. last night, I paid someone a thousand dollars." He read the note attached to the payment. "What is *shhh monnnee*?"

Ashley studied the message. "Drunk writing?"

His jaw tightened, and his body grew tense. He supposed there was a way to deny payment on such things, but he didn't know how. Regardless, he didn't have the time to worry about it now.

"That's only one of the payments you made last night. Please scroll down and read the payments in the order you made them. That will tell us what we did and where we went."

His finger moved the app listing down. A rideshare receipt was the first thing he found. "We have a thirty-eight-minute ride to the Clark County Clerk's office—thank you, Uber, for those details." He then read the next receipt. "Followed by another rideshare receipt to the Strip."

"At least we weren't driving drunk."

"The next receipt is the *shhh monnnee* one." He skipped it and tapped the next receipt, but he knew it wasn't a good sign by the recipient's name, *podweddingchpl*. "A receipt of one hundred and fifty dollars for the chapel with a memo of *wededig*."

"Oh, dear. I'm sure you meant to type wedding."

His chest tightened. The note was for their wedding. "The next two payments are to the same address. This fifty-dollar receipt is…" He had trouble reading the message but finally guessed it to be a minister fee. "The next one is eighty dollars, and it looks like it was for the rings."

The rings had looked cheap, and here was the proof.

The following payment stared back at him. A sum of two hundred and fifty dollars and the recipient *podphotonv*. He was going to be sick. He guessed it was for Pair O' Dice Photography, Nevada. He read the memo. *pcs and cmm vido*.

"What does that mean?"

"Check your email account."

"What? Why?"

If the bar pictures were any indication of their sad state, he could only imagine how they appeared on video. "See if there is an email from the chapel with"— he paused slightly, his eyes narrowing— "a link to pictures and a commemorative video."

Her hand moved like lightning. She had an expression of horror that matched the one he felt plastered on his face. "Nothing," she finally said.

He did the same. "Me, neither. Either we gave them a bad email address, or they have a CD and printed pictures for us to pick up."

"Or they might still email them to us." Her face pinched in concentration. "What if we gave them an email or an address of a family member?"

He didn't look his best in the pictures on her phone. Professional photography or not, he didn't want to explain the photographs or a video to his mother. He didn't even want his family to discover this blunder.

Worse yet, what if they got leaked to social media and his hospital saw them? "We should go to the chapel and see where the video and pictures are," he said.

"They never should have married us. We should sue them for allowing this to happen." Her defeated expression caused him to place his hand on her shoulder. "We can fix this."

Married incorrectly or not, they needed blood tests to prove how drunk they were. His headache had lessened, and he felt capable of moving now. "Regardless of whether or not we consummated the marriage, our blood tests will show how impaired we were."

Her head shot up. "We didn't sleep together." Her voice sounded determined and positive, making his gaze meet hers.

"I only know we woke up in different rooms." He tugged at his shirt. "Fully clothed."

Her jaw tightened, and she took a deep breath, which made her body rigid. "We didn't have sex," she said determinedly.

Her serious expression told him one thing. Whether they had been intimate or not, she would deny it no matter what. They could have had sex at any time last night until they landed back in his room, so it was odd that she was so adamant about it.

Was she ashamed she'd married him, or was the idea of sleeping with him that appalling?

This was new ground for him. No one had ever objected to his attention before. Why would she find him so distasteful?

After an awkward silence, she said, "My clutch purse is just a phone carrier with room for credit cards and cash. It has no other clues. Besides the bars, the courthouse, and the wedding chapel, I only have a few of those three-word combos in my phone's notes app."

His wallet and watch lay on the bedside table. He must have trusted her last night, or perhaps he'd been so drunk he didn't notice leaving them a few feet from her. He opened his wallet, checking the cash first. It seemed to all be there, as were his credit cards.

He removed everything from inside. Perhaps another clue lurked about.

His credit cards and driver's license were the first to hit the bed.

Next came his medical license. He placed it on the comforter on top of the credit cards. He then retrieved the next item. A Platinum Excelsior Club pass to Club Williby. She watched as he set it on the bed with the other things. If she knew Williby was an elite club with loose women and an anything-goes mentality, she didn't say a word. His membership had expired a while ago, so he wasn't sure why he still carried the card.

A parking permit. Some older receipts.

Wedged in the back was a plastic card. "I forgot all about this," he said between chuckles.

"What is it?" She picked up the card and studied it. "United Angelical Ministries?"

The plastic embarrassment was an online officiator license. He and some buddies had entered an awkward contest. The winner won a thousand dollars, which wasn't much, but he'd done it for the challenge. You needed to convince a woman that you were a seminary student and then sleep with her. Women weren't idiots. He had applied online to the United Angelical Ministries and got their wedding officiator license. The package allowed him to marry people in a few states, which was enough proof to convince a woman that he was studying for the priesthood and win the bet. It was odd how the woman he'd slept with had found the idea of him becoming a priest sexy.

He took the card from her and put it back inside the wallet. "Long story." He cleared his throat and noted that the only other item in the wallet was a row of condoms. Their silvery foil packet stuck out of the side pocket.

What the hell? He wanted to know.

He removed the condoms and counted them. All five were accounted for. More were in his suitcase, but he doubted he would have reached for them instead of using the ones conveniently in the wallet.

"I told you we didn't have sex last night."

And that was *her* story. All he knew for sure was that they didn't have *protected* sex last night.

He put all the items away, disappointed that no new evidence had presented itself. He then remembered what Paul had said last night, and his heart sank.

Digging into his pants pocket, he said, "Please, please, please be here." He pulled out a small ring box and let out the breath he had been holding.

"Is that Linda's wedding ring?"

He showed her the black box, the Jay's Jewelers name embossed on it in gold lettering. "Brian left it on the table last night during dinner. Paul didn't trust him with it, so he gave it to me to put back in the carriage house before we left. Of course, I went out with you and didn't even…" He opened the box, and his heart sank. A black slit in the velvet stared back at him. No glittery diamonds, no ring, no nothing.

"Holy shit!" He jumped from the bed and dug his hands into his pants pockets. "The ring…the ring…"

Ashley picked up the empty box. "Dear Lord. Where is it?"

"I don't know. I…it was in the box… I saw it… I… I should have returned it to my room." Thomas slapped his forehead and ignored the pain he felt afterward. "I'm such an idiot."

"Check your purse," he said, his anxious voice an octave higher than usual.

She opened the clasp and dumped everything onto the bed. No ring. "We'll find it."

"How? How are we going to do that?" His relationship with Paul was barely good enough to be called shaky. This would ruin it forever.

Damn. Paul had entrusted him with it. Entrusted him…well, like a brother. It had been their first bonding moment as siblings in ages.

"We know where we were. The bars and chapel won't be open yet, but we can make some phone calls." She took an exaggerated deep breath, likely to get him to take one, as well. "This isn't the end of the world. *This* is fixable."

Every muscle in Thomas's body tensed, and even as reassured as she sounded, he wasn't sure he believed her. He needed to make some calls, and now. He couldn't wait. "I'll give you a few minutes to freshen up in the restroom." His hand nervously indicated down the hallway to the suite's only bathroom. "If we're to keep this quiet, I'll make sure the guys are still crashed so they don't see you. We can then sneak out and fix this missing ring and marriage fiasco." He ripped the top sheet of paper from his notebook. "I'll make some phone calls, we'll get our blood tested, and then retrace our steps. We'll take care of everything."

"That's right. So, don't panic."

Her shaky voice sounded as uncertain as he felt.

8

Thomas had already called the Corporate Room, Yo Ho Ho's, and the Pair O' Dice Chapel and left messages at all three. Nothing opened until after six o'clock tonight, and he already felt sick to his stomach. The only saving grace was that the ring wasn't a family heirloom. Paul had said he'd bought it a few weeks ago. At least, there was that.

Now was not the time to panic over the ring. That needed to be placed on the back burner. It was time to panic that his wife was in the bathroom, and they needed to get proof they'd been complete idiots last night.

Anxiety crept along the length of his spine and camped out in his neck and shoulders. He shouldn't have come to the wedding. He could have just sent a gift.

Why the hell didn't he?

Ashley was quick in the bathroom and emerged with a fresh face and kept hair, which reminded him there was one pleasant aspect to this horrendous comedy of errors: He had a partner in crime. A *beautiful* one.

She touched her ears. "Have you seen my earrings?" She glanced around the room. "They're silver hoops."

He didn't see how a pair of earrings was all that important, but since they could have been a gift from her mother or something, he glanced around. His heart wasn't into it, and he gave up quickly.

She dashed around the room, giving every surface a fast once-over. She wore no makeup yet looked more beautiful than she had the night before. Her skin radiated with a glow that undoubtedly stemmed from her body still processing the alcohol, but her rosy cheeks and tender smile showed she was ready to start the day. Thomas still needed a shower, a shave, and another three hours of sleep to feel even slightly human again.

"I'm sure we'll find them if they're here." Thomas took a cursory scan of the room again, but they didn't have time to search—and they didn't want to wake anyone up. They would have to find them later.

Thomas gestured toward his bedroom door, and she walked past him down the narrow hallway. The renewed scent of an earthy fragrance—warm and spicy—caught his attention once again. He didn't recognize the aroma but remembered being mesmerized by the smell last night. Her clothing, hair, and skin had blossomed with the scent. A weak yet powerful memory came to his mind. He had kissed her milky-white neck. At some point last night, he had kissed her.

She came back into the room a second later. "They're not in your bedroom."

He cleared his throat, not wanting to think of her—his wife—in such a way. An annulment was their only solution. Starting a relationship with her, especially a physical one, would not be the answer. Besides, they needed to find an expensive ring. "We'll look for them later."

Brian's loud snores filled the shared living space, and the two tiptoed their way around him to the door. Mohinder no longer lurked about, and Thomas figured he'd had the good sense to fall back to sleep in his room. There was no sign of Paul or the other two men, either.

Thomas didn't dare make a sound. He only allowed himself to breathe again once he and Ashley were safely outside the carriage house and walking to the main house.

"What time is it?" Ashley shielded her eyes from the rising sun's crimson rays long enough to answer her own question. She glanced at her phone. "It's after nine in the morning."

He figured it was early for her and was surprised to hear her say, "I'm usually up by six." He was an early bird, too. Awake by six. A much-of-the-day-already-done-by-noon type of guy.

"I live a good distance from my hospital, and my workday begins at seven a.m., so I'm an early riser, as well." Thomas focused his attention on the stone path, averting his gaze from the harsh sunlight. "I don't usually feel this bad, though."

"That's right," she said, walking carefully beside him. "You're a doctor." A large lizard crossed her path, and she stopped abruptly with a pitchy gasp. She continued on her way once the path was clear and asked, "Got any good remedies for a hangover?"

"Besides not drinking?" He walked up the stairs of the main house and held open the door. The tiny bell dinged, sounding louder than usual. "We need water and lots of it."

"Good morning," Hershel said as he carried a container of eggs to the buffet table. Once he'd safely placed the eggs in the chafing dish, he looked up. "You two are awake early."

The inquisitive look on his face told Thomas one of two things: Either the man had expected no one from the wedding party to be up so early after the bachelor and bachelorette outings, or he was surprised to see Thomas with Ashley.

"Do you have a lost and found?" Thomas asked.

"Sure. Did you lose something?"

"I did. You didn't happen to find a ring, did you?"

"No, but I can keep my eyes open for it. What kind of ring?" he asked, still preoccupied with the food. "A class ring or something?"

"No, not a class ring. More of a woman's ring...with diamonds." He figured panic would ensue if he said, "*the bride's wedding ring*" and was surprised when Ashley said, "We lost my cousin's wedding ring last night. Have you seen it?"

No mincing of words, then. No games. Straight to the point.

Hershel's eyes widened. "No wedding ring has been turned in."

"It has three diamonds that curve upward to match the engagement ring," Thomas said, pulling the description from his memory.

"I'll ask Brenda, but she's usually good at filling me in on big things like that." His brow furrowed and showed concern. "I'll check the barn. Did you lose it there?"

"Maybe." Thomas wasn't sure if they'd have any luck, but he suspected Hershel would sweep the entire place out and look through the trash to find it.

"We're off to retrace our steps from last night." Thomas bit his lip and imagined the chaos if word got out. "Please don't mention this to anyone. We're on top of things. We'll find it." He did his best not to look too hungover and was impressed by how together Ashley seemed.

"There isn't a wedding or dinner planned in the barn for another two days. I'll search the entire place." Hershel stirred the food on the table, lit the Sterno for the eggs, and gave the servers orders to set out more fresh fruit. The dining area held a dozen tables, and guests filled over half, everybody seemingly enjoying their meals. "Breakfast is served until ten a.m." Hershel gestured at the delicious buffet as he walked from the room. "Dig in. The coffee is fresh. You can't begin your hunt on empty stomachs."

"Coffee sounds great," Ashley said, nearly cooing.

The last thing her body needed was caffeine. "Here," Thomas said, handing her a water bottle from the breakfast buffet. "You need to keep hydrated. The alcohol in your system has dehydrated you, and a med tech will need to find a vein, which is easier with hydration. Trust me. Caffeine won't be your friend right now. It'll also make your headache worse." He needed to hydrate, too, so he grabbed a bottle of water for himself.

"I've known Brenda and Hershel for a couple of years. They'll be on the lookout for that ring." She waved her hand dismissively at the fine food. "They always serve such great breakfasts here, but the smell is making me sick." Ashley unscrewed the cap and took a deep swallow, appearing desperate for an end to her headache.

He understood the feeling. Usually, the smell of bacon—especially if he were on vacation and not counting calories—lured him in. But not today. He could do without the smell. "We're in no shape to drive. I'll schedule a car to pick us up. It shouldn't take long for one to arrive." He gestured to the food on the table.

The scent of eggs and bacon made him want to vomit, but he knew a breakfast biscuit would be good. "Eat some bread. The heavy carbs will make you feel better."

He took out his phone and pressed his rideshare app, only to discover that he had no service. "The Internet is spotty." Doing the please-find-me-a-good-reception-spot dance, he wandered to the window, where he had two bars.

The driver would arrive in ten minutes, which gave him enough time to adjust his work schedule for early the next week. He gazed across the room at Ashley, who sat nibbling on a roll at a breakfast table. He may need to spend a few extra days in town with the wedding and while trying to sort everything out.

So much for his hasty exit on Sunday morning.

He might need to extend his stay at the wedding site or even postpone his flight, but he knew he had surgery scheduled for late Monday afternoon. He hated canceling on a patient, especially that one, but it was best to make arrangements as soon as possible. He knew his schedule held an opening later in the week where he could reschedule the woman's surgery. He'd just have to miss a tee time with some friends.

His hospital app opened but slowed to a halt, showing him only a frozen screen. Good thing he had his assistant's phone number.

He noticed the picture frame near the window was crooked, so he straightened it. He then sipped his water while waiting for his phone service to direct him to his assistant, Tyrone. A mental sigh of relief washed over him as he heard the man's slight Jamaican accent and not the harsh digital voice telling him to leave a message.

"Tyrone, it's Dr. Stallworth."

"Good morning to you, sir. Are you still on holiday?"

Without going into detail, Thomas told the man that his schedule needed to be cleared for Monday afternoon and Tuesday, but he felt confident he would make it back to Chicago by Wednesday morning. "We can reschedule Ms. Brady's next tattoo for Friday afternoon."

Slight clicking noises sounded over the phone, and then Tyrone said, "Ms. Brady has already canceled her Monday appointment. There is a message in her chart. Would you like me to read it?"

Naturally, he did. Tyrone had no clue how much of a headache pounded in Thomas's ears, though. He took a seat and rested his head in his free hand. "Please."

"She is happy with her results and doesn't want another tattooing session."

What? That was insane. "But she isn't done. She needs one more round of work for her reconstruction to be perfect."

"She must be happy with how everything turned out."

Thomas's jaw tightened slightly. "Her body could be perfect. If she's willing to…" He let his words trail off. Even though the man could read her chart, Tyrone didn't need to know all of Ms. Brady's medical details. "Never mind. That's fine, then." Why would someone be willing to settle? He had done a great job of reconstructing her breast after the single mastectomy, but with a few more tweaks, it would match her healthy breast perfectly. No one would even know she had suffered from cancer. Her body would be whole again.

"Thanks for the message. Please clear my calendar for now. Thank you." He disconnected and leaned over more, allowing the weight of his head to stretch his tight neck muscles and give him some headache relief.

"The driver is here."

He turned to see Ashley standing near him. When did she walk over? He was glad he hadn't gone into detail about Ms. Brady's condition. Even if nearly two thousand miles separated them, he shouldn't talk about a patient within earshot of anybody.

"That was quick," he said. "Hopefully, everything else today will be just as fast."

Ashley nervously twirled a curl of her hair around her finger as she glanced out the car window at the familiar Las Vegas Strip. For all intents and purposes, Thomas was her husband. Other than him spending all day fixing noses, she knew nothing substantial about him. He had a good sense of humor and similar interests, but could she trust him?

And, dammit, if she didn't find him sinfully sexy.

Even unshaven and feeling poorly, the man remained desirable. His dark blond hair, steely blue eyes, and—she had to be honest—firm body lured her in. But more than all of that combined, he exuded a sexy masculine presence. He was tall, formidable, and spoke with such a deep voice she felt confident he would be a tenor in any choir.

Her attraction had consumed her the minute she first laid eyes on him at the venue. She hadn't known who he was when he checked in. The Bella Rosa hosted several weddings a week, so how could she have guessed the gorgeous man would soon become extended family to her?

Well, not extended now. He was her husband.

Her throat swelled, and she wasn't sure she could make small talk. She sipped her water, finished the bottle, and continued gazing out the window as her bladder reminded her how much hydrating she had already done this morning.

She had lived in Vegas her entire life, but the place held little interest. They passed the MGM and the Statue of Liberty of New York-New York. Next came M&M's World, which was followed by the Coca-Cola Store. The Bellagio lay ahead on the left, Paris's Eiffel Tower on the right. Tourists were awed at the glitz and glamour, but they didn't see Sin City daily as she did.

She snuck a peek at Thomas, who spent more time studying his phone than taking in the sights—or even trying to make small talk. Could he also be nervous? He had a panicked look, and she wasn't sure if it was due to their marriage or losing Linda's ring. Both were monumental.

He didn't look uncomfortable sitting next to his new wife, though. He clearly suffered from a hangover much like she did, but not from proximity problems. He probably had no issues talking to women. The more, the merrier. She, on the other hand, was sweating profusely. Not knowing what to say to a man who could shoot cologne ads in his spare time added to the wrenching in her alcohol-filled gut.

From the bits and pieces she had overheard last night from the wedding party and what Linda had told her directly, distractions of beauty often turned Thomas's head. From blondes to redheads and every woman in between, his reputation as a ladies' man preceded him. No, his reputation resembled more of a babe hound.

One who had selected her, of all women, to walk down the aisle with.

He let out a slight sigh as his fingers continued tapping on his screen. Ashley didn't remember if Thomas mentioned a girlfriend last night. Perhaps he was texting the current woman in his life some convenient white lie to cover his mistake from last night.

Mistake.

She hated that he might see her as such. But for a mistake, he had not only spent the entire evening with her but had also walked down the aisle and said "I do" in front of a fake Elvis—or whoever had married them.

She studied the handsome man sitting mere inches from her in the car, taking in the determined focus in his eyes as he read something on his phone's display. Rugged jawline. Gorgeous eyes. Scruff of a beard giving him that Calvin-Klein-underwear-ad type of look.

And a doctor on top of it all.

Her mother had always said that a doctor would be a good catch. The profession showed the man was intelligent, passionate, and committed. Obviously, doctors cared for fellow human beings.

She glanced at Thomas's hands. Lifesaving hands. Strong. Sure. Sexy.

Arousal bubbled within her, a sensation she hadn't experienced in a long time. They weren't just strong hands. They were big hands. *Very* big.

His gaze caught hers, and she turned back to the window. Heat flushed her cheeks, and she feigned interest in the city again. Even this early in the morning, people filled the streets. The late-night gamblers had left, as had the sex workers and their tricks. Now, hotel staff, waitstaff, and sightseers with families walked along the pavement. The images were so mundane and ordinary here.

"The streets are filled with people, and it's only after nine on a Sunday morning." Thomas set down his phone, a concerned look marring his handsome features.

"Is everything all right?" The thought that he had a sick patient now crossed her mind. He had been so focused on his phone, and as a doctor, he would be in touch with his office. She had overheard a small portion of his phone conversation while they'd waited for the rideshare, and it now replayed in her mind. *"Her body could be perfect."* He was a plastic surgeon. Maybe a nose emergency from a car accident brewed back in Chicago.

He took a deep breath, allowing himself to smile on the exhale. "Nothing to worry about." He glanced at The Venetian as they passed. "I haven't been to Vegas in years. Different people, different vendors…different places on the Strip. Even so, the city still looks the same."

His voice sounded steady with no criticism, as though he appreciated the town's allure but its charm would not sway him.

And yet, the two had been in a chapel last night, swearing their lives to each other in the heat of the moment.

It didn't get more *swept up* than that.

A flash of memory struck her. Not words or anything concrete, only a feeling that lay just beneath the surface. Thomas was a romantic. Pair O' Dice Chapel aside, he had treated her well and had been attentive. A sense of closeness to him covered her like a trusted security blanket. She had seen the softer side of the man last night, one she'd enjoyed.

He pointed out her side window. "It was winter the last time I visited. The gardens weren't fully in bloom like they are now."

"When was that?" she asked, surprised that the question had popped out. But, honestly, the earlier silence in the car had been nearly deafening.

"Paul and I were here once when we were kids." A smile appeared on his face as though a fond memory had come to him. "A family road trip as we made our way to California for a wedding."

Weddings had a way of bringing families together.

"Paul was too young to remember Vegas, but I remember the lights and the people. I wanted to see the nightlife, even though I was only fourteen and too young to appreciate the place fully."

She wondered if that meant gambling or women.

"But then I've never been much of a gambler."

That narrowed it down.

"Linda and I grew up here," she said, changing the topic slightly and clearing her mind. "She wanted to be married here, not because of the glitz but because of her pastor. She's attended his church for over two decades, though he is retired now, and the church itself is a parking lot. Father Perin is too old to travel, so she needed to be married in Vegas so he could officiate."

"Really?" Thomas's voice held surprise.

"I think he's in his eighties now and doesn't perform any weddings, but Linda convinced him to proceed over hers. Her father,"—she pointed at herself—"my uncle, is good friends with Father Perin." She let out a deep sigh as she thought about Uncle Richard. The man had undergone quadruple-bypass surgery a year ago and had aged considerably since then. "He doesn't need any more drama. He's had health issues, issues at work, issues with Linda...."

"With Linda?" Thomas's focus centered on Ashley, and she felt the heat of his stare, his dazzling blue eyes locking onto hers.

"I'm not saying she is a total Bridezilla, but she can be a bit much and hard to deal with." Ashley felt a tiny sting of betrayal to her cousin, so she added, "She likes things to be done her way."

"The bridal itinerary as exhibit one," he said, his voice holding delight and his eyes capturing the twinkle of his devilish smile.

"She's always been high-strung, but the stress of this wedding is going to make her snap." This was why Linda had asked her to keep Thomas busy and away from Paul, and exactly why Ashley had agreed. Moving her gaze from his eyes to his full lips, she realized that the request had seemed so devious at first but a joy once she met the man. A tingle of excitement shot through her as she remembered him accepting her invitation to leave the party last night to hang out with her. The feeling probably wasn't the same as being voted prom queen but it must have been damn close. Her heart still pounded at the memory of it.

"The bridal flowers," she said, getting back on topic. "They haven't arrived. The invitations were a mess. I won't even go into the chaos of the menu and what the bridal party refers to as the *clown car mess* of a seating chart."

"Honestly, none of what you're saying surprises me."

"Oh?"

He shook his head as though trying to figure out a polite way to say something. "She comes across as someone who puts herself first." His gaze drifted out the window as the car turned down a side street. "Someone who knows what she wants and will get it no matter what."

True. Linda had always wanted what she wanted when she wanted it. She resembled her mother in that way. The two had been close, but Linda's mother always dominated the relationship.

Odd how Ashley now realized she had allowed Linda to do the same to her. Even as children, Linda had always chosen the games they played, then dominated and ultimately won them. The rules were always created on the fly, and the players gladly partook, which precisely why Ashley had agreed to keep Thomas busy. Linda had wanted it done, and Ashley was quick to agree.

A pang of shame crossed her heart. Ashley hadn't

thought of Linda's mother until now. Linda and her mom were close and even looked like sisters because Ashley's aunt was so youthful looking. But she had died in a car crash over three years ago.

She would have loved Paul and been so happy for Linda in her marriage. Even though Linda's parents were divorced, the woman had still believed in love and wanted the best for her daughter.

"I don't want to cause Linda or Paul any more aggravation," Thomas said, his hand resting gently on hers and causing a tingle of excitement to rush up her arm. "We'll get last night straightened out. No one needs to know. I'm not scheduled to leave until Sunday, so hopefully everything will be done by then. But if it takes another couple of days, I cleared my calendar."

Taking his hand off hers, he tapped the pocket holding his phone. "The chapel and bars don't open until six p.m. tonight. We'll have to make another excuse to go down there."

She had memorized the bridal itinerary and knew they'd have an opportunity to do so. "Hopefully, the chapel hasn't filed the paperwork yet." Her head still felt sluggish after last night, and the blood work should prove the two were impaired. He'd be back in Chicago next week, and she'd return to her life.

Single and alone.

She didn't need a man in her life, but a twinge of sadness hit her heart. After being diagnosed with the BRCA2 gene mutation nearly three years ago, she had undergone a double mastectomy, a complete hysterectomy, and an oophorectomy—removal of the ovaries and fallopian tubes—and felt anything but feminine. Accidentally getting married in Vegas was probably the closest she'd ever get to even dating someone again.

Not that she'd dated a lot of men before. Her body had been appealing, at least she'd always thought so, but even with her C-cup breasts, she couldn't have landed a man as handsome and sexy as Thomas. And now? He was way out of her league.

Damn cancer. A tear threatened to escape, but she held the weakness back. She had cried all she would over the deadly disease. She would not shed one more tear over it, would not allow it to consume her thoughts or dampen her spirit. She would not let the monster win.

9

An hour later, Ashley carefully closed the outer door of the Bella Rosa cottage and crept in. A craggy, disembodied voice filled the air and startled her.

"Ashley?" whoever it was asked again.

Her cousin sat at the table in the bridal building, her hand caressing a hot mug of coffee, the brew's aroma inviting. "Have you been out all night?" she asked.

Ashley walked through the darkened room, the morning's rays shining through a side window, illuminating the kitchenette where Linda sat. Her cousin had always been a morning person, but Ashley had figured the woman might sleep in after last night. It would throw off Linda's schedule and her routine, though, and Linda would have none of that.

As if witnessing a terrible accident, Linda's eyes widened, and for a moment, she didn't appear as hungover as she had a second ago. Linda's gaze darted to the far hallway where Ashley's bedroom lay. The door remained closed. "I thought you were in your room," she said and then winced, holding her head. "You look as bad as I feel."

"Thanks, that's reassuring." Ashley set her purse on a side table and noticed Linda's best friend, Imani, asleep on the couch. Evidently, the women weren't faring any better than the men this morning. The bandage from the blood work still squeezed Ashley's arm, so she turned her body so Linda wouldn't see it.

Ashley didn't wear a jogging suit, didn't appear to have been out on a coffee run, and still wore last night's clothes. Linda's eyes widened, and she pointed an accusatory finger in her cousin's direction. "Tell me you weren't out with Thomas all night. That bastard texted me some shitty things, but I thought you had dumped him and came home."

The look unsettled Ashley. She had never been the type of woman to do the walk of shame, and Linda knew it. However, the idea that her cousin believed her capable of a wild night with a Greek god excited her for a moment. "We bar hopped all night."

Linda glanced at her watch. "Until after ten-thirty the next morning?"

Ashley wasn't sure what to say or how to cover her tracks. She had expected none of the women to be awake. She used her hand to cover the bandage on her arm and walked closer to Linda so their discussion wouldn't wake the entire household.

"I kept Thomas away as you asked." Even speaking his name conjured images of his rugged good looks. "We made it back to the carriage house, and he passed out."

"Passed out?" Linda's phone buzzed, and she read the text. "Shit." Her face hardened, telling Ashley that Bridezilla had awoken. "The cake topper, which should have arrived two weeks ago, is still on backorder. The store swore it would be delivered by today."

Ashley put her hand on her cousin's shoulder. "Like I said last week, you can decorate the cake with fresh flowers instead. It will look beautiful."

But there had also been an issue with the flower order.

A forced and fake smile pulled at Linda's lips. Understandable with everything the bride had to deal with. She looked at her cell phone again, and an eyebrow rose. "You sent me texts until well past one a.m." Her finger scrolled down. "Past two a.m. I didn't see this one." Her eyes shifted from left to right as she read. "Well, even if I had, I don't think it would have made sense. What is *paro dichppl*?" She paused, flashing a huge smile. "Looks like you were having a good time."

Ashley hadn't thought to check her text messages to Linda. She took the phone from her cousin before she realized that *paro dichppl* was Pair O' Dice Chapel. The picture that Linda looked at, with her eyes closed and

Thomas barely looking human in the background, was their wedding photo.

"As I said, we went bar hopping." She put the phone to sleep as guilt nudged at her gut. She wanted to confide in Linda and tell her all about last night… what she remembered and had pieced together anyway. But she knew she couldn't. And she especially didn't want to mention the missing wedding ring. "I want to make everything as easy as possible for you."

Linda focused on her coffee as though it were a lifeline. "Thanks for keeping Thomas away from Paul and, I guess, getting him home safely. The man's a troublemaker who enjoys his liquor and women."

"You warned me, and I knew what I was getting into. Besides," she said, smiling, "the night wasn't bad. And I'd do anything for you."

"You're the only one I can trust to keep him away all week. Damn his mother for inviting him and insisting he be a part of the wedding." Linda rolled her eyes. "If you listen to her talk, you'd swear Thomas is a misunderstood saint."

So, she had understood correctly. Ashley had never met Paul's mother but understood that the lonely widow was desperate to keep her family together. Not an easy task considering her sons' rocky relationship.

Linda's reddened eyes did their best to focus on Ashley. "Do you know how much I love you?"

Her wavering voice ended in a full-out yawn.

Ashley hadn't seen Linda this hungover since her prom night, which felt like a lifetime ago.

Being cousins of the same age, living in the same town, and attending the same schools growing up had made them more like sisters than cousins.

God, so much water had passed under their bridge. There was nothing Ashley wouldn't do for Linda.

"You're lucky you didn't hang out with us girls last night. We went to a few bars and then basically camped out at a strip club."

Ashley wasn't a prude, and there was nothing wrong with a beefy man undressing in front of you, but being in a crowded room of women gawking and making lude comments was not her idea of a good time. If a man stripped for you, it should be a private showing. And the man needed to be someone you cared about.

Linda closed her eyes and took a deep breath. After a brief pause, she took another deep breath and sipped from her coffee again.

Thomas was right. Water was the way to go, no matter how wonderful the coffee smelled. She walked to the small kitchenette, slyly removed her bandage, wadded it, and tossed it into the trash. She then got two water bottles from the refrigerator and sat next to Linda.

She set a bottle in front of her cousin, urging her to drink it. "So, Thomas is a troublemaker?" she asked, wanting to know more about the man whose silver wedding band now lay in her purse next to hers.

The man wasn't covered in boils, wasn't dull, wasn't

unkempt—quite the opposite, actually. Ashley found him charming and sexy. Judging by the drunken smile she sported in the selfies on her phone, she had enjoyed her time with him. He didn't seem like an untrustworthy opportunist.

Linda shrugged, her eyelids half-closed. For a woman who perpetually had perfect hair, flawless makeup, and impeccable posture, she slumped in the chair, her rats-nest of hair desperately needed combing, and her smoky eye makeup from last night now had her resembling a badger.

"I don't know the man. Not really." She brushed aside the water, but Ashley opened it and set it in front of her again, insisting she hydrate. "I know Paul doesn't trust his brother. That's for sure."

"Why not?" He had undoubtedly jumped into marriage. Perhaps there was a reason, though Ashley didn't own property or have any money. Her dowry consisted of loyalty and love for the right man, whomever he may be.

A strange feeling overcame her.

Odd that she figured he had suggested going to the chapel. She had no idea whose idea it had been. She assumed she hadn't suggested getting married last night, but she had no clue for sure. Since they had to get a marriage license first, she figured they didn't just happen across a chapel and say, "*What the heck?*"

Linda finally took a long swig of her water. "I don't

think the man is evil. Their falling out all stemmed from Tina."

"Paul's ex-girlfriend?"

"Thomas's ex-wife." Linda shot Ashley a sharp look. "And, yes, Paul's ex-girlfriend. Stolen from him." Linda shot her friend a glance. Imani was still asleep on the couch, and although Ashley assumed the woman knew the story, Linda lowered her voice and said, "Thomas can't help his roving eye. He's that type of man." Linda placed her hand atop Ashley's. "I knew a pretty woman like you...well, he couldn't help but be distracted. Fancy parties, expensive cars, pretty women. But you aren't the type to be lured in by his false charm. And he certainly wouldn't be foolish enough to get involved with you."

Ashley straightened in her chair. "What do you mean by that? Why would being involved with me be foolish?" she asked defensively.

Linda quickly shook her head, wincing as her headache gave her visible grief. "It's just that, after Tina, I can't imagine he would be interested in any woman even remotely connected to Paul." She waved her hand through the air, indicating the couch. "The entire wedding party is probably safe from that man's desire. But Imani was smitten with him the moment she saw him. I knew I couldn't trust her." She then glanced down a hallway where Mindy and Sarah slept. "And don't get me started on the other two."

A strange emotion ran up Ashley's spine, and she

looked at Imani. She had taken an interest in Thomas at dinner last night. Ashley had clearly forgotten that. Imani was younger, had gorgeous dark skin, and was ten pounds lighter than Ashley. She stared at the woman's aerobicized body and realized she was jealous she had been attracted to Thomas.

"Imani certainly is a beautiful woman," she said flatly.

Linda began singing Roy Orbison's *Pretty Woman* louder than a whisper and out of tune.

"Shh. You'll wake Imani and the others." Their doors were closed, but Ashley assumed they had all made it safely home. Imani stirred on the couch, and Ashley could make out the woman's side profile. She was still snoring.

"...you look lovely da da...are you lonely let me be?..." Linda sang, butchering the words.

Ashley was impressed that Linda could sing at all, if only half the words. She wasn't sure why Linda's confirmation that Thomas was a ladies' man had hurt her feelings. They had no deep, meaningful relationship other than the marriage—which didn't count. The blood work would be done in a couple of days, and they'd be able to annul the marriage if the paperwork had been filed.

Linda continued with the song's second verse until Ashley pushed the water bottle closer to her. "Keep drinking. Trust me. It will help."

Linda placed her hands in front of her chest as men

did when talking about boobs. "Imani has big breasts like her. Another reason I thought you'd be safe with him."

Ashley froze, her body stiffening. Linda had never spoken in such a way about Ashley's mastectomy before. "What do you mean? Like who?"

"Bitch Tina. Big-boobed bitch Tina," Linda said, laughing.

It took a second for Ashley to realize the subject was back on Thomas's first wife.

First wife.

Ashley was the second.

"Thomas is a breast man." Linda tried to sit straighter in the chair but then slumped again, a look of horror crossing her face. "I'm sorry. I shouldn't have said that." Her gaze focused on Ashley's chest. "Your foobs give you a great rack. No one can even tell. Hell, you'll never have to worry about aging and having your boobs,"—Linda's hands dropped lower—"droop to your knees."

Ashley's gaze darted to Imani, who still lay asleep. Not everyone needed to know about Ashley's mastectomy. Her expensive fake boobs—her foobs— were medical-grade prosthetics, weighted on the inside to hang like the real things. The perfect C-cup, but fake. "Thanks. Now, you should go lay back down."

Linda shook her head as though that were the last thing on her mind. "We're all going shopping today. Maybe I'll even buy a cake topper." She stood but had to steady herself. "We need to keep to our schedule. Besides, I'm sure I owe you money for last night, so I'm buying today."

"You don't have to pay me anything for last night. I was happy to do you a favor."

"You were a lifesaver." She eyed Ashley sternly. "You still have the week off, right?"

"Brenda said I could take some time, but I'm on call because the other masseuse's daughter was sick the other day. I'm also still working at Massage Envy part-time until Wednesday, but only if they have too many clients and they need me to fill in."

"Good." Linda picked up the coffee mug, not the water, and took a sip. "Paul and the boys are getting their tuxes today." She checked her watch. "Actually, they need to leave soon."

As Ashley was about to say she doubted the men would follow the itinerary, Linda took out her phone and called Paul. "They need to wake up," she said.

Linda had always been high-strung, even as a child. Ashley figured either Paul enjoyed that personality trait or he at least tolerated it in her. He always seemed to follow whatever Linda wanted.

Everybody did.

Even though Ashley wanted two more hours of sleep and a shower, she knew she'd be at the mall shopping for a new cake topper with the rest of the bridal party.

Ashley stood and pushed in her chair, leaning

heavily on the frame when her phone chirped. She read the text, disappointment shrouding her expression with each word. She turned to face Linda, who was now off the phone. "Brenda says they have a massage client. The appointment is at noon, and the other masseuse needs to leave for a few hours." She walked toward her bedroom to gather her clothes and make her way to the shower. "I'm going to freshen up and head into work."

"What about shopping?" Linda's voice sounded sharp, as if everyone's life needed to be put on hold to do wedding stuff with her. The entire world revolved around Linda, not only now but every day. Shopping, lunch, and making sachets of birdseed awaited the ladies today. Honestly, Ashley preferred work to hanging out with four hungover women whose first stop of the day was to get loaded on caffeine at the closest Starbucks.

Ashley shook her head as she made her way to the bathroom. "I'll join you later." She knew she needed to get ready quickly; Linda would see to that. She closed the bathroom door and looked around. One full bathroom for six women. The cottage looked great on paper, but once the women moved in, the tiny room looked like an Ulta store had exploded.

Ashley's dress from last night, as lovely as it had been at the start of the evening, clung to her body and felt nasty. She grimaced at the green stain on the front, figuring it was probably ruined.

Too bad because the style suited her.

She removed the frock and caught her reflection in

the mirror. The green stain had not only stained her outfit but had also soaked through to her bra.

No. No. No.

Grabbing a washcloth from below the sink, she scrubbed as her mind raced. What could the stain be? Mint cognac? A light minty fragrance emanated from her hideous, industrial-strength, only-Mrs.-Doubtfire-would-wear-this brassiere as she rubbed harder at the stain.

Crap. She didn't care about the expensive mastectomy bra. What mattered was the super expensive, insurance-covered, fake prosthetic set of boobs underneath it. She removed the bra and pulled out the foob from the left cup's pocket. There wasn't much of a stain on the prosthetic, but it was enough to leave a sticky mark.

She put the washcloth under the water again and carefully cleaned the foob. Her health insurance, like most, only afforded her one nice pair every six months. At first, she'd thought two pairs of foobs each year would be plenty. She was wrong. The wear and tear on the weighted prosthetics were more than she had initially thought. The foobs had a thin satin cover, but she wore them daily. Use and sweat caused them to change shape, and since you could only spot-wash them, body odor remained—and accumulated—on them.

This one now smelled minty, but not in a good way.

She stopped scrubbing the foob, knowing that if she got it too wet, it wouldn't dry by the time she needed to put it back on, and she didn't want to place it in the bra while it was wet. She couldn't throw it in the dryer due to the metal weight inside.

Stupid thing. The non-weighted ones could be washed but tended to shift out of place, causing her to tug the bra down throughout the day so her foobs weren't floating around her chest. It wasn't uncommon for one of them to be an inch or two higher than the other, giving her a lopsided appearance.

Her finger touched the sticky green residue. She hadn't even felt the goo on her last night. If she had, she would have cleaned herself up sooner. Maybe she had been too drunk to feel the drink. Maybe. More likely, the foobs had created a padded barrier between her outfit and skin, and she'd felt nothing. She would have known if the drink had soaked down to her natural breast. She would have felt it.

The mirror reflected the rest of the horror show. Ashley looked like she had been ridden hard and put up wet. Her chemo-curls were all over the place due to the humidity, her makeup was gone, and her eyes were mere slits from exhaustion.

And Thomas had seen her like this.

So much for good impressions.

A jar of hair mask lay on the counter next to so many other lotions and potions. The product belonged to Imani, who had said she could borrow some. Imani's hair was coarser than hers since the woman had a beautiful natural afro style, and Ashley had heard that some heavy conditioners like this one worked well on her hair type. The mask was the pre-wash kind. Ashley wet her hair at the sink and put some of the thick cream on the tips of her tresses.

In truth, Ashley had a drawer full of treatments and conditioners to tame her now-curly hair. Since it had been straight before the cancer, she'd had no idea the ordeal that curly-haired girls went through to maintain their styles. The worst part? She couldn't even brush it. She'd loved raking her boar-bristled brush through her hair a hundred times at night before bed. But not anymore. A wide-toothed comb through wet locks was all she could do now with the curls unless she wanted them to get frizzy.

God, her hair looked a mess. And now it had white tips on the ends, giving her a porcupine appearance. Yep, she wouldn't be winning any beauty contests anytime soon.

But her hair wasn't the most shocking part of her reflection.

Her bare chest stared back at her, proof of the cost of her cancer. The curved upward scars, now whitened with age and healing, reflected back at her. The breast surgeon had cut the incisions so breast reconstruction could occur later, and Ashley appreciated the skilled doctor's quality work. Still, she hadn't wanted a plastic surgeon to work on her.

She didn't want any doctors working on her anymore.

Her fingers traced the silky scars where natural and beautiful C-cupped breasts once were. Now, only the flatness of her chest remained. After undergoing the double mastectomy, oophorectomy, and complete hysterectomy—plus six months of some of the harshest chemotherapy imaginable—she wanted nothing else done with or to her body.

At least she didn't have to undergo radiation. Chopping off her breasts while the cancer remained at stage 1A had seen to that.

No radiation. It had felt like a blessing.

A knock sounded on the door.

"Hurry up, Ashley. A line is forming to use the shower," Linda called from the hallway. "We all want to make ourselves beautiful."

Beautiful.

The monster inside stirred. Her figure resembled that of a ten-year-old girl. Tears formed, and she inwardly chided herself. She was alive. It wasn't as though she needed breasts. She wasn't nursing a baby. She had always liked children, and had a baby come into her life, she would have gladly welcomed it, even though she never saw herself as the motherly type. Knowing she could *never* have a baby, though? That cut her deeply. There'd be no little Ashleys in the world. Not anymore.

"Yeah, sweetie. I'm up. Hmm? I don't know." Paul's faint and grumbly voice came from his bedroom, followed by the door opening. His eyes squinted as he scanned the living room. "I think…" He cleared his throat and then yawned. "I might be the only one…wait, Thomas is up."

Thomas gave him a curt nod. His brother resembled the walking dead with his bloodshot eyes and slow yet stumbling walk. His Gumby hairstyle resembled his childhood style before discovering girls and deciding that proper hygiene was the way to go. He walked barefoot into the carriage house's living area in his T-shirt and a pair of shorts. No matter how drunk he was last night, the fact that he'd gotten into some semblance of pajamas proved impressive.

Wait. The T-shirt was on, but inside out *and* backward.

"Morning," he grumbled as he walked past Thomas, making his way to the bathroom. Thomas listened to make sure his brother wasn't ill, not that he was Paul's keeper, but the man was family, and Thomas was a doctor. The two may not have spent much time together over the last ten years, but seeing him now—and knowing Paul was trying to get along with him—meant the world to Thomas.

A thud that sounded like a can of shaving cream hitting the floor was followed by some curse words from behind the bathroom door. Thomas could mentally see Paul cleaning the mess and then checking the damages from last night in the mirror. The scruffy start of a beard and the painful squinting of the eyes would be staring back at him. Thomas didn't know how the women were doing, but the itinerary called for a morning bridal party jog, which should have started two hours ago.

He knocked on the door. "You okay, Paul?"

Some mumbling came from within, followed by a curt, "Be right out."

Paul probably would have felt better had he thrown up before bed. Thomas's heart went out to him, and he almost pitied his brother—which surprised him. Even as bad as he felt, Paul looked worse. Thomas may be standing, though not ready to face the day, but Paul was barely walking and had a fiancée to face.

The door opened, and Paul walked out, his face slightly wet, his hair combed, and his demeanor cowed. Paul's hand squeegeed his face, focusing primarily on his eyes as he tried to wake up. "We can do that later, sweetie." A brief pause on the phone was followed by, "I don't think these guys are going to wake up anytime soon." He yawned widely, and Linda's muffled voice sounded from the phone. She didn't sound happy.

"What time is it? We only got like six hours of sl— No, of course not, sweetie."

As a doctor, Thomas wondered how Paul could walk without a spine.

And, evidently, once you got to where rings were exchanged, and the aisle was in sight, you didn't mind talking to each other on the phone while in the bathroom. The thought struck him as odd. Even in the four months he had been married to Tina, they had never become that close.

Thomas wasn't sure if that level of intimacy was sweet or pathetic.

Maybe with the right woman, it would be the former.

His mind refocused on Ashley. She didn't seem plastic and fake but rather honest and genuine. At some point in her life, and he believed she deserved it, she would find a man like Paul. Someone whose heart and bathroom door lay open to her.

As Paul began reciting where they'd gone and how much he had drunk—swearing he was in relatively good shape for their busy day ahead, even if his rough voice indicated otherwise—Thomas gathered his phone. He decided now would be a good time to shower. He'd feel more human afterward.

"She what? Just now?" Paul's gaze darted to his watch, even though he clearly knew the time. His face was surprisingly alert, and he appeared wide awake. "What did she say?"

Thomas froze, knowing that Ashley had not been able to sneak back into the cottage without notice. Did their night on the town remain a secret? Had Linda given Ashley a verbal beat down to where the elopement had been revealed?

"I'll ask," Paul said, his voice accusatory and raw.

"What did you do last night?" he asked with a glare once he ended the call. The timbre of his voice sounded the same as their father's when he caught them doing something they weren't supposed to do, and for a moment, Paul looked very much like the man. Thomas had never noticed the resemblance so much before as he did now. The tone and stony glare were not appreciated, especially not from his *younger* brother.

"Me?"

Paul stumbled into a chair and pointed accusingly at Thomas. "You were out all night with Ashley?" His voice pitched higher when he said her name, as though the man wasn't surprised Thomas may have invited a woman to his bed last night, more that he just couldn't believe it was Ashley. Paul gestured at the room with a wildly waving hand. "And she slept here last night?"

The rumor mill ran fast. He hadn't fabricated a joint lie with Ashley. He didn't know they would need one—at least not this early on—and he wasn't sure what she may have told Linda. His hands went up in surrender, not that he owed his brother an explanation, but the two were trying to get along. "Ashley slept in my bed. I slept out here."

Brian's snoring filled the room, making his presence known to Paul. He checked around the sofa and saw the man.

"He had to sleep on the floor because I was already on the couch," Thomas said.

"I don't remember seeing you here last night." A

stern look crossed Paul's face, followed by one of disgust mixed with the pained expression of a hangover. His face was hard to read, and Thomas wasn't sure the man believed him. "Tell me you didn't…" Paul's eyebrow rose in a way that Thomas couldn't interpret. Was he about to ask if he had married the woman or only slept with her?

Thomas wasn't stupid enough to give the former away. "Do you want to know if I slept with her?" Thomas filled in the hopefully obvious—and less damning—blank. His jaw tightened as he stared at Paul. How could his brother think that any woman Thomas was romantically involved with was any of *his* business?

"Did you?" Paul's hand touched his temple, and he squinted his eyes as the light from the window shone in and assaulted his hungover brain.

Mohinder's bedroom door opened. "You all want to keep it down out here?"

"I didn't sleep with Ashley," Thomas said, hating that he had to tell his brother anything about his private life. Now, the question of whether he'd married the woman… But that was something Paul would hopefully never discover.

Thomas shifted his gaze slyly toward Mohinder, who walked through the living room to the kitchen to get a bottle of water. The man's loyalty was to his cousins, not to Thomas or Paul. Hopefully, he wouldn't rat Thomas out.

"Sounds like a heated discussion. Does this mean we're not getting our tuxes this morning?" Mohinder's tone and his unforgiving expression said one thing: He didn't want to pick up his tux. He probably didn't want to have lunch with the women, either.

It was too early to do anything. Heck, Brian was still crashed on the floor.

"I told Linda we'd get them later." Paul's voice then muffled as he said, "I didn't tell her that the next available time was on Friday morning, so don't say anything to her, or she'll freak out."

Mohinder raised a single eyebrow that hid under dark bangs. "Look at you. Not taming that shrew." The corners of his mouth curled up in a knowing smile. He gestured with his hand as though controlling a whip and made a snapping noise. "You know you'll pay for that later if she finds out."

Thomas wondered exactly how often Paul crossed Linda, and what her controlling demeanor caused her to do when and if he did.

Linda.

Crap.

He needed to tell Paul the truth about his fiancée, and soon. The convention in Colorado was five years ago, but he'd instantly recognized her in the engagement picture his mother had sent to him. Linda Higgenbothem. With all her curves and charms. The woman—and her name—was hard to forget.

Paul's eyes narrowed and a scowl appeared as he

rubbed the back of his head. "I got some weird—and insulting texts—from you last night," he said, directing his attention to Thomas.

Shit

"I was drunk. Stupid. I didn't mean…Please ignore them. The texts were just my frustration with having lost the wedding party last night, nothing about you…"

"Or Linda?"

"Yes, about that…" Here was his opportunity. Just blurt out what he knew about the bride, break up the wedding, and leave Paul…a mess.

God, he was weak.

Right now was probably not the best time to destroy Paul's world. Not with him feeling so sick and already upset that Ashley had spent the night at the carriage house.

"I was just lashing out. I didn't mean anything by the texts."

Paul's lips pursed and he began to nod his head. "For Mom's sake, I'll ignore them. But don't ever call the woman I love a bitch again. You don't even know her."

"Of course." Thomas stretched, and his back popped, still protesting having slept on the couch. The truth would come out later.

"We'll meet up with the ladies for a late lunch." The way Paul grimaced at the thought of food brought out the doctor in Thomas again.

"You should drink some water. I left a bottle by your bed with some ibuprofen."

"Oh?" Paul's face softened. "That was nice of you." Paul mumbled something about keeping to the itinerary as he made his way back to his bedroom. They'd have lunch with the women and then leave for dinner at six o'clock.

"I won't be able to make dinner tonight," Thomas said.

"You have to." Paul stopped in his tracks, turned, and shook his head. "Linda may understand one wrinkle in the schedule, but not two. Definitely not on the same day."

Thomas didn't care what Linda wanted. He glanced at Mohinder, hoping he could use the man as a lifeline. "I can't make dinner."

"It's only a meet and greet for the bridal party. It's fine if he misses it." Mohinder came to Thomas's rescue, his voice calm and soothing. He obviously understood that Thomas needed to go with Ashley to the chapel and clear up their mess.

Paul rubbed both temples, and his expression told Thomas that he was in store for many marital headaches in his future. "Linda wants everyone—"

"And I said I can't come," Thomas said again, knowing he couldn't help Paul grow a spine.

"Why?"

"He's a busy doctor. Leave him alone." Mohinder gave Thomas a sly look. "The man dropped all his patients and changed his entire schedule to spend a week with you. Don't you think he might be video chatting with some of them?"

Paul let out a groan but seemed to understand. Regardless, Thomas needed to get to the chapel and retrieve the paperwork. Hopefully, he had left the ring there. Given enough time, he could join the bridal party after dinner.

"I'm sure everything will work out." Thomas could have been upset by Paul storming out of the room, but he didn't have time to placate his brother. He was just glad Paul didn't ask for Linda's wedding ring.

He had a few precious hours now due to the schedule change, and the weight of the world lay squarely on Thomas's shoulders. He couldn't do anything for hours, and since his back and head were plotting to kill him, he figured he'd put the massage coupon from his wedding bag to good use.

10

The wedding march played in the background, catching Ashley's attention as she made her way from the cottage. The Bella Rosa hosted several ceremonies during the week, even on weekdays. Brides flocked in from all over and bought one of seven package deals, with family and friends booking rooms at the resort.

Linda had chosen the most expensive Wedding Bliss package. A week-long stay in the carriage house for the men and the cottage for the women, with the I Do bridal suite reserved for the night of the couple's wedding. As well as the rehearsal dinner, reception, and main event all in one luxurious place.

Truly an all-inclusive spot for weddings. Ashley couldn't afford much in terms of a present for her cousin, especially since she had to buy the bridesmaid dress, shoes, and jewelry herself, but she'd received a hefty employee discount for the couple, which had saved them hundreds of dollars.

And the venue exuded elegance. Convenient and absolutely beautiful, especially once the flowers in the garden bloomed like they were doing now.

The bridal march ended, and Ashley saw the happy couple standing in the floral gazebo in the lover's grotto with rows of chairs filled with guests. Linda and Paul would be standing there shortly.

The bride was easy to spot in her white gown, but two women were in white, not one. Two breathtakingly beautiful women stood at the altar to pledge their love to each other.

The world had finally caught up. Hershel and Brenda had been among the first to offer bridal packages to the LGBTQIA+ community, with several shops in town following suit. Even the bakeries had hers-and-hers and his-and-his wedding cake toppers.

Absolutely a move in the right direction.

Her thoughts drifted to her cousin, Mohinder. He had hidden his boyfriend from extended family for so long. Now, Nick would attend Linda's wedding as Mohinder's date. It would be nice to finally meet the man who had captured her cousin's heart, primarily since she had heard so much about him over the last several years.

The two brides kissed, and Ashley realized she stood in the background of the photographer's view, so she continued her trek to the main house and walked in and over to where Brenda waited.

"Is it noon ready?" Ashley asked, taking the clipboard from the registration desk. Her body was only going through the motions of being at work. Her uniform was clean and pressed, her name tag securely in place, but her heart and focus remained on Thomas and the nightmare they had woken up to.

Well, that and going back to bed to get more rest. A dose of acetaminophen on top of the ibuprofen and about a gallon of water were helping. She nearly felt human again. But the last place she wanted to be was at her massage table, making someone else feel good.

Well, the second to last place. At least she'd gotten out of shopping with the rest of the bridal party. There would have been an inquisition about what she'd done last night, and she didn't have a convenient lie, nor had she coordinated one with Thomas. She'd have to do that before everyone met for dinner.

"Linens are on the table, the lights are dimmed, music is playing, and the man is getting undressed." Brenda checked her watch. "I know I called you at the last minute. We're lucky he only just now arrived."

The clock on the wall showed 12:03 p.m. Ashley didn't remember the last time, if ever, she hadn't been able to get herself together to start her workday by nine. She didn't need her boss—good friend or not—thinking she was slacking off. "I'm sorry." Her gaze quickly scanned the medical documents the massage client had filled out. Sloppy penmanship, barely legible, and yet totally complete. Even the muscle groups were listed correctly. Honestly, it looked as though a doctor had filled out the forms. "In his early forties, athletic...no sports injuries." She flipped the top sheet over and continued reading. "He wants a deep-tissue massage."

Deep tissue.

Her strong fingers did such massages easily. But today? On an athletic forty-two-year-old man? She'd have to press her whole body into him.

"He paid for a full hour, not a half," Brenda said.

Of course, he did.

"Thanks for helping out. I wasn't expecting a massage to get scheduled today, and Carol had an emergency."

"Is she okay?" Carol's emergencies tended to be of the family variety. The woman had many children and continuously needed to run to the daycare for one of them.

"She'll be back within the hour."

Within the hour? Thank God. Ashley didn't know if she could work an entire shift, but she could manage one client. He was probably the groom for another wedding or maybe the best man. Probably not the father of one of the brides, which was good since they were the chattiest.

"I'm sorry to have called you in. I know you're busy with the wedding."

"It's fine," Ashley said as she continued scanning

the documents. "I know you gave me the week off, but I could use the money and the break from the wedding stuff."

A devilish smile curved Brenda's lips. "And what about Paul's brother? Thomas? I noticed the two of you were hitting it off last night."

Were they? She had felt a spark but assumed it existed only on her side. Even after he agreed to hang out with her last night, she'd still suspected he had done it more because he didn't want to spend the evening with his brother. Perhaps heat had existed between them from the very start.

Well, there must have been some heat. He *did* marry her.

Marry. She had a husband.

A second husband.

"Are you okay?" Brenda's voice sounded concerned. Her eyes widened as she studied Ashley. "Are you hungover?"

She took a cleansing breath. The shower had done wonders, but she still probably looked like hell. She bit her lip and did her best to push aside the fact that her husband was picking up his tuxedo and about to have lunch with the wedding party. "I'm fine." She flipped to the back of the last sheet of paper. The client was prolific in his muscle strain description. It was like reading a novel she kept trying to skim but couldn't.

Brenda's face pinched. "Hershel said he saw you and Thomas this morning. Did he do something to upset you?" She briefly paused and studied Ashley's wet hair. "Were you out all night and just getting in this morning?"

"No." Ashley didn't know how to explain what had happened, but she desperately wanted to confide in her friend. Whatever she could share would have to wait, though. She finally finished reading the last bit of the paperwork. "Look, I have to get to work."

Grabbing her arm, Brenda held her back. "He can wait another minute." A worried expression crossed her friend's face, and even though Brenda wasn't old enough to be Ashley's mother, she had mother-hen tendencies. "I thought you were interested in Thomas last night. I mean, the man is handsome, a doctor, and available." She glanced at the massage door and then back to Ashley. "Did he upset you?"

"No." Her voice came out louder and sterner than intended. "I had a great time with him. At least, what I can remember of the night. I know I enjoyed myself."

Brenda's head tilted, and she stared at Ashley. "It was that kind of night, huh?"

"No, this was different." Ashley leaned in and swiveled her neck, surveying the room. She knew the entire wedding party, both the men and the women, were likely out running errands, but she still wanted to make sure nobody was around. Only a handful of guests were downstairs, and they weren't with her party. "Thomas and I got married last night."

"What?" Brenda's hand went to her gaping mouth,

much like a mask, only her friend's bulging eyes glaring at her. "You got married?"

"An accident. One we're going to correct as soon as possible."

The clock now read 12:08 p.m. She needed to get into the massage room. The Bella Rosa didn't have a policy for reducing the massage rates if the appointment ran too far behind like the other places Ashley worked, but she knew never to keep the client waiting. If nothing else, her tip would suffer because of it.

She clutched the clipboard. "Don't tell anyone. We're going to get the entire thing annulled. No harm, no foul. We just need to fix this mess and move on."

"But, Ashley…" Brenda pointed at the door. "You should know—"

Ashley went to the door and knocked. "Keep my secret. At least, for now." Brenda's muffled complaints about the client faded into the background.

"Come in," a male voice said after she knocked. The smell of calming essential oils filled the room and greeted her as she set the client's paperwork near the sink and made her way into the dimly lit room to the oils on the table.

"Are there any areas you'd like me to focus on or avoid?" she asked in her professionally low and soothing *work* voice, which sounded a lot like Phoebe Buffay's voice from the show *Friends* whenever she did a massage.

"My lower back needs some work. I flew in

yesterday on a cramped airline. And once I arrived, non-stop stressful wedding stuff happened, followed by some poor sleep." He let out a deep sigh. "I have an even worse day ahead of me today."

"I'm happy to help." She guessed him to be a groom. Usually, she asked when the wedding was and wish the couple a happy and long life together, but not today. She didn't need to get the man talking. This was his massage, and it should be peaceful.

Grooms tended not to talk about the wedding unless asked. The brides were a different story. They'd endlessly talk about everything that had gone wrong, offering countless stories about wedding-day horrors. The flowers, the cake, the invitations… It now occurred to Ashley. The brides rarely talked about the things that went *right*. They always focused on the doom and gloom.

Maybe there was something to be said for a drunken night at a wedding chapel. It cut out a lot of the painful planning.

She walked around the table and took in his frame. He lay face down with the sheet covering him from the waist down.

Muscular and strong. Her last client was a sixty-year-old grandmother who had fallen and twisted her back. This man wasn't frail or hurt. No. His body was in great shape.

She warmed the oil in her hand and paused before touching him. Her job had her touching men all the time. Her clients weren't typically as well built as this man, though. She was now a married woman, and even though she didn't owe Thomas any explanations, she felt odd.

Married to a Greek god, about to touch another Greek god... Men were falling out of the sky now that she wasn't looking for one. This one wasn't wearing a wedding ring. God had a sense of humor.

She worked her client's shoulders, his smooth skin taking the oil and glistening in the dim light of the room. Her expert fingers quickly felt the knots' pressure points and worked them out, gaining moans of pleasure from her client.

At least she could still do her job, even with how hungover she felt.

Not a single freckle marred the man's flawless back. His body was muscular and cut. Her fingers strategically moved along the length of his muscles, spreading the oil as she went, eliciting another soft moan from her client.

"Oh, yeah...can you work a little more on that spot?"

A large knot lay in the muscles of his lower back. She used her elbow to work out the kink. She pressed the pressure point to the base of the muscle and back down with her arm until the tension in his body subsided.

She worked on autopilot. Soft music played in the background, and she made out the face of the clock beside the oils. She'd begun the massage at 12:11 p.m.

Shoulders, neck, delts. Ten minutes later, she had moved down the left side of his back, followed by his right.

"Some more pressure would be nice," his muffled voice said.

Immediately, her steel-like fingers sank deeper into his tissue. The man felt rock-hard, and she figured he must spend every extra minute at the gym. She was building up a sweat.

She eyed his dark blond hair. From the back, he looked a lot like Thomas. Poor guy. He was sticking close to Linda's insane schedule.

Had Ashley even kissed Thomas? She must have at the altar. The wedding pictures and video they'd hopefully collect tonight had probably caught the moment. His arms around her, their bodies close, their lips pressed firmly together.

Excitement flushed her skin and awakened long-dead feelings.

She breathed in the calming mist of the diffuser and allowed the essential oils' fragrance to calm her as she dug her palms into the man's back muscles and glided her hand down to his waist. She worked her magic and distracted herself by imagining the long flight her client had sat in. The airlines packed people in so tightly, and she knew exactly where to apply pressure to relieve him of that pain.

He had also mentioned a poor night's rest. He must have slept crookedly since his back held knots.

A few minutes later, she shifted the sheet to reveal

his left leg, carefully tucking the sheet...oh, her client wasn't wearing underwear. She folded the sheet and placed it gently under the curve of his firm left buttock.

She worked her way down the leg, focusing on the muscles but hearing the man moan again.

The gorgeous, naked man.

Perfection or not, he was a client, and more importantly, she *was* legally married. Guilt swept over her—thick and slimy—as she continued her job.

Thomas had paid her some attention last night. He was the first man in years to do so, and now some deep primal she-beast wanted to be released? She understood that she wasn't cheating on her husband by enjoying massaging a man who took care of himself. The granny she'd last seen had needed to be touched with a feather. She kept complaining that Ashley's pressure was too hard, even when she had only laid a hand on her back.

And it was nice to hear someone moaning in delight rather than flinching in pain.

"My glutes need some work, if you don't mind."

Oh, she minded. Even his voice, though strained and muffled from lying with his face in the hole of the chair, sounded heady and masculine. Something deep inside told her she needed to envision him hideously deformed when he rolled over. He was more than likely someone's groom, and she had no business enjoying this. Heck, there had been a spark between her and Thomas last night, and he had been an eligible bachelor when she met him. Her gaze darted to the clock. She was thirty-five minutes into the massage. She would spend two or three minutes on his glutes, but that would be it, and only because he requested that she do so.

She uncovered the most perfect butt cheek she had ever seen. His tan line ran below the rounded flesh. Athletic, outdoorsy…Adonis-like.

For women, she would make a pressure point and move the leg out to help stretch the muscle. This man's leg was massive and too heavy for her to lift. Besides, putting her hand on his upper thigh to maneuver his leg felt too intimate.

Doing what could only be considered the worst job imaginable working on glute muscles, she lifted the sheet to give him privacy. "Please turn," she said in her professional, Phoebe Buffay voice.

She lowered the sheet, not wanting to make eye contact with the man.

"Ashley?"

Her heart skipped a beat when she stared at him as he sat up. "Thomas?"

Even in the dim room, she saw a gleam in his eye as he smiled at her. "I didn't know you were a masseuse." His head tilted, and he squinted his eyes. "Wait. I do remember that now. But I didn't realize you worked *here*." He covered himself more with the sheet. "I thought you'd be out with Linda and the others."

A blush heated her face. The gorgeous man on her table, the one she'd fought so hard not to think about, was her incredibly handsome husband. *Her* husband.

She bit her lip and stared at her hands. Had she known she was touching Thomas, she…well, honestly, she would have allowed herself to enjoy it more.

"I called after you left and spoke to the woman who owns the place. Hershel's wife…what's her name?"

"Brenda," Ashley said, giving him her name and finally understanding the look in her boss's eyes when she had moved to the door to meet her massage client. She felt confident that her co-worker didn't have a family emergency. Brenda had set up this little rendezvous.

"Right. She said a woman named Carla would be the masseuse."

"Carol."

He snapped his fingers. "Yes. She said Carol was the masseuse on duty."

"Carol had a family emergency, and even though I have the week off, I'm on call in case Brenda needs me to fill in."

A genuine look of sympathy crossed his face. "I'm sorry to ruin your day off, especially since I know how you must be feeling." He rubbed his back. "That couch last night…" he said, straightening his tall frame and towering over her from his seat on the table. "You're a good masseuse."

"Thanks. I mostly do chair massages at companies, but bed and breakfast places are big business for me. I met Brenda a few years ago and have worked here part-time ever since."

God, it felt like naked small talk.

"She's lucky to have you." Even in the dimly lit room, his blue eyes seized her. She got lost in them for a moment and didn't turn away.

He glanced down, breaking the spell, and gripped the sheet tightly. "I should probably get dressed and go."

"You're not done with your massage."

He went from painful back to throbbing need with one seductive look from her. Her fingers had danced up and down his spine, had touched him in intimate areas, and had given him pleasure—and he hadn't even known it was her.

The massage needed to end. He needed her to be done. If he lay back down, he'd tent the sheet and show her exactly how much he enjoyed her touch. And that shouldn't happen since they couldn't consummate their marriage.

The look in her eyes had shown him one thing: She seemed happy to see him. Her face had gone from a dull work burden to one of glee when she realized it was him she had been working on for the past half hour.

"Lay back. I can work on your chest," she said in her normal tone. He'd only known her for a day, but he would recognize that voice anywhere.

"I think I'm done." He tucked the sheet under his legs but allowed for a bunching of sorts around his crotch. A faint memory of being back in high school came to him. Being stiff and hard and doing his best to cover himself. Books back then, a sheet now—the sheet being much thinner, and he knew precisely how naked he was.

"You paid for an hour. You should get what you paid for." She picked up his arm, and he allowed her to do so. She placed his palm upward and massaged the center of his hand.

"The skilled hands of a surgeon." Her thumbs radiated outward, stretching his hand muscles. He hadn't realized his hands had held so much tension. His other hand balled into a fist and pressed against the table, so he told himself to relax. His fingers loosened from the fist, and he took a deep breath.

"Do you still have a headache?" He didn't know what to ask and thought this would be safe. His head wasn't pounding anymore. That was the one thing about waking up with a hangover. The moment you woke up was the worst you'd feel all day. With each passing hour, you would feel better.

"It's gone. I just need more sleep." Her fingers traveled up to his forearm but then stopped. He thought she might say something, but she switched to his other hand, stepping closer to him and massaging that one, as well.

His gaze drifted to the counter, where his clothes were neatly folded. He should end the massage, get dressed, and move on with his day—meeting her later to annul their marriage—but then the earthy citrus scent of what he guessed were essential oils greeted him. The fragrance mixed with the scent of the room felt calming and peaceful.

"Paul was getting ready when I left. Mohinder was trying to wake Brian. My guess is they'll be leaving soon to meet Linda and the ladies for lunch." Her eyebrow rose slightly, and she continued to work the palm of his hand. Her movements felt good. This was so much better than being out with Paul.

"You seem to be in less of a panic right now. I'm glad you came in to relax."

The massage had been more about increasing blood circulation since he had drunk so much last night, but it was also about needing to relax.

An awkward pause settled between them, so he said, "I don't fit in with Paul and his group, so I thought I'd come in for a massage." He pointed at his head. "To get rid of my headache."

"I'm glad to help. Linda is determined to stick to her daily plan, no matter what. Tonight is dinner with everyone. I think we can manage to skip it."

"Good." He inhaled deeply and enjoyed the calming effect of the room, especially since she stood so close to him, and his heart was beating faster. "The chapel opens at six tonight. We'll get there then and hopefully end this…issue."

He almost said *ordeal* but held back. Ashley was a working girl, but not what one usually meant when discussing Vegas. According to his faulty memory, Ashley worked hard for her money and had just put herself through school.

A smile appeared on her face, and he wondered what exactly had happened for him to wake up on the couch alone. Was she a good girl like Mohinder had suggested and couldn't even sleep—not have sex with—but simply sleep next to a man in the same bed? Was she sweet and innocent and not a raving, crazed psycho like so many other women got when they discovered he was a bachelor doctor?

One horrible date came to his mind. Actually, a series of them with the same woman. She wanted a discount on a *boob job* from him. He did breast augmentation and reconstruction, not just boob jobs, but that was all people ever saw. Telling people that he worked on noses was easier. Of course, then everyone wanted a free nose job.

Ashley's hands touched his bare chest, ready to move on to the next phase of the massage. "It'll be easier if you lay back down."

He moved the loosened sheet around his hips and tied it off so he'd be safe to stand. "You sit," he said, patting the massage table.

"What? No. I—"

Before she finished her sentence, he placed his hands around her tiny waist and lifted her. "Are you drinking plenty of water?"

She gave him a wry smile. "I've already peed five times today."

His eyes had become accustomed to the dim light in the room, and he could make out the blush crossing her cheeks.

His hand touched her head, a thumb at each temple.

"What are you doing?"

"Shhh," he said in a soothing tone. "You may claim your headache is gone, but I can see you still suffer."

"It's not that bad anymore."

Even with the complaint, she relaxed her neck muscles and leaned into the massage. A thought occurred to him. He liked making her feel better. Taking care of her. She was definitely no wounded bird or damsel in distress, she wasn't some helpless person in need. But he liked being near her and making sure she was all right.

"You should be on the receiving end. You're the customer."

In a joking yet reassuring way, he said, "But what kind of husband would I be if I let my wife suffer?"

11

Thomas stood in the parking lot next to the carriage house with Mohinder. He scanned the area, making sure no one else from the wedding party was about to see him meeting with Ashley. Mohinder was somewhat of an ally in all of this, but Thomas reminded himself that even though Mohinder knew about their secret marriage, he didn't know about the missing wedding ring.

And hopefully, he wouldn't find out. With any luck, they'd find the ring. If not, well, he had a plan B.

Ashley approached and studied the heavy clouds. The temperature had dropped significantly, and the smell of rain lingered in the air. "A storm is coming."

"We're supposed to have a thunderstorm later tonight," Mohinder said, studying the sky like a meteorologist. "It's coming from the east and should be here soon."

Thomas rubbed his head and felt the final remnants of last night's hangover dissipate. "Tell my brother I'm meeting an old friend…maybe a work colleague."

Mohinder squinted at the sky, where a thick cloud now covered the late-afternoon sun. "I'll figure something out. Although you should be able to get to the chapel and back for tonight's activities." He pulled out his worn, multi-folded, and somewhat abused wedding schedule. "Linda has us following this damn thing like clockwork."

"Was tonight the get-together dinner and movie night?" Ashley asked as she joined them.

Looking at the teal-colored piece of decorative cardstock, Mohinder read, "Joint movie night." Mohinder's face lit up. "*Love Everlasting*." A slight smile crossed his face. "I've seen this movie before. It's not great, but it's okay."

"Total chick flick," Thomas said, letting the words escape with some derision. Naturally, the film couldn't be an action drama, Paul's favorite genre. Surely, Linda must have picked this movie out as *their* movie and insisted they watch it during this week.

Mohinder's head tilted slightly, and his lips moved as he read the paper. "Three years ago, on a cool autumn night, Paul and Linda had their first date…yada yada yada." He took a deep breath. "First date, first movie… knew they were meant to be together…" His voice didn't sound mocking or resentful, just like someone too familiar with the details. He folded the paper and placed it back into his pocket. "Nice love story or not, Linda has told me about her first date with Paul at least three times. I wouldn't be surprised if she gave a speech at the wedding explaining how they met."

Linda seemed like the type of woman where everything had to be about her. She didn't seem like an action-adventure-movie type, so Paul probably rarely got to see anything but chick-flicks and rom-coms.

Thomas didn't want to watch the movie, but it did sound better than going to a chapel to retrieve life-changing paperwork—hopefully—and he certainly didn't want to scour the city for a lost ring. He gently nudged Mohinder's shoulder, feeling closer to the man due to his help and understanding. "Your evening sounds better than ours."

"The movie really isn't that bad Nick enjoyed it."

A moment of awkward silence, brief but still there, hung between the three.

"Well," Mohinder said, looking past Thomas without making eye contact. "You should probably…"

Nick wasn't one of the men in the bridal party. Judging by the look on Mohinder's face, he hadn't been invited. The fact that Mohinder wasn't making eye contact with him now told Thomas one thing: Nick was important. "Is Nick your husband?" When Mohinder's face blanched, Thomas added, "I hope he can make it to the wedding so I can meet him."

Mohinder's face brightened, and he gave a curt nod. "He's my boyfriend. He'll be here for the rehearsal dinner." He looked at Ashley and then back to Thomas. "Ashley and Linda have never met him, either, although they've heard a lot about him."

"He sounds wonderful," Ashley said. "I'm glad he's coming. He's family and should be included."

Mohinder let out a sad sigh full of what sounded like pain he had carried for years. "My parents will be here on Saturday. They've never met him. And they've never been interested in meeting him."

"They don't understand," Ashley said.

Thomas had heard this story too often. He had hoped more people would understand in today's age, but he still ran into this type of closed-mindedness. "I'm sorry they don't understand Nick's importance to you."

Ashley lay her hand on Mohinder's shoulder. "I'm sure they'll reconsider once they meet him."

"Thanks." He pursed his lips, and his head tilted in sad defeat. "The chapel opens at six p.m., so you should be on your way," he said, changing the subject. He pointed at Thomas. "You're visiting a colleague." He then gestured to Ashley. "And you are…?"

"Working. I sometimes do late hours at a yoga studio. I already told Linda, so don't worry about covering for me."

Thomas thought he felt a raindrop but ignored it. They couldn't be thwarted by bad weather right now. He opened the car door, which generated a slight smile from Ashley. He figured most men didn't open car doors for women anymore. In one sense, it was a shame, but it did make the small gesture stand out even more when he did it.

Once in the car, she held both wedding rings in the palm of her hand. "We might as well see if we can get a refund on these."

He didn't care about the cost of the rings but was grateful she had them. They needed the paperwork, pictures, and video. That remained the main focus. They pulled onto the highway as Ashley asked her smartphone for directions. "We should be there in twenty minutes."

A citrus-mixed-with-sandalwood scent filled the car, and he inhaled it deeply. "I like the perfume you wear," he said, not knowing what else to say to make small talk as he drove.

"It's essential oils, an autumn blend." Her voice sounded faint, and he figured she felt the awkwardness, too.

"I spoke with Linda today—that is when she wasn't going crazy with wedding issues." A slight chuckle escaped Ashley's lips as Thomas turned onto the second highway. "I'm assuming she's already downing a glass of wine and feeling better."

Ashley cleared her throat and said, "She said your mother invited you to the wedding, not Paul."

Shame covered him, making him feel dirty. He had suspected as much, but the painful truth hadn't been proven until now. Paul didn't want him at this bachelor's week. Hell, the man probably didn't want him at the wedding.

"Yeah, well," he said, his voice wavering, "let's just say I doubt Paul will miss me at the movie tonight."

She must have heard something in his tone because her gaze darted to him. "I'm sorry. I didn't mean—"

"It's all right," he said, brushing her off with a gesture of his hand and keeping his eyes on the road. "Paul and I haven't gotten along in quite some time." He probably should have stopped there, but he wasn't sure how much of the details she was privy to. Obviously, Linda knew about the rift. Since she and Linda were close, she could have shared the story with her, as well...and Ashley probably thought the worst of him.

"The fight was over my ex-wife," he finally said. He pursed his lips, not understanding why he didn't want Ashley to think less of him. If she knew the story, at least she should hear it from his viewpoint. "Tina and Paul were an item and had dated for nearly a year when he introduced her to me." He thought back to the woman he had been married to for only four months. At first, her childlike ways had been exciting, but her lack of maturity—and bed-hopping—made for a short relationship.

"I heard you broke them up."

Thomas had always told himself a person couldn't break up something that was already smashed to pieces, but he *had* played a considerable role, and he had to admit it. "She *bumped into me* in Chicago," he said, taking one hand off the steering wheel long enough to make air quotes. "I was picking up some dinner to bring home and thought our meeting was accidental. I hadn't talked to my brother in a few months, and she led me to believe they had gone their separate ways. She said she was in town for a job interview and didn't know anyone."

He had been stupid. Her sad brown eyes, tearful sniffles, and the please-save-me, maiden-in-distress act had gotten him. She'd played him like a fool. A simple call to his brother would have cleared everything up, but he'd been too busy playing the knight in shining armor. Ten years had passed, and while he could claim some stupidity on youth, he knew he was fully responsible.

His hands clenched the steering wheel even tighter. "One thing led to another that night. Dinner, drinks…" He paused, realizing the situation with Ashley was similar. Lately, his weekend drinks with friends had become happy hours starting on Friday night, followed quickly by after-dinner drinks nearly every night to unwind after a hard day. He'd binged last night and had already thought about having a drink during lunch today. He had never before thought he might be an alcoholic. After all, he was a doctor. He would have detected the early warning signs. He knew better than to abuse his body with alcohol. He…

His gut clenched. He knew he was lying to himself, not wanting to believe his estrangement from his family bothered him that much. In truth, he hadn't been happy in years. "I think I might have a drinking problem," he said in a hushed voice. To his surprise, Ashley placed her hand on his arm.

"I eventually talked with Paul when I realized my mistake with Tina. He wouldn't tell me the details but said they were on-again-off-again and that he hoped they would reconcile. My affair with her was only one night... I never planned to see her again after Paul told me he still loved her, but she..." He bit his lip and sucked in a deep breath, still feeling the pain of the phone call he had received all those years ago. "She called me and claimed to be pregnant."

"Pregnant?" Ashley's eyes widened, showing the unspoken shock he'd known would be there. Sleeping with your brother's love was terrible enough. Getting her pregnant? People would view him as a monster, so he never told people the entire story.

The GPS had him turning off the main highway, so he put on his turn signal. Some misting raindrops fell on the windshield, and he turned on the wipers.

"She *claimed* to be pregnant. But it was a lie." He thought back to the lengths Tina had gone to in order to convince him—the nausea, moodiness, always touching her belly. She even had a pregnancy test with a plus sign on it. It must have been easy to fake that with a blue marker.

He'd been a sucker.

"We got along. She enjoyed the same hobbies I did.

She rooted for the same sports teams and watched the same types of movies. She became the exact woman she needed to be to endear herself to me. We were married within a month, and in the process, I lost my brother. Of course, I thought I had a child on the way. What was I supposed to do?"

"So, she wasn't pregnant but used the lie to trap you?" After he nodded, she asked, "Why? She was already dating Paul. Why not trap him instead? I mean, you're both handsome, both well educated, both—"

"Paul isn't a doctor. He planned to become one but then dropped out of medical school and became a pharmaceutical rep while dating Tina. Evidently, that wasn't what she had in mind for a husband. Their relationship ended when he made that change. Of course, he doesn't see it that way."

Ashley's body went rigid, and she sat straighter in her seat, causing Thomas to briefly turn to see her pinched face and the scornful look in her eyes. "She's one of *those* women," she said, disgust in her voice. "They push back gender equality by generations with their actions. I call the ones who succeed *Mrs. Prestige*."

Thomas lifted an eyebrow, and she added, "A woman who wants prestige through marriage. Women marry for money all the time, and, in a sense, marrying a politician, doctor, or lawyer is the same thing. They even get the title that comes with it." Her jaw tightened, and she added, "Some women don't understand they can have the prestige by going to school and *becoming* a doctor or lawyer themselves."

Looking into Ashley's eyes, Thomas saw something he had not seen before. The look wasn't self-righteousness or girl-power pride. No. It was something else.

"Why be a cheerleader on the front lines when you can have people cheer for you?" Her cold gaze landed on his, and he recognized the exasperated expression: self-worth. Ashley had put herself through school. She had worked hard. She had enough self-respect not to use someone to get ahead.

He rarely saw that in women.

Now at a red light, he stared deeply into Ashley's eyes, and a revelation came to him. He rarely saw that look in women's eyes because he always dated the wrong types of women. He dated those who were arrogant and self-centered.

An odd feeling tingled up his spine and lightened the heaviness he always felt in his chest when it came to the opposite sex. Self-sustaining, strong, and worthy women were not unicorns. They were out there. He just didn't know the fields in which they ran.

"Tina sounds like a total loser."

He turned on the car's blinker once again and switched lanes. "She was. After a while, it became obvious that she wasn't pregnant." He shrugged and had to admit defeat in selecting his first bride. "I didn't think she'd lie about something like that. We went to the courthouse and got married. About a week after the honeymoon, we started fighting. She didn't like sports, didn't have the same interests as me, and didn't enjoy the types of movies I did."

Now he understood why tonight's movie selection had bothered him so much.

"You went to a courthouse the first time? So, you have a habit of not wanting elaborate weddings," Ashley said with a certain levity that he suspected she'd meant to lighten the mood in the car.

"I guess so." He felt his lips curl upward into a genuine smile, which surprised him. Spending thousands of dollars on a wedding never sat well with him. The venue, the cake, all those guests... Just for one day, when you should be focused on the marriage, where you'll live, and how to afford a lovely honeymoon.

He had never thought about why he had gone with Tina to the courthouse. He was just thrilled that the money they would have spent on an elaborate wedding would instead go toward the cost of a newborn.

A baby he was happy didn't exist.

Kids were not in his future. One day, he'd love to be the fun uncle to some nieces and nephews if he ever got the chance with Paul's future kids, but he didn't want the responsibility of raising his own set of little rugrats.

He'd leave that task to those who would be good at it.

"We should have the drug screens back by Tuesday

or Wednesday," he said, getting back to their initial problem and his reason for skipping out on his brother. "Mohinder won't say anything to Linda or Paul. None of the other men know anything, so nothing should get back to them."

"Or to our parents."

Very true. He didn't want to explain yet another wedding fiasco to his mother.

"You just missed our exit," she said, pointing behind her. "But we can still get there if we take the next turn. I know of a parking garage we can use."

He put on the blinker and followed her advice, which led them to a three-tier park-place only a few blocks away from the chapel. He paid for parking, and the two exited the garage.

KABOOM!

They had started down the sidewalk for their trek to the chapel when a clap of thunder startled them both.

"I don't suppose you have an umbrella in the car?"

He glanced at the darkening clouds above them. "We should move quickly."

Before they managed a single block, rain pelted them in sheets.

"Over here." He ushered her aside, and the two took cover under a green-and-white-striped awning. The pawnshop was closed, and the tiny scrap of hanging fabric was the only haven in sight.

Rain tapped the awning and poured down in front of them, making a wet curtain that kept them huddled together at the pawnshop's door. His arm gripped her around the waist, and he pulled her closer. "Our feet are getting soaked."

She leaned into him, her face nestled against his chest. A slight move in either direction, and they'd be drenched. "At least the temperature isn't too bad right now. The storm has cooled things off."

Cooled off? It was anything but.

Ashley hiked her purse higher on her shoulder so it wouldn't get wet. The action caused her right hand to encircle more of Thomas's back, where it was pressed into his finely cut figure. She thought back to the massage. If she had…

She took a deep breath and tried to think of something else. Nothing came to mind.

With another thunderclap, Thomas held her tighter. "Don't be afraid. This won't last long."

"I'm fine." He held her tighter and physically moved so his body blocked more of the rain, pushing her against the dry brick wall. When he stroked her hair and said, "Shhh," she asked, "Are you afraid?"

"What?" He pulled away slightly, only enough to make eye contact, and said, "Of course, not."

Lightning lit the evening sky, and she felt his body tense.

"It's okay if you are."

"I'm fine," he said in a not-too-reassuring tone that made her ask again. He finally said, "Astraphobia affects two percent of the population. I'm not afraid. I just don't like storms."

"Astraphobia?" Leave it to a doctor to make the fear of thunder and lightning sound scientific. "How bad is your fear?"

The rain came down at an angle, drenching their feet. He had sandwiched her against the building so she avoided the worst of it.

"Thunder and lightning don't bother me that much—"

Another flash of lightning streaked across the sky, this one larger than the others. It brightened everything in its path, including the terrified look on Thomas's face as he held her so tightly she could hardly breathe. He closed his eyes and was as white as a sheet by the time the thunder came.

And it came within three seconds. She heard Thomas counting, his warm breath coasting across her skin as the large boom followed.

"That lightning struck only three miles away." He scanned the skies and saw nothing comforting.

She held him tighter, her arms around his back, her head pressed to his chest where she heard his heartbeats over anything Mother Nature was dishing out.

"It's all right. We're safe here." She stroked his back, comforting him. "The weather wasn't so bad a few minutes ago." With one hand, she retrieved her cell phone from her back pocket. Opening her local news app, she selected local radar and watched as the time-lapse tool showed the storm coming into their location. Mostly red splotches were above them, but some were purple. The storm had come in so quickly, she wasn't surprised that it looked like it would move north of them and out of their way soon.

He shifted his weight until her back pressed against the building, his body pinning hers. He buried his head in the wet curls on her neck, and she suspected he had tightly shut his eyes. She rubbed his back gently. "It will be over soon."

"I'm fine. I just want you to be safe." The warm whisper danced on her neck, causing a shiver of goose bumps to prickle.

"I'm not afraid," she said in a reassuring tone. "Now, if a spider were under the awning with us, I'd be screaming at the top of my lungs. We all have fears, and it's fine if you have astraphobia."

She now realized how she slowly rocked him. Surprisingly enough, the movement helped. His tightly wound body relaxed, and he sank deeper into her. "How long have you been afraid of thunder and lightning?"

He took a deep breath and made eye contact. "I'm not afraid of the storm. I just want everyone to be safe."

"Okay, so how long have you needed everyone to be safe during storms?"

His eyebrow lifted as if he didn't usually talk about such things but was now willing to. "Before Paul was born, we had a dog named Oslo." His face lit up as he thought back to his childhood pet. "She was a beautiful greyhound mix, about the same height as I was at four years old." A smile came to his face, one that twinkled in his eyes. "I thought she was a horse and tried to ride her so many times, but she was gentle and tolerated me."

Thomas scanned the sky, and she noted that it took more time for the thunder to sound after the lightning. "One night, we had a bad storm like this one, but it lasted for hours. My parents thought I was asleep, but the weather kept me up. I heard Oslo whining from the hallway and my parents telling her the storm was nothing to be afraid of."

His eyes narrowed as if remembering something terrifying.

"The whining stopped." He looked at Ashley, and his eyes widened. "All of a sudden, Oslo was deathly quiet, and I didn't know what was wrong. I snuck out of my room to get her. I thought she'd be happier with me in my bed, under the covers. I found her crying and hiding behind the couch near the back door. She was too scared to continue pacing the hallway. She shook uncontrollably and wouldn't stop drooling. I thought she was going to die."

He shuddered at the memory. "I've never seen an animal so scared before. My parents were in the kitchen, so I got her out from behind the sofa and cleaned her up."

He paused and let out a nervous chuckle. "I thought it would be best to let her go outside to use the bathroom before coming to bed. So, stupid me, I opened the doggie door, and she ran out."

"Oh, no!"

"She escaped and was out in the storm." He glanced at the sky. "Out in the harsh elements."

"What did you do?"

"I followed her. I was small enough to get through the doggie door. I crawled through but didn't see her anywhere." He touched his shirt, and the rain's dampness clung to his chest. "My pajamas were soaked in seconds, but I didn't care. I ran after her. It took my parents a while to realize that Oslo was gone. Much longer to realize I was outside with her."

"How long?"

He shook his head to tell her the time didn't matter to the story. A scared little boy was out in a storm. Even five minutes would seem like an eternity. "An hour or so. Somehow, I managed to find her. She was two blocks away, but in the dark, I didn't know how to get home. We lay together under a car to stay safe. I had to hold on to her collar and comfort her so she wouldn't run away." He pointed at his forehead. "She gave me this scar and another one near my right ear, trying to bolt again."

Ashley touched his forehead, not seeing the scar but believing it was there. "She was terrified, and you were trying to calm her."

He closed his eyes and smiled. "Much like you're comforting me now."

"You were a little boy out in bad weather, trying to care for a loved one." She rubbed his back more and held him closely. "You're safe here with me. We're both safe."

He allowed his body to sink into her more. "I've never told anyone that story before."

"You haven't?"

He smiled as he shook his head. "My parents found Oslo and me. They were also drenched from the rain, and I forced Oslo out from under the car when I heard my father yelling my name. I'll never forget my mother's face when she saw Oslo and me."

Ashley could imagine his parents' worry and then relief after finding them—and the relief on *his* face knowing his parents had come to rescue him and his dog. The current storm wouldn't continue for too much longer.

They just needed to remain safe and stay in place.

12

Their trek to the chapel was full of mad dashes between awnings and under storefronts that offered protection, but their clothes were still wet. It was the sticking-to-your-skin, must-get-out-before-you-catch-a-cold type of drenched that you wouldn't want to spend all day in.

Ashley hated the feeling, especially since her jeans from the knees down and her sneakers were soaking wet.

Thank goodness the worst of the weather had passed. It had been a long thirty minutes under that awning, but a glorious time getting to know Thomas. The sky had lit up with Mother Nature's splendor, and she had his protection, even though she wasn't scared. He was more composed and much more at peace now that the weather had passed, although he hadn't stopped holding her hand since they had left the security of the pawnshop's awning.

His hand was strong, and he seemed determined. Even though she had just met Thomas, he gave her a sense of security and protection—something she had lacked since being diagnosed with breast cancer a few years ago. The cancer had been a threat from within, and even though family members sat with her during her chemo treatments, she had fought the battle alone.

No one could understand what an infusion felt like until they sat in the chair. The numbing of the skin on top of the port, the prick of the needle going in, the beeping of the machine as it pumped in the chemotherapy drugs and steroids. The beeping of those little machines still sounded in her ears when she closed her eyes, and the monster came out to torture her.

Mohinder and Linda had stood by her and held her hand. But her body had experienced weight gain and neuropathy to the point where she lost feeling in her toes. Then there was the dreaded hair loss.

Losing all her hair. That was the most painful of all. Certainly emotional pain, but losing her hair had the same sensation as being a little girl and keeping her hair in pigtails all day before releasing it from the tight pull of the hairbands. Except the chemo hair loss felt a hundred times worse and lasted for a solid week without relief. She still had the black T-shirt she had used to collect the hair. Spreading it out on the rug in her bathroom, leaning over it, and gently running her fingers across her sensitive scalp to collect the hair. Seeing how much came out—several times a day—and knowing it wouldn't stop until none remained.

She had suffered that and so much more alone.

All alone.

The words of her oncologist came to her. "*Stop focusing on cancer.*" The doctor saw people who were far worse off than her, and even though he may have been right, it'd proven difficult for her to live each day as it came and be *grateful*, especially when she still experienced the numb toes.

"We're almost there," Thomas said as they dashed from one safe spot to the next.

He was so focused and determined.

Even though she needed to fix the problem of their accidental marriage, it had given her...something. She couldn't put her finger on it, and even though it would be a pain to fix, it distracted her and gave her a purpose.

In any event, it was something other than a wedding and seeing other people blissfully happy. If it weren't for a legally binding marriage and a missing ring costing thousands of dollars, her outing with Thomas, including the downpour, would have actually been fun.

She rethought that. No, it *was* fun, regardless of the issues.

"I'm sorry I didn't have an umbrella in the car," he said.

"We're not going to melt." There was no reason to apologize. Her umbrella lay in her suitcase at the cottage, all safe and dry. She could have easily brought it, but she hadn't.

"We're finally here," he said once the porte-cochère of the Pair O' Dice Chapel covered them. Unfortunately, the sign on the door still read *Closed*.

"They must be late opening due to the weather." Ashley noticed the time. The place should have opened nearly half an hour ago. She peered through the tiny window on the door and knocked loudly. "There is a light on inside."

Thomas let go of her hand, shook his arms, and inspected his wetness level. Shaking his head, his hair reshaped into a sexy, by-the-pool style. Why did men always look good with wet hair?

"Your hair is so curly." He nodded and indicated her mop of hair.

A quick smile came to her as she touched her tresses. Curls always tightened when refreshed by water. She always thought the wetter her hair was, the better it looked. She'd had difficulty styling her curls as they grew out and needed to learn proper curl care. Now that her hair was shoulder-length, it took minutes in the morning with many products for her to prepare for the day.

He removed a handkerchief from his pants pocket. "Clean and mostly dry." He gazed into her eyes and asked, "May I?"

She wasn't sure what he meant, but she nodded. He wiped the rain from her face, much like a person would take care of a valuable treasure they didn't want to see spoiled by water. His hands were gentle and thorough. "You all right?"

She had never been one to want a man to protect her, but something deep inside her appreciated Thomas foregoing his fears. He dried her off as best he could when his own face still dripped with water from his wet hair. "I'm fine."

A stillness grew between them until she finally turned away and said, "Pair O' Dice Wedding Chapel." Ashley read the neon sign and felt her heart sink. The place was a dive. They could have gone to a famous Las Vegas chapel or any of the other nicer venues in the city. But no. They must have been on a mission to find the cheesiest place Las Vegas had to offer—especially since they would have had to go down several side streets to get here.

"I have no idea how we even found this place last night."

She didn't either. It wasn't a historic landmark or one of the more ideal venues. Her last wedding took place at the well-known Little White Wedding Chapel. The wedding had been impulsive, quick, and not what she truly wanted. No family attended, and they had no pictures. Only she and her high school boyfriend being stupid and running off. If someone was with the right person, there was nothing wrong with eloping, but Roger was anything but that. He incurred gambling debt, wiped out her college savings, and finally put pen to paper and told her in a note that he was leaving her.

It had been a crazy and regretful—not to mention expensive—six months. Thankfully, she was able to track Roger down long enough for him to sign the annulment paperwork. She hadn't seen him since, had never gotten a penny from him, and even had to pay for the termination of their ridiculous yet completely legal and binding union.

She stared at the locked door, not remembering it at all from last night. "If we're married, how much do you think it will cost to get the marriage annulled?" It wasn't as though she hurt for money, but she wasn't blessed with an abundance of it, either.

"Shouldn't be that much, but I'll pay for it."

She quickly turned and faced him. "You don't have to do that."

"Consider it a wedding gift." He tested the door. When it wouldn't budge, he knocked again. "They should be open in a minute. I can hear someone inside."

Ashley tapped her purse where she kept their wedding bands. "Maybe they'll take the rings back." Deep down in a pit of her stomach, she knew they were married. There was no paperwork here to retrieve, no last-minute reprieve, nothing hopeful to believe.

They were screwed.

"I cleared my schedule so I can stay in town on the Monday after the wedding. Just in case we need to file some legal paperwork downtown."

There was that. The paperwork would take months, but both would initially have to sign the legal documents. "I'm sorry if this is interfering with your patient schedule. I understand you're a plastic surgeon…a specialist. People are probably on a waitlist to have their surgeries."

His features relaxed, but not in a defeated type of way. More a life-goes-on kind of look. "My patients go through a lot. They are…"

His expression became pensive, as though he searched for the right words. "My patients tend not to let the little things in life get them down. I work with them for years sometimes, ensuring they get perfection when they're on my table."

She hadn't realized nose jobs took that long. Rhinoplasty seemed like a procedure that would only take a few visits with a doctor. But then, people in car accidents sometimes needed to have their faces rebuilt. Surely, that could take up to a year.

"Thanks for staying the extra time. Hopefully, we can get everything done."

He glanced outside the tiny building and stared at the steeple and what looked like cheap stained glass running the lengths of the building's sides. He then pointed to the iron gate that led to a small concrete patio. "Do you think we were married inside or out here?"

The rainy weather had now given way to stifling humidity. Her hair would go from beautiful curls to a frizzy mess within the hour. She pulled a coiled scrunchy from her wrist, the most convenient place to store them, and pulled her hair into a sloppy bun. "I'm hoping we weren't married anywhere and they turned us away."

"Well, there is that."

Once again, Ashley peered through the small window in the heavy wooden door that led into the little chapel. "Someone's coming."

"Is it Elvis?"

She stifled a chuckle but peered back, concerned the King might be coming to let them in.

"I'm sorry," the photographer said as he searched the lost and found. "No one found a ring last night." He pointed to a slip of paper attached to the box. "Anything of value is put in the safe and registered on this piece of paper. The only thing found last night was a watch and a lost pearl earring."

"Were two silver hoop earrings found?" After the photographer gave her a look that said he'd already explained what was found, Ashley added, "I don't know where I lost them last night."

Thomas had wanted to talk to the minister, but a couple walked in a minute after they arrived. Now, they needed to wait. "Please, have a seat. When Father Dougherty finishes this ceremony, he'll be able to answer your questions." The man studied Ashley for a moment and then added, "I remember you." His voice pitched higher, and he studied Thomas. With his finger pointing from one of them to the other, he said, "You were both drunk when you walked in here."

Ashley, who had been inspecting the tiny chapel from floor to steeple, stepped forward. "You knew we were drunk? Yet we still ended up married?"

"You passed the breathalyzer test."

"We what?" Thomas's voice held bold defiance. "I don't see how that's possible."

"Regardless, you two were holding hands, acting giddy, and laughing—just like half the people who come in here. I'm an experienced photographer, and I couldn't get you to smile at the camera at the same time." He dismissively waved his hands in the air. "Even a serious stare would have been fine, but you two barely stood straight."

Thomas's mind focused on one word. "I'm never *giddy*." Thomas would have taken that as a sign of his drunkenness, but no one here knew him, not even his bride.

"Regardless, you seemed in love. Especially the cute pet names you had for each other."

Good God, there were pet names? His heart sank. Did he even want to know?

"Sugar Pants and Hot Lips. I'm not sure which was which."

"Oh, my." Ashley raised a hand to her mouth. Her initial gasp turned into a chuckle.

Neither name suited him, but he suspected a story existed behind them. He now understood the scribbling next to their names on the license. The words weren't *Surgeon* and *Hotel*. Nope. He was Sugar Pants. And his bride was Hot Lips.

Not that he knew how hot her lips were. If he'd found out last night, the memory was lost in his drunk vault. He didn't even want to know why she'd called him Sugar Pants.

He paused and thought about that. Actually, he might want to know.

"If you're the photographer, what pictures were taken?" Ashley asked, obviously not interested in any nicknames. Thank goodness she wasn't a woman who couldn't joke about such things.

The assistant pulled out a pamphlet and wrote on the back. "Here. You need to check what email addresses you gave the minister when you talk to him, but that's the video and picture uplink website. You should get an email with your secure login within forty-eight hours of the wedding. Typically, it's only about twenty-four hours."

He turned the flyer around. "This will help you understand annulments in the state of Nevada."

Thomas read the title of the flyer. In big letters, it read: *Annulments*. Evidently, there was a need for such reading material if they kept it handy. The stack he'd pulled it from was quite large.

The wedding march played, and the photographer turned to leave. "The minister doesn't allow pictures during the ceremony, so I'm up next. I'll be busy in the main chapel for about twenty minutes. You can talk to the minister once he's done posing with the couple."

Thomas quickly scanned the document. *Both parties must agree to the annulment.* No problem there. As hot and sexy as Ashley was, she didn't know or understand how to abuse her womanly powers. He had been stupid enough to marry her without a prenuptial agreement, though he doubted she knew how wealthy he was. A natural assumption would be that he had money due to his profession, but he had carefully bought real estate for the past twenty years and had quite a few investments. His home in Chicago was worth well over two million dollars.

Cost of the annulment - $500. Not a problem. Even if Ashley hadn't mentioned the price ahead of time, he would have insisted on paying for it. Not because he was gentlemanly enough to do it but because he wanted it over with.

One party must live in Nevada for at least six weeks before requesting the annulment, or the marriage must have occurred within the state of Nevada. Ashley lived here, so they were good there. He assumed she wasn't planning on leaving the state anytime soon. Plus, they had been married in Nevada.

Must be filed with the city. He'd assumed as much. The chapel wouldn't do that for them.

There was also a time limit in which to file. They would meet that, as well.

Overall, the paperwork's brevity held just enough information to provide a checklist of what to do, and that was all they really needed.

Then he saw the list of approved reasons for filing an annulment, which was what he wanted to see. He hadn't misrepresented himself to her. Neither of them was already married, but they qualified for impaired judgment. Plus, if he could believe Ashley, the two had not consummated the marriage.

Ashley had wandered into a section he would describe as the gift shop area of the place. He joined her at a glass counter where a selection of rings was displayed.

"Looks like we splurged and got the nicest set. The sign says no exchanges if the rings are engraved."

"I doubt the name of the chapel inside our rings counts as an engravement."

Regardless, the cost of the rings was nothing.

She shivered, the air conditioner hitting her. They stood under an air vent, and more of the light, flowery scent of the chapel surrounded them. He wished he had a warm jacket to take off and offer her.

Sliding her hand up and down her arm for warmth, she checked out the variety of shirts and shorts that hung on a rack. The Pair O' Dice logo marked each one, as did the titles *Bride* and *Groom*. The clothes weren't what he wanted to wear, but they were dry.

"These shirts have *I'm the Bride!* and *I'm the Groom!* on them with the Pair O' Dice logo, but the printed titles are small. It's a set with matching shorts." He grabbed a medium woman's set and handed them to her. "We should put on some dry clothes."

She accepted the clothes and walked to a basket. "There are socks, too."

Naturally, everything was purity white. Thomas would expect nothing else. They'd be walking out of here like walking billboards. "We'll have to ensure that no one sees us wearing these things."

The minister, an older man with gray hair and kind eyes, walked out of the chapel and closed the door. "Welcome to the Pair O' Dice Wedding Chap—" His eyes widened, and a spark of recognition grew. "I figured I'd see the two of you again."

13

Ashley was grateful the minister allowed them to buy the outfits and change into clothes that weren't wringing wet. Her irritated skin had turned that pale, whitish color, and the air conditioner had chilled her.

Thomas changed and met her in the chapel's entryway, where the minister waited.

"Father Dougherty says he remembers us being drunk last night." Ashley wasn't sure if that was a good or a bad sign, but it sounded promising that the man might not have filed the marriage paperwork.

"I married a Hot Lips," he said, pointing at Ashley, "to a Mr. Sugar Pants," he continued, now pointing at Thomas. Another couple entered the chapel. The woman in a flowing white gown held on to her groom, who stood smiling from ear to ear. They came with six others, with more standing outside the building and coming in.

"I have an appointment in a few minutes," Father Dougherty said. He greeted the couple and asked them to speak with the wedding coordinator cleaning up the chapel area. Ashley hadn't even noticed the woman before, but she wore a pleasant dress and a name tag, obviously an employee. The smile she plastered on her face seemed fake but nice enough until she noticed Ashley.

The woman blanched white, and she turned away to face the wedding party that had just come in. She busied herself with them, showing them into the chapel.

"Please, I don't have much time." Father Dougherty ushered them into his private office, where Ashley took a seat directly across from the man. The marriage license was in her purse, so she took it out, unfolded it, and placed it on the desk between them.

"We were here last night and found this license. We believe you officiated and married us," Thomas said, pointing to the paper and taking a seat next to Ashley.

Father Dougherty barely glanced at the paperwork before handing it back. "We are usually too busy to perform many walk-ins and prefer our couples to schedule ahead of time. Late last night, the two of you barged in here with this license and demanded to be married."

Demanded? Ashley found it hard to believe that she

would have been so aggressive. She gazed at Thomas. Maybe he had insisted the minister marry them.

"When Dorothy," he said, indicating his assistant outside, "asked you two to leave, you were incredibly rude to her."

"Rude?" Ashley folded the license and placed it back into her purse. "What did we do?"

The minister pointed at Thomas. "Sugar Pants didn't do anything. It was you, Hot Lips."

Having a man of the cloth use that tone of voice and call them by their drunken names from last night sent chills down her spine. She wasn't sure what had been said or done; she only wished the entire night could be erased.

"I'm not sure what you said to her, but by law, she conducted a breathalyzer test on you both. You were under the legal limit and—"

"Your photographer mentioned that," Thomas said, his voice showing his irritation. "I don't see how that is possible since neither of us can remember even being here last night."

"Legally, we tested you. You paid your money and were married."

Father Dougherty picked up another annulment flyer, obviously not realizing they'd gotten one from the photographer. The minister glanced at his computer screen and typed something on the keyboard. The clicking of the keys filled the tiny room until he wrote something on the paper.

"I'm betting these emails are incorrect, so your packet of pictures and video were not sent out." He gestured out the door of his office. "Dorothy can put them on a USB drive for you." He pointed at the code he had written across the brochure. "Give her this number."

"What emails did we put down?"

Ashley was glad that Thomas had asked and hoped she had been too drunk to write her mother's address.

"Seems to be a joint email, *hotlips@sugarpants.com*." His eyes traveled from Ashley to Thomas, but his thin lips and stoic gaze remained humorless. "Is that a good email for either of you?"

"Thank God, no." When the minister glared at her, she lowered her head. Was that considered blasphemy? They were in a house of the Lord. What she'd said was probably okay. She didn't want the minister, who probably already had a low opinion, to think any less of her.

Father Dougherty took a highlighter from his desk and opened the pamphlet. "The license was already sent and registered with the recorder's office. That's the beauty of living in the age of the Internet." He moved the highlighter across the page and marked it as he read. "You have thirty days to file a complaint for annulment. In the complaint, you need to have another adult personally serve—meaning hand-deliver—a copy of the complaint and the accompanying papers to your spouse.

Whoever served your spouse must fill out an affidavit of service, which you must file with the court."

He set down the highlighter for a moment and glared at them. "Are you two getting this, or are you still drunk?"

"We're not drunk, sir. Thank you for your help," Thomas said sheepishly.

Ashley's heart sank. The paperwork had been filed, and even though she had undergone an annulment before, the procedure felt daunting. Her first husband, Roger, had been resistant and absent, but at least he lived in Nevada. Having Thomas living in Chicago would make the process even more taxing.

"Your spouse can answer the claim or make a counterclaim. If your spouse files an answer, you will have a meeting with the court within ninety days. After that, the judge will schedule a hearing to determine whether an annulment is appropriate. You and Mr. Sugar Pants will have to testify at the hearing, and you can give the judge other evidence to support your case."

"Mr. Sugar Pants and I were completely drunk when you married us." Ashley's voice rose, and her tone was that of a lecturer, even though she tried to sound calm. "You should never have married us in the first place."

"You went to the courthouse and got a marriage license. You then came here to get married. You passed a breathalyzer test," he said, counting off on his fingers. "You showed foreknowing, intent, and were legally able to be wed." His expression hardened, and Ashley assumed this wasn't the first time the minister had needed to have this conversation with a couple. He pushed his glasses farther up his nose and handed her the brochure. "I only perform the wedding ceremonies. I don't ensure the marriage will last."

He then gave her a harsh glare. "Marriage is not to be taken lightly. Hopefully, the next time you two enter into the sacred union, whether it be to each other or with different partners, you won't take your vows so lightly."

"Of course, sir." Ashley accepted the brochure and the lecture. She had heard it before when she ran off to marry Roger. She hadn't learned from her mistake, and Father Dougherty unknowingly called her on it.

The minister removed his glasses and sized the two of them up. "You both seem eager to annul your mistake, but if your spouse doesn't file an answer to your annulment complaint, you can ask the clerk to issue a default against them. The judge can then enter a decree of annulment for you. Of course, this takes at least ninety days, and either you both must sign the paperwork or the one not in default signs."

"I'm sure neither of us will be in default," Ashley said, glancing at Thomas.

"We have lab work to prove our state of intoxication," Thomas said.

Ashley clutched the pamphlet. Everything had been discussed on how to get unhitched legally. There was still one more matter to discuss. "We would also like to have the annulment filed with the church."

"I'd suggest you speak to a priest who knows you. They can handle that. In fact," he said, showing a bit of compassion on his face, "it wouldn't hurt to speak to him and maybe get some counseling."

That was a religious tongue-lashing Thomas didn't want to hear. Especially since it may take as long as ninety days to get the annulment. What were they living in? The Dark Ages?

"If you'll excuse me. I'm needed to marry a couple who *scheduled* their wedding. They took the time to consider their actions and are ready to commit themselves to each other."

Thomas clutched the plastic bag he held that contained their wet clothes. Minister or not, the man, although correct, was a… Nope, he would not say the man was a dick. He wasn't even going to think such an insult in a chapel, even if what the man had said was salt being rubbed into the wound.

"We'll be seeing our family preacher on Saturday. I can ask him after the ceremony about filing our annulment with the church." When Thomas nodded, Ashley added, "Let's talk to Dorothy and get those horrible pictures we paid for." She stood and walked with Thomas to the chapel entrance. They found Dorothy seated behind a desk, her head down, doing paperwork.

It then occurred to him that Dorothy was the dot6vegasmom he had given the thousand-dollar Venmo payment to.

Yeah, he wanted to talk with her.

Thomas's shoes squeaked across the floor. "Ma'am? May we speak to you for a moment?" He did his best to use his most polite voice, even though he wanted to demand she tell him why she had extorted a thousand dollars from him.

The woman barely made eye contact. "How can I help you?"

"Do you remember us from yesterday?" By the guilty look in her eyes, he felt certain she did.

Dorothy glanced away and slightly to the left, which was a sign she was forming a lie in her head. "There were several couples here late last night. I…"

"How did you know we came in late and not early in the evening?" Ashley asked. Her eyebrows knitted together, and Thomas figured she'd also made the connection to the Venmo payment and suspected the woman was hiding something.

As if Dorothy suddenly grew a spine, she sat straighter in the chair, raised her head high, and asked, "How may I help you?"

Ashley showed the woman the brochure with the photography code. She took the paper and moved toward her computer. Her fingers danced across the keys, and then she tilted the screen toward them. The wedding images appeared, and they were worse than

Thomas had feared. Inhibitions had left. Dignity, too. When they were open, their eyes were red and held the dull look of a trapped animal. Even their mouths gaped open in some pictures, hinting at how bad their speech and reaction time must have been.

Within minutes, Dorothy had pulled the images and video from the computer and stored them on two matching white USB drives. The Pair O' Dice Chapel was written in gold across them. If an additional fee existed for the service, she didn't ask for one.

Her eyes narrowed, and she moved her head closer to the computer screen. "I only have one email for the two of you," she said in a way that told him that she didn't think the first email was accurate. "Do you want to put down a second one so we can email you the images, as well?"

"Sure."

Ashley's answer surprised him. These were not images he wanted to cherish, but he gave Dorothy a good personal email once she had taken down a valid one for Ashley.

When it became apparent the two weren't leaving, Dorothy glanced at the main chapel doors. They remained closed. "Is there something else I can help you with?"

Her voice sounded hushed and laced with a tinge of panic. She glanced at the floor when a slight cough sounded.

Thomas noticed a small child asleep on the rug

behind her. A little boy, no more than three years of age, lay curled up in a powder-blue blanket, his head on an overstuffed pillow. He wore Spider-Man pajamas and held a tissue in his hand. His nose and face were flushed red with a fever.

"Is he your son?" Pictures of several kids and a child's drawing sat framed on her desk. And even though the woman was well dressed, Thomas saw the worn look in her eyes that said she needed a nap. The look was common with working mothers, and he now recognized it in her.

Regardless, she had extorted money from him.

She knelt and checked on the boy, who still slept. She removed an empty sports drink bottle next to him and placed it on her desk. "The lady who watches my kids doesn't accept sick children. Father Dougherty doesn't like for me to bring my babies in here, but I didn't have anywhere else to take him." She then added, "A friend of mine is coming for him. He'll only be here an hour."

"Have you taken him to see a doctor?" Pediatrics wasn't his specialty, but he could examine the child if needed. When she stared oddly at him, he could only imagine the impression he had made upon her last night. "I'm a doctor."

She still looked skeptical until Ashley added, "He really is."

Her face relaxed, as did the shocked expression in her eyes, and she focused once more on her little boy.

"I've already taken him. He has a viral infection. No antibiotics. I just have to give him over-the-counter medication until he's better."

"You're a single mother?" Ashley asked.

"Yes," she said, her neck swiveling to survey the room and ensure no one stood within earshot. "I need this job. So, please don't... I mean..." She took a deep breath, and near panic showed in her eyes. "You insisted. I should have said no, but you two would have gone elsewhere. I know it was wrong, but you kept raising the amount, and..."

"I insisted?" Thomas asked.

"After you both failed the BACtrack...."

"The what?" Ashley asked.

"The breathalyzer. If any couple looks drunk, I have to check if your count is over point-zero-eight. You both failed but wouldn't take no for an answer."

"We asked you to lie about the results?" Thomas asked.

"You *insisted*. Said you'd go somewhere else because you wouldn't let a unicorn escape." She shook her head. "I wasn't sure what you meant by that, but the two of you were calling yourselves pet names, hanging all over each other... You said it was your destiny to be married."

"I said it was our destiny?"

Dorothy pointed at Ashley. "No, Hot Lips did. But you agreed. You offered me a bribe, and I said no. You kept increasing the amount until..." She pursed her lips and looked even more guilty. "Until I finally agreed. You don't understand,"—she glanced at her son—"I shouldn't have done it, but that is a lot of money. I swear, I've never done this before, and I won't do it again. I promise."

The main door to the chapel opened, and the photographer left the room. As the door slowly closed, the ceremony began.

While the photographer stood outside of earshot, Dorothy whispered. "I need this job. Please, don't."

"It's all right." Thomas took the two USB drives and pocketed them. "We understand."

Ashley considered the young boy who began a coughing fit. "We hope he feels better soon."

Thomas walked to the exit door, and Ashley followed, obviously believing the woman. He could have insisted that Dorothy return the money. He could have even filed a complaint and had her fired—or worse, thrown in jail. But what was the point? They would still be married, and Dorothy didn't seem to be a terrible person, despite having done a bad deed.

And, especially for being in a chapel, wasn't forgiveness expected?

"After all that humble pie," he said to Ashley once they were outside, "how about some dinner?"

14

"Leave it to Vegas." Free of the chapel, Ashley held out her hand and gazed at the disappearing clouds. "Pouring rain one minute, and then not a cloud in the sky the next."

"Just like Chicago." Thomas glanced down one side of the street and then the other. "Do you know of a good restaurant nearby?"

"We were at a nice bar and then the pirate pit last night. Let's head to the Corporate Room." Their wedding stuff aside, they still needed to find Linda's ring, and the only way to do that was to retrace their steps. "We can check their lost and found and also have dinner." Ashley pressed a button on her phone. "Show me how to get to the Corporate Room."

The results showed her rentable business conference rooms but no bar. "Show me how to get to the Corporate Room bar." When the results were still less than desirable, she said, "I'll have to type in the name."

Thomas gently touched her arm to stop her. An odd expression, followed by a huge grin, captivated his face. "We already know where the place is."

"We do?"

"We have the exact coordinates." He took her hand and led her to the intersection with more traffic. "What were the first What3Words in the texts from last night?" Thomas let go of her hand and raised his arm to hail a cab.

It was so evident that it practically stared them in the face. She felt silly for not having thought of it earlier. "We saved the What3Word locations!" She opened her texts and read the first trio of words to him as he put them into his app. "This is brilliant."

"That location is a few miles from here." A cab arrived, and he opened the door to allow Ashley in. He sat beside her, and the scent of disinfectant and vinyl hit her nose.

Glancing at the three-word combo's actual address, he gave the cab driver the location. "I'm betting this triple pair is for the first bar we went to. I left a voicemail at both places, asking about the lost ring but never heard back from either."

"Hopefully, they serve food at the Corporate Room." Ashley hadn't realized how hungry she had become. She'd lived in Vegas all her life but was unfamiliar with the place when they arrived a few minutes later.

Restaurants and bars held a high turnover rate. Judging by how packed this one was on a Sunday night, it was doing well.

"The Corporate Room." Thomas read the marquee and then paid the driver before stepping out of the cab and waiting for her to join him. "This looks like the place from the pictures last night."

"The timestamp on the selfies shows this was the first place we stopped yesterday. How on Earth did we know about this place?"

Thomas gave her a playful shrug. "There's a Corporate Room in Chicago. Very upscale for a bar. It's downtown in the business complex and does extremely well. I think maybe we came here on my suggestion."

Once inside, Ashley realized they weren't up to the dress code. This wasn't a T-shirt and shorts type of place. Men and women, some in suits, sat at the tables, sipping colorful cocktails and champagne. The sounds of chatter and laughter surrounded her, as did the scent of sliders and nachos.

"Welcome to the Corporate Room." A woman in a black-skirted suit and a white button-down shirt greeted them. She eyed their outfits and then glanced around. "I'm sure we can find a spot for the bride and the groom."

Ashley gazed at Thomas's shirt that proudly announced he was *the groom* and nearly laughed. Well, they were married yesterday. So, technically, he *was* the groom.

Her groom.

"This table in the back is nice and quiet," the waitress said. Ashley assumed the *quiet table* was more on account of their comfortable attire than any privacy concerns for being newlyweds.

"Can we have that table against the wall?" Thomas pointed to a spot not quite so private, but it *was* empty. The waitress smiled politely and said, "Sure. Newlyweds should get the table they want."

"What3words shows you a three-meter area." He pointed at the table as they walked over. "We were sitting here last night." He took his seat in the booth, and she slid in on the opposite side.

"Your waitress will be right with you. Our house specialty is the lemon shots." The hostess set down two menus and then left.

Ashley glanced around the room. "Does anything look familiar?"

The twinkly glass-covered place, with its expensive framed art and rows of expensive alcohol bottles, may have hinted at some recognition. Still, she figured anything he remembered might get confused with his Corporate Room back home.

"Not really," he said after scanning the room. "I'm going to talk to the manager about Linda's ring and see if anyone found it last night. Why don't you look at the menu and get us some water for the table?"

She watched as he left. They still needed to talk about the annulment and who would hand-deliver the paperwork. She assumed Mohinder would fill that spot since he was the only one who knew about the marriage. He'd do it, no questions asked, no judgment, and no lecture given.

The waitress came by, and Ashley asked for some water. She was surprised to see quite a variety of food on the menu. Everything was expensive, especially the drinks. After last night, she needed to lay off the alcohol for a while.

A list of salads caught her attention, and she figured her body needed something healthy. Plus, the picture of the meal looked appealing. Setting the menu aside, she glanced at the artwork on the wall that hung next to their table while she waited for Thomas to return. A local artist had done the artwork. The abstract painting was decoupage with decorative items glued onto the canvas. The color scheme was primarily gray and blue with some gold thrown in. Not precisely her taste, but better than some other paintings around the room. The price of the painting was a whopping five hundred dollars. Since the other artwork looked the same, she figured the Corporate Room featured artists and rotated them on a set schedule.

"No luck," Thomas said, rejoining her at the table. He placed his water glass squarely on the coaster and straightened his silverware next to his empty plate. "Nothing was turned in."

"That's a shame."

He studied the room, and she figured nothing was

coming back to his mind either. After sorting the white, pink, and yellow sugar packets in their container to be grouped by color, he glanced at the painting. It was crooked, so he straightened it. "This looks vaguely familiar."

"I was thinking the same thing."

"I guess it's a local artist." He stared at the price tag. "A local artist who thinks very highly of themselves."

"The piece likely isn't for sale. That price probably ensures no one will touch it."

Thomas opened the menu. "I can't believe it's already so late." His gaze fixed on the salads.

"I'm going to have the garden salad with the house dressing. I'll add some grilled chicken to it."

He closed the menu. "I've had their garden salad before. It's fresh and tasty."

"Welcome to the Corporate Room." The waitress walked over, ordering pad in hand. Her head tilted from side to side, and then she said, "Congratulations! We have a specialty drink for newlyweds. On the house."

Ashley glanced at their outfits, the Pair O' Dice logo brazenly displayed. She didn't need to explain to the young woman that while they were married, they weren't interested in celebrating. "We'd rather have water."

"If you don't want a drink," the waitress said, pointing to the menu, "we have our newlywed appetizer. Chicken fajita nachos with all the fixings. Also on the house."

"Their nachos are fantastic. That sounds great, thank you," Thomas said. "And we'll take two of your garden salads with grilled chicken. House dressing on the side."

Healthy salad aside, the nachos did sound good. And to be honest, part of the reason she'd thought to order a salad was because Thomas was a doctor. How could she eat something unhealthy in front of him? He had ensured she was hydrated today. He didn't seem like a cheesy nacho type of guy.

"Dinner is on me," he said once the waitress had left with their orders.

"You paid for the clothes. Let me at least get dinner."

He raised his hand and stopped her. "If I could afford to pay dot6vegasmom off last night with a hideously huge bribe, I can afford to take my wife out to dinner."

Thomas's boyish grin won her over. "My guess is that she has six kids." Ashley couldn't fathom being a single mother with so many mouths to feed. "She must be desperate to risk her job by taking a bribe."

Thomas shrugged, evidently agreeing with her. "I'm glad we stopped off here first. I can't imagine what kind of food Yo Ho Ho's serves."

"I'm thinking frozen seafood, microwaved to something less than perfection."

And there was his smile again. For someone who'd spent a thousand dollars on a bribe, several hundred for a wedding he didn't want, and still had an expensive ring to find, he seemed to handle stress well. So many others would be crabby and impatient, but he remained easygoing. That demeanor probably went over well with his patients. "I doubt we'll be at the pirate place for long, but we should check their lost and found, as well."

The waitress came back with a massive platter of nachos and two plates. Two glasses of water were also on the large tray. "Your appetizer." She placed the food in the center of the table, then set down the plates and glasses. "Your salads will be out shortly."

Ashley scooped some nachos onto her plate. The gooey cheese draped across the expanse from the main platter to her dish, and her stomach growled in anticipation. "This looks amazing."

"At least, it's hot." Thomas took a portion and dug in.

Funny how comfortable she felt eating with her hands in front of him. Typically, she would get a salad or a nice piece of fish on a first date. At Mexican restaurants, she would order something more refined than a taco. No one looks sexy or pretty when eating one of them.

Yet she went in again and grabbed another chip loaded with nacho cheese and salsa. What was it about Thomas that allowed her to let down her guard?

"I thought we would ask Mohinder to do the paperwork. He's also a lawyer. That probably won't hurt. We can sign the affidavit tomorrow, and you can either petition me for an annulment, or I can petition you for one," he said between bites.

Disappointment pulled at her. No matter how close she felt to her *husband*, he had a life back in Chicago to return to. Possibly even someone… She fidgeted with her necklace, and her chest tightened. "Do you have a girlfriend?"

Had she really just blurted out that question? She scooped up a big bite and put it into her mouth. Most wives would want to know if their husband was romantically involved with another woman. The information wasn't entirely out of the blue, but she still felt her cheeks flush.

He was in mid-chew, so he picked up his napkin and wiped his mouth as he finished his bite. "I don't do the boyfriend/girlfriend thing."

Was it a thing? "What do you mean?"

He took a sip of water as though trying to find the right words. "I've been married before, and that didn't work out. I've had a few nice romances that were exciting for a time but eventually ended. I date, but there is no one special." He pointed at the remaining nachos on the platter, and she nodded for him to finish.

"So, you haven't been lucky in finding the love of your life."

He eyed her questioningly. "Does that statement mean that you believe in finding the love of your life? Your one true partner and soulmate?"

His tone surprised her. His words weren't

judgmental or filled with pain from having searched for true love and never finding it. He could have easily asked her if she believed it would rain tomorrow.

"Yes, I think there is a perfect match for everyone," she finally said.

"A soulmate?"

She had thought Roger was her soulmate the day she'd married him. She had been so young and naïve. A man like Thomas was a much better fit. Strikingly handsome good looks aside, Thomas was patient, kind, and mature. Sure, not what letters to Dr. Ruth were filled with, but to her, having an educated, career-oriented, and playful man seemed so much more important.

"I believe there are many wonderful matches for everyone out there. You only need to find one of them. I haven't found mine yet." She leaned forward and gazed into his beautiful blue eyes. She could get lost in them. Four years had passed since her last date, so she was out of practice. Were they having a moment?

His gaze moved from her eyes to her lips but then roamed slightly south. Even though a small part of her hoped he was thinking of her as more than just an accidental wife, she still felt uncomfortable with him noticing her chest.

She abruptly sat straighter and adjusted the collar of her shirt. Her mastectomy bra, as hideous as it was, covered all her scars except for one. Her port scar marred her skin above where her right breast had been.

Now faded to a silvery line across her clavicle, it was barely visible but could be seen given the shirt she wore. V-necks or open collars were tricky. A movement like leaning forward could reveal the telltale sign of having been a cancer patient.

Her fingers traced the opening and tugged at the fabric, ensuring the scar remained hidden. But had he seen it already?

He smiled at her, and she completely forgot what they had been talking about.

"Here are your salads. Do you want some grated parmesan cheese?" The waitress carried a serving platter and placed it on a stand to help her serve them their meals. She then grabbed the cheese and held it, waiting for an answer.

"No, thanks," Ashley said. Thomas shook his head.

Once alone again, an awkward silence fell. She nibbled on her salad and tried to steer the conversation back to the topic of their annulment, specifically how Mohinder could help them, but the table's mood had changed.

There had been a moment. And she'd blown it.

She tilted her head and studied the painting again. "Is that...?" She leaned in and stared at the thin, shiny object that reflected the light from the table. It couldn't be.

She caught her breath. "That's my earring!"

She pointed at a section of the painting closer to Thomas. "I must have sat on that side of the table last night. I pinned my earring there." She suddenly realized she had defaced an expensive piece of artwork. Even though it wasn't her style, she didn't want to pay for any damages. "I pinned my earring onto this five-hundred-dollar painting." Her hushed voice was laced with guilt but hinted at how surprised she was for having done such a thing.

Thomas leaned in. One eyebrow rose as he recognized the item.

She scanned the crowded room. Many people were about but either engaged in conversations or not looking in their direction. The waitress was nowhere in sight. "Okay," she said.

He quickly retrieved the earring. "You may want to wash this before wearing it."

"I hope we find its match. These are my favorite." She placed the earring into a side pocket of her purse next to their wedding rings so it would be protected. She checked the art some more, and didn't find the other earring. "I lost two earrings last night. You lost a ring."

"Do you think we were just throwing jewelry away?"

The hoops weren't extravagant, but they had been expensive enough. She wouldn't have just left them behind, mainly because they were her favorite pair. She stared at the table and its square shape.

Square.

"What3words is a three-meter by three-meter area."

She pointed at the painting. "This painting is within our first set of words on my phone."

Jewelry. Treasure.

A bubble of excitement rose within her, and she saw his face light up with understanding and hope. "We were geocaching last night." She held up her phone. "We know exactly where to go to find Linda's ring."

"I'm betting we hid either the ring or your earring at Yo Ho Ho's."

"And we probably went there because they had a treasure map for us to use later. We were probably excited to be modern-day pirates." Ashley dove into what remained of her salad, her fork scraping the plate. "Let's finish and go to the next spot."

His expression wasn't as joyous as she had hoped. An expensive diamond ring should never be lying about for someone to find, but perhaps they hid it well enough —in plain sight—that they still might get it back. "I'm sure we can find the jewelry together," she said.

"It's not that." He set down his fork and looked off into the distance. "I already ordered Paul another ring."

"What?"

He wiped his mouth with his napkin. "He bought the ring from Jay's Jewelers. I saw the ring close up last night at dinner. After a message chat with a manager, I went online earlier and tracked down another ring."

"Linda picked the ring out herself. She'll know it's not the same one."

"I bought an exact match. It turns out the ring wasn't unique."

That didn't sound right. "Wedding rings aren't unique?"

"Sometimes, they are, but I took a chance since he bought it from an outlet store and told me it had a special name. Linda's ring was basically a knockoff of a designer one. Jay's Jewelers makes a few hundred of a design and then sells the rings in different regions of the United States. It took me nearly an hour today, but I found one in Memphis and had it engraved. It will be overnighted to the Bella Rosa by tomorrow morning."

Just like that. She wasn't sure whether to be impressed or saddened. "I know we haven't found the ring yet, but how much did you pay for the replacement?"

His lips thinned into a straight line. "You don't want to know."

She had no idea if she was responsible for losing the ring or was only an equal partner in the loss. Still, she felt the need to say, "I can't afford the replacement cost of the ring. I know Linda. That ring couldn't have been cheap."

He quickly leaned forward, his eyes widening. "I don't expect you to pay for any of it. Not at all. *I* was responsible for that ring."

This explained why he wasn't going crazy to find it. He wanted the ring back, but he had seemed calm about the loss. "When—not if—we find the ring, you can return it."

"Not with the engraving."

Her heart sank. "Oh, I'm so sorry." She now remembered that they were going to return their wedding bands, but had quickly left the chapel, their tails between their legs.

"Don't be sorry. It's fine."

Thomas had made this decision. He'd spent the money. She shouldn't feel guilty about the cost, but she did. "The most expensive part would be the diamonds. You could resell them."

He gave her a curt little nod. "I'm sure I can."

Suddenly, she wasn't in the mood to finish her salad. Their marriage, the cost of this second ring, and the fact that they were missing wedding-party activities came crashing down on her. "We should probably head out."

Thomas followed his phone app's instructions to the next What3Word spot. "I'm glad Yo Ho Ho's is within walking distance."

"Congratulations," a passerby said, obviously noticing their attire.

"We'll need to change clothes before anyone at the Bella Rosa sees us." Ashley pointed to the bag of wet clothing Thomas still carried. "I can put on my shirt and get to my room before anyone sees me."

"I can do the same." Three men stood on the street corner eyeing them, another man stared at them when they turned down another street, and a woman standing near a closed store asked a man walking by if he wanted a date. "Stay close to me. I don't think this is a good neighborhood."

Ashley moved closer to him, obviously feeling the dark-alley vibes. "Maybe we shouldn't...."

"This is the place," he said, interrupting her. "Yo Ho Ho's."

"More like Yo Ho *No*."

Fast food wrappers lay on the asphalt of the small parking area, and cigarette smoke hung in the air. In one corner near the door, he spied a pair of cockroaches running among some dried leaves.

"The earring or ring is somewhere inside." He opened the door and let her in, even though he didn't want to touch the worn metal frame that probably swarmed with germs. "Let's not touch anything," he said, wiping his hands on his shorts.

"Agreed."

Darkened corners lay before them, each decorated with plastic Halloween decor rejects. One ornament was a skull with a snake emerging from its empty eye socket. The other decorations were even less appealing.

He had never liked gross Halloween imagery.

"Arrgh! Welcome to Yo Ho Ho's." A man dressed as a pirate greeted them. He cocked his head and read their shirts. "Congratulations! Are you here for drinks or dinner?"

The place was empty, save what looked to be two regulars slumped over in barstools, their lifeless bodies not even caring where they were. The foul smell of rotten fish hung in the air, making him want to gag.

"Just answers to some questions." Ashley stared at the parrot resting on the bar, eating what Thomas hoped was birdseed and not stale nuts. "Were you working last night?"

The pirate held a pitcher of something green and filled two glasses. "I was off yesterday." He handed them the green drinks without indicating whether he thought the question odd. The smell of mint wafted from the glass, but there was also the scent of bourbon. "Everyone gets a glass of grog." The man then pointed a finger upward. "But only one. You'd be flyin' high on a second."

Thomas sniffed the drink and wondered if they had been double-served last night. God, he had actually drunk this crap? Even with the minty liquid inches from his nose, he could guess it was nearly one hundred percent alcohol.

"This is what was on my dress last night." She placed the tumbler down and stared at her hand before wiping it on her shorts.

Thomas's glass was stained, there were flies on the bar, a dead roach on the floor, and the parrot walking across the counter had probably been pooping everywhere. This was a health inspector's wildest story in the making.

"Hey! It's Sugar Pants and Hot Lips!"

They both turned to discover another pirate behind them, this one all smiles, his hands up and looking like he wanted to hug them. The man wore a red bandanna across his forehead, and his dirty brown hair lay in dreadlocks under it. Thomas had never been a fan of the *Pirates of the Caribbean* movies, but this Johnny Depp wannabe must love the entire franchise. "You remember us?"

"Are you married?" Before Thomas answered, the man motioned to his co-worker. "Dinner will be on the house. Bring the happy couple a plate of our crab cakes and," he said, giving Thomas a wry smile, "I'll get them two island margaritas. Just like last night."

"You worked last night?"

"Aye."

Thomas was willing to bet this place remained empty even on Saturday nights, likely losing money like a sieve. Any patrons would be easily remembered.

"We didn't come for dinner. We're looking…" Before Ashley finished her complaint, the man walked behind the bar to make their drinks.

"Dear Lord, I can't believe this place," Thomas whispered. He draped his arm across Ashley's back, holding her close to him by the waist. He figured they were safer here than on the street, but this was a dirty dive. A place someone as sweet as Ashley shouldn't be.

Ashley pointed at the phone Thomas still carried. "Quick. Let's find the What3Words spot and get the jewelry back."

"You didn't notice?" He found it odd that he had seen it and she hadn't, but the pirate was a tall man—the same height as Thomas—so perhaps he had a better view standing to the man's left.

"What? His nose?" She glanced back at the man. "He's probably been in a few bar fights."

"Nose?"

She pointed along her own bridge and moved her hand to one side. "It's totally crooked."

He'd have to straighten her out later about what he did for a living, but for now, he wanted her to know that he had won this round of the geocache. Not that it was a competition. This was a joint venture. "That pirate is wearing your earring."

"No!" Ashley's gaze darted to where the pirate stood behind the bar mixing their drinks. Her eyes widened in recognition. "I gave him one of my favorite earrings?"

It wasn't a funny situation, but her look of horror made him chuckle. "What do you want to do?"

"Besides leave and take a long shower to scrub this place off me?" The pirate belched and placed the drinks on the bar. Ashley leaned in and whispered so only Thomas could hear, "I can buy another set of earrings."

The bartender let out an exaggerated *arrgghh*. "If these drinks aren't to your liking, I can get you a second glass of grog." He leaned in. "But just like last night. Don't tell my boss."

"Good God." Ashley's hold on Thomas's arm tightened. "We had two of those nasty large drinks?"

Probably at least two, which explained why they'd felt like sunken ships this morning. "Let's ask about the ring, but I doubt it's here since the second earring is." Thomas waved his hand and got the bartendar's attention. "We lost a ring last night. Was one turned in by any chance?"

"What sort of ring?" the bartender asked throatily.

Thomas didn't like his answer. Had a ring been put in lost and found, one would think the answer would be that a ring *had* been discovered, not what type it was. "A nice one," he said, giving no details.

The second pirate returned with a nasty plate of crab cakes—or he assumed there were crab cakes buried under the oily sauce.

"Thanks for the food and drinks, but my wife and I are going to head out."

"Come and have a seat. The drinks are on me since you're newlyweds. I had no idea when you said last night you were here for a wedding that you were talking about your own."

"Yeah, it's crazy. But we only stopped by to say hello and see if you had the ring, so...we're going to head out," Thomas said again.

"Afraid you'll wear your drink again, Sugar Pants?" The pirate let out a raucous laugh. The smell of booze became stronger. The man was stinking drunk and probably the owner of the place. Perhaps up to his eyeballs in debt.

The parrot let out a squawk and caught Thomas's attention. He stared at the island margaritas that rested on the bar. The parrot had made its way over to them and pecked at the sugared rims. "Let me guess. I spilled an island margarita on my pants yesterday."

"Not just yours, Sugar Pants," the pirate said between fits of laughter. "Mine, too."

A fly landed on the red sauce covering the crab cakes. Thomas had to ask, "Are the crab cakes spicy?"

The second pirate answered, "We put a Cajun spice on them, and the heat level is mucho hot." He then looked at Ashley. "You loved them last night, Hot Lips."

"I think I'm going to be sick," Ashley murmured.

"We need to head out."

The heat and humidity hit them once they left. The sun had come out, but now it had sunk below the horizon. The ground was still wet, and Thomas's skin felt sticky as he walked to the sidewalk's edge.

A group of men stood on the street corner, and the hairs on the back of Thomas's neck pricked up. He and Ashley knew where the second earring was. Thank goodness this wasn't where they'd left the ring. They may still find it as long as the What3Words locations didn't progressively become less desirable places.

"You'd better stay close." He extended his hand to pull her closer to him when she slipped. He swung his arm out and caught Ashley's thin waist before she fell and hit the sidewalk. He dropped the bag he carried and his phone but managed to remain upright. "Are you okay?"

Her green eyes widened in surprise as she stared back at him. "The rain made the cement slippery." She leaned into him as he supported her. "You have great reflexes."

He would never have caught her if he hadn't already been reaching for her. The spill would have been a nasty one. He practically felt her heart racing as he steadied her. "The sidewalk sloped downward a bit where you were walking."

"I guess I should be more careful." She stared back into his eyes and found concern in them. "Thank you."

"Are you newlyweds all right?" a stranger asked as he approached, his hand open to help. The man didn't necessarily look threatening, but the street corner men were also walking toward them now.

"We're fine, thank you." Thomas picked up the bag and his phone, wiping his cell on his shirt.

Ashley tested her foot and limped. "It's not too bad."

His body went rigid, and he went into doctor mode. He supported her by keeping his hand on her lower back as he knelt to get a better look. "Don't be silly. You can't keep walking on it." He didn't think she'd broken anything, likely only a minor sprain. Still, he said, "You need some ice."

"We have one more place to go. Let's do that and get

home."

He was about to complain, but something about the look in her eyes told him she didn't want the night to end. At least, he *hoped* that was what he saw.

He stood and let his arm drop to her waist to support her. "Let's see how far away the third place is."

Keeping an eye on the three men now back on the street corner, he checked to see where the next What3Words location was. "The wedding ring is inside a building." He tapped on the phone and brought up a map displaying a satellite image. "It's a planetarium." He tapped on the building image and discovered it wasn't open on Sundays after six p.m.

A memory of lasers came back to him. Flashes of light mixed with images of the stars. "The What3Words location is in the middle of a planetarium that doesn't open until noon tomorrow."

"Noon tomorrow? But we need to get the ring." She put weight on her leg and winced.

He tightened his grip around her, and she allowed her body to sink into him again. A rideshare would take a good five minutes to arrive. "The ring is safe in a locked building. We'll have to come back tomorrow for it."

Glancing around, he saw a cab turn down the street. He raised his arm to hail it. "We'll go back to the Bella Rosa, change our clothes before anyone sees us in these, and then I'll get you into bed with a bag of ice."

"You're the doctor."

15

———

"**D**o you need another ice bag?"

Brenda halfway got out of her chair before Ashley could stop her. The two sat in Bella Rosa's main dining room, the kitchen just a few feet away. "My foot's been half-frozen since last night." She removed the ice pack, the melted ice sloshing in the rubber pouch, and took her foot off the chair. "It really doesn't hurt anymore."

"I'm glad it wasn't more than a sprain. Good thing you had a doctor with you." Brenda's expression was a mix of serious and giddy. "I still can't believe you two got married."

Neither could Ashley, who had spent the last half hour recounting everything she knew to her best friend.

"Tell me more about Thomas. What were you doing when you got hurt?" Her eyebrows waggled suggestively as if there were a juicy tale to share, and her tone implied that perhaps she had suffered a bedroom accident before.

"I slipped in the rain, nothing more."

"Nothing more? Hmm." Brenda's coffee cup clinked when she set it on the table. Her lips pursed, and she waited expectantly.

She could wait all day. There was nothing to tell.

Well, almost nothing.

It would have been an awkward moment of silence, but another group of guests had pushed four tables together and had been loud throughout breakfast. They were now gathering their purses and phones and standing to leave.

"This isn't over just yet." Brenda excused herself to say goodbye to the guests. They grabbed more brochures from the counter and asked her about the helicopter rides to the Grand Canyon. It was early enough in the day, the bad weather had stopped for now, and they should have a good tour. All Ashley was grateful for was that none of them wanted massages. Carol worked back-to-back from a packed appointment book, and Ashley used her foot as an excuse not to lift a finger to help today.

Besides, she was on vacation.

"Want more eggs? Coffee?" Brenda had pushed the tables the other guests had shoved together back, and a busser cleaned the mess. The eggs, bacon, side of French toast, and the heavenly coffee were more than enough, but Ashley handed over her mug and asked for another cup.

Ashley didn't know how Brenda managed everything.

"Things certainly seemed cozy last night when I brought the ice bag to the cottage." Brenda set down the hot beverages and then stacked the breakfast dishes in the corner of the table. "Other than discovering that you didn't hurt yourself here, I didn't get too many details. Linda and all the other ladies were swarming all over you."

The cottage had been a madhouse. She and Thomas had both put on their wet shirts in the cab, which covered the Pair O' Dice wedding logos and bride and groom labels on the shirts. The shorts had an image of a pink pair of fuzzy dice for her, and a pair of blue fuzzy dice for him. Thanks to a black marker the cab driver had, they marked out the small bride and groom from their shorts without stripping in the car.

"Last night was crazy."

"Crazy good?" Brenda leaned in. Besides an elderly couple several tables away, the two had privacy in the dining room. "Thomas wouldn't let anyone touch you. He was like a mother hen with the ibuprofen, propping your foot up on a pillow and giving you instructions to stay in bed."

Ashley relived the incident in her head. Thomas had asked the cab driver to pull around to the front of the cottage and then carried her inside. He had lifted her effortlessly, took her up the stoop, and then walked with her in his arms to her bedroom.

The scene was all too familiar—a groom carrying a bride across the threshold and going straight to bed to begin the honeymoon, except four women followed them to the boudoir, asking many questions. And nothing romantic had happened. She couldn't even change her clothes until after Thomas left. Luckily, she was able to convince everyone that she needed some rest.

"I can tell by that smile on your face that it was crazy good." Brenda's smile widened, and in the gleam of her friend's eyes, Ashley saw motherly warmth. Brenda was only fifteen years older than Ashley, but the wisdom in her gaze spoke volumes.

"Thomas is a great guy." Brenda's eyebrow rose. "And a doctor."

"Yes, a doctor." Ashley's cheeks grew hot. She wanted to share her feelings about Thomas with Brenda, and even though she knew the woman could keep a secret, Ashley still needed to sort them out for herself. "It's complicated."

"Why? Because he lives in Chicago?"

It would be a problem. But it was the monster inside her that kept alive the ordeal she had been through. The one that reminded her daily that cancer could come back, and not just breast cancer, but others, as well. The monster tugged at her innermost thoughts and concerns. "I'm not ready."

Brenda's eyes narrowed as though a motherly lecture was soon to follow. Before she could get a word out, though, Ashley shifted nervously in her chair and said, "You know I never reconstructed."

"So?"

"Something like that would matter to a man."

"Not if he cares about you." Brenda put a hand on either side of her breasts. "These don't define you or make you a woman, honey."

"You told me you researched plastic surgeons and found the perfect doctor before you did your reconstruction." Ashley gazed at her friend's chest. "You had a double mastectomy after your breast cancer, and your reconstruction took place at the same time."

"My cancer was different. My body is different." Brenda placed her hand atop Ashley's. "What did I tell you in the ABC class I taught?"

"You said I'm more than the sum of my parts. That what's on the inside is more important than what's on the outside."

Saying the words brought tears, but she held the monster back. She grabbed her napkin from the table and wiped her eyes. "I know I'm brave for what I've gone through, but with a mastectomy, oophorectomy, and hysterectomy, I feel chopped up and cored out as a woman."

"Honey, you are young and beautiful. Any man, even a doctor as handsome as Thomas, would want you."

She had heard it all before. "While I was going through chemo, losing my hair, and having surgery, I never thought about the possibility of having another man in my life. I just wanted to beat cancer and live."

"You were focusing on you. That was what you needed to do at the time. But now,"—Brenda's hand gently caressed Ashley's face so they could make eye contact—"you've beaten cancer, and you can live a little."

"You don't understand. You have Hershel, who already loved you when you went through it all."

"Hershel stood by me every step of the way. You were brave to go through what you did alone."

Everyone told Ashley that. That she was a fighter. Strong and capable. Why didn't anyone understand that she just wanted to scream?

"I know you said you wanted to wait until your five-year survivor mark before even thinking of reconstruction, but it's been four years since your diagnosis. If you want to reconstruct, you can."

Ashley knew that Brenda loved how her breasts had turned out. Her surgeon had done a fantastic job, but she had shared with Ashley the drawbacks of reconstructive surgery. The feeling of the breasts was different since belly fat was heavier than breast tissue. The numbness of the area and the fake nipples meant she wouldn't even feel them. When Brenda gained weight, she gained it differently and sometimes felt like a linebacker, always having to wear a bra because of the heaviness of her chest.

And then there was the scar. A two-foot line from one side to the other where they had removed the replacement tissue. The utter lack of feeling in her midsection alone sounded terrible, even if it did come with an excellent tummy tuck side effect.

There was another option, but there was no way she would put silicone or anything else fake into her body.

"It's been seven years since my cancer. I finally feel like I have my body back."

"Back? Or have you just gotten used to your new normal?" Ashley asked, using the term from the ABC class that Brenda had taught.

Brenda caressed Ashley's hand more. "The BCRC offers great counseling. I think you should talk to someone."

Ashley regretted saying *new normal*. She didn't want to talk to a counselor. How often had she talked with other survivors, and they said they had a *second chance* and were *more focused on what matters in life*? Most weren't in their late thirties and alone.

"If the first thing you still think about in the morning, and the last thing you think about at night is that you had cancer, then you need to talk to someone. Because you *had* cancer. The disease lost. You won the battle."

The monster was still inching forward and ready to pounce. Ashley felt her fear and didn't mind being vulnerable in front of Brenda. "Every morning and every night when I lay down in bed, I wiggle my toes."

Brenda's face pinched, knowing what Ashley was about to say.

"It's been four years. Right after chemo, I had a sixty-five percent loss of feeling in my toes. It's been years, mostly with physical therapy and supplements, to get me back up to only a five percent loss. And I still can't feel the tips of my toes. Every time I'm in bed, I wiggle them, feel the chemo-induced neuropathy, and remember what I went through."

"Then stop wiggling your toes and be grateful for that sixty percent of feeling that came back. Most chemo patients never regain feeling in their extremities. I still have some loss myself." She touched her scalp gingerly. "My hair came back, but not as full as before, and my scalp still hurts if I brush too hard. You were spared that."

It was true. Ashley's scalp didn't hurt. Her hair, although curly now, was thick, lush, and extra soft. It was, after all, the hair of a three-year-old. When it first came in and was so short, it felt as soft as what she imagined a baby duckling's feathered little body would feel like. Her skin was also extra soft. Her elbows had never felt so smooth.

But she was tired of being told to feel grateful. She was grateful to be alive but wanted her old body back. But being BRCA2 gene mutation positive, her body had carried the possibility of cancer her whole life. It was a part of her.

"Even though you had an eighty percent chance of getting cancer, you did everything to ensure it wouldn't come back. The surgeries, the chemo…you did everything. And you caught your breast cancer early at stage 1A."

True. Cancer hadn't even spread to her lymph nodes. She did get lucky, but still. "My gene mutation gives me a higher chance of skin cancer, ovarian cancer, and pancreatic cancer. New research shows that thyroid, stomach, bladder, and colon cancer might also be linked to this damn gene mutation—s+o I now have four more specialists to see."

"Your ovaries are gone. You took care of that, and you get screenings every six months to catch all the others." She gave Ashley a reassuring smile. "What are you more afraid of? Finding a man or getting cancer again?"

An awkward silence fell between the two as Ashley sat, deep in thought.

"I can tell Thomas likes you. He thinks you're beautiful and desirable because you are. Women wear fake eyelashes, pushup bras, SPANX, bootie padding, and even have veneers put on so their teeth are sparkling white. Having prosthetic breasts is not that unique in the world."

The door opened, the little bell chimed, and Thomas

came in. His running shorts showed off his lean, muscular legs.

"Good morning." He pointed at Ashley's foot. "How are you feeling?"

Before she could finish saying, "I'm fine," he stood by her side, inspecting her ankle.

He gently touched her skin and compared one foot to the other. "The swelling has gone down."

"It's a little sore, but it's not bad." She glanced at Brenda. "Mother hen over there insisted I ice it again, although I can walk just fine."

"You came into this room limping?"

"Barely." Her gaze went from Brenda to Thomas and then back again. She knew he hadn't heard their conversation thanks to the closed door and the little bell to announce his presence. Talking to Thomas when they were on a mission to find missing jewelry was easy. Other than that, they talked about their mistake of a marriage. Talking about getting a second annulment while helping her cousin marry the man of her dreams depressed her—more than she wanted to admit.

"Do your best to stay off it today. I'd invite you along, but I'm going for a run." He gave her a brilliant smile that lit up the room and danced in the light reflected in his eyes. "I'll see you at the escape room thing later."

Thomas grabbed a bottle of water and left.

"An escape room?" Brenda asked. "Those places where you have an hour to get out of a locked room?"

"Neither Paul nor I have done an escape room before, but Linda suggested it. The groomsmen don't know the bridesmaids, and they thought it would be a good way to mingle."

"That's not a bad idea. Tell you what," Brenda said and then pointed to the counter where the brochures lay, "if that place has extra, bring back some flyers and we'll put them next to the hot air balloon rides and tours of the Vegas Strip. You never know what kind of excitement you'll find when inside an escape room."

Thomas stepped onto the deck and finished stretching, grateful to be back into his exercise routine. The decadent pasta dinner the other night, the heavy drinking, the complications of his wedding... The stress was too great—and his mother hadn't even arrived yet. He needed to pace himself better.

He stretched his calf and heard a noise from the side of the main house. He figured it was another guest until he heard someone swearing and muttering under their breath in what he believed was Yiddish.

"You doing okay?" he asked once he walked around the building.

Hershel wiped his brow with a handkerchief. "Fine. Fine." His pants were covered in mud at the knees from where he had been kneeling on the ground. "The rain last night ran off from the hill," he said, pointing to the back end of the property. "We have an old well over there for smaller weddings. It's only good for taking rustic wedding pictures now, but last night's storm caused a bit of a mudslide."

Thomas studied the path Hershel had come from. The land was far enough away not to disturb the guests. Before he could say so, Hershel added, "We're getting another storm this weekend, unfortunately." He wiped his hand again and removed the mud from it, soiling his handkerchief even more. "I need to place some boards to hold back the drainage and halt the erosion."

Even in the morning's cooler air, the temperature was rising. Hershel appeared to be a man in his sixties and seemed healthy for his age, but he was getting up there in years. "Don't you have any help?"

"Oh, no." He waved his hand. "I like to take care of the gardens myself." He pointed to the gazebo, the lover's grotto, and the small fountain and pond. "I put in the sprinkler system and did all this landscaping. I like to work with my hands."

Thomas gestured to two chairs in the garden. "Tell you what. Take a break for a few minutes. Then, instead of me going for a run, I'll help you with that mess near the well."

"I couldn't ask you to do that."

"You didn't. I offered." He gestured to the seat again, and Hershel sat. Thomas took the other one and handed him the unopened water bottle, which the man accepted. "The place is amazing. Practically a Garden of Eden."

Hershel took a slug of water and then smiled widely at Thomas. "Brenda does the cooking...well, most of it. We have help with that. But she does all the bookings, mailers, and advertising for the place. She has a good head for that sort of stuff."

"Sounds like a good division of labor."

"It is. Together, we manage the contractors like the massage therapist, the caterers, florists, and such." His voice contained pride, and his eyes shone as he surveyed the grounds.

"Sounds like a huge undertaking."

Hershel nodded. "Brenda always dreamed of owning such a place."

Marriage was filled with compromises. Hershel seemed happy, but Thomas still asked, "Was it your dream, as well?"

"Mine was to have the love of a good woman and provide her with whatever her heart desired."

That wasn't what Thomas had expected to hear, and he felt a little lost trying to understand having that type of love for another human being. He comprehended such a love, but to truly understand it?

"We were both software engineers at IBM when we met. Long hours. Cubicles. Computers." He rolled his eyes. "And the commute. We'd drive an hour one way only to sit in a windowless area of a building and never see the outdoors. It was so crazy that we'd leave for work early in the morning when it was dark outside, then leave to go home in darkness again, buying a fast-food dinner on the way."

"Sounds awful."

"Then we had kids. That changes things. Overall, completely for the better, but trying to work and maintain a family life—even with two committed partners—was difficult. We promised ourselves that when we became empty nesters, we'd treat ourselves right."

"By buying the place of your dreams."

"By not waiting until we were at death's door to finally enjoy living. But then Brenda got sick with breast cancer. Our daughter was a junior in high school at the time." He thought back to what must have been a terrible memory because his eyes appeared sad. "Brenda told me she wanted to live long enough to see our baby girl graduate from high school."

The woman seemed so healthy and vibrant. Thomas would never have guessed. "I'm sorry to hear that. She must have caught it early."

"She discovered it in the shower one morning."

Many Stage-1 breast cancers were caught by self-exams and confirmed by the doctor. "And she saw your kid get through high school?"

"Our daughter graduated from college last May and"—he looked around and tapped his knuckles on some nearby wood—"Brenda is still doing well."

"That is good news."

"You don't get a better wake-up call than facing death. We quit our jobs, took our savings, and bought this place right after our daughter went to college."

"You ever regret leaving the rat race?"

"Never." He glanced at Thomas's hand. "No wedding ring. You never took the plunge?"

"Once." He found talking with Hershel easy and comforting. "The marriage didn't last long. In theory, marriage is fine, and it works for some, but I don't believe there is one person out there that is *the one* for everybody. My ex-wife wanted to be a doctor's wife. Any doctor would have filled the role. I was the unlucky sap she fixed her sights on."

"Did you love her?"

It was hard to admit and a question he had thought about often. "No."

"Then she wasn't the one."

Thomas let out a slight chuckle. Hershel had dismissed his story so quickly, as if love were easy to find. "Let me guess. You hit the jackpot with Brenda right away. What were you? High school sweethearts?"

"I was married before Brenda. I married a nice Jewish girl, the one my parents chose for me. I thought life worked like that. You grow up, marry, have kids, then grandkids. But I never thought about whether I was happy."

The information surprised Thomas. "And you weren't."

Hershel waved his hand, and his expression soured.

"I was miserable. I didn't want to admit it. The marriage lasted five years. I was happy to escape without kids to tie me to her."

"Whatever became of the ex?"

He shrugged. "I think she moved to Omaha. She's married and has a family." He took another sip of water, and Thomas waited for him to continue. "I met Brenda, and I didn't care what her religious beliefs were, didn't care if my parents liked her, didn't care about anything but how much I loved her. My only thoughts were if she would make me happy and if I loved her. Love would make everything else work out in the end."

"I used to think the same way. Brenda is a rare breed of woman."

Hershel shook his head. "Women like her exist. You just need to know where to look."

16

———

The group stood together, men on one side, women on the other, facing the escape room's closed door. Posters of the different games hung on the walls, and the difficulty level ranged from simple to catastrophically hard.

"I've done many of these in the past, and there are plenty of tricks to help you win." Linda pulled out a box of items and went through them. "Does everyone understand their roles?" Linda passed out small pads of paper and pens.

Mohinder handed the last pad of paper to Thomas. The blue pads were for the men, the pink for the women, and each was marked with the wedding date and the bride's and groom's names.

"Is this for real?" Thomas flipped through the book and glanced at the blank pages, ten in all. "She had special stationery created for this?"

"Shh. Do you want her to hear you?" Mohinder's jaw tightened as though he had been on the receiving end of Linda's temper in the past. "I've done several of these, and they've always been fun. I doubt this one will be enjoyable."

"All your names are in these bags," Paul said, pulling the drawstrings on each and holding them awkwardly in his hands. "Linda will draw the name of one groomsman and one bridesmaid to be partners."

"We're getting partners?" Mohinder shifted from foot to foot. "I've never teamed up to do this before."

"I've played with partners," Thomas said. Even the bags were color-coded. He couldn't read if there was anything stitched onto the bags but figured they, too, had likely been marked with at least the wedding date. "Partners can provide a strategy that has some benefits."

Linda pulled out a name from each bag. She called the matched set and had the couple stand next to her. It all seemed so elementary school-ish, but a part of Thomas hoped his name would be matched with Ashley's.

"Mohinder and…" Linda reached in and pulled out a slip of paper from the pink bag. "Ashley."

And so the name drawing went, filled with pageantry and school-yard suspense. Matt with Sarah. Connor with Imani. And, of course, Paul would be matched with Linda.

Thomas gave a courtesy grin at the last woman standing. Mindy, the one bridesmaid he didn't know.

Since there was an odd number of women to men, Brian was also unpartnered.

"You three can be a team," Linda said.

Once Thomas and the other two joined the group, Mohinder made his way over. "Here," he said in a near whisper. He handed Thomas his slip of paper. "I'll take Mindy and Brian. You can have Ashley. You know, in case her ankle hurts and she needs your help."

Thomas didn't complain. He just made the same lame excuse to Mindy and Brian as they switched.

An employee came into the room. He held a clipboard and checked the paperwork. "You're the Stallworth wedding party?"

The man's smile appeared fake as he congratulated Paul and Linda on their upcoming nuptials. He clearly didn't care why they were there, only that he needed to give them the rules and have everyone sign paperwork relieving the escape room company of any responsibility if anyone got hurt during the game.

The man collected all the paperwork and then handed out masks. "You're blindfolded, so you can't start the game until the whistle blows. We don't want anyone looking around or taking notes before the start of your hour."

Once blindfolded, the staff member instructed them to turn to their left and place their hand on the person's shoulder in front of them so he could lead them all into the room. Thomas leaned forward and whispered in

Ashley's ear to make sure she watched her step due to her foot.

"The mad bomber has left a bomb in a church. You're a detective squad that needs to find the combination to unlock the cage where the bomb is housed at the altar. Hints are all around the church, but not everything is a valid clue. There are items to deceive you."

He led them to a pew and told them to sit carefully. "You're in the church, and the bomb is directly in front of you. I will be watching and giving hints if you need them, but everyone has to agree that you want a hint since I can only give you three. We will begin in a minute. Before I leave, are there any questions?"

The room fell silent, so he bid them good luck and left.

A moment later, an alert sounded, followed by the man's voice over an intercom. "Detectives, remove your masks and start looking for clues."

Thomas removed his blindfold, his eyes adjusting to the dim light of the room. Ashley sat to his left, and a pulpit, choir pit, and wired bomb lay ahead of them. He also saw a pipe organ, a small room in the corner, and some lockers containing choir robes nearby.

Everything familiar and precisely the same.

"This is the bomb," Linda said, as though the team hadn't heard where it would be from the game master. The fact that it had several wires sticking out was another obvious clue.

Linda stood in front of the group, twirling her pencil with an authoritative flair. "Typically, you need to find a combination lock with a series of numbers or a riddle. There are usually four or five different things to focus on." She studied the church and pointed with her pencil. "Like that coat rack area or the Bible station. Each team should pick one area and bring all the clues to a central spot." She walked to a table near the bomb where a whiteboard hung. "We can decipher the clues here."

As each group scattered, Ashley and Thomas were left alone at the altar with the bomb. She eyed the place like a true gamer, taking in all the nuances of the atmosphere, from the police-taped pews to the hymnals opened to specific hymns. She then grinned a smile of approval. "This is so extravagant."

Thomas took out his phone and turned on the flashlight app. "It's dark in here. Make sure to watch your step." She nodded but focused on the room. He watched as her mind raced with the possibilities of all the clues to find. She was a gamer at heart, and he loved that. "Have you ever done an escape room before?" he asked.

"I've always wanted to but never found the time." She stepped forward and studied the metal cage surrounding the bomb chained to the altar.

She was adorable walking around the caged bomb and inspecting every wire, every chain link, going over every possibility. He touched the lock and said, "I've done a few of them, including this one."

Her face lit up, and she moved closer so no one else could hear. "You know the solution?"

He leaned in, the fresh scent of her perfume teasing him. "I don't know the exact combination, but I know how to find the clues." He studied the bomb and then pointed at the wires. "One hint is that when you pull the red wire to defuse the bomb, you need to ensure the yellow wire is grounded."

She studied the bomb. "These are blue and white wires."

"Exactly. Same escape, but with subtle differences. When I played, the wires were a different color. Just make sure not to pull a wire without confirming you have all the instructions from inside a boot. The boot is in the chaplain's office."

A gleam emanated from Ashley's eyes, even in the darkened room. "Oh, I think we're going to defeat this mad bomber."

Mohinder walked to the clue collection table with a calendar. "April 5th, September 9th, and October 4th are circled." He took the quick-erase marker and made a note on the whiteboard beside the table.

"These three numbers must be important," Mindy said.

Brian grabbed the calendar and inspected the clue. "So, is it the number of the months and the days?"

Thomas knew the answer was only the days, but he'd let them figure it out. "The bomb casing needs five numbers, so if you get the correct order of those three numbers, it might unlock the footlocker in the corner."

"You think so?" Mindy seemed excited about the game. Perhaps the entire group consisted of gamers.

Brian searched through a hymnal they had also found. "Maybe this will tell us the order."

Thomas tugged Ashley out of earshot. "It won't." He moved her away from Mohinder's group and walked to the corner of the church.

"We need to focus on one set of numbers so we can contribute to the game." Ashley walked to the organ and sifted through the paperwork lying on the seat. "Let me try to win this on my own." Her devilish smile caught him off guard. She enjoyed winning, but the joy was in the play. Her zeal for gaming allowed him to watch over her and the entire group.

"What are you looking at?" Linda asked, her voice commanding as she removed the metal candlestick from Paul's hands. "Let's see if this matches the other ones on the table." She left with Paul trailing behind, his found clue now safely in Linda's hands.

"She's always been militant like that," Ashley whispered. "Paul doesn't seem to mind."

"People, don't be afraid to use your flashlights." Linda's voice boomed from the opposite side of the room. "We're ten minutes in. Let's move it." She gave orders to Matt and Sarah, who were walking around looking lost. Linda was larger than life and determined to win.

"This organ looks out of place even in a church." Ashley touched the keys, and they didn't sound. Thomas remained quiet even though he knew the answer.

She reached around the side of the instrument and pulled out some sheet music. "I'll bet there is a clue on this music." Her expression turned hopeful. "I can read music."

"You won't need to." Then, pointing at the pipes, he asked, "Notice something odd?"

She studied each of the pipes as it left the instrument. "This one isn't connected." She touched the pipe, and it came loose from the organ. One end's shape looked like something to put your eye up to. She peered through the pipe and studied the sheet of music. "These numbers are jumping out."

The excitement sounded in her voice. She enjoyed the game and wasn't shy about showing it.

She wrote the two numbers in her notebook. Evidently, it wasn't so silly to have paper and a pen handy.

"There are music books laid out in a numbering scheme." Ashley put them in order. "Don't help me with this clue like you did with that pipe. I can figure it out myself."

"I wouldn't dream of it." She studied the books and seemed mesmerized by the puzzle. Her lips pursed, and her eyebrow lifted as she pieced the clues together. She made an incredibly sexy detective.

"Book number three is missing. That is the third number," she said, grinning at him.

"Detectives. You have used twenty minutes of your time," came the announcement over the speaker.

"Okay, don't tell me the order to put them in." Ashley knelt and studied the organ's foot pedals. He knew no clue was there, so he suggested, "Why don't we check the pockets in those choir robes?"

She gave him a wry smile. "Don't spoil this. I was about to check those robes." She stepped toward them. "Did you save the church last time?"

"We died. The yellow wire, remember?"

The time went by quickly with team Matt-Sarah, Mohinder-Mindy-Brian, and Connor-Imani, all finding clues. Oddly enough, team Linda-Paul was lagging, even though Linda was a self-professed expert.

Thomas and Ashley hadn't found a clue either, but she was doing this alone. The group wasn't discovering the clues fast enough. Worse yet, they were wasting time on false ones. "Maybe you should tell Paul to look closely at the stained glass and where the statue of Jesus is looking."

Ashley glanced at the image of the Lord. Linda stood near the likeness but had ignored it entirely. "I think Linda will explode—like this bomb—if we don't win."

"You have fifteen minutes left," came from over the speaker. "And only three of the five digits have been discovered to unlock the five-number combination lock on the cage. The window might be of interest if you need another clue."

"Paul," Thomas said, gaining his brother's attention. "Look closely at the stained-glass design. I think the pattern is off, and something may be stuck to the glass." He raised his voice and said, "Linda, check to see where the statue of Jesus is looking. There may be some clues there."

"I'm looking at the empty bottles for the sacramental wine," Linda announced with authority in her voice, not moving toward the hint he'd given her.

"I'm guessing Jesus is looking at a clue for that fifth number?" Ashley said.

Thomas wasn't much of a churchgoer, but since Ashley wanted their annulment filed with the church, he assumed she'd appreciate this. "Jesus has the answer."

17

Ashley sat in Thomas's car as he drove to the planetarium. The wedding itinerary had them doing the escape room, followed by a victory lunch, which felt hollow since the bomb had blown up. "I can't believe we didn't save the church from being destroyed."

"I can't believe Linda cut the blue wire even after I told her not to." Thomas let out a chuckle and then said, "Actually, I do believe it."

Ashley ran through the scenario in her head once more. They'd had two minutes left, Thomas had the instructions from the boot, and Linda still wouldn't listen to him. "Linda thought she knew the solution. Once she has it in her head to do something, there's no stopping her."

"Do you think she even enjoyed the game?"

To Linda, as far as she could tell, the game was more of a check-this-off-the-list type event to have the wedding party get to know one another. "Probably not, but I had a lot of fun. I wouldn't mind doing more escape rooms."

"You were great with the clues."

She watched as he focused on the road and turned down Avery Street. She'd always found something attractive about a man behind the wheel of a car. And this wasn't just any car. The man rented a Lexus. Leather seats and a good forty computers ran the vehicle. Powerful and strong.

Feeling a flush coming over her, she adjusted the air conditioning vent to point directly at her. They were on a mission to get Linda's ring back. Then they'd ask Mohinder to serve the paperwork to annul them. Even if Ashley were interested in Thomas, he was returning to Chicago after the wedding.

"What excuse did you give to get the afternoon off?" he asked.

"I'm not working this week. I did your massage to help Brenda." Another flush filled her cheeks. Brenda had arranged that massage for the two of them, but Thomas didn't need to know that.

"No, what excuse did you give to get out of wedding stuff?"

"Oh, that. Linda thinks I'm working this week. She was upset because I told her I had the week off, but she knows I can use the extra money."

A twinge of pride smacked her in the face. She was sitting in a luxury car with a wealthy doctor headed to retrieve an obsolete ring he had already paid to replace. She rarely felt self-conscious about such things but added, "I recently finished my degree. I should soon be able to change jobs."

After she'd said it, she felt stupid. Thomas had never said or done anything to make her feel any less significant than him. He hadn't flaunted his money or made her feel bad for not contributing monetarily to the searches as he did. Stupid pride made her feel uncomfortable.

"Your degree is in kinesiology?" He gazed at her briefly before focusing once more on the traffic.

"Yep. After the wedding, I plan to fill out applications for positions with some local doctors." Actually, she had already sent in applications but hadn't heard anything back. A lot of applications. She wouldn't worry about that just yet, though. She had time.

"Physical therapy is a good field. I know many doctors in the area. Maybe I can help."

She never accepted help for such things. She could do it on her own. "I can't ask you to do that."

"It's the least I can do for my *wife*." He gave her a smile that showed off his playful side, and she again figured pride was getting in her way. Sometimes, it wasn't *what* you knew but *who* you knew that helped you move ahead. "Thanks," she finally said. "I'd appreciate that."

She didn't know what else to say, so she asked, "What was your excuse for leaving Paul and the guys today?"

"I'm being considered for the head of surgery at Ian Ostern Memorial Hospital. I told him I had a meeting with the board." He gave her a wry smile. "Actually, I've already been offered the position, but Paul doesn't know that. I have a meet and greet with the staff later this week."

A ray of hope hit her. Ian Ostern Memorial was only about an hour away. "You're moving to Nevada?"

"I haven't accepted yet. I have until the end of the month to decide, but I think I'll take it." He glanced at her. "You know what?" He paused, and a smile came to his face as he focused on the road again. "They mentioned childcare incentives and other stuff in the package."

It'd never even occurred to her to ask. "Do you have children?"

"No, but the hospital mentioned several perks to me about joining their staff. I'm betting I could tap into and take advantage of them."

"What do you mean"?

"I could ask that my wife also gets a position in their nice physical therapy center if I take the position. They opened a place next to the hospital, and it's supposedly one of the best facilities in the area."

"The Champion Physical Therapy Center?" she asked, knowing darn well which facility he meant. The place held the gold-star location high on her list. She had filled out an application but hadn't heard back. She kept her words steady and even to hide her excitement. "They already have my application. That's my first choice for a new job, but I can't ask you to do that for me."

"You're my wife for the next few weeks. By the time you start work and dazzle them with your abilities, it won't matter if the marriage is annulled."

"I…" It would be a dream to work there.

"They'd probably increase my moving budget and even offer me more perks for you. So, you'd be doing me a favor."

"Really?" Jobs like that existed? She supposed if you were high up enough, anything was possible. "Well, if it isn't any trouble, then sure. I'd love the help."

"I can't guarantee anything, but consider it done. I'm also going to see about the elder care places they're affiliated with. My mother is still in relatively good health, but I'd like to be near her in case of anything."

No matter what warnings Linda had given her, Thomas was a caring man. His childhood dog, a job for her, buying a replacement ring for Paul, and now moving for his mother. She rarely ran into a man who put his family first. "You're a good son."

He grimaced. "I haven't always been. I've been absent these past ten years because of my marriage to Tina."

He had mentioned the ex-wife several times. The rift

that she-devil had wrought must weigh heavily upon him. "I can see how that would be awkward with Paul, but he's happy with Linda."

"Is he?"

"I think so. Few men could tolerate her strong personality, but he seems to do fine."

Thomas parked the car and inwardly grinned as the two walked toward the planetarium. A job for Ashley, near him. He didn't know where the relationship would eventually lead, but she was a hardworking woman with a good work ethic. Any clinic would be thrilled to have her on staff.

And he could help her. Take care of her. It had been a long time since he had put someone ahead of himself. He enjoyed the feeling.

Doing something for his mother would also please him. He wished there was something he could do for Paul that wouldn't destroy his world.

The air conditioning hit him when he held open the door for Ashley. For being a Monday, the planetarium had several people in the lobby waiting to enter the 3:15 show.

"Tickets are thirty-five dollars per person." She stood in line with an unspoken question in her eyes. "I don't remember seeing a receipt for a show. Did you see this in your Venmo account?"

"No, but I remember lasers. I guess I could have put it on my credit card. I didn't think to check for any charges there, and I doubt this place accepts Venmo." Taking out his phone, he opened his What3Words app. "The last triple set has the location in this building. He scanned the room and then pointed to where the theater room was. "Looks like it's several feet beyond that wall."

"The show is an hour long. We have time to watch it, but I doubt we'll be able to hunt for the ring while everyone is in their seats."

Thomas studied the room's layout: restrooms on one side, offices on the other, a hallway marked off, and many people milling about the front entryway looking at planetary displays. This would be a perfect date-night spot if he weren't on a mission to find an expensive ring.

He heard it the minute the thought crossed his mind. He didn't take women to places like this. He took them to dinner, play productions, or performances that reeked of money, and then to bed. This nerdy venue held no interest to women. Even the crowd here reflected that. The women in line were all mothers taking their children for an educational experience while on summer break. Other than a few elderly couples—who were probably here with their grandkids—this wasn't a couple's place.

Ashley read the banner and said, "I wouldn't mind watching the show. Looks pretty interesting."

Really? He'd had the same thought.

"We could have snuck into the theater or were let in," she said, eyeing the door with an *Employees Only* sign. "We should probably make sure to pay, though, and not risk getting caught and thrown out before we find the ring."

He took out his wallet. "Good point."

Once in the theater, they followed the app to the back wall, where the exit door was. "What3words is showing the ring's location beyond this far wall." He showed her his phone's display. "The ring isn't even in this room."

The lights flickered. "We need to take our seats," Ashley said. "The show is about to start."

They found two seats together in the back. The room held nearly eighty people and resembled an old-style theater, complete with black velvet curtains lining the walls. The seats were cushioned and easily leaned back when you pressed your back into them, so you were staring at the ceiling.

"Welcome to the universe," the guide said as he began the presentation. To Thomas's surprise, Ashley seemed to cling to his every word. Her eyes twinkled as she stared at the ceiling and waited for the impressive movie to begin that showed the big bang and explained how the universe had begun.

He had to admit, the show was good. He even enjoyed the section where they showed the moon's waxing and waning phases through all twelve months of the year.

The crowd cheered during the laser show, marking the performance's end. Van Morrison's *'Moondance'* played, and lasers danced across the black theater ceiling. What was more beautiful than the laser light display was how the bright lights reflected in Ashley's eyes.

He watched her face as she enjoyed the show. She seemed much like a child watching fireworks for the first time. Her mouth opened slightly as she looked on in awe.

What was it about her that was so playful and fun?

He took her in. There was wonderment in her eyes, and a playfulness about her lips.

Her blouse gaped a little at the neckline, and he took a peek at her perfect skin. The black lighting in the room illuminated her alabaster complexion.

He cocked his head and looked closer. Peeking out from the right side of her shirt was a scar, illuminated due to the lighting in the theater—an inch-long silvery line right above her clavicle bone.

A port scar?

He had seen them enough to recognize them from a mile away, but a part of him was hesitant to believe what he had seen, even though he thought he had noticed it yesterday when she wore the v-neck shirt during dinner.

He glanced away and pretended to watch the laser show, even though it now held no interest to him.

He needed to know.

Turning to see from the corner of his eye, he checked again.

His heart sank as he confirmed what he didn't want to know. She had been a cancer patient.

18

The lights came on in the auditorium so they stood and left ahead of the crowd.

"There is more on display upstairs to your left. To the right is our gift shop," the presenter said pleasantly. The show was well done, although not a single person, not even a child from the audience, had any follow-up questions or showed any real interest in the subject. Thomas had to admit, once he'd confirmed Ashley's port scar, the display didn't hold his attention, either.

He thought he had seen the scar yesterday but wasn't sure and hadn't wanted to stare at her chest to confirm it. Nor had he wanted to ask outright if she had been a cancer patient. He spent all day with women with such scars and had thought—no, he'd *hoped*—he had imagined the one on Ashley.

It wasn't as though he pitied people who battled the disease, especially women with breast cancer, but he respected their strength and what they had endured. Many women became empowered by their experiences. They understood life to be short, that second chances were rarely given, and that holding on to pettiness did no one any good.

But he wouldn't have thought someone as young as Ashley could have gone through such an ordeal. Of course, the port scar didn't have to mean cancer. People had infusions for many reasons. He hated to think of her lying in an infusion chair undergoing *any* treatment.

Treatment or surgery. Her breasts were…perfect.

Ashley squeezed through the exit door a few feet ahead of him, smiling at the other exiting planetarium patrons. The light from the gift shop shone through her hair, the beautiful curls he had noticed the moment he'd first laid eyes on her, and he felt stupid for not piecing it together earlier.

Chemotherapy had left her with those curls. It was common for the drugs. Most hair resumed its natural flair after a few years, so if Ashley wasn't born a curly-haired beauty, it gave him a timeline. She was probably still within her five-year window of survivorship. The first five years were the risky ones where cancer had a good chance of returning.

What stage had she been in? How young was she when the disease struck her?

He barely got through the door when Ashley approached him. "The place is clearing out. Looks like everyone went to the gift shop."

"The gift shops are always at the exit to catch people as they leave." He gazed into her green eyes and saw more depth to them than ever before.

"So now that we're on the other side of the wall, where is the ring?" Her gaze drifted toward the gift shop. "Please tell me it's not in there. Someone could accidentally buy it."

The ring. Right. It was why they were here.

Thomas took out his phone and checked the app. "It's not at the store." He turned his head and studied the floor several feet beyond the stairs leading to more of the exhibit. "It's here in the lobby."

She followed him to where the app indicated. A potted tree stood in front of them.

"We buried it?" she asked.

Thomas studied the app. Nothing else but the tiled floor stood within the three-by-three-meter area. "It has to be in the dirt." Checking the soil, he saw no part that had been disturbed. Surely, Hot Lips and Sugar Pants would not have dug a hole and cleanly patted down the telltale signs. "The soil is dry. Maybe the dirt was wet last night, and it was easy to cover up any holes. Of course, it wouldn't need to be very big."

The tree's planter wasn't that large, but searching through the dirt would get them noticed and possibly thrown out.

"It's not in the dirt." Ashley stared at the tree. "Its branches reach the second story, and there is a sitting area above us."

He shifted his gaze and studied the full branches, not understanding why a tree would be in a planetarium. There was certainly room for it—it wasn't a California redwood—but still. "You think we put it on a branch?"

"I know we did." She took his phone and sorted through his pictures. "We took a picture of a tree last night. Not the trunk of one, not the roots, but the leaves at the end of some branches. We could only have taken this image if we were standing at the same height as the top of the tree."

Ashley walked to the staircase and held onto the banister as she carefully stepped up.

"How's your ankle?" He watched as she shifted her weight from her good foot to her bad one. Her gait seemed reasonable, and so were the strides she had taken thus far.

"My ankle is fine. I hardly feel any pain at all."

They went upstairs to the couch-like seat. The square box shape, draped in fabric, did not look familiar but would have been ideal for sitting on and touching the tree branches that hung over the side railing.

"I'm surprised we didn't fall last night. We must have put it on one of the closer branches."

She stood at the railing, her hand holding the phone in front of her. She was so focused on the game, so determined to win. He took a deep breath and found himself physically and emotionally attracted to her. She was both sexy and playful. The combination beckoned him.

"This bunch of leaves over here looks the same and would be a good hiding place for..." She turned, and the biggest smile stretched across her face. Her expression lit up the room.

"You found it?" Excitement filled him, and he dashed over to stand next to her. The ring lay behind a leaf on a thin branch. They had placed it a good six inches onto the branch with the leaf securing it in place so it wouldn't fall.

"I can't believe we did it." She plucked the ring from the tree and held it in her hand. "It's by far the nicest treasure I've ever recovered while geocaching."

"Right?" He felt practically giddy, and he was *never* giddy. Perhaps this was something new that only Ashley brought out in him. "A six-thousand-dollar ring just sitting in the open like this, and we found it!"

"Six thousand dollars?" Her mouth gaped, and she stared at the ring with wide eyes. "Even drunk, if I had known how expensive this thing was, I wouldn't have suggested we leave it for anyone to find accidentally."

He placed the ring in his pocket. "I don't know how much Paul paid or how much only this ring cost, but the replacement set was over six thousand dollars."

"For a ring?"

Her eyebrows knitted in disbelief, as though she couldn't understand anyone spending that kind of money for a piece of jewelry. He felt even more embarrassed by the forty-dollar ring he had bought her only a few days ago from the Pair O' Dice Chapel.

She was worth more than a ring like that.

Perhaps taking the job at Ian Ostern Memorial Hospital would be the best. A new start in a new town. The pay and prestige were good. He certainly coveted the position. His thoughts drifted to Ashley and how he had laughed and had a good time with her, no matter how expensive and stressful the last two days had been.

Taking the chief of plastic and reconstructive surgery position would mean staying close to his family and seeing to his mother's needs if they moved her to the state.

He could date his soon-to-be ex-wife.

A smile curled his lips as he emotionally committed to the new hospital position. He wouldn't have to let Ashley go. That alone was worth moving to Nevada.

"Let's hope this is the last snag at this wedding. I don't think Paul or Linda could handle any more upset."

He didn't share the excitement in her voice. He knew that one more hiccup existed, and *he* was the cause. He needed to tell Paul the truth about sleeping with Linda. He also realized that if he wanted to pursue any relationship with Ashley, he had to tell *her* that he had slept with her cousin.

Ashley sat with Thomas in the parked car, and Thomas seemed to hesitate. He turned on the air conditioning and placed his left arm on the door's armrest. "Can I ask you something?"

He appeared pensive and distant. "Sure," she said.

"Do you think Linda keeps secrets?"

"Linda?" The question surprised Ashley, but she knew the answer. "She isn't one of those women who hides things from someone she loves. She shares everything with Paul."

His eyebrow lifted suggestively. "Everything?"

The way he asked indicated he knew a secret Linda was keeping. "What do you know?"

He seemed almost guilty, which made Ashley's heart beat faster. "Spill," she said.

"Is Linda… I'm not judging here, not at all, but is she…?" He pursed his lips as though trying to find the right words. "Before Paul, would you say she liked to party?" His eyebrows rose again, as did his inflection on the last word.

"Drugs?"

"No, not drugs." His face pinched as though he were rethinking how to phrase things. "Do you think she had many one-night stands with men?"

"Linda?" The question was rather personal and something that Ashley, even as a favored cousin, wouldn't know. She knew about the long-term relationships Linda had had, but nothing fleeting. If Ashley had to guess, Linda's number of ex-lovers would be around five or six.

Ashley didn't want to betray Linda's confidence.

She wasn't even sure she should talk about something so personal to Linda's future brother-in-law. "Are you asking if she's a virgin?"

He took in a deep breath and stared at the dashboard. "No, that's not what I'm asking." After a moment, he said, "Promise you won't think less of me when I tell you this."

His blue eyes beseeched her, and for a moment, she found herself drawn to him even more. Pain lived within his gaze—a pain that had no answer. His pursed lips, hunched shoulders, and the defeated expression on his face haunted her.

"You also can't repeat this to anyone."

His tone worried her. "What could be so bad that—?"

"Five years ago," he said slowly, interrupting her, "before Paul met Linda....*I* had a one-night stand with her."

Ashley's gaze darted away, and she couldn't breathe for a moment. Had she heard that correctly?

She replayed each word in her head, feeling her muscles tighten. Thomas had slept with Linda. Her cousin.

Squeezing her eyes shut, she tried to wrap her mind around what he had said, but her focus remained on how her heart had stopped beating and how tightly she had her teeth clenched.

"You…and Linda."

"Me and Linda."

Betrayal, but it wasn't as though Thomas owed her anything. Husband or not, they didn't have more than a one-night stand, sans sex, between *them*.

Her body stiffened, and she found it difficult to look at him.

"Linda doesn't even seem to remember me," he said sheepishly.

Like that was any consolation.

She had been warned. A player like Thomas…so many women, so little time. Why was she so stupid?

"You slept with Linda?" Ashley sat straighter in the seat, the air conditioner no longer hitting her face. She knew Thomas to be a hound, and here was the proof. "Good Lord, you slept with the bride, and Paul doesn't even know."

"A chance meeting at a convention before they knew each other. It was only one night."

The scenario didn't sound like Linda. She'd had her fair share of ex-loves—the term now sickened Ashley's stomach when thinking of the two together as lovers— but Linda didn't do one-night stands. She was a relationship woman. Always had been.

Ashley gazed at Thomas but then shifted her focus elsewhere. Anywhere else. She turned her head to face the neon planetarium sign, not him. Linda had been with him. Had touched him. More to the point, *he* had touched *her*.

His hands had been on her body. His lips… Ashley squeezed her eyes shut again and held back her emotions. Linda had warned her that Thomas used women. Ashley now understood why she had said that. Firsthand knowledge.

"Your reaction is exactly why I need to tell Paul." His voice fell to a mere whisper. "The encounter didn't mean anything to me. I'm sure it meant probably less to her."

It meant nothing? Sex with a woman was meaningless to Thomas?

She snuck a peek at him as he stared out the window. He had slept with Tina on their first date. He'd practically admitted that. How many women did he use and throw away like that?

"I've been trying to tell Paul since I got here, but I haven't found the right time."

The conversation she'd had with her cousin raced back through her mind. *"Keep Thomas away from Paul."* Linda hadn't wanted Thomas hanging around his brother. Thinking about it now, keeping Thomas apart from the wedding group meant keeping him away from Linda, as well.

She doubted Linda was tempted. After all, she planned to marry Paul.

Was she tempted? Did she want Thomas?

She stared at his strong jaw, blue eyes, and devilish good looks. Every woman probably wanted—and evidently got—him.

"How many women have you slept with that having sex with Linda meant nothing to you?" Her hardened voice surprised her, but she wanted to know the answer. "How many?"

He took in a deep breath, probably trying to do the complicated math. Take a number, multiply it by weeks in a year, and multiply that by…what? Decades at this point?

His body shifted, and he pulled away as best he could in the confines of the car. "I don't really want to have this conversation with you."

"What? You can't count that high?"

His gaze now matched hers. "The number doesn't matter. What matters is that years ago, before Paul met Linda, I slept with her. And that information will tear Paul and me apart even more as brothers. Which is why I don't want to say anything, but Paul needs to know the truth—especially since Linda has been avoiding me."

Ashley no longer cared if Thomas had a good relationship with his brother. But Paul didn't deserve this. She had gotten to know him over the past few years, and he was a decent and hardworking guy who doted on Linda. "If this *event*," she said, nearly hissing out the word, "happened years ago and meant nothing, then Paul doesn't need to be told."

"Possibly. But what if she's hiding it from him, and he finds out one day? I have to tell him because of Tina. It'll be worse if he finds out after the wedding, especially if Linda lies to him about other things." He took another deep breath, inhaling the cool, air-conditioned air and letting it out slowly. "I wish I knew if she remembered me or not."

"I think it's a good bet she does," Ashley blurted out, not thinking.

"What are you talking about?"

Linda had played Ashley. Just like when they were kids. Linda performed as the puppet master, pulling strings, and Ashley danced to whatever tune Linda wanted. "She asked me to keep you away from Paul. Even paid me money to take you out after dinner that first night."

Thomas's face paled as he processed the information for a quiet minute. "That confirms a few things for me," he finally said in an icy tone. "I know what I need to do now."

19

Thomas had made an excuse to duck out of dinner last night. He hadn't seen Ashley since she'd confessed that she had asked him out because Linda paid her to do so. He wasn't sure how to process that information.

Well, other than being pissed.

He'd needed time to cool down last night and this morning. His mother would be here soon, and being seconds away from exploding emotionally would not help since she knew where all his buttons were.

He inhaled the fresh air deeply and counted to ten several times.

The Bella Rosa's porch boards creaked again, the sound pitching to the exact volume that grated on Thomas's nerves. The noise sent shivers up his spine like nails scratching on a chalkboard. "I'm sure she's fine," he said, his tone showing irritation. Concentrating on his mother's arrival was difficult while Paul paced the length of the wooden platform.

Paul stopped and stared at him, giving him the irritated-little-brother expression that'd been so well practiced since they were kids. Regardless of his discontent with Thomas, the man stopped and gave the boards some rest. He pulled out his phone and stared at the display. "She's five miles away."

Thomas looked at him questioningly.

"A few months ago, I visited her and got access to her phone. I track her with the Life360 app. I can see anywhere she is in real-time as long as she has her phone on her." Anger gleamed in his eye as he added, "And, no. She doesn't know." He put the phone in his pocket, but Thomas suspected it'd be out again before the time it took to cross the five miles was up. "I've been watching her since she landed at the airport today." Paul turned and focused his gaze south toward the main road where his mother would be coming from. He gently tapped his neck and took in a deep breath.

Their mother had always been independent. Learning about such a breach of privacy would wound her, and there was no reason to hurt her feelings. She was a widow and alone in the world. Paul had moved from California to Nevada a few months after meeting Linda, which left their mother with no close relatives nearby if an emergency occurred.

The Life360 app was a good idea. And their secret.

"You need to relax," he told Paul, although the stress

of the last few days laced his words. Paul may be the one about to be married, but Thomas juggled a mental mess himself. His mother, the annulment, the wedding, the job offer, and, of course, Ashley. She and her deceit had consumed his thoughts since last night. She had actually been *paid* to go out with him. Paid. Like a common sex worker.

And a bad one since sex hadn't been involved.

He wanted to scream, leave. Disappear.

Linda and her lies could go to hell. She had probably told everyone her own warped side of the story, painting him as the villain and saying the night they'd shared never happened, all so only he'd be ostracized by the group.

Did the entire wedding party view him as a joke?

His mistrust of Ashley had him not wanting to hang out with her last night, so he'd tried to blend in with the men. Bad mistake. All he did was drink three beers and go to bed early with the excuse that he had work on his mind.

So much for giving up alcohol.

A cool breeze blew through the trees, ringing the wind chimes in the garden and bringing the scent of fresh flowers to him. The wedding march played for another set of nuptials, these taking place near the reflection pond. The tune carried on the breeze and turned Thomas's stomach.

The place focused on weddings and love. He had gotten caught up in the allure and the spell of the fake oasis, even though he had promised himself he wouldn't. Fifty percent of marriages ended in divorce. This place was the start of so much misery. His parents had lived until death did them part with his father's passing, but role models or not, that wasn't today's world. People didn't stay together.

He crossed his arms and glared out among the flowers and winding paths before him, barely making out the wedding party near the pond. He and Ashley's marriage would be annulled. It wouldn't even count toward that fifty percent failure rate. It'd be like it never even existed.

Thomas stretched, hoping his muscles would loosen and relieve some tension, but they didn't. He needed a massage. He mentally cringed as he thought back to his last one. Had Ashley switched places with the regular masseuse just to endear herself to him? Had it all been a lie?

Paul stood and tapped the side of his neck with his finger again. The small, irritating motion bothered the hell out of Thomas.

Paul rechecked his phone as he resumed his pacing. "She's three miles away. You haven't seen Mom since Dad's funeral, so be prepared. I think he was the rock that held her together."

"So you've said a dozen times already this morning." The added stress from the mental image Paul painted didn't help Thomas's mood. His mother, at least the woman he'd known before she became a widow, had been strong and self-reliant. A world traveler who didn't like asking for help. She could certainly manage to get from the airport to the wedding venue.

"I think she has Alzheimer's. She forgets a lot of things."

"I'm sure it's not that bad," Thomas said, even though he had only seen her briefly at the funeral. It had been a good year since he'd last visited his parents.

"Thomas," Paul said, stopping mid-pace and glaring at him. "I told her eight or nine times this past month when and where the wedding was. I swear, she didn't remember."

It was more likely their mother was lonely and wanted to talk. Thomas didn't need Paul's unprofessional diagnosis. "If you're so worried about her, why didn't you meet her at the airport?"

"You know how she likes doing things her own way."

A shiver ran up Thomas's spine. Linda was just like their mother. It was all so Oedipal. Paul's choice of bride, how he put up with Linda…it all made sense.

"Besides, Mom yelled at me when I said I'd get her."

"She yelled?" That didn't sound like his mother. She may be controlling and the best at laying down guilt trips, but she never raised her voice. "I think you're exaggerating things."

Paul's face flushed, and his jaw tightened. For a moment, Thomas saw the stubborn kid his brother had been as a child. He was definitely their mother's son. "Mom is aging quickly without Dad. I don't think all the days alone are good for her." He took in a deep breath. His hands were balled into fists, and every muscle seemed tight. "She can't stay out in California alone. We need to move her to Nevada to be closer to Linda and me." His eyes met Thomas's. "Or she needs to be in Chicago with you. Either one."

The offer from Ian Ostern Memorial Hospital was solid. Thomas's if he wanted it. The position had seemed so appealing a short while ago, but he wasn't sure he should take it now. Ashley would be less than an hour away. Closer if he got her that dream job at the physical therapy center.

He thought about that. He'd still help her.

"I think I see her."

Thomas could barely make out the car as it turned down the dirt road. "That's not a cab. It's probably another bridal party."

"Maybe, but Mom took a rideshare."

Two words that didn't belong together. "*Mom* took a *rideshare*?"

"Sure."

"You're so worried that she's mentally falling apart, and the woman can work the Uber app?" His brother was losing it. Their mother hadn't embraced technology since she found most things with the Internet confusing, but a rideshare app?

The car approached, and his mom waved to them from the back seat. She looked the same to Thomas.

Paul waved to her but then turned around to face his brother. "I ordered and paid for the car," he said in a rush. "She called and was so turned around at the airport that she didn't know what to do once she left the terminal."

The excitement in Paul's voice gave Thomas pause. "Rideshares are common at the airport."

"I know, but she didn't go to the rideshare lanes. After landing, she caught a shuttle to a car park center, thinking she'd be able to get a ride. She was confused when I asked her why she was at a place called The Spot.

"She was probably confused because she doesn't know you can track her phone and get her exact location. She probably questioned why you knew where she was."

"It wasn't that. When I called, she asked me if I knew where she had parked her car."

The words hit Thomas, and he waved back at his mother as the car stopped. "She thought she'd find her car?"

"Yep. She said she couldn't find *her* car." Before Thomas commented, Paul added, "Once she got there, she thought she had parked her car and needed to find it. She completely forgot that I had a car service waiting for her."

A heaviness settled in Thomas's chest and tugged at

his heart. If what Paul said was true, they may have severe issues with their mother.

Paul shot his brother a serious expression. "She needs help." He opened the car door and helped his mother out. Her slender legs appeared thinner, her hands as they reached for Paul seemed frail, and her hair, always luscious and full, was lackluster and whiter than Thomas remembered. She stood and needed to hold on to Paul and the car door for balance.

"The flight was awful," Karen Stallworth said once she exited the car and composed herself. "The airport was under construction. I got so turned around. Can't they schedule their repairs at night so they aren't so disruptive on the travelers?"

Paul kissed his mother on the cheek. "LAX has been under construction for nearly a year, Mom. Don't you remember us talking about it when I last visited you?"

Thomas watched as no recognition appeared in his mother's eyes.

"Remember?" Paul said. "When I saw you earlier this year. I flew out to visit you."

"Of course, sweetheart. Of course."

Thomas leaned in and gave his mother a hug and a kiss on the cheek, unsure if she actually remembered Paul's visit.

Her lips were thin, the skin of her hands papery and nearly translucent, but her eyes glistened with happiness as if she were glad to be here.

The driver pulled the suitcases from the trunk and

set them on the ground. Thomas tipped the driver and took her bags.

"Look at my two boys," she said, her craggy voice filled with excitement. "Together again."

The three hugged awkwardly, with Thomas still holding on to a carry-on bag. He had leaned in for the hug, bowing at the waist and trying to keep the load on his back without it flinging forward and hitting his brother, but something seemed odd.

He stood tall again and did a height assessment. Had his mother shrunk since his father's funeral?

"Mom, I told you one of us would have met you at the airport. You didn't have to do this on your own." Paul glanced from his mother to Thomas. He tilted his head slightly and raised one eyebrow.

Message received. Thomas nodded back. He would have to take her to the airport for her return flight since Paul would already have left on his honeymoon. The last time he had seen their mother, she had been grieving the loss of their father but had otherwise seemed fine. She took care of all the final arrangements for their father—had actually insisted on doing so—and refused to leave the home where she had raised her family.

A two-story house with a staircase leading straight to a tiled floor.

He had not gone home for Christmas. Now, thinking about it, had he done so and found her like this, he would have at least accident-proofed her house as much as possible.

"Paulie, sweetheart, it's your wedding. I still have the strength to get from an airport to a car." She pulled a well-folded and worn piece of paper from her pocket. "I have all the directions you gave me."

Paul took his mother's arm, and the two walked side by side to the Bella Rosa's main house. "I thought we'd have lunch, but why don't you lie down? The ordeal at the airport sounds horrible."

A floodgate opened. Their mother took a deep breath and recited every disagreeable turn of events. Why did the airports have to be so big and maze-like? Why did she have to pay for her checked luggage? Why did they not serve drinks on board the aircraft?

Paul helped his mother up the porch steps. "Mom, you can always ask for some water or something. The flight attendants have juice and sodas, too."

"I asked for a shot of Four Roses. They don't have that on board. Evidently, that airline is too conservative for whiskey."

Thomas paused when he heard that. His mother had always been a teetotaler, not a drinker. When had she started boozing it up?

Paul opened the main door to the resort, the little bell chiming. The air conditioner hit them as they walked in and caught Karen's silvery-blue hair, making it fan out in the breeze. Her curled locks were pinned in an elegant style, and Thomas figured she had treated herself to a spa day before coming to her son's wedding.

Karen held the cardigan she wore and pinched it closed by her neck as they walked farther into the building and around some people from another wedding party who were checking out. A second group stood at the elevators waiting to go to their rooms. "This place is lovely, Paul. It's so quaint and charming."

His mother always used the words *quaint* and *charming* for small and disagreeable. She had used those words to describe the treehouse their father had built in the backyard, Thomas's first apartment, and the energy-efficient car he'd bought after med school.

Even though he now believed there was some cause for concern, his mother was still his mother.

"Where is that beautiful bride of yours?" Before waiting for an answer, her head pivoted to the right, and she addressed Thomas, "You should find someone as nice as Linda. Are you seeing anyone right now?"

It hadn't even been five minutes. And no matter what he said, she'd find a problem with it and offer to fix it. He certainly couldn't say he had gone on a bender and married the first woman he got his hands on in a drunken stupor.

His thoughts immediately went to Ashley. After returning to the Bella Rosa last night, he had ghosted her. She hadn't looked at him and hadn't said a word about his confession regarding sleeping with Linda. The entire wedding party split into a *girls' night* and a *guys' night*, which had been fine by him.

A part of him wanted to blurt out Linda's secret to make her pay for what she had done.

"A good woman—and I mean a good one who knows how to cook—would do you wonders, Thomas. You're too thin." His mom pivoted in the lobby and skeptically eyed him. "You're too single."

She had not stopped talking since she'd gotten out of the car. Had they really only walked from the outside into the main house before she asked about his dating life?

"Thomas is doing well for himself, Mom."

And now Paul was throwing himself under the bus for him? Everything felt so *Twilight Zone*-ish.

"Thomas paid for your room already." Paul led them to the elevator once the crowd had squeezed into the last car. He pressed the button hard, not once but four times. "It's a beautiful room. We scheduled lunch at the resort for the three of us, but maybe you should rest."

The smell of grilled chicken filled the air, not that Thomas was hungry.

"Don't be silly. I'll just drop off my bags, and we can have a lovely meal." Her gaze ping-ponged between her two sons as they waited for the elevator. "These are the best of times. If only your father were here."

Six minutes.

"I can drop these things off at the room if the two of you want to sit in the dining room." Thomas glanced at the hall where people sat and dined. There were a few tables left. Besides, he had his mother's key in his pocket already. "I'll be right down."

Paul flashed him a frustrated expression but said, "That sounds good, Thomas." He held on to her arm and carefully turned her around. Thomas noted how much his mother leaned on Paul as they walked away. Her feet shuffled against the floor, and her gait was uneven.

After struggling for years for a second child, she had been forty-six when she gave birth to Paul. The doctors called a pregnancy like that a mature maternal age, but it meant one thing: His mother was now in her eighties, alone, and with the start of health issues.

As frustrating as she could be, she needed more from him. And he needed to give it.

Several minutes later, Thomas returned and found their table. Paul had selected a quiet spot near the window that overlooked the garden.

"What took you so long? Mom and I have already ordered drinks for the table."

Thomas took his seat, trying hard to decipher the hidden messages in that statement. He had only been up to the room and back, yet Paul looked like he had gone through the wringer.

He then noticed the amber-colored liquid in a glass in front of his mother. "Is that scotch?"

"On the rocks," Paul said. "Evidently, Mom prefers single malt to double."

"Double malt isn't nearly as good." She shifted in

her seat and faced Thomas once he sat. "A lovely woman sat next to me on the plane, Thomas. She is a teacher in Chicago." Her face lit up, and she placed her hand on his. "I told her you'd call her."

"What?"

"I told her all about you. She's single and beautiful."

"Mom, I'm sure she's nice, but you don't need to find me dates." It wasn't the *date* part that bothered him. She was trying to find him a wife. The mother of her future grandchildren—kids Thomas didn't even want.

"So, I hear you had a floral fiasco," Thomas said, reflecting the focus onto his brother.

"Oh, no. Paul? The flowers?" their mother asked questioningly.

Paul's expression changed once he was tagged as being *it*. He took his right hand and gently tapped behind his right ear with two fingers as he took a deep breath. Thomas figured it was an anti-anxiety movement.

Maybe he should try it sometime.

The conversation shifted from the floral fiasco to the gorgeous gardens of the Bella Rosa, then back to how the airports had been under construction.

Their salads were served, and his mother, who had definitely lost weight over the last year, only had a few bites. Her skin was thinner, and she even had trouble holding on to the fork.

"It's so nice to see the two of you getting along." She took another sip of scotch. Even soaking wet, his mother wouldn't weigh more than a hundred pounds. At least she took in the drink slowly.

"When did you start day drinking?"

Paul answered the question with a sharp kick to Thomas's shin under the table.

A nearly guilty expression crossed his mother's face. "I only have nightcaps to help me sleep. That house is so big and lonely without your father."

"It's noon, Mom." Before he even asked the question, he'd figured the answer was connected to his father's death.

"Flying to Paulie's wedding alone hit me pretty hard." Her face showed the raw pain of being widowed. "It's so nice to have you together and getting along."

She looked on the verge of tears.

"I'm so glad I insisted you invite Thomas to your wedding, Paulie."

"Of course, Mom. Thomas is my brother. He had to be here."

Thomas felt a connection with Paul for the first time since he'd arrived for the wedding. The two needed to take care of their mother. In this, they would always be united.

A server placed three chicken plates in front of them before refilling their water glasses and leaving again.

"This is so much food." Karen's frail hand waved over her lunch. "Do either of you want half?"

"Mom, eat your lunch. Thomas and I have plenty."

The conversation ping-ponged from the wedding to

the weather to how thin Paul was and how single Thomas remained. The table banter played out like a weird opera, with both brothers deflecting questions by redirecting their mother's attention on the other one.

Paul's deflective comments to get the conversation's focus back on to Thomas and his single status made one thing perfectly clear: Paul didn't know about Ashley and the wedding. Mohinder remained the only one who knew and, evidently, he could be trusted.

Thomas shifted gears and talked about a white paper and medical trial he was about to start in the field of breast cancer. Anything to get off the topic of him still being single was preferred.

"Is this a study of women who are triple-negative post-surgery and chemo? The one with all that grant money?" Paul asked.

"Have you heard about the study?" Overall, Thomas wasn't surprised. It had been discussed within the medical community for months. Breast cancer carried three receptors. Being triple-negative meant the receptors were all negative and the patient wasn't given pharmaceutical treatment after chemo. There were always studies to find new treatments, especially for people with gene mutations prone to getting the disease.

"Some of my pharmaceutical carriers are awaiting answers from the study. They're hoping to carry that family line of drugs one day," Paul said.

"It's so nice that the two of you can work together." Their mother beamed a proud smile at the two of them, but Thomas suspected that she didn't follow the conversation and possibly didn't understand it. He would have mentioned the escape room event to her but figured she might get lost in a conversation about preventing a church from blowing up.

Paul finished his meal—a bit rushed, in Thomas's opinion. "The wedding party is doing a helicopter tour of the Grand Canyon later today. Everyone is leaving soon, so I need to get going."

Their mom's face showed caution and worry. Evidently, she hadn't been given an itinerary. Was there one for the parents?

"We're going on a helicopter tour?" Her gaze shifted between Paul and Thomas.

"We know you don't like heights, Mom," Paul said. "Besides, we thought you'd probably like to rest at the Bella Rosa before this evening. Remember, you and I are having dinner with Linda and her father tonight."

She appeared confused but gave them both a smile. "You're both leaving now?"

Thomas couldn't leave her alone. Had he known the state of her health, he would have insisted on picking her up at the airport. "I think I'll stay behind. It's been a while since we've talked, Mom."

"Oh, that's nice." The muscles of her face relaxed, and she seemed delighted at the idea. He touched her hand, feeling her petite frame as she wrapped her fingers around his.

She then said, "It'll give me a chance to tell you

about this wonderful woman who sat next to me on the plane. She's a school teacher from Chicago."

A string tugged at his heart. This was his mother. The woman who had been his biggest cheerleader his entire life. There was more at work here than just old age. She had always been headstrong and invasive in her sons' lives, but he suspected she had the onset of dementia.

20

The sound of the wedding march played again.

The tune had found its way into Ashley's bedroom window at the cottage. Through the paned glass and her hands, which now did their best to block the unpleasant melody from her ears.

Ashley glanced at the clock on the wall. Only thirteen minutes. Her nap wasn't long. This was the third wedding at the Bella Rosa today. There had been one yesterday and two the day before.

She never thought she'd be so sick of weddings.

She got out of Linda's wedding party outing by faking a migraine and insisting she had seen the Grand Canyon dozens of times. She wanted the world to disappear. She had no reason to lay claim to Thomas besides the wedding ring that hid in her purse, but she still hated that he had slept with her cousin.

A tear threatened to escape, and she chided herself for her weakness.

There was nothing between her and Thomas.

He was a successful plastic surgeon with tons of noses to fix in Chicago. She lived in Las Vegas. Nothing could happen between the two.

Nothing *should* happen.

And yet, she felt the loss.

The wedding march ended, and she knew another bride stood by her significant other to share vows.

Two fairy-tale weddings had happened already today. Two happy futures.

And all she had was a cheap ring, a cousin she didn't want to be near, and a commitment to annul everything.

And she was stuck at the Bella Rosa until Sunday morning.

The ugly monster that lived within her was ready for a pity party, but she shoved him into a dark mental closet and locked him away. She didn't want to think about the past. She didn't even want to focus on what a louse Linda was.

She rolled over, and the tear-soaked spot on her pillowcase touched her cheek. Flipping the pillow over, she tried to forget about Linda's wedding. Tried to forget about Linda's lies to hide the truth from Paul. Tried to forget that Linda wanted another *wedding meeting* later today to discuss some choreographed dance moves she had designed for the official first dance.

Someone needed to tell the bride she had two left feet. No amount of practice over the next few days would change that, especially since the groom had no rhythm. But Linda had seen another wedding party's prepared sachet down the aisle, followed by their nearly perfect theatrical number in the barn at the reception, and she had it in her head that their ragtag team of coordination-challenged people could put on a production that rivaled *Mama Mia*.

She'd have to talk to Linda and change the woman's mind. That would involve talking to her, and there was a good chance—as angry as she was with her cousin—she would blurt out that she knew Linda's secret and why she needed Thomas away from Paul.

An icy shiver ran up her back. Thomas had touched Linda. Had lay in a bed with her cousin, and...her mind went dark. She knew how built Thomas was. Could imagine his muscular body lying in bed. Could almost feel his strong arms around her.

Her heart twisted.

Those strong arms had been around Linda. Whether it was one night or not, Thomas had chosen Linda to be intimate with—and, evidently, most women in Chicago if her cousin could be believed. But not her. She had been drunk in his bed, yet he'd chosen to sleep on the freaking couch.

She understood that she should be grateful not to

have been molested by some lecherous creep. Her *husband* had honorably kept his distance from his drunk *bride* and did not force himself on her.

So why did she feel this way?

Footsteps sounded on the cobblestone path outside her window. They stopped abruptly, and she heard two people talking outside the cottage. The rose garden's comfortable benches were only a few feet away, and she figured the loud talkers would be there for a while.

So much for continuing her nap.

Ashley grabbed her book and sunglasses from the nightstand and left the cottage. The weather had become slightly cooler with the rain from yesterday, so she hoped the well's swing was dry. Since Hershel had roped off that area until he could finish the repairs, and because it lay in the northernmost part of the resort grounds past the main house, she hoped to find some peace and quiet.

She sidestepped the yellow tape that stretched from one tree to the other, its *Under Construction* sign not hindering her need for isolation. The ground was mostly dry, the air crisp and fresh. Exactly what she needed.

She walked around the umbrella swing. The seat was big enough for two so she could lie down. She might even set the alarm on her watch and maybe take another short nap.

"Ashley?"

She jumped back, her foot slipping on the muddy

ground and sending new pain through her nearly healed ankle.

"I thought you'd left with the rest of the party an hour ago." She found it difficult to make eye contact with Thomas. She had been so mad at him last night for his lustful horny ways that she wasn't even civil to him. But one glance from him now reinflamed a passionate desire she should not have for the man. How had he put it? Sex meant nothing to him.

"Have a seat." His voice sounded somber, melancholic. He resembled Eeyore on a bad day. He took a sip of beer, and two empty bottles sat on the table beside him.

He had said he might have a drinking problem and had sworn he'd try to give up the booze. So much for that. He clearly had no control.

She sat next to him and gestured to the empties. "I thought you were quitting." Her voice held a disdainful and frosty tone.

His jaw tightened, and pain flared in his eyes. This wasn't a casual beer or a guilty pleasure. He lay slumped in the swing. Something was wrong. "What happened?" Her heart skipped a beat. "Oh, God. Did you tell Paul?"

His head lowered, and he set the beer bottle down. "Didn't have a chance. Our mother arrived today."

She understood how mothers had ways of hitting every button their children owned. But this seemed more than a routine annoyance. She didn't know Paul's mother but understood she was recently widowed. "Is your mother all right?"

"I think she has dementia or the onset of Alzheimer's."

His words had been said in a hushed tone as though speaking them aloud worsened the conditions. It was the same way her mother had said Ashley had cancer.

She sat closer to Thomas on the swing, setting her anger at him aside. "I'm sorry. How old is she?"

"She'll be eighty-two in October."

"She's so young. Are you sure she has one of those diseases?" She felt stupid for asking a doctor if his diagnosis was correct, but she hoped he was wrong.

Thomas described the last hour he'd spent with his mother before she left to take a nap. Karen had difficulty remembering things, couldn't answer simple questions, and had nearly failed a memory test he'd slyly performed on her. Worse yet, she repeated the bit about the teacher on the airplane two additional times.

"I think the loneliness of the last fourteen months since my father died has been tough on her emotionally and mentally. She's still very functional but lives alone in my childhood home." He lowered his head, and his face appeared ashen. "She can't live alone in that big house. It has two stories and hard tile everywhere. She shuffles when she walks and could easily trip on the throw rugs all over the place."

"She may not want to leave behind her

independence. You might need to safety-proof her home."

His gaze fell on her, his eyes reflecting his worry. "I've searched memory care places for her since I sat on this swing." He clutched his phone like a lifeline. "Paul and I have had our differences in the past, but I know we'll work together to take care of her." His eyes glistened with tears. "She's our mother."

His legs stretched and rocked the swing. The comforting motion seemed to soothe him.

Without thinking, Ashley lay her head on his chest. To her surprise, he wrapped his arm around her shoulders and held her close. She felt the tension in his body through his tight grip.

"I decided to take the position at Ian Ostern Memorial Hospital, which is only an hour away," he said. "I was on the phone with them today after my mother went down for her nap. There's just so much to do. I have a dinner meeting tonight with some board members, a tour of the hospital and staff tomorrow, and Thursday, I'm meeting with a real estate agent for housing for me and a place for my mother. I'll be able to transition into the new role within the next few weeks." He then added, "I'll be able to continue wedding stuff Friday morning when we get the tuxes."

She felt him nod as he spoke as if mentally checking off a list of what needed to be done. She focused on him moving from Chicago. He'd be close by.

Although he would be gone tonight and tomorrow,

she'd enjoy the time with her cousins, but Thomas had made the last few days memorable. She'd miss him.

"There are some good retirement centers up there. Mom will be close to me and near Paul, as well."

She sensed his vulnerability. His mom was important to him, and he was a good son. "I'm sure there are many suitable places she'll like. Some even affiliated with Ian Ostern Memorial." Memory care was expensive. She figured the price was not a problem for the two brothers. They'd take care of their mother no matter what.

Thomas sniffled and then cleared his throat. "I do have some good news." His foot kicked off, and the swing's motion grew stronger. "The blood results are in. My state was hammered. You should get the results emailed to you, too."

She nestled in, and the scent of his cologne mixed with the garden flowers and the beer's hops. "One problem at a time."

They sat together for a moment, and a sense of anxiety bubbled through her entire body. He would be living in Nevada. Would only be an hour away, perhaps less if she got a job at the physical therapy center. She felt like she was about to explode when she finally said, "Taking Linda's money and doing her a favor gave me the courage to ask you out. I'm not even sure I would have been able to say hello to you that night if she hadn't pushed me to do so."

She glanced at his full lips that had slightly parted.

"I enjoyed going out with you that night. I've enjoyed the geocaching and finding the lost treasures together since. I've had more fun this week than I've had in a long time, and I can't believe you will be gone for the next two days. I understand, of course, but I'll miss you. I know our wedding was a mistake and that you date many women"—she fought for the right word —"casually. But messy annulment aside, I'd do it all over again."

His expression softened, and it seemed like an eternity passed before he said, "My feelings aren't casual when I'm with the right woman. Someone who means a great deal to me."

His gaze moved to her lips, and he leaned in. She closed her eyes and shifted closer, shortening the distance and meeting him halfway as her heartbeats thumped in her chest.

"Sorry, I didn't realize anyone was over here."

The words caught her off guard. Her eyes opened, and she sat up. Hershel stood near the swing, his wheelbarrow full of soil, mulch, and flowers.

"I put up the tape so no one would venture over here." He checked out the mud and mess from the previous storm, but she knew he was slightly embarrassed about disturbing them.

"It's fine," Thomas said. "I should check on my mother anyway."

21

Thomas walked past designer tuxedos at the Best Dressed tuxedo shop. Brands such as Hilfiger, HUGO BOSS, Gucci, and Armani snugly fit each headless, still perfectly fit mannequin.

His thoughts weren't focused on wedding-duty activities. Over the last few days, Ian Ostern Memorial Hospital had wined and dined him until late every evening. The days were filled with meetings with staff, touring the hospital, looking at houses and memory centers, and, of course, dinner parties at night. They were surprised by the fact that he now had a wife. He must have initially told them he didn't, but there would likely be an open position for her at the clinic. It wasn't guaranteed, but the coordinator had said there had been some employee turnaround and he could look into it.

And that was another cause to celebrate. At first, one

glass of champagne sounded appropriate. But then there were more cocktails with the board members, some old networking acquaintances who wanted to toast him, and then the nightcap. Three more days of drinking.

Could he even go a week without booze?

Paul's wedding was tomorrow. There'd be champagne to celebrate. Perhaps he should test himself once he returned to Chicago. No alcohol for the duration before he moved. It wasn't long, but he felt that if he could manage that test, he could handle a lifestyle change of no alcohol.

A new hangover headache still pinched his face. His body would thank him for the trial run. And if he failed, there were undoubtedly AA meetings in Vegas.

"It's not like she'll wear it again anyway. Those dresses are usually hideous."

"I know, but you have no idea how much that thing cost. And the shoes needed to be a size bigger because…"

Thomas turned his head and listened to Matt and Connor, the two groomsmen who mostly kept to themselves and he really didn't know. They'd arrived at the Bella Rosa just before he did and were Paul's college buddies. Connor's wife expected their first child soon, and Matt already had two little ones, the oldest already in kindergarten.

The conversation turned to the weird things kids thought were food, and as entertaining as that topic sounded, Thomas realized why he hadn't gotten overly familiar with the two men, even though they seemed like great guys. All they talked about were their wives and children.

A world that Thomas didn't belong to.

Two clerks came out from the back room, each struggling to carry tuxedos safely zipped away in garment bags. They smiled at Paul and the wedding party, but they *were* the only customers in the shop.

"Dr. Thomas Stallworth," one lady read from a tag and looked questioningly around at the group of six men. The expression her face held was *which man is the jackpot?* with a glimmer of *hopefully not the groom.*

After all, doctors were at the top of the dating food chain.

When Thomas raised his hand, she nodded in an acknowledging way and handed him the bulky bag. He thanked her for the outfit and smiled back politely.

She swung the second bag around to read its tag, not reconsidering Thomas.

Did she dismiss him? He stood taller, sucked in his gut, and puffed out his chest. His hand went to his belt, and he shifted to a Gucci-cologne-ad pose all before he realized what he was doing. No interest on his part existed, yet he couldn't believe she wasn't at least making eye contact with him.

Was he on autopilot mode around women? He hadn't been like this around Ashley. He had been himself. She didn't care about his job or status. She only cared about him.

Then again, maybe the attraction women had for doctors was only in his imagination. Perhaps he was getting older and not the catch in his forties that he had been only a few years ago. Women still saw him as a money ticket, but they were getting fewer and farther between.

He *was* getting older.

He rubbed his chin, realizing he hadn't trimmed his beard. He liked the shorter length, which seemed to fit his face nicely. The longer length made him look more like a lumberjack. He had been out with the hospital board members all night and had barely made it to the tuxedo shop on time. That had to be it. He inwardly chuckled at his stupidity. Had he been adequately groomed, the woman certainly would have noticed him. Would have taken a second or even third look at him. Would have wanted his number.

She didn't even glance in his direction. Neither did the other clerk.

A twisting in his gut told him the truth.

He saw what he wanted to see.

He was a man in his early forties who still played around. A man who carried an additional ten pounds, drank too much, and had been estranged from his family for the better part of a decade. Doctor or not, his life was a mess, and women of quality didn't see him as a serious person in the romance department. He had one failed marriage behind him and an annulment waiting in the wings.

It didn't get more real than that.

"Mr. Matt Klein," the second woman said. "Mr. Connor Reed?"

The clerk that had helped Thomas then read the name on her remaining outfit's tag. "Mr. Mohinder Partha…"

"Parthasarathy," Mohinder said, completing his surname so the clerk—who was now smiling and happy not to crucify the pronunciation—wouldn't need to. He took the outfit and slung it over his shoulder.

Thomas sized up Mohinder. The younger man had no gray hair. He was built. Plus, he had that tall, dark, and exotic look. And he was a lawyer. That had to be a draw for women. Matt and Connor were also handsome men—and younger. And Paul was undoubtedly taken. Linda was beautiful.

Thomas was the oldest man in the wedding party.

The oldest and single.

Sort of.

He was the old fart. The relative who had to be included.

"Do you have my tux?" Paul's gaze moved through each of his four groomsmen and Thomas, who all held tuxedo bags in their arms. "Mine has a white vest," he said, his voice filled with anxiety. "The pants length was being altered."

The lady who had handed Thomas his tux checked

all five of the tags. "These were all hanging together." When she didn't see Paul's outfit, she looked woefully at the second clerk, who was older and possibly more her senior at the store.

The second woman disappeared into the back before Paul could question her. The clerk who had handed Thomas his tux smiled politely and told them where the fitting rooms were.

Before the men disappeared, Paul let out a nervous chuckle, his pinched face showing concern. "Last night, Linda said the lace on her veil ripped. Wouldn't it be the last straw that sent her over the edge if my tux went missing?"

As though realizing the possibility existed, his face drained of color. He stood taller, and his gaze darted to the door of the back room. "We can't have another thing go wrong. I found out this morning the vegan dish we ordered for one of Linda's family members was written in as veal cutlets."

"We heard Linda yelling about the veil all the way from the carriage house last night," Matt whispered to Thomas. "You missed quite the show."

"Should be a double feature when she learns about the veal," Connor added.

"I took care of the meal," Paul said, his eyes widening and showing the stress of the last few days. "She doesn't need to know about that." His posture changed in a take-charge sort of way, as his gaze traveled from one groomsman to the next. "If they can't find my tux, no one here can tell her. I'll figure something out because she doesn't need this grief. I'll make sure everything is perfect." He waved his hand in the air. "Now, go try on the tuxes and make sure your clothes fit."

Paul's voice wasn't filled with fear of Bridezilla running rampant but rather with love and concern. His eyes softened and showed how much he wanted his bride to have her perfect day. Paul had always been protective of those he loved, caring for their mom like a worried mother hen. He had visited her several times, scheduled weekly calls with her, and texted her several times a day.

The men gathered their shirts, cummerbunds, and ties, then disappeared into the dressing rooms. Thomas looked back at his brother. He stood alone in the waiting area. Even from this distance, Thomas saw how anxious Paul was.

Thomas closed the changing room door and quickly swapped outfits. He had worn tuxes enough to know what went where, and his mind drifted to Paul as he suited up.

Paul's care of their mother had let Thomas off the hook, so he selfishly focused on himself. His brother picked up the pieces and became the man of the family.

Guilt covered Thomas, thick and syrupy as he put on the pants.

He missed his brother and having him around. For

Paul's sake, he didn't want anything else to happen with this wedding.

Thomas buttoned his shirt and started in on the tie. If Linda had screamed with a torn veil, she'd probably go postal about Ashley beating her down the aisle and creating more of a rift between the two brothers. Thomas had to keep his wedding a secret, but he still needed to warn Paul about Linda.

He put on the jacket and did a quick inspection in the mirror. Good enough. He needed to go back and check on Paul.

As he approached, Paul rocked from one foot to the other, and Thomas felt sorry for him. "I'm sure they have your tux," he said, placing his hand on his brother's shoulder. "Don't panic. Not yet, at least."

"Right. I need to pace myself."

Thomas grinned. Paul had a great sense of humor when he didn't take life too seriously. Thomas hoped marrying Linda wouldn't squash that part of his brother. "That's the spirit."

Paul took him in from head to toe and nodded. "You clean up well."

Straightening his tie, Thomas thought about clothing alternatives if a problem with Paul's tux existed. Certainly, there were other tuxedo rental places.

The other three men emerged in their tuxes, Connor doing his best to straighten his tie. The three men belonged on the pages of *GQ* magazine. The sales clerk checked the sizing and fit. She gave the men the typical you-look-dashing comments and asked them how the rentals fit.

Rentals.

Thomas hadn't expected to be part of the wedding party, but had he given it more thought, he would have brought his designer Hart Schaffner tux. The suit wouldn't have matched the others in the wedding party, but at least he wouldn't have to wear rented pants.

He had bought the tuxedo years ago for a black-tie formal engagement party for one of his best friends who had decided to finally tie the knot. His second best friend went a less traditional route when he made his way down the aisle. He'd have another chance to wear it once he officially moved to Nevada. Ian Ostern Memorial would throw a fancy shindig for him...and his wife.

A bubble of excitement welled up within him. He wanted to see Ashley again. They had tried calling each other, but their schedules never seemed to line up. Either she was out on a mini putt-putt range or horseback riding, or he was with the hospital staff or talking to a real estate agent.

As Matt complained about his jacket bunching and Mohinder assured him it was his imagination, Thomas wasn't sure how to help Paul. His brother did his best to hold it together, but Thomas recognized Paul's threshold window. He was old enough not to run crying to their mother. He was an adult and could handle things on his own. Hopefully, Linda would prove to be a good wife and help Paul with the stresses of life.

Maybe.

Matt, Connor, Brian, and Mohinder left to change, but Thomas stayed behind. He stood beside the tie table, collected the boxes by color, and arranged them in neat rows. He needed something to do while he waited for the next snafu in this wedding. The woman was taking a long time in the back room, which wasn't a good sign.

"Sir, how does your tux fit?" the clerk asked.

"Fine." Even had the suit needed alterations, Thomas would have said nothing as long as it didn't cut off his circulation. Slight changes wouldn't take long, but Paul didn't need any more issues.

As Thomas straightened the ties, he thought about his old *Three Musketeer* gang in Chicago. The other two also had children now. Thomas was the last bachelor holdout among the group. Forty, single, and alone.

Everyone in his inner circle had found their life partners.

Where had the time gone?

"I can't believe they're having trouble locating my tux." Paul stared at his watch and then paced. "I knew we should have gotten them on Sunday."

The clerk and a man came from the back room empty-handed. "It'll be another minute," she said in a comforting tone as she scanned the invoices and left again.

They waited for what felt like an eternity. Then, one

by one, the wedding party emerged in their regular clothes, their tuxes safely stowed in their garment bags.

"This is insane." Paul's voice was pitched higher, near panic levels now.

"Don't freak out." Mohinder swung his tux around his shoulder and stood by Paul. "We ordered the tuxes months ago." He nodded at Thomas. "Thomas got his tux in a week."

Paul took a few deep breaths and let them out slowly. He then closed his eyes, took another breath, and held it before shaking out his arms and exhaling.

"What are you doing?" Thomas asked.

Opening one eye, Paul stared at his brother. "Breathing exercises to calm down." He hit a button on his watch and repeated the motion.

Mohinder eyed Paul. "Is that helping?"

"It isn't hurting." Paul stopped the exercise and glanced at his watch. "I just don't want to get too upset, that's all."

Before Thomas could ask if there was a reason behind the exercises, Mohinder pointed at the sales clerk across the store near where Brian had wandered off. "Is Brian getting it sorted out?"

Thomas spun around and saw the best man. He'd been the first one back from the fitting room, and Thomas had lost track of him. Brian leaned toward the woman, and his body posture and calm demeanor meant one thing. He was hitting on the clerk instead of reassuring Paul. But guessing by the smile on the woman's face, she was flattered.

It was the same woman who had handed Thomas his tux. The one whose smile had been hollow.

"He's getting another number." Paul let out an exasperated sigh that held no ounce of hope. "He'll add hers to his collection. I think he's picked up a good seven or eight this week." He studied the woman as though seeing her clearly for the first time. "Brian has a wide range of types. I would have thought she'd have turned your head, Thomas."

This was a new development. Paul never talked in passing about Thomas's dating life. The subject had always remained a taboo topic between the two of them since Tina.

He must really be rattled.

Glancing at the sales clerk, Thomas wondered if she was his type. She was, yet he hadn't noticed her, other than her dismissal of him. His hottie radar was off. He gazed around the store and found two more sales clerks —both beautiful—that he had not noticed. One, with her light skin tone and red hair, resembled Ashley, but she wasn't as pretty.

"I'm surprised you haven't collected a few numbers yourself this week. Although, I noticed you didn't come home the last few nights."

Paul knew Thomas had been at Ian Ostern Memorial Hospital on business. Did he think the trip was a ploy to get out of wedding duties and hook up with loose women on the Strip?

He waved his hands dismissively. "I'm only teasing. I know you said you were out on business. Of course, you could have found a hot nurse."

Paul gave him a sly smile as though he knew Thomas had hooked up with some random stranger. This was lighthearted banter coming from his brother, something that—typically—he would have taken as a good sign. But not anymore. No other woman turned his head. Ashley had changed all that.

"What is this about a hot nurse?" Mohinder glared at him with anger in his eyes as though Thomas had crossed a line. Of course, Mohinder knew about the marriage between Thomas and his cousin.

"I had a meeting at Ian Ostern Memorial Hospital. There were no hot nurses. The hospital offered me the chief of plastic and reconstructive surgery position, and I accepted—with a few negotiation topics left to discuss. I toured the hospital, met the staff, and was treated to two dinner parties. It's an hour away, so I thought it best to stay up there until this morning." He then added, "Alone. As I said, no hot nurses."

"A job?" Paul's ashen face showed some hope. "That'd be great. Mom seemed okay while you were away. She only repeated stories a few times and managed to stay focused on the conversations, between her naps anyway. I think she did well because she was trying to make a good impression and not really being herself—like when we were alone and having lunch. When she's more relaxed, she shows more signs of dementia. Maybe we could research some nice homes for Mom near both of us to meet her needs."

"I've already considered that." Thinking of his mother needing a memory care place hurt him, but he knew they should make the move sooner rather than later. The hospital had some recommendations, and he had visited a few facilities. A couple seemed perfect for her.

"Someone's coming," Mohinder said, indicating the manager and sales clerk. "He's carrying your tux."

The man approached with the tuxedo wrapped in a zippered fabric bag. "Sorry for the confusion."

Paul's body visibly relaxed, the smile on his face became broad and cheerful, and he left to try on his outfit.

With Paul distracted, Brian still hitting on the woman, and the other two groomsmen across the store, Mohinder cornered Thomas before he could disappear into a dressing room to change. "Ashley asked me to do the paperwork for the annulment."

They needed someone to perform the role. Mohinder was the perfect choice. But something in the finality of having someone appointed to the task grated on Thomas. Perhaps if Ashley didn't consume his every thought, he would see other women and notice their existence. But something had changed.

"Thanks." He forced a slight smile as he kept his voice down.

"Ashley figured it would be easier for you to charge her for the annulment since she's in town. I can serve her the paperwork at any time. It'd be more difficult to serve you in person once you're back in Chicago." He gave Thomas a sheepish look. "I wasn't aware of the job position at Ian Ostern Memorial. Congratulations, by the way."

"Thanks." Thomas glanced away. Paul and the other groomsmen weren't within earshot. "That's still a good plan. It'll be weeks before I can officially move anyway."

"I printed the paperwork last night. You can sign it when we get back."

Nodding, Thomas realized that was probably what Ashley had been doing the last few days, even though they'd had a moment. She had been preparing the paperwork for the annulment. The moment, as lovely as it had been, had probably only confused her. He moved a chair and placed it in the row of other chairs in the store's small sitting area. He then moved the second one in line with the first. "Thanks for getting all that set up."

"Are you all right?" Mohinder tilted his head and studied Thomas as he straightened a third chair. "Are you having second thoughts about the annulment?"

He let out a nervous laugh, surprising him. Crossing his arms in front of himself, he feigned a slight smile. "Not at all. Ashley needs the paperwork signed so she can move on. She deserves to find the love of her life and—" He let out another nervous chuckle. "She should find someone better than me."

Mohinder's eyes narrowed, and he studied Thomas. "You're nothing like I expected."

"How so?"

"Paul described you as"—he pointed at Brian, who had gotten the woman's number and was now hanging out with Matt and Connor—"a more polished version of Brian."

"Of Brian?" Brian's hollow personality and insincere ways were nothing like Thomas. As the best man, he should have shown more support for Paul during the tux issue.

Thomas's chest felt heavy as he watched Brian and his colossal ego. He hadn't heard the pickup lines the man used and wasn't even sure what profession he was in, but Thomas figured he had seen far worse throughout the last few years and all the women Thomas had bedded. He had even played games with fellow hounds to see who could get the most phone numbers, who told the wildest stories and still managed to get laid, and who had the most notches in their bedpost.

His headboard was a splinter of wood from the past few years.

"Paul said you were a player like Brian. I don't know. I don't see it—hasty marriage to my cousin aside."

Naturally, that is how his brother saw him. Thomas knew it probably all stemmed from him marrying Tina.

"I don't see the comparison," Mohinder said. "You have a more loving nature to you. Ashley told me about your mother. I hope you don't mind. We've had some nice, deep discussions over the last few days."

Deep discussions? Thomas wasn't sure if that was good or bad, but he liked Mohinder. He was a good man. His thoughts drifted to Ashley, and he knew—thanks to the itinerary—she was out with his mother. All the ladies were getting their nails done, and he trusted her. She would make sure his mother was taken care of.

Okay, so maybe the itinerary wasn't a stupid idea.

"I haven't seen Ashley this happy in a while," Mohinder said. "She enjoyed some sort of treasure hunt you did."

A smile quickly spread across Thomas's face. "I enjoyed it, as well." The geocaching was probably the most fun he'd had in years, and the most expensive. The game had been over too quickly, just like the entire whirlwind week.

Nothing existed on the schedule for later this afternoon—for either the men or the women. Everyone was free from lunch until the rehearsal dinner. Perhaps he could spend more time with Ashley, not just because he needed her help in telling Paul the truth, but also because he wanted to spend time with her.

That was if she forgave him for sleeping with Linda. They hadn't had time to talk about that yet.

"She showed me the pictures on her phone and the chapel site. Besides the truly horrible wedding pictures, the two of you make a good couple."

"She showed you the wedding photos?" He had only glanced at them, more to confirm he had actually gotten married than anything else.

"And I watched the video."

Thomas had skipped the video and hated the idea of anyone watching it. He didn't want to see himself so sloppy drunk. But it did sound like the adequate proof he needed to help with his drinking problem and finally put the bottle down.

Mohinder gave him a sincere smile—one that lit up his face. "I enjoyed listening to your vows."

There were vows?

"I wasn't sure I liked you or even trusted you until I heard what you said to Ashley."

Thomas needed to watch that video.

The tiny dryer beeped and let Ashley know that her manicure had dried. She wasn't the bride, she didn't need to have her nails done, but at least she wasn't in the back room like the other ladies. The one good thing to come from chemo was that the hair on her legs—or anywhere else south of the border—had barely come back. Baby-fine hair that took forever to grow didn't need to be painfully waxed away.

Plus, she wasn't about to embark on a honeymoon where a husband would see her up close for any type of inspection.

"How beautiful. I love it."

Karen's voice nearly echoed in the salon shop. As the only people there, the wedding party had taken over the place. Thomas's mother had had her hair done and loved her wash and set, which brightened her face.

Oddly, she now thought of the woman as *Thomas's mother* and not Paul's.

"I think I'll do this deep red nail polish." Karen sat at the manicure station next to Ashley. "I wish I had such natural curls." She seemed openly friendly, and for a moment, Ashley thought the woman might touch her hair, but she didn't.

Ashley gave the woman her usual polite smile. It was her these-are-my-chemo-curls grin she gave people whenever they talked about her hair being naturally beautiful or, worse yet, when they asked her how she managed such beautiful ringlets. Going from wavy hair, to bald, to short hair with tight curls and eventually to long, loosely curled hair all within three years was not a hairstyle journey she'd recommend to anybody.

But now that she was at the other end, she had to admit that her hair had become darker and baby-soft. The new hair made her look younger. Her hairstyle hadn't really changed since high school, and the curls gave her a new look.

A look that, if she managed them correctly so they didn't frizz, she liked.

"I pay so much money to have my hair look like yours." Karen looked past Ashley to a large mirror on the wall and inspected her hairstyle.

No matter how much Karen paid, Ashley knew the cost of chemo treatments was far higher.

"I keep my hair shorter than you, dear, but I have to use a hair wand to get my hair to do what yours does."

A hair wand?

Nobody called curling irons that. At least, not anymore.

Karen set the nail polish on the table and began chatting with the nail tech who joined her at the station. Looking closely at Karen, Ashley noticed the signs of aging. The woman had kept herself trim and fit—and looked good for a woman in her early eighties—but she was mentally older than her age.

"It's so nice to have you as my daughter-in-law."

Ashley's head spun, and she gazed directly into Karen's eyes. Did she know? Thomas wouldn't have told her about their drunken marriage, and she studied the woman carefully. Finally, she figured the dementia was at play. "I think you're confused. I'm Ashley. *Linda* is marrying Paul, Mrs. Stallworth."

She had guessed right, and Karen's expression tore into Ashley's heart. The woman appeared both embarrassed and ashamed, especially since she and Linda looked nothing alike. Linda got the blond hair and blue eyes from the family, whereas Ashley took after her grandmother with the red hair and green eyes. And Linda was a good two inches taller. "Honest mistake. After all, she is my cousin, and you just met the entire wedding party."

Karen smiled, but Ashley knew the mistake still hurt the woman. She wondered if Thomas's mother knew about her condition and was concerned about it. On some level, you would think a doctor would have diagnosed her and told her about what would come.

Then again, Ashley only assumed the woman kept her yearly checkups. Fixed income. Newly widowed. Living alone. She may not.

"So glad that is over with."

Ashley had been so preoccupied with Karen that she had not noticed Linda making her way out of the back room. Judging by how she walked, she'd gotten all the hair below the belt taken care of.

"Your nails are already done?" Linda inspected Ashley's hands and then shook her head. "I thought you were getting your nails done, not just painting these short stubs a light pink color." The expression she had was one of slight disappointment. "It's a wedding. Splurge a little."

True. Ashley rarely spent money on pampering and the luxuries of life. She treated herself to a modest yearly vacation and some niceties of life—mainly after she had survived cancer and understood how precious life could be. But there was a practical side to her. "I can't massage people with talons like yours."

Holding her hand so the fingers folded under, Linda studied the waning effects of her last manicure. "I need to get these filled." Her eyes sparkled. "I think I'll put a clear rhinestone on one of my nails."

A plastic gemstone would cost way too much and be accidentally ripped off within hours, ruining her entire manicure. This was precisely the decadence Ashley refused to waste money on.

"Won't a gem distract from your wedding ring?"

"Thank you, Karen. I was going to say that myself," Ashley said.

"Good point. I'll go with a classic red shade." Linda stared at her engagement ring, and her expression told Ashley one thing: She was envisioning the actual wedding ring placed beside it on her manicured finger. Thank God Ashley and Thomas had found it.

Removing her engagement ring, she tentatively looked around. "I didn't bring a purse."

Her cell phone barely fit into her back shorts pocket, and she had nowhere to store the jewelry. "Can I put it in your purse?"

"Sure." Ashley took the ring and placed it in the inner pocket of her bag. "It's right here for when we're done." She glanced at the door leading to the back room. "Are the others almost done, Linda?"

Linda gently sat next to Ashley, wincing a bit from

the waxing. "They're a woman short today. Imani is only now getting waxed."

This outing would take all day. It wasn't as though Ashley had anywhere else to go, but she didn't like the smell of nail polish.

"You two ladies can start on your pedicures." A woman, who Ashley suspected was the place's owner, came from the back room and smiled politely at Linda and Ashley. She walked them to a section of the place with four-foot tubs and two employees waiting for them.

"I think I'll pass on a pedicure." Ashley took the seat next to where Linda now sat. "I can enjoy the massage chair, though."

"Get your feet done. It's all a part of the girls' spa day.'"

An unfortunate side effect of having chemotherapy was the loss of the nerve endings in your fingers and toes. Ashley's hands had been spared the effects, but her feet had not. "I still have numb toes." She wiggled her toes inside her shoes, feeling the loss of sensation.

"It hasn't gotten any better?"

"I've been working with a physical therapist, doing light therapy, and taking supplements to stimulate nerve regrowth. I still have about a five percent loss on the right side. Less on the left."

"Didn't you say you were over a fifty percent loss about a month after your treatments were done?"

Ashley hated how she'd felt during and after chemo, but years had passed, and she had done her best to detox her body. She needed to be grateful for where she was now. "Don't remind me. With every step I took, my numb toes reminded me of the cancer."

She took her hands and mimicked walking. "You had cancer. You had cancer," she said every time a hand came down as a step.

"Or, as I told you at the time"—Linda made the same hand motion—"you were cured. You were cured."

Ashley couldn't help but smile. Linda had been there through the entire ordeal. She had sat with Ashley for a couple of the infusions and understood what she had gone through. Rows of recliner chairs, each with IV poles, small tables, and wastebaskets next to them. People lying down with tubes sticking out of the ports in their chests where the needles could be more easily inserted. Infusion nurses, kind and compassionate, busy taking care of the heavy workload in a room that smelled like disinfectant and medicine.

It was a place Ashley never wanted to go again. The last time she had been there, she'd taken pictures with the nurses and proudly rang the bell by the door. She still had the poem on it memorized:

Ring this bell three times well. Its tune to clearly say: My treatment's done, my course is run, and now I'm on my way.

She received a certificate signed by all the nurses stating she had achieved health and wellness—a cherished reminder of her fight that now hung framed in her home. Everyone cheered as she walked out the door, just as she cheered for those that had rung the bell before her.

Ashley had made good friends during her treatments. She gently touched her port scar and caressed the small spot on her chest. The port, a piece of plastic with a thin tube running the length of her neck through her vein and directly into the upper part of her right atrium, had been surgically sewn to her muscle. Ports saved the veins in patients' arms from being destroyed by too many infusions. As much as she hated the device, it'd served a purpose, and the scar was a small price to pay for all it had done.

Linda leaned toward Ashley and held her hand. "I know that look on your face. You're worried your cancer might come back. It won't. You did everything to ensure it never returns." She smiled, and for a moment, Ashley recognized her mother and her aunt—Linda's Mom—reflected in her loving expression. "Besides, your feet aren't saying anything right now except that they want to be painted and put into beautiful shoes for a wedding."

She always did know what to say to make things better. Ashley smiled and sat back in the chair. "We can do that." Chemo killed all growing cells, which was why your hair fell out. But it also destroyed your nails. Most of Ashley's nails were fine now, but one of her toenails had fallen off and had never grown back correctly. It was a mangled mess and twice as thick as the others.

But it would look good with some nail polish.

The foot water was ready, and Ashley removed her shoes and sank her little piggies in. It had been a long time since she had treated herself like this. She needed to be more generous to herself and give in to the little pleasures in life, even if they seemed frivolous.

"By the way," Linda said, "great job keeping Thomas away. Hell, I haven't even seen him for a few days."

It was the one subject Ashley had done her best to avoid. She just wanted to enjoy the day, but since Linda had mentioned it... "He was out of town for business but should be back today and hanging out with Paul."

"Oh? Well, it's good he's back. They needed to get their tuxes." Linda's expression hardened. "I can't believe Paul postponed it until the last minute."

Scheduling anything after a bachelor party was ridiculous, but Ashley didn't want to mention the absurdity of the wedding itinerary. "There were reasons."

"I know, but Paul lets things fester in a last-minute type of way. I don't want him to feel stressed."

Ashley had known Paul to be high-strung in the past, but he had mellowed out over the time she had gotten to know him. Linda had a lot to do with that. Not with her schedules and checklists but with her careful planning and preparedness. "I'm sure he's enjoying spending some time with his brother."

"Don't be fooled by Thomas. He's a womanizer who

hurt Paul deeply." As if it only now occurred to her, she asked, "He isn't bothering you, is he?"

Bothering? Quite the opposite.

"He's been a perfect gentleman, and I've enjoyed spending time with him."

Linda nearly splashed her lady with the foot water as she turned her body to face Ashley. "No." Her eyes grew wide and held an accusing look. "You're not falling for that brute, are you? Tell me you're not."

Ashley looked away, not because she didn't want her expression to tell the story but because Thomas's mother was now moving to the nail dryer. She remained out of earshot, but Ashley felt the need to nod toward her and say, "Shhh."

"Thomas isn't a one-woman type of man," Linda said in a hushed whisper.

"He got married to Tina. Looks to me like he isn't afraid of commitment."

"And he probably cheated on her."

"What?"

Linda adjusted her legs so the woman could continue with the pedicure. "Well, I don't actually know. But that marriage broke up immediately, and typically there is only one reason for that."

"You don't know the whole story." Evidently, Thomas hadn't made the false pregnancy well known to the family. It made her feel even closer to him since he had shared the entire story with her. Of course, he had shared more than that. She had to ask, "Are you sure there isn't another reason you don't like Thomas?" *Maybe a more personal one,* Ashley thought.

"Like what? He stabbed my Paulie in the back. That's all I need to know about that loser."

Perhaps it was Ashley's expression of hurt mixed with anger, but Linda added, "Successful doctor aside, he hasn't been there for his mother since his father's death." She checked to make sure Karen could not hear their conversation. "Paul has done everything for the woman. I don't even know if Thomas cares what happens to her."

"He cares about his mother."

"He doesn't show it." Linda took a deep breath as though preparing to assault Ashley with more ammunition against Thomas but then shook her head. "I'm sure the man has some good qualities. Heck, I only just met him this week."

For a moment, Ashley almost believed her. Thomas had no reason to lie about the night he had spent with Linda, so why would he have fabricated the story?

"Besides, I would think you'd have more issues with him than I do."

Linda's snippy tone held a secret. "Why is that?" Ashley asked.

"He's a plastic surgeon."

Ashley had no problem with that profession. A demand for nose jobs existed, and not just due to vanity. People were involved in car accidents and needed facial reconstruction. Thomas helped people look and feel normal again. Even if someone had their nose done due solely to appearances, they had every right to feel good about themselves and raise their self-esteem.

"I don't care that he does rhinoplasty. So he fixes noses for a living. So what?"

Linda's face paled, and her jaw slightly slackened. "He isn't that kind of specialist."

"What kind is he?"

"He does breast reconstruction for people who have had cancer. People like you."

22

P eople like her.

    Ashley didn't know what to think about Thomas. He was the one type of doctor she had avoided during her months fighting cancer. All she could focus on during the pedicure and the lunch they went to afterward was how she had mistaken his specialty. Why had she been so sure he did rhinoplasty and not breast reconstruction? Was she so predisposed to think of plastic surgery as being only for the face?

Then again, when you heard hoofbeats, you thought of horses, not zebras.

Well, she wasn't thinking. That was her problem. But hadn't he told her he worked on the face? Or had she assumed, and he'd never corrected her?

Had he lied?

It all felt like such a blur now. They certainly could

have discussed his vocation at length during their drunken night.

But then, she hadn't told him everything about her job either, which was why the surprise massage had happened.

She thought about that day and how good his perfect body had felt under her fingertips. Pure fantasy had her thinking of him rolling over, removing the sheet, and pulling her toward him. How she could have felt the heat of his body against hers. Felt his hands on her body. How they could have made good use of that massage table.

She now sat outside the Bella Rosa in the cool breeze, rocking on the swing she had considered their spot. The well remained taped off and she sat all alone. She shifted positions, crossed her legs, and stared at the dark clouds hanging low in the sky. They matched her mood.

It was crazy to fantasize about the one man she could never be intimate with. Not just because she needed the marriage annulled and bedding your husband was a no-no offense to proving you didn't belong together, but because he would see her as a patient the moment she took off her shirt.

Since it was a part of the counseling from the BCRC, Brenda had encouraged her to at least speak to a specialist about breast reconstruction. She had reviewed pamphlets, seen videos, and knew exactly how the procedure was performed. She'd even met with a plastic surgeon before her mastectomy. The man's office was immaculate, and everything was perfect. Even the man's desk was organized and tidy. He had explained how many procedures his patients underwent—the reshaping of the new breast or breasts, the origami folding of the skin into a nipple, the endless tattooing for the right shade of red for the areola—that told her he was skilled and also a perfectionist.

Thinking back to Thomas, she figured he, too, suffered from perfectionism. The profession probably brought out that trait in all doctors. They were rebuilding a private and intimate part of a person's body. A part that had been stricken with illness and misshapen or removed. Those doctors paid attention to detail and because the patients wanted perfection they demanded it, as well.

How could she ever think of being intimate with a man who would only see her physical flaws?

A rumbling sounded in the distance, and the smell of rain became intense. The forecast called for thunderstorms tonight. Possible tornados tomorrow. Even though the weather had cooled, it would make for an unpleasant wedding.

More drama.

As she pushed off on the swing, her feet rhythmically tapping against the dirt, she wanted to escape. There was too much drama going around, and she hated it. Thomas still needed to tell Paul the truth. Linda had slept with Thomas, and…her breath hitched as she thought of Thomas. She needed to get the annulment done.

Then Thomas could return to his practice, and her life would resume its new normal.

She'd seen a breast surgeon for the mastectomy, an oncologist for the breast cancer, a dermatologist for the threat of skin cancer, a specialist for her potential pancreas issues…her geneticist helped her understand her BRCA2 diagnosis, and even an acupuncturist had helped her get through the worst of the chemo. And, after chemo was done, she'd added on the neurologist to help her with her numb toes, the place she went for ion foot baths to detox, and the fact that she'd done cryotherapy to freeze her body a good dozen times. That added up to a lot of doctors.

But not a single plastic surgeon was in the mix.

"I thought I'd find you here."

She knew it was Thomas before she even glanced up. The scent of his musky cologne was like a beacon that drew her in. In the crisp pre-stormy weather, the scent was piercingly good. He stood firm and handsome before her, and she wondered if he would tell her the truth.

"I sent you a text."

He had left her four.

She couldn't look at him. He was a cousin-screwing, breast-fixing liar. "I needed some alone time before the craziness of the rehearsal dinner tonight," she lied. She glanced at the sky. The rehearsal would have to move inside the barn. The Bella Rosa staff would be busy setting up chairs tonight, and the wedding schedule would be back-to-back to accommodate every wedding party. She wasn't sure how many weddings were scheduled, but a typical June Saturday held at least two.

It would be chaos.

A slight breeze caught his scent and wafted it closer to her, so she gazed at him. His hair was tousled, and he stood before her with a look of concern on his face. She did her best not to sound accusatory but composed. "Why did you have me believe you were a plastic surgeon that fixed noses all day?"

His expression changed to one of surprise. He stood taller and took in a deep breath, pausing before answering. "You assumed."

His answer wasn't the one she was searching for. "But you never corrected. Why?"

He nodded to the seat on the swing next to her, the same place he'd sat a couple of days ago. She slid over to make room for him, and he lowered himself. The swing creaked with his added weight and rocked forward.

Damn, he looked good.

"When people hear *plastic surgeon*, they always assume noses. They think my patients are vain people striving for that perfect profile."

His tone sounded prepared, as though he gave this answer often.

"People in car accidents need their noses and faces fixed. It's not about vanity. What is the real reason?"

His gaze shifted downward, and he let his body sink into the hard wooden boards of the swing. "People tend to view me differently when they know I do breast augmentations. If people think nose jobs are vain, you should see what people think of women who want..." His hands gestured toward his chest, his palm cupped as if silhouetting breasts. "It's not about vanity or that...I mean, I *do* breast augmentations on perfectly healthy and beautiful breasts that women want modified. But that's not why I...it just...I mean." He took a deep breath. "The women I help... I..."

Her eyes found his. "What?"

"The majority of my work is reconstructive. Women who have had lumpectomies, who have breasts that are different sizes, or whose breasts are misshapen due to the surgery." He glanced at Ashley, and his eyes wandered toward her chest. "I also work on women who have had mastectomies, both single and bi-lateral, where both breasts have been removed."

Ashley crossed her arms in front of her chest, her arms brushing against the two foam bumps. "I guess I understand that with all the women you date, some might feel awkward dating a man who handles breasts all day. I guess it'd be like dating a gynecologist. But why didn't you tell me?"

"I wanted to, especially when we were geocaching and getting close, but..." He bit his lower lip, and she could tell there was a secret he kept from her. One he didn't want to let out.

"But what?"

"Why didn't you tell me about your breast cancer?"

A thunderbolt clapped, and lightning streaked across the sky just as he said the word *cancer*. The display made the word even more devastating.

She glanced away, her body going rigid. Having had cancer was her secret. Hers to tell if she chose to. Something she didn't like to talk about and didn't want him to know. "Did Paul tell you?"

He pointed to her scar that lay hidden behind her blouse. "I saw your port entry the other day. You also have the softest skin and hair I have felt in a long time." He touched her hand and smiled at her curls. "I'm guessing your hair hasn't always been this curly."

Tears threatened to escape, the monster wanting out. She studied the darkening sky and did her best to hold them back as one finger coiled around a curl.

"You never mentioned cancer to me."

"Because I don't have cancer. I *had* cancer. I took care of it."

Dammit. A tear escaped and rolled down her cheek. Before she could wipe it away, his hand brushed her cheek and removed it for her. He now sat closer to her, his hands inches away…from foam.

"I love your attitude. You *had* cancer. I work with many women who live in fear and can never get to that point."

She had heard the same from Brenda, but her friend thought that she wasn't quite there yet.

"I didn't correct you when you thought I worked on noses because I thought you might feel awkward knowing what I do for a living—especially once I suspected you had breast cancer."

He was right. She had felt odd ever since finding out his profession, but mostly because of her personal situation. "Just because you handle breasts all day...I mean...I don't think that should make a difference if a woman were interested in you."

Obviously not, the man was gorgeous.

"It's just that..." She glanced down at her chest and took a deep breath, trying to find the right words.

"You never reconstructed."

Her gaze darted to his, triggered by the word 'reconstructed.'

"Breasts are never completely identical to each other. Yours are identical and perfectly shaped."

The breast foams were a 'left or right' matching set. Same size, same shape, same everything. Interchangeable for either the right or left side of the bra.

She wore the stupid expensive foobs so *no one* could tell. She wore them on the hottest days when they felt like pillows on her chest. They were high quality, weighted, and perfect. "I could have reconstructed. I just didn't want any more surgery. Besides," she said, once again glancing at her chest, "these are medical grade prosthetics. They're supposed to fool everyone."

He placed his hand on his thigh and seemed to care about his chosen words. "My career has me spending my days with women wearing partial to full prosthetics. I can spot natural, augmented, and fake from a mile away." He glanced at her chest but not in a lustful way, more so like a doctor. "Your prosthetics are exceptional. So much so that I can tell they are fake. They are perfectly symmetrical, and their weight has them hanging at exactly the same shape—even when you stretch and move your body, like when you plucked Linda's ring from the tree. They don't move like real breasts."

Had he been staring at her chest? Was it a sexual or professional interest? She honestly didn't know which she'd prefer.

"If you can't afford the surgery, you're still Mrs. Stallworth. I can put you on my insurance until the annulment. You could get your body perfect."

"Perfect?"

His eyes held a glimmer of hope, and his smile told her he genuinely wanted to help her. Help the poor, cancer-stricken massage therapist who couldn't afford to be put on a payment plan. She sucked in a deep breath, and her jaw tightened.

"Yes, perfect in a not completely symmetrical way."

"Perfect."

"I wouldn't work on you myself, but I can

recommend some great surgeons in the area. They do excellent work with transplanting the subcutaneous tissue, connecting nerve endings, shaping, nippling, and tattooing."

He sounded like all the doctors she'd gone to. Abstractly talking about her body, like it was clay and not flesh and blood. "I chose not to reconstruct because I'm done altering my body. This body," she said, waving her hand across herself, "has been put through too much already."

"You can reconstruct at any time. You can choose what size you want, as well. Insurance will cover it, and it's never too late to get the body you want."

"The body I want?"

"And the body you deserve."

His words sounded like a commercial.

"A doctor can reconstruct you so that no one can tell the difference unless they're close and touching them."

Her body recoiled from the idea of someone like him seeing her naked, let alone touching her. "The body I *want*?" Her body tightened, and she wanted to explode. "I don't want fake breasts. I want *my* breasts." She touched her chest and poked at the foobs she wore. "My breasts were lopsided, uneven, and absolutely beautiful." She wiped at the tears forming. "More importantly, they were mine. The body I *want* is the body I had to give up to survive."

His eyes beseeched her. "You can have everything that cancer took away."

He had no idea what cancer had taken from her. There was no way in hell she wanted to be cut side to side across her stomach—tummy tuck pleasantries aside —and have a dead zone of feeling where the huge scar would be. No nerve endings, no sensation. She didn't want fake boobs that would have no sensation, either. At least being flat allowed her to feel her chest.

"I am more than just a patient on your table. I am more than just a cancer survivor." She took a deep breath to steady herself. "I am more than the sum of my parts. And I don't need to reconstruct to fit into anyone's ideal image of what a woman should look like."

23

Ashley stormed off and left him at the well alone.

Thomas wanted to follow her, to throw his arms around her and comfort her, but all he could do was sit there and watch her leave as it started raining.

How could he have hurt her so much? All he wanted to do was help her, and now she was in tears.

He didn't understand women.

His words were the same as he used on all his patients. They all cried joyfully at his firm belief that he could give them what they wanted. The women were eager to reconstruct. Eager to have him restore what they had lost. Eager to move past their cancer and put it behind them with a new set of beautiful breasts.

Ashley was a unicorn. In every way.

He slowly walked in the opposite direction, back to the carriage house. The rain grew in intensity, and he made it to the porch before a downpour. He had already signed the paperwork that Mohinder had delivered for the annulment. He would suffer through Paul's wedding, return to Chicago, and prepare for his move and career change.

Life would go back to normal. New location. More responsibilities with his mother, but back to normal.

He hadn't even wanted to come to this wedding and knew nothing good would come of it.

He thought about the real estate agent he'd hired to search for a beautiful house—a house big enough for two people.

He had been a fool.

Opening the carriage house door, he found Paul fiddling with his tie. "Have you seen my tie tack?"

Matt and Connor were in their rooms, also getting dressed, and he wasn't sure where Mohinder was. When he didn't answer Paul, his brother asked again about his tie tack.

"I don't know, Paul. You can borrow mine. It's in the top dresser drawer of my room." Taking a seat on the couch, he knew he needed to get ready for the rehearsal dinner, but he didn't feel like doing so. Ashley would be there.

A knock sounded on the door, and a part of him hoped it was her, but he wasn't sure what he would even say to her.

It was Linda, wet umbrella in hand and a sour expression on her face.

Of course, it was Linda.

"Is he ready? The wedding coordinator is waiting."

She was the unhappy little B-side to this entire week of hell. Another woman he didn't understand and didn't care to. "He needs another minute," he said, gesturing for her to take a seat inside and wait.

He could have said hello. He could have told her she looked beautiful since she was all dressed up. Heck, he could have commented on the weather. He could have done many things, but all he could focus on now was how the time was running out for him to tell Paul the truth.

The rehearsal would be followed by a dinner and the wedding the next day. Paul would be married and off on his honeymoon after that. A trip with a two-faced liar who was likely using him.

Linda placed her dripping umbrella outside the door and entered. She paced the floor, and it was clear her anger at waiting grew. Staring at Linda's cold blue eyes, Thomas knew she'd never tell Paul the truth. She had paid Ashley to keep him away. She knew who Thomas was and exactly what she had done in that bedroom all those years ago.

"I'm sorry to hear about your mother's death," he finally said, trying to figure out a way to have her open up and confess. He crossed the room and stood closer to her. He couldn't ask her directly about their night because of her temper, so he thought he'd trip her up with small talk. "I noticed that your father was alone. Paul told me your mother died a few years ago."

Her eyebrows knitted together. "I always thought she'd be here for my big day." She bit her lower lip and appeared deep in thought. "She would have loved Paul."

For a moment, Thomas felt sorry for her, but he didn't know how to comfort her. Hell, he didn't even want to. He managed to say, "I'm glad your father is still with you."

A slight smile pulled at the corners of her lips. "My parents didn't get along. They'd probably have spent the entire time fighting if she were here."

"I'm sorry to hear that." He slowly walked around her, circling her.

"They had a troubled marriage that ended five years ago in a bitter divorce."

She was opening up. That was a good sign. "Sometimes, marriages don't work out." He was aware that Linda knew he had married—and divorced—Tina. Of all people, Linda should be grateful that Paul hadn't married the shrew. Of course, that's not usually how people saw things. He wasn't sure how much she knew but assumed the entire story was from Paul's perspective.

That probably accounted for her defiant posture and put-out expression.

They heard shuffling in the bathroom and Paul yelling that he'd be out soon. Linda smiled and nodded politely to Thomas.

That was when he caught sight of her tattoo. The ink rested on her upper arm; he had not seen it due to her outfits this week. "That's a nice tattoo." He stepped closer, knowing he had seen that exact shape before.

She glanced at the moon design on her right arm. "It's called a—"

"Celestial pair," he said, finishing her sentence.

"Yes." Her eyes narrowed as she gazed at him questioningly. "The sun is the other half. Are you interested in tattoos?"

"Not really." He wasn't sure if he was boasting and didn't want to be happy about the situation, but he had her exactly where he wanted her.

That tattoo was the final proof he needed, although he had thought it was a picture of the sun. He had been drinking that night, so it might have been the moon. Regardless, the artist's style was prominent.

Her phone rang, and she excused herself while checking her text messages. "The coordinator is getting impatient." She nervously glared at the closed bathroom door and then back at her phone. She seemed piqued but willing to wait. Until her eyes widened in what he believed was shock. Her fingers then flew into action on her cell phone.

She looked agitated until her phone buzzed again.

Had she remembered?

"Do you even remember me?" he asked.

"What?" An impatient tone sounded in her voice as she walked to the door.

"Five years ago," he said. "In Colorado." His voice

pitched higher and became more demanding as he stepped closer to her. "Sound familiar?"

"I don't know what you're talking about." She reached for the doorknob. "Can you please rush Paul and bring him to the barn, not the reflecting pond as it states in the itinerary. As soon as possible?"

She didn't wait for an answer. She opened the door and let herself out.

"No problem," he called after her. He didn't need to hear her confession. The expression of shock and the look of guilt she wore was evidence enough. She remembered.

As her high heels clicked quickly away, Thomas knew he couldn't wait anymore.

"Paul, hurry up," he said, knocking on the bathroom door. "We need to talk."

24

The world had changed in a bad way.

Paul hated him now more than ever. But at least his brother knew the truth.

It had only taken twenty minutes to go through the entire rushed rehearsal because another bride and groom needed to do theirs.

A quick walk down the aisle, some placement tweaks where the groomsmen and bridesmaids were told to stand on a piece of blue tape on the floor, and they were back up the aisle in a blur.

Probably for the best. Paul shot daggers out of his eyes at both him and Linda the entire time. The loathing look he gave Thomas and the seething disgust directed at Linda were painful to witness.

But what else could Thomas do? His brother needed to know the truth. But seeing him angry at the altar made Thomas want to leave. He had made things so much worse.

Deep down, he knew he didn't deserve to stand with his brother at the altar. He watched as Brian stood beside Paul. The man may be an ass, but he had his brother's back. Matt and Connor did, as well.

Despite his mother wanting him to be a groomsmen, Thomas's job would be that of an usher. Helping Linda's and Paul's friends find their seats. Nothing special. Nothing grand.

Thomas should never have come to the wedding. Right now, he was bearing the elements to drive to a restaurant for a festive dinner that would be anything but jovial. Paul had refused to get into his car for the short ride and had gone with Connor instead. No one but his mother wanted to ride with him. Even Ashley had ghosted him.

He was the relative no one wanted but tolerated because of the special event.

"This is so lovely," his mom said as he escorted her into the private dining room. Two large tables draped in white linen sat in the center of the room. Tiny tea lights reflected light through their glass candle holders, white place settings with gold trim lay stacked at each seat, and crystal goblets for water and wine were at the ready for what promised to be a beautiful evening.

"This is your seat, Mom, next to Paul and Linda."

Thomas sat his mother down at the place setting with her name on it. She sat across from Linda's father and the rest of the key players: Linda, Paul, the maid of honor and her date, and Brian and his date. Thomas found his name at table number two with the other two bridesmaids, Ashley, Matt, Connor, their significant others, and Mohinder. He didn't know the other party members well, so he quickly switched his placement. He now sat beside Ashley and Mohinder. It also offered him the seat farthest away from Paul and would possibly give him a chance to talk with Ashley.

"Daddy, you made it." Linda walked into the room and hugged her father. She and Paul made the rounds and greeted all the guests as they arrived. The small talk ate away at him. Paul couldn't have appeared more upset, which turned Thomas's stomach.

And then, Ashley walked in wearing a ruffled dress that showed no cleavage, a matching purse, complementing jewelry, and a smile that lit up the room. Simple elegance. Classy. Stylish.

And totally pissed.

She had ignored him as much as possible during the torture of the rehearsal. Even now, she barely made eye contact with him. She greeted everyone but made a point not to say hello to him.

Once everyone took their seats, he held out Ashley's chair for her. If nothing else, she'd sit near him for a meal. He'd be able to talk to her. Be able to apologize.

Ashley glared at the name on her seating placement and noted that she sat next to Thomas. "Brian," she said, turning to the other table and pointing at the seat next to him. "You said your date didn't arrive because of the bad weather. Can I sit next to you?"

Thomas tightened his grip on the back of the chair he held for her as Brian cheerfully said she could sit at the grown-ups table. Ashley even giggled at the lame joke.

Before she left, she shot Thomas a quick glance. The type that your opponent had when they won a point off you. But the game wasn't over yet.

Thomas pushed the chair in and took a seat.

"Thomas, this is Nick." Mohinder's voice filled with pride as he introduced his boyfriend. The man was lean and handsome—a perfect match for Mohinder. The two made a beautiful couple and seemed happy together.

He wished Ashley had wanted to sit next to him. "It's nice to meet you, Nick. I'm glad you could make it to the wedding."

Taking a deep breath, he needed to find a way to get Ashley alone.

The salads came with a side dish of chitchat. Matt's and Connor's wives talked about the kids and how they never had time to see each other—they then both promised to do better and to make time. Judging by Matt's and Connor's conversations, they worked together doing something boring.

Nick leaned closer to Mohinder and got Thomas's attention. "Is the redheaded one Ashley?"

Mohinder quickly said, "Shhh," and then whispered into Nick's ear. He then leaned toward Thomas. "I'm sorry. He saw your signed document in my room and asked."

Overall, Nick knowing didn't matter.

Ashley laughed at something Brian said and seemed so engrossed in talking with him that she must have decided to move on. Whatever they had between them, no matter how special Thomas had thought it was, obviously hadn't been as important to her.

The waitstaff entered with trays and served the main course, taking away the salad dishes to make room. A salmon filet now sat in front of him while others at the table were served either chicken or beef. He figured the meal selections had been made ahead of time. He'd never talked to anyone about what he wanted to eat, but he loved salmon.

But he knew Paul didn't. Disgust now replaced the scowl Paul had worn throughout the meal. Thomas heard little from the first table but could make out Paul's protest about eating the fish.

Paul's face reddened, and everyone stopped talking to stare at him.

"I told you I wanted the steak, but I guess what I want doesn't matter." Paul pushed the plate away and glared at Linda.

"You need to eat more fish." Linda studied him carefully and added, "You've been in a bad mood since the rehearsal. What is going on?"

Paul's eyes narrowed, and his gaze shot straight for Thomas. "We can talk about it after dinner."

Linda followed Paul's stare. "Oh, no." She stood and pointed to Thomas. "Has he upset you again?"

In a look like hellfire, Linda fixated her hatred on Thomas to where, for a moment, he was actually scared she might explode. "He shouldn't have come to the wedding."

"Why?" Paul stood and turned Linda around so she faced him. "Why shouldn't *he* have come?"

Thomas saw the profile of her face, and she seemed to be in shock. He supposed no one had ever spoken to her in that tone of voice before.

"Because he aggravates your blood pressure." Anger laced her words.

"Never mind my blood pressure."

"Someone needs to keep you healthy, because heaven knows you don't watch out for yourself."

Paul's fingers tapped behind his ear again as they had the other day, and Thomas understood the motion. The tapping, the non-beef meal. Paul had a threat of high blood pressure, which ran in their family. Their father had even died of a heart attack.

"I've done everything I can to keep that man away."

"That wasn't all for me, Linda, now was it?"

"What the hell are you talking about?"

Paul's gaze darted from her to Thomas and back again. "Five years ago. In Colorado. A Hilton hotel room. Ring any bells?"

Thomas thought his salad might come back up. He

stood and said, "Paul, we can talk about this back at the resort."

"We'll talk about it now." Paul pulled a small box from his pocket. "I asked Thomas to hold on to your wedding ring until the wedding tomorrow. I borrowed a tie tack from him and opened his dresser drawer. Imagine my surprise," he said, opening the box and holding it up to her face, "when I saw not just your wedding ring in the drawer but also your engagement ring."

"This ring?" Linda held up her hand, and the light caught the diamond from the engagement ring on her finger. "I don't know what that ring is."

Thomas gasped. He had placed the replacement ring in his drawer and forgot it was near his tie tack. Linda's real wedding band was in his nightstand. They were in identical boxes, and he had kept them apart. "I can explain."

"Shut up," Paul said, dismissing Thomas. He tossed the ring box onto the table and faced Linda. "Are you going to deny that the two of you slept together?"

The room fell deathly silent. And if Thomas thought Linda had looked angry before, it was nothing compared to how her reddened face contorted now. Her body went rigid, her fingers balled into fists, and she had slits for eyes. She stormed to the doors of the private room. "Everyone but Paul, out." She then pointed at Thomas. "The ass in the corner stays, as well."

The people in the room scurried like mice as

Thomas felt his legs grow weak. This was it. Paul would hate him forever, but at least the truth would be out.

"You stay, too." Linda grabbed Ashley's arm as she was about to leave the room. She closed the door with a heavy thud, and Ashley looked as scared as Thomas felt.

With everyone else gone, Thomas said, "It happened a long time ago."

"Like never!" Linda leaned in. Her eyebrow rose behind her bangs. "What makes you think I slept with your brother? I'm not Tina."

Throwing that name in Paul's face only angered Thomas more. Bitch or not, she was going down. "Linda, I know you remember because of the expression on your face right before the rehearsal when you stormed out of the carriage house." He pointed his finger accusingly at her. "Your face went as white as a sheet, and you scurried out as fast as possible when I mentioned Colorado."

"I stormed out because I wasn't wearing my engagement ring." She turned to Paul. "I didn't take it off because I was unfaithful to you. I took it off because I was getting a manicure, and Ashley was holding onto my ring. I left the carriage house to get it out of her purse." She gestured at Ashley. "Tell them."

Ashley's gaze went from one person to the next. She even made brief eye contact with Thomas. "She's telling the truth. She asked me to keep her ring in my purse while we had our nails done. She texted me right before the rehearsal and said she didn't want to practice the wedding without it. I told her my purse was on my bed in my room and said to get it out."

That explained her reaction, but Thomas still questioned it. "Regardless of the ring, I told Paul everything." His eyes narrowed in on Linda. "*Everything*."

"Everything?" She closed the distance between her and Thomas and put her fists on her hips. "Well, please enlighten me."

He didn't want to go over details and certainly hadn't done so earlier when he told Paul about the two of them, but he felt like he had no choice. "We were both a bit drunk. I doubt drunk enough that you wouldn't remember. It was five years ago at a conference in Denver."

She shook her head, her blond locks grazing her shoulders. "I wasn't in Denver five years ago. What conference?"

"You don't have to deny it now. We should get everything out in the open before we get married."

"Hush, Paul. I want to hear from Mr. Sleaze. What conference?"

Linda had walked him back into a corner of the room, so he stood taller and confronted her. "The Laztec Medical Conference. End of day three. Boring lectures. I was at the hotel bar when we bumped into each other. Your name *L. Higgenbothem* barely fit onto your name tag. You had a room on the fourteenth floor. We were in the elevator already"—he glanced toward Paul and then to Ashley—"we barely made it to the room," he finished in a more hushed tone.

"Really? From what I know about you, you sleep with any woman breathing. Are we to believe that you remember *any* of their names?"

"That's the takeaway you got from that story?" Paul accused.

"No," she said, holding up one finger on her hand, telling him to wait a minute. "He can't keep it in his pants, and he makes up a story about me with such vivid details like this? It's a complete lie."

"I know the name on the name tag. *Higgenbothem* was such a unique name. I was drunk—"

"Drunk? Yeah. Because you always make good decisions when you drink," Linda spat back at him.

Thomas felt a bubble of anger rising. What caught his attention was that Ashley glanced away. He didn't want her to hear any details about the night, but the truth needed to come out. "I joked at the time that your name seemed similar to hug-a-bottom, and you said, 'By all means.'"

Her mouth gaped open in what looked like feigned shock.

"That's another look I remember well." Thomas didn't want to pitch a war with Paul's bride, but she had thrown down the gauntlet.

She took another step toward him. "Well, maybe it was another L. Higgenbothem. Have you ever thought of that?"

"Another L. Higgenbothem?" Ashley asked.

"Sure, why not? My mother was an L. Higgenbothem. There are probably many women with that name."

Paul crossed his arms, and his jaw tightened. "Women who look exactly like you?"

"Evidently." Her tone tightened, but she wasn't backing down.

"With a celestial pair tattoo?" Thomas countered. Linda's arrogance ticked him off. How much longer would she perform this charade? "Give it up, Linda. The name, the body, the ink...it was you."

"Oh, God." Linda's face turned ashen, and her body nearly crumpled. She steadied herself with the back of a chair. "Oh, my God."

She did remember. As much as Thomas loved being right, a part of him felt sorry for Paul. His bride had slept with so many men that she couldn't even keep track of them.

"No, no. Oh, God, no."

"Linda, it was a long time ago," Ashley said in a reassuring tone. "We all have pasts. You and Paul can get over this. I'm sure of it."

Ashley was right. Thomas wanted his brother to be happy. Maybe now, with no lie between the couple, they might have a chance at a good marriage. Maybe. "I'm sorry, Paul. I didn't want to ruin your wedding day. I just wanted you to know the truth."

His brother's expression showed his defeat, yet he

held out his hand and placed it on Linda's shoulder. "It was long ago, and I can tell you didn't remember. You weren't trying to lie to me."

"It wasn't me," Linda said in a raspy voice. "I wasn't the one." She took a gulp of air. "I might be sick."

Enough was enough. She was a good actress, but there was one more piece of evidence, and Thomas wasn't afraid to use it. "So, if it wasn't you, why pay Ashley to keep me away from you and Paul this week."

"You did what?"

"She paid me, Paul. She wanted me to keep Thomas occupied."

Linda glanced up, her expression confused. "I wanted you away from Paul, not me. His doctor diagnosed him with high blood pressure. I wanted him to get through the wedding without a lot of stress. When your mother insisted you be invited, Paul was so agitated I thought he'd have a heart attack like your father."

"My blood pressure is fine." Paul's tone suggested one thing: He didn't want to talk about his health. He tapped behind his ear again.

"Paul, I never slept with your brother." Her face creased as though she were about to cry. "My mother was *Laura* Higgenbothem. She was a physician's assistant for years. *She* attended that conference."

Ashley gasped.

"You mean...?" Paul's eyes widened, and he glared at Thomas. "My brother slept with your *mother*?"

"A celestial pair tattoo. She had the sun. I have the moon." She glared at Thomas. "Was the tattoo of a sun?"

Thomas could barely breathe. His knees felt weak, and he took a seat at the table. "Yes."

The three joined him. "Your mother." Shame crawled up his body, and he hated the feeling. "I slept with your mother. Wait, there is a huge age difference. I would have known."

"They looked like sisters," Ashley said.

"Sisters?" Thomas nodded his head, trying to take in everything. "Your mother, who looked exactly like you, slept with me."

"You don't have to keep saying it." Linda's body shook in disgust. Her face contorted, and she let out a *bleh* sound that resembled gagging. "I can't even look at you."

Thomas focused on Paul. His mad, reddened face was now pale, and his stance was no longer defiant but sympathetic to Linda.

"This is so much worse," Thomas said.

Paul, whose eyes were still widened with surprise, shrugged. "I never met Laura." He put his hand atop Linda's and gently patted. "I think you sleeping with Laura is better than you having slept with my Linda."

Linda opened the palm of her hand and allowed

Paul's fingers to slide between hers. "She…after my dad…" Her voice trailed off. "My dad."

"Shh," Paul said in a comforting tone.

She gasped for air and got out, "After she and my father divorced years ago, she had a wild side." She quickly held up her hand while trying to compose herself. "Don't tell my father. I know it was years ago, but we don't need to bring this up." Her eyes had daggers in them. "Especially don't mention it at our wedding."

"Nobody will say anything," Ashley agreed. "We'll say tonight's argument was all a misunderstanding."

Ashley had always been easy to read, but not now. Thomas figured she, too, was disgusted by him.

God, he had slept with Linda's mother. Ashley's aunt.

A shiver of disgust ran down the length of his spine.

"Don't worry," Paul said. "I'm not going to say anything to upset my future father-in-law." Paul's eyebrow rose as though he suddenly remembered something. He then pointed at the ring box on the table. "Then how did this second wedding ring set get into your drawer, Thomas?"

So much for dodging the second bullet. But after the news about Laura, how could this be all that bad? "I temporarily lost Linda's wedding ring."

"You what?" Linda nearly shrieked.

"We *temporarily* lost your ring, Linda," Ashley said, taking half the blame. "But we found it again."

"That's right," Thomas quickly said, noting that Linda's face was gaining a reddish hue again. "It was only gone for a day, but I wasn't sure we'd get it back. So, I searched online and ordered a replacement. I was lucky it came so quickly."

Paul picked up the ring box with the name Jay's Jewelers on it. He opened the box and inspected the bling. The light from the overhead fixture caught on the diamonds' facets and sparkled. "I know a guy and got a great discount. You paid retail for this?" He let out a whistle. "Damn. I should have become a doctor." He removed the ring to read the inscription, which matched Linda's ring. "Carelessness aside, you love me enough to replace this thing?"

"It's your wedding, Paul." Thomas didn't know what else to say.

Paul's face lightened, and a glow came about him. "Wow, I misjudged you. Here I thought you and Linda were pulling another *Tina* on me."

"Paul." Linda gently placed her hand atop his. "You're my Paulie. My Paulie for life, baby." She planted a kiss on him and hugged him.

Thomas felt tears welling up. He had misjudged Linda. The two made a sweet couple, and once the embrace ended, she was actually smiling.

But it didn't last long.

"And that brings us to something else I wanted to discuss." Linda reached into her pocket and held up another ring set. Two single bands with diamond chips. "Would you mind explaining these?"

"What is it?" Thomas asked.

Ashley sucked in a deep breath, and Thomas turned toward her. Her head now rested on her hand. "It's my ring." Her shoulders sank. "Our rings."

Now he recognized the set. They'd never returned or exchanged them. He could barely breathe. It was as if the air got sucked out of the room.

"Why do you have one of Ashley's rings?" Paul asked. "And one of Thomas's rings?"

Linda didn't exactly looked pleased with herself but rather proud that she had uncovered a secret. "When I got my engagement ring from Ashley's purse, I found these in the same side pocket. Both from Pair O' Dice Wedding Chapel."

"What?"

"They got married, Paul." Linda set the rings on the table, and they both looked at Thomas and Ashley for answers.

Thomas shot Ashley a glance that she picked up on. She was good about knowing what he was thinking, and she nodded as she took her ring off the table and held it. Since the entire wedding party was still locked outside, Thomas came clean about everything.

25

A shley gulped down the mug of coffee, not even caring that the brew had gone cold.

She and Linda had stayed up all night talking. The drunken night, the lost ring, the geocaching. It answered many questions Linda had about why Ashley had been MIA so much.

The one that remained unanswered was whether Ashley was in love with Thomas.

That question hurt too much to put words to, and it had kept her up long after Linda had gone to bed.

And now, in the light of day, she still didn't have the answer.

She pinched the fabric of the teal bridesmaid dress, and her fingers grasped inches of material. There was too much dress in certain areas and much less in others. Her foobs did their job and held up the dress's form, but the cleavage and sides were lower cut, and the bra's material peeked through.

Why had she agreed to wear such a revealing dress?

God, why did Linda have to pick out such a low-cut style? It was summer, but… She inspected herself in the mirror again, not enjoying her reflection.

A sloshing sound came from the cottage's deck just before the door creaked open. Brenda stepped in, her shoes and hat dripping with rain.

Linda's big day or not, the weather was not anyone's friend today. The women were on weather duty last night, watching the local news station's radar maps. The storm wouldn't clear until Monday afternoon at the earliest. Now that all the secrets had been shared, the next big drama to focus on was the storm and where the ceremony would occur.

But wasn't it good luck if it rained on your wedding day?

"It's coming down in sheets." Brenda shook her coat and removed it, which caused a spray of rain to fly off. "We set the barn up last night as a contingency plan for the wedding. It'll have to serve as both the venue and the reception." She placed her dripping umbrella by the door. "We have one more wedding this evening, and they are marrying in the gazebo. Their guests will be under that big tent we have."

A giant thunderclap sounded.

"If the tent doesn't blow away that is," she added.

It was only nine in the morning. Ashley knew Brenda would worry about all the Bella Rosa brides, but Ashley could only focus on this wedding. In particular, the dress showing too much of her stupid mastectomy bra.

"Do you have a safety pin?" she asked, knowing the chances were slim. None of the bridal party had one, and right now, she'd settle on a bulky clothespin to close off the cleavage of the drape-of-a-dress she wore.

Brenda tilted her head and took in the gown. She grinned and nodded. "Girl, you are wearing that dress."

The compliment was nice to hear, but Ashley had eyes. She knew better. "I want to make sure I *keep* wearing this dress when I'm standing at the altar."

Studying the way the teal cascading fabric fit, Brenda said, "It fits you like a glove. Why do you need a pin?"

Ashley raised her arms and showed the imperfection. "You can see this hideous thing. All the other women have those boob tapes or bras with low cutbacks. But no." She raised her hands and turned to her side. "You can easily see my disgusting bra in this dress."

"Then put your hands down."

Brenda was no help. She was familiar with mastectomy bras and how ugly—and expensive—they were. No one wanted to sport one of those nasty things. Ashley had even dressed in her own room, not wanting to be part of the bridal party getting ready with their lacy bras and stuck-on ledges. It was bad enough the open-toed shoes showed the toenail that had gotten screwed up from the chemo. She didn't need everyone to see her delicates that resembled what Robin Williams wore as Mrs. Doubtfire.

"Seriously," Brenda said. "The dress looks great on you."

"Whatever." Ashley waved her hands like a fan in front of her face. The weather had cooled considerably since the rainstorm had struck, but she felt flushed.

Brenda took a seat on the couch. "What's got you all in a tizzy?"

What bothered her had nothing to do with the wedding. Rain pounded on the cottage's roof and streamed down the window panes. Getting the women in the bridal party to the barn would take umbrellas and rain smocks, but it was doable.

What wasn't doable was spending the day with Thomas. Confessing to Paul and Linda that they'd drunkenly gotten married was embarrassing enough. But at least no one knew about him wanting to *fix* her body.

"Does your mood have anything to do with that hunky doctor husband of yours?" Brenda's eyebrows waggled suggestively, and Ashley remembered the massage Brenda had orchestrated. Brenda's heart was in the right place, but Thomas wasn't the man for Ashley.

"Thomas…"—she shrugged—"it's nothing."

"Sounds like a little something." Brenda's eyes widened. "Is that it? Is it a *little* something?" She held out her hand flat toward her. "Because, honestly, he has big hands." She moved one finger across like a measuring tape and nodded approvingly.

Ashley's mood had nothing to do with that. Not that she knew the size of anything on Thomas. She sat with Brenda on the couch. Briefly, she filled her in on the chaos of the last few days, including more details of her unintentional wedding, the ring mix-up, and how Thomas had slept with her aunt. Moreover, how the bride and groom had learned everything during a dinner party that could only be described as a horror scene.

Ashley was impressed that she summed up the chaos so quickly.

Brenda's eyes widened, and her jaw fell slightly agape. "They need to make a movie out of that."

A smile curled the corners of Ashley's lips. One day it will be a funny story, but not yet. "Husband or not, Thomas thinks I need to be *fixed*." She made air quotes with her fingers, and Brenda had to ask why.

"Oh, I forgot one important detail," Ashley said. "Thomas doesn't do rhinoplasty. He does breast reconstruction—mostly for women who had breast cancer."

Brenda let out a burst of laughter, followed by a snort that she apologized for. "I see Anna Kendrick playing you in the movie."

"It's not funny. He said I could have the *perfect* body if I wanted." Again, she used air quotes. "He's a perfectionist who thinks a woman can't be a woman without boobs."

Brenda's eyes narrowed skeptically. "Are those *his* words?"

"No, but you should have heard him." Ashley thought about what he had said, but she fixated on the word *perfect* more than anything else. "He went on and on about how I can have the body of my dreams."

"I see." Brenda took in the information and seemed deep in thought. She finally said, "And a woman doesn't need breasts to define herself as a woman."

Ashley heard the words as they were said. They resonated with her and hit her in the dark place she went to whenever she had a pity party. The dark place where the monster lived. "Okay, I get it. I know I feel…" She paused and searched for the words. "I don't feel complete without the foobs on."

Honestly, she didn't go out without her foobs, not even to put her trash can outside on collection day. She even had a pair made of plastic beads for when she went swimming. Hating her flat chest, she hid it from the world, even though she didn't want to reconstruct.

"But *you* don't need breasts," Brenda said.

"Of course, not."

Patting the cleavage of the dress, Ashley inspected its fit. The chest would sag without her prosthetics. Comfortable T-shirts were more her style when she lounged around at home.

"You are an extremely beautiful woman, even if you took those foobs off right now. I doubt the men attending this wedding would even notice the bride or the other bridesmaids if you were in the room."

Brenda was a highly recommended counselor at the BCRC and helped many women through their breast cancer journey. Her comforting voice, reassuring smile, and personal history with cancer had drawn Ashley to her.

She studied herself in the mirror. She was a survivor. She could handle anything. She needed no one to feel sorry for her. "I've totally got this." She sat straighter, pushing the monster back into a dark mental cave, and felt empowered. "I don't need Thomas to..." She paused and then nodded, strengthening her resolve.

"To what?" Brenda asked.

Ashley held her head up high. "To approve of what my body looks like."

"Do you really think that was what he was trying to do?"

The question made her pause. Thomas wasn't the type to belittle her. He had been wonderful over the past week. But his words. *Perfect body*. It made her stomach twist in disgust.

"You've had a bad body image since your surgery." When Ashley complained, Brenda held up her hand to stop her. "Do you remember how you described the women who sat in the infusion room with you getting their chemo?"

Ashley stared at the floor. Of course, she remembered. Sitting in that chair and getting those chemicals dripped into you for hours was something you remembered every detail of.

"How did you describe them?" Brenda prodded.

"They were like exotic, frail birds lying there, all beautiful and helpless," she said in a hushed tone.

"Exotic. Beautiful." Brenda reached for Ashley's curly hair and caressed it. "And how did you describe yourself."

Shaking her head, Ashley refused to answer.

"You lay in that chair. No hair. No eyebrows. A good thirty pounds heavier due to the steroids you were on." Brenda paused slightly. "You always said…"

Ashley rolled her eyes. "That I looked like Darth Vader dying."

"Like the *evil* Darth Vader. Burned. Pasty, sickly skin. No eyebrows. Lying there dying."

Ashley wiped away a tear. "I can't cry right now. I'll ruin my makeup."

"Then ruin it." Brenda handed her a tissue box from the side table. "You were hard on yourself then, just like you're hard on yourself now. You've often told me how you'd like to find a good man like my Hershel." Her eyes widened. "Well, honey, you found one. You need to talk to him."

"Uh, didn't you hear what he said to me?" She used air quotes again. "Perfect body."

Brenda's hand went to her hip. "You heard his words, but did you listen to him?"

"What?"

367

She shook her head and let out a sigh. "You often say that Hershel is a dream husband. So supportive, so loving. His most compassionate trait is his ability to listen."

"Yeah." Ashley's eyes widened, and she nodded exaggeratedly. She then waved her hand toward her friend. "*You* got the only good guy around."

"Puh-lease." Brenda rolled her eyes. "Men, in general, like to fix things. It's in their nature. Years ago, Hershel and I had our biggest fight ever. I was upset about my boss, my job, you name it. Hershel kept jumping in and telling me to quit the damn job or demand a raise. Hell, he even told me to try to get my boss fired."

"Sounds bad, but I don't see how that—"

"I'm getting there. I don't even remember what I was so hot about. But"—her hand went up, and she paused and made sure she had Ashley's attention—"we weren't fighting about the job."

Ashley couldn't even imagine Hershel raising his voice. Brenda, on the other hand, was a passionate and formidable woman. "What was the fight really about?"

She nodded like the answer was obvious. "He wasn't listening. He jumped in and tried to fix my problem for me. Like I wasn't woman enough to handle it myself."

Ashley understood that completely. Every man she'd ever dated had done that to her. "That's what Thomas did."

"Of course. All I wanted was for Hershel to listen to me. Now he understands that when I vent and get nearly irrational over something, he just needs to listen and agree that I'm absolutely right in feeling that way. I may be wrong, but I need to know that he is on Team Brenda and agrees that I have a right to *feel* the way I do. Still, men want to fix our problems."

"I don't need Thomas to fix my problems."

Brenda's eyebrow rose, and she pointed at Ashley. "And you're just as guilty. You weren't listening to him, either." Brenda leaned in and placed a hand on Ashley's shoulder. "Fixing our problems is what men do when they are in love."

"In love?"

"Honey, the way Thomas's face shines when you enter a room..." She made a satisfied noise in the back of her throat. "That man has it bad for you. He just doesn't know how to listen and step back so you can make your own decisions."

"But the way he went on and on about how the new medical breakthroughs can fix me...." Her voice cracked. She had been sliced open and robbed of her femininity. There was no way to fix what she had been through.

"Is he a good doctor?"

The question threw Ashley. "He's at the top of his field."

"So, a man whose specialty is to reconstruct breasts

wanted to jump in and help you, and that was a bad thing?"

"Well…"

"You're mad because he tapped into one of his strengths. He probably figured you were like all the other women who come to him for help. And he wanted to help you because he cares about you."

Her breath hitched. She remembered the concern in his eyes as he asked her why she hadn't told him about the cancer. He had known for days but hadn't said anything. He'd waited for her to initiate the conversation.

But did he truly understand how she felt?

"I haven't seen him since after the rehearsal dinner. He knocked on the cottage's door several times last night, but the ladies did me a solid and didn't let him in." She thought about how soaking wet he must have been standing in the rain.

He had stood outside in the middle of a *thunderstorm*. For her.

Brenda's phone rang. The ringer was a sound bite from the song, *Holding Out for a Hero*, which was the song the device played when Hershel texted her. She glanced at the text message. "This isn't good."

"Is Hershel okay?"

"Yes, but we might have a problem. I gotta go."

"We're still waiting for the minister to arrive." Brian checked his watch and didn't look hopeful. He, Matt, and Connor were dressed in their tuxes and staring out the window at the downpour. "The weather is terrible. Are you sure Father Perin can make it?"

Paul tapped the side of his neck. Again.

Thomas figured by the time the man said "I do," his neck would be raw.

"The wedding will be fine," Thomas reassured him. "Hershel and his crew set up the barn last night. It'll be great."

Lightning lit the sky and brightened the entire room, but Thomas stood his ground. "There are only tornado watches in the area. No sightings."

"And it hasn't even begun to hail," Connor said.

Matt was on his phone. He hung up and shrugged. "Becky isn't coming. She and the kids are staying home."

Connor's wife had done the same thing. Brian had a similar excuse, but Thomas wondered if the man had made up his plus one for the wedding.

"It'll be fine." After everything that had happened over the past week, how could the weather stop his brother from having the perfect wedding?

And there was that word again. *Perfect.*

His thoughts immediately went to Ashley, but he shouldn't focus on her right now. She had refused to speak to him last night. She'd probably do the same today. He needed to stay focused.

"Mom is already at the barn," he told Paul. "She's doing okay. Of course, she already started her day drinking.

"She may have the right idea."

Thomas let out a chuckle once he realized Paul had made a joke. When his brother relaxed, he was always fun to be around. They'd have to talk about the high blood pressure, but not today. Today was all about him and Linda.

Linda, the woman who probably still didn't want to lay eyes on Thomas. Holiday meals would be challenging unless the two could work something out.

And then Thomas paused.

Holiday meals?

A warmth spread through him. He wanted holiday meals with his family. Wanted to move to Nevada and enjoy spending time with his loved ones. Wanted to see Ashley and...

His gut twisted, and he could almost taste bile in his throat.

Well, maybe he could get over Ashley in time.

Maybe.

He had downloaded his and Ashley's wedding video. Maybe it was self-loathing or the need to kick himself while he was down, but he sat quietly in the corner of the room and hit the play button.

Even sloshed and unable to stand, Ashley looked divine in the video. He, on the other hand, was a hot mess. He searched ahead until the video showed a closeup of him.

"Ashley…" his recorded self said and then broke into laughter. "You compete me."

They were hiding jewelry, so Thomas wasn't sure if what he wanted to say was, "You *complete* me" or acknowledge that she offered stiff competition for him with gaming.

Mohinder heard the video and joined him on the couch. "Have you seen it yet?"

"No." Thomas had hit pause and wasn't sure if he should continue. Matt and Connor were busy texting their wives and checking the weather. Paul was pacing a hole in the carpet. "I'm not sure I want to."

"Watch it. Don't just listen to the words. *Watch* who you *are* in the video. See what's important and how comfortable you are together." Mohinder saw his boyfriend Nick avoiding Brian and talking with Paul. He smiled at Nick, and a twinkle appeared in his eyes. "You should be with someone who has seen the worst of you and still wants to be near you." He faced Thomas and put his hand on his shoulder. "Be with someone who allows you to be who you are." His warm smile comforted Thomas, but then he motioned to Nick. "Let me calm Paul down. I love Nick, but he lacks certain people skills. Paul looks even more agitated now."

Sitting alone on the couch, Thomas resumed watching the video. His face in the recording changed. He viewed himself as a longing gaze replaced his laughter, followed by some heavy sighs. Sullenness overtook him, and his face pulled into one of sadness. "Ashley, you're my Hot Lips. I want to share my loneliness with you for the rest of my life. I don't deserve you, but I hope you want me anyway."

And then the video showed him nearly falling over and laughing. "Seriously." The recording continued, and drunk Thomas did his best to compose himself, even though he now sat on the floor. "It's not just wanting to share my loneliness…" The video zoomed in on his face. "I want you. You're the one. The only one for me. I just want you." He then shook his head and smirked. "I suck at sweet words, but I love you. I'll be there for you. I'll even…" His eyes narrowed. "Do you need me to hold back your hair?"

Ashley's voice off camera claimed she wasn't going to throw up and that she loved him, too. The video then ended with the two sloppily kissing each other.

Even drunk, Thomas knew what he wanted. Knew what he had. Knew what he needed.

And he had lost it all.

He stared at the frozen image of the two of them locked in a heated kiss, knowing the moment was gone forever.

BUZZ-BUZZ

A text came in, and Paul set his cufflinks aside to check his phone. His face blanched as he read the message.

"What is it, Paul?" Thomas asked as he placed his phone in his tux pocket.

"Brenda said there might be a problem, and she was right." Paul set the device down and had a seat. "It's confirmed. Father Perin isn't coming. The weather is too dangerous, and the authorities are shutting the road down due to flooding." His voice deflated, and whatever sparkle he had in his eyes left. "We can't get married without a minister."

The room fell silent.

"Bride. Groom. Rings." Paul took the paperwork from his tux's breast pocket and threw it on the table. "The marriage license is to be signed by the officiant in front of witnesses." He stared at the ceiling. "The little flower girl probably isn't coming either."

"Don't these things happen all the time?" Brian asked. "Your wedding can't be the first rained-out ceremony in existence. What do people do?"

The men, all dressed and with nowhere to go, stared at each other as the rain pelted on the roof, and the whooshing sound of wind beat against the windows.

"Unless we can find someone to marry us, we can't get married today." Paul sucked in a deep breath and tapped on his neck once more. "So, unless one of you is an ordained minister, I will have to tell Linda." He gazed out the window into the darkness of the outside. "I need to tell her in person. She's probably all dressed up, makeup done, ready to go."

An ordained minister?

A flush of adrenaline surged through Thomas's body. He took out his wallet and sat on the couch. He emptied the contents and searched for the minister card he knew he had. *Please,* he thought. *Let this be an answer.*

He remained quiet as he silently read the plastic card. He had taken the test online for that stupid bet last October. He remembered the month because the deadline was Halloween, and he had rented a priest costume to seal the deal. It'd taken him a month of prepping to win the bet since the online class lasted four weeks. The course granted him the right to marry people in five states. He didn't even remember which ones.

He found the card, and his eyes fixed on the expiration date. He still had months left.

Holding his breath, he flipped the card over and discovered *Nevada* written on the back. He nearly dropped the card, and his heart skipped a beat.

Paul undid his tie. "I'd better go over and give her the bad news."

"Wait," Thomas said, his voice pitched high with excitement. "You're getting married today, Paul."

26

"Your makeup looks great," Imani said, touching up Linda's cheeks with more blush. "See? I told you you didn't need to hire someone else to do your makeup." She held a hand mirror, and Linda inspected herself.

Linda gave a half-hearted smile. "You did a great job. Hopefully, the rain won't wash it off by the time I get to the barn." She looked half-heartedly at the window and Ashley. "Is it calming down any?"

"Dark clouds still," Mindy said.

"But it isn't raining as hard now," Sarah chimed in.

"All right." Linda took a deep breath and adjusted the bib she wore over her lacy bra in case of a makeup mishap. "Time for my hair." She gave Mindy a sour look. "The makeup lady has the pins. I was going to wear my hair in a French twist with"—she touched strands of hair by her cheeks and twirled them in her fingertips—"spiral curls cascading down the sides."

"Don't cry," Ashley said, handing her a tissue. "You'll ruin Imani's hard work."

"It doesn't matter. No one is coming to this wedding."

Ashley had to admit the weather would keep many away. "Your father is here. We're here. Most importantly, you and Paul are here. You don't need anyone else."

They got Linda's hair done and carefully maneuvered the dress so she could step into it and put it on. The last touch was the veil.

The Disney princesses had nothing on her. She was a vision.

"Do you remember when we were kids and would wear my mother's white silk pillowcases as veils, pretending to be brides?" Linda asked.

Ashley smiled and said, "Yes." This was the first time since last night that Linda had mentioned her mother. Last night, the conversations about her at the cottage ranged from being sad that she couldn't be here, to fury for what she had done. The two had stayed up after the other women went to bed. The only thing keeping them awake now was the strong coffee they had drunk this morning.

Carefully, the women moved from the cottage to the barn, making sure the men had arrived before them so there'd be no chance of Paul accidentally seeing the bride.

The barn had been transformed since last night. The lights still twinkled from above, and the candelabras still sectioned off the room, but the tables were gone. In their stead, rows of white chairs faced forward. The flowers had not come to decorate the place, and the wooden altar seemed empty without them.

The women were then sequestered in a small room in the back of the barn so no one could see them until the wedding march played. Since Ashley found the tiny space too snug with five women wearing yards and yards of fabric, she left to see if Brenda needed any help.

After Brenda had received that strange text, she'd fallen silent and become secretive about it. Ashley knew that something was wrong, and she was determined to discover what it was. The trick was not letting Linda know that something *else* had happened to ruin her day.

The groomsmen were huddled near the barn windows, scanning the skies for any sign of a clear-up. She figured there would be no cars coming down the drive. No guests would need to be seated. No huge gala event.

But with the right man, you didn't need all those things.

She lifted an eyebrow questioningly at Matt and Connor. Connor shrugged in answer, indicating that he, too, didn't know how this would end.

Wandering past the rows of chairs, each tied with a teal ribbon, she strolled down the aisle—passing rows of mostly empty chairs—save for her uncle talking with Thomas's mother. The two sat in the first row with the empty rows trailing behind them.

So many seats.

She wasn't even sure she knew enough people to fill each one. She didn't have a big ceremony for her wedding and didn't need one.

She paused. Make that for her last *two* weddings. Of course, she didn't have the money to splurge for anything super fancy, either. Her ex-husband's gambling debts had taken most of her financial resources. Her schooling after that had pretty much wiped out her bank account.

But she could dream.

Standing at the altar, she allowed herself a tiny fantasy. Rain or not, this place was beautiful, and Brenda and Hershel should be proud of their business. They had created a fabulous destination wedding resort.

She imagined walking down the aisle, her father proudly escorting her. The flowers would be wildflowers or violets, and the color scheme would be purple. Every chair would be filled with a loved one with happiness in their heart for her. And then Thomas would be waiting…

She blinked, pulling her out of the fantasy. A man, *someone*, would be waiting for her. There was no one else in her life right now, and, she had to admit, it was easy to fantasize about a handsome man like Thomas. So, she allowed herself another minute of decadence.

Her dress would be ivory-colored with baroque flowers woven into the fabric. A veil like Maid Marian, the kind that encircled the head with flowers and then draped down the back, would be atop her head.

And her favorite music would be playing softly in the background. *Edelweiss*. She wasn't sure why she loved the tune so much, but she did. The ceremony would be an intimate affair with only family to share her big day.

Someone behind a partition swore, interrupting her fantasy. It sounded like Thomas, and it was a good thing the building was a barn and not a church. Taking a look, she found him holding his phone and searching for reception. He already stood over six feet in height. With his hand up as high as he could manage, he was like a towering hunk of manhood.

Her eyes traveled from tip to toe while he had his back to her. Perhaps she owed it to herself to explain to him what she had gone through and why she had decided not to undergo any additional surgeries. Breasts gone. Ovaries gone. Fallopian tubes, well, what use were they if the cervix and ovaries were removed? Add on that some lymph nodes and her appendix had been removed as a child, and her body had already undergone too many changes.

Oddly enough, she still had her tonsils.

The thought made her chuckle, which caused Thomas to turn around.

"Hey," he said, lowering his hand. The concentration on his face disappeared once he realized it was her. His expression now held a sweet smile, one filled with optimism.

"I was hoping we could talk," they both said.

She glanced away. "I'd like to explain." She realized that wasn't quite the word, so she rephrased. "I'd like to *share* with you what I've been through."

He closed the gap between them. "I'm so sorry for what I said."

"Thomas!" a voice shouted from across the room. "Did you get the ceremony script? We have no Wi-Fi."

Turning, he yelled, "Not yet."

The barn was probably the worst place to get reception, especially with a storm. "What script?"

He checked his watch. "The guests should be arriving, but I doubt any are coming." He gently shook his head as though what he was about to say was obvious. "Everyone—family and close friends—who needs to be here arrived earlier this week. So at least there's that."

Why did he look so nervous?

"Do you have any bars?" He held up his phone, showing no service.

She took her cell from her purse and noticed it was limited, but she had access to the Internet. "What do you need?"

She listened as he made an odd request. It took two tries, but she eventually found what he needed. He took a snapshot of the page from his phone.

"Father Perin isn't coming," he said.

Her eyes widened, and she let out a quick gasp. Overall, she shouldn't be too surprised, but this was the worst thing that could happen. "Well, I guess not *everyone* who *needs* to be here is here. How are we going to have a wedding?"

"Paul put me in last minute as an usher." He waved his arms across the air at the empty seats. "I have no job to do. But," he said, holding up one finger and grinning, "I do have a minister's license for the state of Nevada."

An image of the card he had in his wallet sprang to her mind quicker than the vast smile that now spread across his face. "That card wasn't a joke?"

"No. I really was ordained." His gaze shifted, and he added, "For a bet." He shook his head dismissively. "Just something stupid, really. But I am ordained and can perform marriages in Nevada."

All the pieces were coming together. Brenda must have received a message about the weather and had told Paul. Yeah, she would have done that. Paul wouldn't shoot the messenger.

And they had Thomas! He was jumping in and saving the day. A modern-day hero.

A *sexy* modern-day hero.

"It's serendipitous, then." Yes, it was kind of a clergy role, but…. Damn! He just got hotter. The room grew warmer, and Ashley inspected him in his beautiful tux. "You know what?" she asked, walking to the upright piano. "Ministers and priests tend to have a…" She had no idea what the right word was, so she said, "…scarf they wear."

Loud thunder rumbled above them, but Thomas stepped closer, oblivious to the noise. "A clergy stole?"

Damn! He knew that? He was getting hotter by the minute.

Why were men of the cloth so tempting? Probably due to them being taboo and off-limits.

She removed the long table runner that rested on top of the piano. "It's colorful. It'll look good in the pictures."

He took it and draped it around his neck, a kink in the fabric catching on the back of his collar. "How's it look?" he asked as he ensured it hung equally in the front.

She stepped into his personal space and put her arms around his neck. Her fingers tugged at the makeshift clergy stole, and she straightened it, pulling him closer. "You look handsome."

"Are we ready? No guests are coming." Paul and the other men stopped watching the dark skies and joined them at the altar. "How is Linda?"

"She's doing great." Ashley laced her fingers together and cracked her knuckles. "It's been a long time since I've played piano, but I can probably manage a wedding march."

"Do you know it?" Brian asked.

She picked up a sheet of music from the top of the piano. "No, but I can read music."

"We can take pictures," Matt said, volunteering him and Connor. The bridesmaid, Mindy, was already snapping away, so there'd be plenty of wedding coverage. "I'll do pictures with Mindy, and Connor can record the ceremony."

"No problem." Connor took out his phone and stood at the ready. "Sarah," he said, glancing in her direction. "Can you gather the candlesticks and bring them up here? Maybe those ribbons, too."

"Sure," she said. "They'll look nice as a backdrop."

Ashley sat at the piano, her fingers depressing a few keys. They could do this. A quiet, intimate wedding. It was perfect.

Brenda and Hershel appeared out of nowhere, their dripping clothes showing they had only now come in. "The road is out. There won't be any guests." Hershel stared gravely at Paul. "The other wedding for today canceled." He scanned the room. "You can have this room all day if you need it."

"Our other guests are hunkered down in their rooms," Brenda added.

"No caterer, either," Hershel said. "But we do have food at the main house." He glanced at the lights that twinkled above and the warm, low-glow electric candles around the room. "We have a backup generator. We should be fine. But," he said, then scratched the back of his neck, "we can discuss postponement."

"The wedding will proceed." Paul stopped thumping the side of his neck, though he seemed genuinely happy. "I'm marrying the woman of my dreams today."

Hershel nodded as if he understood. Ashley had known the couple for years, and she knew nothing would stand in his way from having Brenda by his side if this were his day.

"We need to get back to the main house." Brenda glanced at Ashley and tilted her head, checking if everything was all right.

Ashley fingered a few more keys on the piano. "It's a little out of tune, and I'm out of practice, but I can manage. Everything will work out."

Brenda smiled back, obviously understanding. "Do you want me to give the bride a message?"

Paul straightened the jacket of his tux. "Tell her I'm ready if she is."

Minutes passed, but then the door at the back of the room opened. Ashley wanted to stare at Thomas but focused on the piano. It was more challenging to play the tune than she had first thought, and she made several mistakes that would forever be captured on Connor's video.

But it didn't matter.

Linda looked like an angel walking to the altar. Her father was a drippy mess, mostly his hair and jacket, but the beaming smile on his face showed the excitement in his heart.

Out of the corner of her eye, Ashley watched as they made their way up the mostly empty rows and saw how Paul's face lit up. She could capture enough of the movements to know when to stop playing once the couple stood at the altar together.

"Dear loved ones," Thomas said, "if you love each other and you want to get married, then you should go ahead. Get married."

From where Ashley stood, Linda's happy smile grew even wider. Thomas had selected the ceremony speech from *Love Everlasting*, her favorite rom-com movie. His focus was on the picture on his phone, which he took of the website Ashley had found for him. Thomas didn't do the voice of the character, thank goodness. His deep voice had made the silly yet romantic ceremony speech sound even more beautiful.

It was perfect.

"Ladies and gentlemen. I present to you, Mr. and Mrs. Paul Stallworth."

The two turned and faced the small crowd.

Thomas had done it. He had never made such an important speech before and felt grateful to have found the ceremony online. Afterward, he'd have to sign the marriage paperwork, file it with the state, whatever.

A surge of pride filled him. He had just married his little brother to the love of his life. Paul had never looked happier.

"When did you become a priest?" his mother asked, quickly getting through the short receiving line and hugging him.

"I'm not a priest, Mom."

"Good. Because I brag to everyone how you save lives by being the best surgeon in Chicago," she said, her words filled with pride.

"Great job, man." Paul came up, arms wide, and hugged Thomas. "The best gift you could have given us." He pulled away and choked up. "You bought the replacement ring to save the day, just in case. You performed the ceremony," he said, his voice cracking. "And to think, I didn't even want to invite you."

"I'm sorry for being absent for so long." Thomas's chest filled with love. This was his little brother, now a married man. He had never mentioned this to him before, but he said, "I'm proud of you, Paulie. I like the man you've become, and I'm honored to be a part of your life."

That did it. Paul started crying.

"You okay, honey?"

Paul took Linda by the arm and kissed her cheek. "Just great."

"You look beautiful, Linda." Thomas leaned in and hugged his new sister-in-law.

Gone from her eyes was the hatred she'd had for

him, the disregard, and the belief that he was someone who needed to be kept away. He saw in her what Paul had always seen. She was a caring woman who took care of her family. "The ceremony was perfect. Thank you."

Perfect.

There was that word again. Everything he did, everything he had, his very demeanor…everything was perfect. And yet, his stomach was more twisted with the feeling of butterflies than when he stood in front of the small group to perform his first—and probably last—wedding ceremony.

"Excuse me. I need to find Ashley."

Linda caught his arm before he took off. "I can tell that you care for her. Please be patient. She doesn't need a doctor's advice, but she could use a good friend to talk to. Perhaps even someone more than just a good friend."

Thomas patted her hand and nodded.

Connor placed his iPhone on the altar. He and Matt had been busy clearing away the chairs and making room for a dance floor. "We have no cake to cut, but we can do a father-daughter, mother-son dance."

"And a couple's first dance," Matt added.

The music played, causing Ashley to let out an "*aww*" sound as she saw how everyone was pulling together and making the day special.

"Can we talk?" Thomas asked, getting her attention and nodding to the tiny bride's room in the back.

27

Thomas closed the door. Raincoats, umbrellas, and shoes littered the small space. Hairbrushes, makeup, combs, and all the last-minute items a bride might need sat on the small table.

Ashley moved some clothes from the sofa and made room for them to sit. He saw himself in the full-length mirror as he took a seat. He saw a lonely man reflected. Someone who had been an idiot to hurt a woman as wonderful as Ashley.

"I'm sorry," he said before she could say anything. "You are such an amazing woman. You're full of life and joy." Many cancer survivors were. Some grew bitter due to their journey. Some got rougher around the edges because life was too short. Some saw the disease as a wake-up call or even a second chance. The little, day-by-day annoyances became less stressful.

No matter what, cancer changed you.

"You're embracing life after the disease, and I..." He paused, still seeing his head in the mirror's edge. He could say the right words and not mess this up. "I can help you financially if you need."

Her face pinched, and she glanced away. "You don't understand at all."

"I know you've been through a lot. You're scared." He thought about how he would feel if he'd had to deal with such a disease. The thought was hard to wrap his mind around, but he had thought of it before. "I don't know how you did it. How any of you women do it." He swallowed hard, and his patients' faces flooded his mind. "I've seen hundreds of women, each so strong and determined to move past the disease."

He sat back on the couch and allowed his body to sink into the cushions so he no longer saw his reflection in the mirror. Seeing his thick mane of hair and thinking of what his dear patients had gone through was too much. Losing their hair. Having body parts removed. Having to stop working for months because of nausea— or worse, working through it because there was no other option.

God, the bills. They were enormous.

"It's not just breast cancer." She caught his gaze with hers. "I had skin cancer a few years ago."

Two cancers? You should never have to hear from a doctor that you have the terrible disease. But to hear it twice? The very idea made him appreciate how beautiful and strong she was.

A sense of fear gripped him. He could have already lost her. Could possibly *still* lose her. "Was it a melanoma or a carcinoma?"

"Melanoma. Small and deadly. Right here," she said, pointing to a spot on her right prosthetic breast. "That damn breast tried to kill me twice."

Being the largest organ in the human body, the spot where the melanoma had appeared wouldn't need to be directly affected by the harmful sun. He doubted she sunbathed topless.

"That's right," she said, nodding as though she had read his mind. "Right where the sun never shined. At least not since I was maybe two years old and playing in a wading pool in my backyard."

"Two cancers." He tried to wrap his mind around that fact. She was so young. "I'm sorry you went through that."

"Thomas." She reached over and held his hands within hers. "I'm BRCA2 gene mutation positive. I have a higher risk of skin, breast, ovarian, and pancreatic cancer. Plus, maybe, other cancers."

"You can have surgery," he blurted, the doctor within him coming through. Gene mutations were often causes for people getting multiple cancers, but he had never known someone who was BRCA2 positive—at least not someone who hadn't been a patient. Ovarian cancer was difficult to diagnose and held such a low survival rate because of that fact. The disease was coming for her. He needed to see that it didn't. "The procedure is called an oophorectomy, and your ovaries can be removed."

She closed her eyes, and he guessed that she had heard the information before. A young woman like her. Such a procedure meant she would become barren, but the chemotherapy had probably already put her into menopause. Her ovaries were only ticking time bombs.

"I already had a complete hysterectomy and oophorectomy. Everything is gone."

Very few of his patients were BRCA1 or BRCA2 positive. Rarely did he talk about the cancers, more about what he could do for those women to regain their feminine shape. He only dealt with the loss of the breasts. Not reproductive organs.

As sorry as he was for her loss, he felt a sense of relief. Those procedures severely decreased her chances of getting breast cancer or ovarian cancer. Chances were unlikely cancer would come back, spread, or that a new cancer would take hold. But there was one more organ exposed, and he was surprised by how his heart now pounded. He didn't want to lose her. "You can't easily remove your pancreas." His mind raced, and he then thought about the Whipple procedure. He had assisted with one as an intern years ago. "Well, it can be done. It's been done successfully for years. You just need to be careful."

"I know." Tears formed in her eyes, and he gently stroked her hair.

"The chance of getting pancreatic cancer is low," he

said, pulling from his memory what he knew about the gene mutation. "With proper monitoring, you should be able to catch it early if you ever even get it." He wanted to be here for her, and his move to Nevada could ensure that. "I'll be moving to Nevada in a few weeks."

He thought it would make her happy. Instead, the floodgates opened, and tears streamed down her cheeks. "You don't have to do this alone." He held her closely, her sobs vibrating against his chest.

"I can't. There's no way…" she said, sobbing.

"I'll be right here for you."

"No." She pulled away. "We can't see each other anymore."

He couldn't have heard her right, but he knew he had. His heart sank. He could be the man she needed if she wanted him to be.

Ashley accepted Thomas's handkerchief and wiped the tears away, feeling vulnerable. She had put on her expensive earrings, her brightest lipstick, and the biggest chip on her shoulder to attend this wedding. And here she was, falling to pieces and crying in front of the one man she had dared to care for. A tug in her gut made her want to throw up for being so weak. There wasn't enough air in the room, and she gulped in breaths to stop herself from bawling like a child.

"What do you mean we can't see each other?"

She didn't look at him. Couldn't.

"Ashley, I don't want what we have to end."

She mustered the courage to sit straighter on the couch and face him. "I can't be with anyone. It isn't fair," she managed to get out.

"Fair?" He cleared his throat, and his brows knitted together. "I've enjoyed our time together. So much so that I was actually disappointed when we found Linda's ring and the geocaching ended. So much so that when they offered me the position at the hospital, my first thought was that I'd be near you." He swallowed hard, and she could tell he was searching for the right words. "I'm sorry for what I said about the reconstructive surgery. I'm sure it isn't for everyone."

His soulful blue eyes implored her for answers. Things she'd only now realized for the first time. It wasn't about body image. It wasn't about the prosthetics. It wasn't about being *fixed* and *perfect*. She knew the dark monster that hid within her heart. The beast she locked away but was always present.

"I can't burden you, or anyone, with my problems," she said, her voice cracking and her tone soft as she finally admitted the root of her loneliness and pain. "I can't give you a child. I'll only bring you sorrow and be a financial and emotional burden to anyone who loves me."

Her heart split open, and the monster consumed her with fear.

"If the cancer comes back, or if another one

strikes…No one should have to be with a woman who…" She sobbed. "Who…who is like…me." Her voice broke as she said the word *me*. She had fought cancer and had won the battle, but what about the war?

She leaned into him, and he stroked her hair. "A woman like you? A wonderful, full-of-life goddess? Any man would be happy." He kissed the top of her head. "*I* would be happy."

He didn't know what he was talking about. She may put on a brave face, but she didn't want to sit in the chemo chair again. Didn't want to have doctors hovering over her. Didn't want surgeries, needles, and pain. She didn't want to put a loved one through it, either.

She felt like half a woman at best.

"I can't have children."

"I don't want children."

"You're only saying that."

He fell silent, and at that moment, she admitted that she probably should have accepted the counseling Brenda had encouraged her to get. But talking to a stranger about being afraid to die, living half a life, seemed pointless. Whenever she mentioned her fears to her oncologist or the people at BCRC, they always said, "But you're not dying *today*" and "you need to find your *new norm*." She was sure that most patients found solace in those words, but she didn't.

"Don't think less of me," he finally said, "but I don't want to be a father." His hand caressed her back. "I can't believe I'm admitting this out loud, but I've never wanted to be one."

His voice sounded sincere enough, but what if he was only saying that?

Using his foot, he maneuvered the standing mirror so it faced them squarely. God, she hated how ugly she looked when she cried.

"What do you see in that mirror?"

The reflection sickened her, but she said, "A woman who needs to buy waterproof mascara."

She saw a slight smile curl his lips in his reflection. "What do you really see?" he asked.

She took a deep breath and gave the usual reply, the one everyone expected to hear. "I see a strong woman who fought cancer and won."

"No," he said, his tone heavy and deep. "If I wanted to hear someone recite, I'd go to a play." His hand nudged her shoulders. "Try again. What do you see?"

The waterworks poured out and wouldn't stop. She barely recognized herself physically. She no longer saw the image of Darth Vader—bald and sickly with no eyebrows—dying in Luke's arms. But the image wasn't hers, either. Her hair had grown in, she now had eyebrows, and the moon face of chemo was gone, but she had changed. She had once had long, wavy hair, had been ten pounds lighter, and was a woman who enjoyed wearing lacy bras and underwear even if no one else saw them. All she saw now was a woman terrified of dying who lived in the shadow of a monster.

"My body is hideous." She waved her hand over herself, mainly focusing on her chest. Under her clothes, two U-shaped scars marred her body where her once-beautiful breasts had been. "I'd frighten any man who saw me naked."

"Not true."

It absolutely was.

"My job has me seeing patients who've had their breasts removed. I often see my patients while still on the operating table right after the breast surgeon removes the breasts, and their chest is still flayed open. Trust me. Your body isn't *hideous*."

Again, he pointed at the mirror. "I'll tell you what I see." He studied her through the reflection. "I see a beautiful woman. Smart, funny, and sexy as hell."

"Sexy?" She nearly laughed and needed to blow her nose into her very wet handkerchief.

"Yes, sexy. If you remember, I jumped at the chance to go out with you after the bachelor party dinner. Partly because I didn't want to hang out with a group of guys I didn't know, but mostly—clearly the majority of my decision—was because this beautiful, auburn-haired, geocaching, goddess of a woman asked me to go out with her."

"And that's why I woke up the next morning in your bed alone?" Her heart stopped, and she couldn't believe she had uttered those words aloud.

She felt his body grow tense and his chest expand as

he took in a deep breath. "Okay. Let's talk about that." His face reddened, and he gave her a short nod. "First, I want to say that I'm glad I didn't get into that bed with you."

Her heart sank. Of course, he'd be glad. Who would want her?

"I'm glad I didn't because I wouldn't want our first time together to be lost. I want to cherish and remember it forever."

"First time?"

"Of course. I know you now. A few days ago, I didn't. On the way to get the blood work done, I kept staring at you in the car and wondering how drunk I had been to not get in bed with you. Even with my head pounding, all I thought about was getting you back into my room and under those covers."

Before she could wrap her mind around what he had said, he continued. "I told myself to keep my distance because we needed the annulment. I knew I shouldn't allow myself to get close to you. But that rainy moment under the awning when you comforted me, all I wanted to do was get you against that building and take you, hard and rough."

Ashley heard the desire in his voice and focused on the words *hard and rough*.

"When you leaned over to retrieve the ring from that branch, I noticed how tight your body was and wondered how I hadn't slept with you yet because my body had ached for you for days."

Days? The room was getting warmer, and she felt heat coming off him.

"And when I told you about my mother that day on the swing, I knew everything had changed. Because I didn't just want to hold you, I wanted *you* to hold *me*. The feelings I have for you became different, more powerful because I didn't want to just have sex with you. I wanted to make love to you."

Leaning against him, she heard his heart racing. She saw the steely gaze in his eyes as he stared at her through the mirror. He wanted her as much as she wanted him.

"And if the cancer comes back? What then?"

"Then we face it together. You've done everything you can to make sure it doesn't return. I'm sure you see a dermatologist for skin cancer, right?"

"Yes."

"You still see the breast surgeon and oncologist for your breast cancer?"

"Uh-huh. Every six months."

"You've removed your ovaries before cancer got to them. That was incredibly brave of you." His hand stopped rubbing her back.

"What?"

"I'm sorry if you wanted to be a mother."

She had always thought that if she were meant to be a mother, she'd be a good one. But she'd never really thought of herself as being a mom to someone. "I'm okay with not having children." She sniffled and took in a breath. "I figured I might have kids one day, but it wasn't something I truly wanted."

It was hard to admit, but it was true.

"I have a team of specialists," she said, thinking of all her doctors. "One watches for thyroid cancer, another for stomach cancer. Two watch for the dreaded pancreatic cancer." Her voice trailed off and showed her fear of the last one.

"If I remember anything about BRCA2, pancreatic is only a small chance."

"It's twice as likely to strike me than anyone else," she said.

"But that would still be under...what? A ten percent chance? Especially since you don't smoke or live a lifestyle that would increase your chances of getting that disease. Besides, there is a surgical procedure called the Whipple that helps people survive that cancer—especially when detected early, which is what all your scans are doing."

She leaned into him and admitted, "My scars are pretty deep. Both emotional and physical." She looked away, and he had to ask why. She pointed to the foobs and mastectomy bra, which peeked through the dress's cleavage. "I know it sounds silly, but you can have any woman out there. You're a doctor." She felt tears welling up again. "Why do you want me? I don't even have breasts for you to touch."

He pulled her closer so his lips were mere inches from hers. "You may not have breasts, but I'd rather touch your heart." He leaned in, and his mouth found hers. His passionate kiss tasted salty due to her tears. His lips were demanding, and his kiss was full of want and need. She matched his desire and kissed him back, putting her whole heart and soul into it.

A knock sounded on the door.

"Ashley? Are you in there? Linda is about to throw the bouquet."

As the footsteps retreated, Thomas straightened his tie and jacket. He then stood and offered her his hand. "Let's see if you catch the bouquet and where this relationship is headed."

She pulled him back to the couch to kiss him some more. "Actually, I'm not single."

THE END

If you enjoyed 'Bachelor Doctor' and would like to leave a review, please visit https://reginamorris.com/bachelor-doctor-info

To purchase the next book in the Rich Indulgence Series, please visit https://reginamorris.com/bachelor-book-5-info

To begin the series and purchase the first book, please visit https://reginamorris.com/bachelor-heart-info/

ACKNOWLEDGMENTS

Special thanks to my husband and our children for their love and support; to my sister for believing in me and encouraging me to follow my dreams; to my critique partners, Jean and Pennie, for being with me every step of the way; to my editor Chelle (Literally Addicted to Detail); and my proof reader team. I also want to thank my beta readers, and street team. This book would not be possible without the support I have had from all of you.

ABOUT THE AUTHOR

Dear Readers,

I hope you enjoyed reading my novel, Bachelor Doctor: A Rich Indulgence Billionaire Doctor Romance. Please leave a review on the retailer site where you purchased the book.

You can find a link to all retailers at: reginamorris. com/bachelor-doctor-info

Please visit my website (http://www. reginamorris.com) for more information about my other novels and short stories. A list of my books and descriptions are below.

Please feel free to contact me through my website, through my many social media sites (see my website for the a list) or by email at mailto:regina@reginamorris. com?subject=Email from fan.

I like to play games and have fun in my monthly electronic newsletters. Please sign up at newsletter.regi-namorris.com

By day, I work in a small cubicle as a computer programmer, but at night I write about vampires, billionaires, and other romance combinations. I capture my creativity on the pages of my passionate stories. I write about second chance romances, mature romances (where the characters are 40+ years of age), and about vampires.

My contemporary romances are mostly sweet romances (please check descriptions to confirm). The romances build a connection between two people with happily-ever-afters. No cliff-hangers, but complete stories.

The books in my series are all stand-alone novels that can be read in any order.

My Vampire Secret Service series is about vampires who can alter their aged appearances by the amount of blood they consume. The series is about a covert team of sexy vampires who protect the President of the United States. This series' success prompted me to launch another series ("Vampire Embrace") that involves the same world, but about civilian vampires who live among unsuspecting humans.

The heat level differs from mild to hot in my books. My stories involving the Historical Preservation Agency and time travel are mild. My two vampire series, my Rich Indulgence bachelor billionaire series, and some of my contemporary romances are hot. These hot stories have an age warning of 18+ on them. My contemporary short stories are mild. My contemporary novels vary.

I live in Austin, Texas with my husband and two children. I graduated high school in Germany and I attended the University of Texas at Austin, where I received a degree in Computer Science with a minor in

"Do you know it?" Brian asked.

She picked up a sheet of music from the top of the piano. "No, but I can read music."

"We can take pictures," Matt said, volunteering him and Connor. The bridesmaid, Mindy, was already snapping away, so there'd be plenty of wedding coverage. "I'll do pictures with Mindy, and Connor can record the ceremony."

"No problem." Connor took out his phone and stood at the ready. "Sarah," he said, glancing in her direction. "Can you gather the candlesticks and bring them up here? Maybe those ribbons, too."

"Sure," she said. "They'll look nice as a backdrop."

Ashley sat at the piano, her fingers depressing a few keys. They could do this. A quiet, intimate wedding. It was perfect.

Brenda and Hershel appeared out of nowhere, their dripping clothes showing they had only now come in. "The road is out. There won't be any guests." Hershel stared gravely at Paul. "The other wedding for today canceled." He scanned the room. "You can have this room all day if you need it."

"Our other guests are hunkered down in their rooms," Brenda added.

"No caterer, either," Hershel said. "But we do have food at the main house." He glanced at the lights that twinkled above and the warm, low-glow electric candles around the room. "We have a backup generator. We should be fine. But," he said, then scratched the back of his neck, "we can discuss postponement."

"The wedding will proceed." Paul stopped thumping the side of his neck, though he seemed genuinely happy. "I'm marrying the woman of my dreams today."

Hershel nodded as if he understood. Ashley had known the couple for years, and she knew nothing would stand in his way from having Brenda by his side if this were his day.

"We need to get back to the main house." Brenda glanced at Ashley and tilted her head, checking if everything was all right.

Ashley fingered a few more keys on the piano. "It's a little out of tune, and I'm out of practice, but I can manage. Everything will work out."

Brenda smiled back, obviously understanding. "Do you want me to give the bride a message?"

Paul straightened the jacket of his tux. "Tell her I'm ready if she is."

Minutes passed, but then the door at the back of the room opened. Ashley wanted to stare at Thomas but focused on the piano. It was more challenging to play the tune than she had first thought, and she made several mistakes that would forever be captured on Connor's video.

But it didn't matter.

Linda looked like an angel walking to the altar. Her father was a drippy mess, mostly his hair and jacket, but

ALSO BY REGINA MORRIS

Rich Indulgence Billionaire Bachelor Series

Bachelor Heart (Book #1)

Deborah Baxter, personal assistant to a powerful CEO, never expected her boss would want her to pose as his fake fiancée. She is plenty attracted to him, but she's a 38 year-old single mother—now turned empty-nester—who hasn't dated in years. Does she really want to go on romantic dates with her boss at the city's glitziest spots? She says yes anyway.

At 49, Daniel Ellington has everything a billionaire could want—except maybe romantic happiness. And that's only because he doesn't really want it—there's much to be said about shallow affairs when you are a busy man. But now reliable sources are telling him he is about to be named one of the country's ten most eligible bachelors by People Magazine, and that kind of tabloid attention is the last thing he wants. Having his assistant pose a his fiancée seems to be the ideal answer, at least at first.

Their whirlwind fake—or is it real—romance explodes on social media. The loss of privacy drives Daniel nuts. But these troubles are nothing compared to Deborah's refusal to date him for real. What is his assistant keeping secret? And more importantly, how can he change her mind?

Bachelor Soul (Book #2)

Billionaire Scott Holister's ambition is to become a senior partner at his law firm. His track record is good and he has seniority at the firm, but he doesn't have the appropriate corporate image. He needs a house, an attitude adjustment, and, most importantly, a wife.

He finds a woman interested in dating him—not his wallet—but the woman he is falling in love with is a waitress at a local diner, who has mistaken him for being a homeless man after he has a mishap wile jobbing in the park.

When the restaurant she works at caters the Christmas party held by Scott's law firm, passions explode as they discover who they are and what truly matters.

Bachelor Dad (Book #3)

Billionaire James Nielson plans to close many of his business's installations, including the original factory started by his grandfather in the small town of Newbury, when a woman—whom he had a sexual fling with over a year ago—abandons her baby at his company's headquarters claiming he is the father.

He and his baby daughter visit Newbury during the holidays where he hires a local woman, Melanie Frank, to be his nanny. She has been furloughed from her job at his factory, and, like everyone in the town, relies on the company for her livelihood. She wants to be an artist, but is financially trapped in the town by the company.

It is obvious to Melanie that James is uneasy around his daughter, isn't finding the town charming, and doesn't feel any Christmas spirit. She's plenty attracted to James, but will this city mouse really be interested in a country mouse? As

James discovers lost family members, the warmth of a small community spirit, and the compassion from his daughter's nanny, he develops a stronger sense of family and his romantic feelings for Melanie grow.

He decides he must keep the factory running, and after buying Melanie's artwork at the local Christmas auction, she has renewed interest in her studies. The two search for the perfect Christmas gift for each other while trying to save the factory, which leads to a Christmas miracle.

Bachelor Doctor (Book #4)

Chaos ensues when billionaire Thomas Stallworth, the leading breast reconstruction surgeon in Chicago, has to stop his brother's wedding in Las Vegas.

Thomas needs to reveal a shocking secret the bride is hiding which will create a rift between the brothers. Worse yet, Thomas drunkenly gets married after the bachelor party to the bride's cousin and must annul the union without anyone finding out.

The bride has an agenda of her own and curtails Thomas's efforts with the one bridesmaid who would hate him the most.

Ashley Uxer, a breast cancer survivor who chose not to reconstruct, attends her cousin's wedding. After the bachelor party, she finds herself drunkenly married to the handsome groomsmen she has been led to believe is a plastic surgeon whose specialty is rhinoplasty.

In this romantic comedy, Thomas and Ashley lose the bride's wedding ring, their emotional baggage, and their hearts in Las Vegas.

Contemporary Sweet Romance Short Stories

Taking Chances

Broken engagement, a disappointed father, an emotional mother, what else could a wounded soldier ask for? Tommy has no idea that his sweet nurse remembers him prior to his injuries. Always professional, Abby treats Tommy no differently because of their awkward past. Once the truth is out, what will become of their friendship and budding romance?

Christmas Joy

Jake needs to clear out his father's old cabin and sell it. He's prepared to deal with the freezing cold weather and the remote location, but not with the sexy woman, who was once his late father's nurse, still living in the place.

More Than Puppy Love

Ex-wallflower, now veterinarian, Kacie Preston is eager to go to her ten-year high school reunion where she can meet up with the boy she crushed on for years. But then his dog, her patient, shows up at the event mistreated. How well does Kacie really know her old heart throb?

FANTASY / TIME TRAVEL BOOKS

Just in Time (Short Story - Prequel to 'Time Historian')

Managing teams to send recorders back in history is stressful enough, but when the government makes a play for proprietary technology from the Historical Preservation Agency, Caleb must rely upon a well-connected, and sexy, developer at a government agency for help. Can the two of them keep time travel in the hands of historians?

Time Historian

Hank McConnell's is having a bad day at the office. First, he just destroyed history. He finds himself living in the Confederate States of America, Lincoln was convicted as a war criminal, and slavery existed for another fifty years. Secondly, his blunder erased his family from existence and his alternate self works as a lonely tenured professor instead of at the Historical Preservation Agency.

He doesn't have much time. He travels back to Lincoln's presidency to right what went wrong. Unfortunately, correcting time is like herding cats and one fix leads to more and more changes.

Is he willing to do the unthinkable to make the world whole again?

PARANORMAL (VAMPIRE) ROMANCES

Vampire Secret Service Series Books (codename: COLONY)

Vampires exist among us. They can be our neighbor, our best friend, our child's teacher...

They alter their aged appearance based upon the amount of blood they consume. They move to a new area, drink a lot of blood, and appear young. Slowly they limit their intake of blood and age, right in front of our unsuspecting eyes. After decades, they fake their death, move, and do it over and over again.

Most live quiet lives in an effort to blend in.

Some, however, want power and control.

The COLONY is an elite group of vampires sworn to protect the President of the United States from these rogue vampires. Few humans are privileged to this knowledge.

Eternal Service (Book #1)

Vampire Raymond Metcalf has too many balls to juggle and life is getting more complicated by the minute. As if working with a covert team of sexy vampires to protect the President isn't enough, he has to deal with his rebellious half-breed son, save the President from a crazed vampire, and break in a new director for his team since the last one, his best friend and the only human he trusts, has decided to retire. Why does his friend's replacement have to be the most beautiful human woman Raymond has ever seen?

Career military woman, Alex Brennan, is being offered the promotion of a lifetime, and with it a romance that she has desperately been seeking. Does she dare accept the position as Director of the COLONY, an elite group of deadly creatures of the night and risk a dangerous romance with a man who isn't even human? Together, can they save the President?

United Service (Book #2)

Sterling Metcalf is a modern–day vampire who clashes with his father's antiquated ideals. Being the half–breed of the COLONY group, Sterling hates being the team's weakest link. He jumps at an opportunity to do some fieldwork rescuing kidnapped vampire children and is accompanied by Kate Spencer, the nanny of one of the children.

Kate is a purebred vampire with a secret of her own. Can Sterling put aside his bad–boy ways and woo the lovely Kate? Will Kate accept the advances of a half–breed? Together, can they save the children from a religious cult who wants to kill them?

Enduring Service (Book #3)

Vampire Secret Service Agent Sulie Metcalf, the President's private physician, has been in love with the same human man for nearly thirty years. She refuses to allow herself the joy of true love because her feelings are unrequited by her human boss, Jonathan Dixon. As Dixon's retirement looms near, and his memories of Sulie and the last thirty years of his life are about to be erased, does she confront her fear of intimacy and take a leap of faith before it's too late?

Dixon has decided to retire and enjoy what time he has left. When his best friend Sulie, a vampire team member, is kidnapped during a medical emergency, Dixon realizes that retirement means giving up everything, and everyone, he's known for the last three decades. Will he risk his life, and his heart, to save her?

Equality of Service (Book #4)

Fifteen years ago, Vampire Secret Service Agent William Wardell met his future wife Jackie Pearlman. She's sexy, opinionated, and finds him to be a mockery of the American dream of equality for all.

Can a past Freedom Rider and racial activist from the 1960s, now turned vampire, prove to the love of his life that he's not a political puppet?

Reliant Service (Book #5)

After faking his death from an assassination attempt on the President, and retiring his first and only alias with the Vampire Secret Service, Daniel Brighton discovers the mandatory sabbatical to be less than exciting. He chooses to do a favor and act as a security guard for a fading pop–singer,

Lori Austin, whose career is winding down. He travels across Europe with her and discovers her past to be one of deception and intrigue with a history leading directly back to the team itself.

Lori Austin is struggling to keep her career alive, and is willing to do what is necessary to save it. From bad press and scandalous stories, she travels across Europe on a relief tour to revitalize her career, but doesn't realize she is traveling with a vampire. Discovering a hidden family secret, she realizes that the one man who can save her is the handsome security guard she fought so hard not to hire.

Echo of Service (Book #6)

After the President of the United States is poisoned, Vampire Secret Service agent Mason Warner steps in as the man's double. He manages the President's hectic schedule just fine until the political party sends in a public relations expert to clean up the President's image. She is the one woman from Mason's past whom he has never forgotten—the woman who is the measuring stick he compares all other women too—but he compelled her decades ago to forget their one night together.

Nicole Banner is assigned by the party to do a makeover on the one man from her past she despises the most. Years ago, her short-lived secret fling with the Senator of Massachusetts, now President of the United States, left her with a son to raise on her own.

Mason can't risk her remembering their tryst from decades ago since she believes him to be the President. Nicole has always hidden her affair from prying eyes, until now.

He still desires her. All she wants is revenge.

Vampire Embrace Series Books

These vampire romances feature vampires from the Vampire
Secret Service world, but these vampires do not work for the
government.

Winter Wishes (Book #1)

Sammy needs a holiday miracle. The Vampire Council is
after him, he's falling in love with his best friend's mother–
in–law, and there's artwork hanging on the wall that was
stolen by the Nazis. Life is spiraling out of control for this
Jewish vampire as he spends the Christmas holiday baking
cookies and wrapping gifts for the needy.

Louise is busy with her charities and hosting her annual
Christmas party. Putting a smile on her face proves difficult
when her soon to be ex–husband arrives with a bimbo on his
arm, her proposed divorce settlement is far from fair, and the
sexy stranger she's starting to fall for believes she's a Nazi.

Destined Desire (Book #2)

After a car accident nearly kills his immortal father,
Alexander rushes to his father's side only to discover that his
parents want him to marry and stay closer to home. He's
already been down this path once before with a less than
desirable outcome, so he refuses. He's steadfast in his
decision until his parents threaten to financially cut him off

and he's forced to approach the Vampire Council for a new marriage contract.

Dionora is enjoying her new job at the Vampire Council Marriage Office. The holidays take an exciting turn for her when she discovers the next match she does is for her ex–fiancé.

Revenge is sweet with this sensual romantic comedy.

Sins of the Father (Book #3)

Due to his father's crimes, Stephan is marked as a second-class vampire citizen by the Vampire Council and is forced to hunt for food during an international blood shortage. He stumbles upon a chance encounter to gain membership in the elite Phoenix Verband vampire organization, which can solve all his financial and blood-related problems. To win the membership, he must compete in an archaic competition where the contestants pretend to be Persian Princes and fight in computer-generated war games. He feels he can hold his own in the games, but the only food on the island is the stolen harem of women. They are assets in the games and are traded as spoils of war.

Breanna is looking for the vampire who murdered her stepfather when she is kidnapped by the Phoenix and sent to an island to become a blood Donor to the vampires. She's on a mission to save herself and all the harem women, but can she trust the handsome Crown Prince she's been assigned to?

*This book does NOT contain any descriptive sexual or physical abuse of women. All sex scenes are of mutual consent and shown in a loving way.